I0676245

SYNCOPATION

TWISTED WISHES
BOOK 1

ANNA ZABO

Syncopation

Second Edition

First edition published by Carina Press, 2018-2025

Copyright © 2018, 2025 by Anna Zabo

Edited by Mackenzie Walton

Cover design by L. C. Chase

Print ISBN: 978-1-947550-20-9

CONTENT NOTES

THIS BOOK CONTAINS:

- consensual kink, including bondage and pain play
- on-page consensual sex
- talk of alcoholism
- talk of drugs
- minor violence (items thrown in anger)
- homophobia / queerphobia
- slurs
- involuntary drugging
- anaphylaxis
- hospitalization
- bullying
- invasion of privacy
- ableism

To Ray. Thank you for all the years of friendship.

CHAPTER
ONE

Ray Van Zeller stared at the tabloid website headline on the tablet their band manager held out for him. "What the *fuck* is this?"

DRUNKEN VAN ZELLER ATTACKS SCHMIDT AS TWISTED WISHES IMPLODES

"What does it look like, Ray?" A sigh and a hint of a sneer, but then Carl always assumed Ray needed to be spoken to using small words, the prick.

Ray wasn't stupid. He was, however, too pissed to see straight. The text on the screen blurred and tumbled, just like his gut. Just like his life. "It looks like a shitty, lying headline." He hadn't been drunk at all. And he hadn't attacked Kevin, their drummer—ex-drummer now.

Carl heaved another sigh. "They have a video of you." He set the tablet down on the coffee table between them.

Of *course* they did. Fucking paparazzi. Ray clamped his mouth shut and shook his head.

"Ray wasn't the one who was drinking," Domino said. He was dressed casually—looked more twink in his button-down and glasses than guitar rock god—but that was Dom. Out of sight, like in this fuckhole of a hotel, he stripped his persona off. "Kevin started in on that bottle *before* the encore. Ray didn't touch a drop!"

Mish grunted her agreement.

Their no-good band manager knew that, too. They'd been excited to get a manager when the record label had sent Carl. Not so much now. Didn't know why, but Carl's animosity rose damn quick, like the band, and Ray in particular was wasting his time.

Fucking thing was that Carl knew Kevin had been drinking on their tour. Hell, Ray had even approached Carl and asked for help, but no—he'd blown Ray off.

You're the leader, Ray, Carl had said.

He was. That night, he'd been the bandleader when he'd stalked after Kevin, off the tour bus, a two-thirds-empty fifth of Jack in his hand. It had been full before the concert. There'd been yelling—Ray at Kevin to get his act together, Kevin back at Ray, all about how he didn't give a fuck about the band anymore and a trained monkey could play his sets.

Wasn't true. Kevin had been a fantastic drummer back when they'd started the band, his rhythms complex and stunning. Then he'd started celebrating a little too hard and never stopped. Maybe it was a way to cope with the pressure they all felt after "Dark Dreams" had hit the top five, but it didn't matter.

His playing had gone to shit. Kevin now drummed out simple patterns that barely matched the songs they'd built around his original complex drumming. The more he drank, the worse they sounded.

The small tour they were on was supposed to show the label that Twisted Wishes could hack a major one. It had only proved they couldn't play in a fucking Walmart parking lot.

Yeah, Ray had taken that mostly empty bottle of Jack and thrown it at the wall behind Kevin. Felt so good, the crash and splash, the shimmer as glass and golden liquid burst against the concrete wall. Like razor-edged confetti. Kevin had gotten quiet then. Told Ray to go to hell. He'd replied that it was rehab or leave the band. Kevin marched back into the bus, packed his bag, and left that night.

Ray scrubbed his face. The tablet had gone dark, but the headline still swam in his vision. "How bad is the video?"

The snort that came from Carl set Ray's teeth on edge, and he ground them together while Carl woke the tablet, scrolled, and clicked the video clip.

After one of the most excruciating forty-five seconds of Ray's life, the clip ended and he didn't look up. Couldn't, especially since he *knew* Carl wore that fucking smirk of his. Yeah, the video was *that* bad. Whoever had shot it had been far enough away, but the yelling, the anger, those had carried even if the words hadn't. And from the angle, it did look like he'd thrown the bottle *at* Kevin.

"Fuck." It came out like a mantra, slow and long, and the word echoed in his aching head. So much for being in control. Being a leader.

"And now you have no drummer," Carl said. "Whatever will you do?"

Ray lifted his chin and met Carl's gaze, and lo and behold, the fucker flinched. Guess Ray still had that *I'm going to murder you* look down. "Hire a new one." Ray didn't look away from Carl's dark eyes. "I would think a manager of *your* caliber would know that."

Silence in the room until Carl cleared his throat. "Of course. And there'll have to be some other changes as well, to smooth things over in the press."

Dom shifted next to Ray, and Mish muttered something low that was probably profanity. She had a mouth worse than his and Dom's put together.

"What changes?" Ray ground the words out.

"No more drinking for you," Carl said. "And you'll make some kind of statement about getting help for your problem."

The hell he would. He opened his mouth, but Mish beat him there.

"That some fucking bullshit and you know it." She rose from her seat at the edge of the bed, and all six foot one of her towered over Carl. "Why the *fuck* are you punishing Ray for Kevin being a drunken piece of shit?"

Carl craned his neck back to take in Mish, his immaculately styled blond hair shifting into imperfection. "Because without a fucking drummer and with this—" he waved at the tablet "—making the rounds, we have to control the damage."

We meant the record label. It *never* meant the band.

God, the band. They needed the tour the label dangled in front of them, needed it far more than Ray needed his dignity or ego. "Fine. I'll do it." He rarely drank anyway, and he did need help—some way to keep from destroying the chances they'd been given.

Silence. Carl sat back against the ugly hotel chair and stared at him. Mish sank down to the bed. "Ray, honey, are you *sure*?"

He nodded and locked eyes with Carl. "But I'm not admitting I'm an alcoholic when I'm not. I'll—say something about anger management. Or stress therapy or something."

Carl raised his chin. "That would be an acceptable alternative."

"And we need to put out a call for a drummer. Schedule auditions." God, where they would find someone who could play as well as sober Kevin, Ray didn't know. But they *had* to.

"We'll have that ready to go, once you make your statement."

Wonderful. Ray swallowed bile and the urge to throttle the man across the table. "Guess I better go write one, then." He rose, put his back to Carl, and marched out of the room.

Outside the run-down hotel, the air was hot and dry.

Scrub and dust and too much sky as far as the eye could see, plus the ever-present roar of the nearby highway. They were somewhere in the middle of nowhere. He wasn't even sure what state they were in—only that it was off the beaten path so they could avoid the press.

He hoped, anyway. Because he probably looked like shit. Felt like it. Wanted to scream or curse or cry. They'd made it this far, the strange little band he'd put together. Dom, his best buddy from high school. Mish, the red-haired, bass-playing crooner he couldn't stop watching at a bar because her performance had been so exquisite, and Kevin, the kid on YouTube who'd rapped sticks against whatever he could to beat out such intricate patterns.

He'd brought them all together and they'd done the impossible.

He swallowed the lump in his throat and stared at the wavering heat mirage in the road. Kevin hadn't survived the pressure of a surprise hit, all the publicity and touring. Maybe that was Ray's fault—he'd gone on and on about practices and looking and sounding their best. They hadn't had a break in months. Hell, it wore *him* down.

Like Kevin, he'd turned to his favorite vice after too many sleepless nights. Once he'd discovered which of the men in the road crew didn't mind being drilled down into a mattress, meaningless sex had become his escape from the stress of being in the spotlight nonstop. He didn't worry too much about being caught. The gossip sites expected gratuitous sexual exploits from rock stars, and he'd been open about his sexuality from day one. The crew had kept silent about it, though.

On the nights he'd fucked the stress out of his nerves, he slept.

Ray wiped the sweat from his brow and paced.

He didn't know what to write. *I'm sorry I'm such a shitty bandleader. I didn't ask for this. It's hard.* That wasn't any good.

Sounded like a whiner, and he could just imagine the responses. *Oh yes, you poor thing, becoming famous is so very difficult.*

He kicked a stone across the parking lot, and much like with lyrics, the right words began to form and merge and break apart and connect. He whipped out his cell phone, opened the note app, and started typing.

He didn't know how long it took to write the damn thing, only that the door to his hotel room opened and closed twice. The second time, boots scuffed against the pavement, and Mish's Doc Martens came into view underneath his phone.

"Honey, you're going to fry to a crisp or drop from heat exhaustion if you stay out here any longer."

He typed the last words and looked up. "I'm done."

Fleeting horror shimmered like heat across her features. "The band?"

"God no." He rocked back, and maybe she was right about the heat. Or it was the stress that had his head spinning. "My apology to give to the press." He handed the phone over to her.

It took her far less time to read it than he'd taken to write it. When she finished, her shoulders dropped. "You sure you want to do this? It's bullshit."

"It's bullshit that will allow us to get a drummer and keep going. This is—a little thing."

Something in his voice must have given him away, because Mish stepped forward and wrapped him in a hug. "Oh, hon. Don't do this for us."

At five foot nine, he could press his eyes against her shoulder, so he did. "But I *am* sorry." Sorry he couldn't keep them together. Sorry he couldn't keep himself together.

The words might be bullshit, but the feelings behind them weren't.

CHAPTER
TWO

There are times in my life that replay over and over in my mind. Points when my life cracked apart, broke, and rearranged into something new and terrifying.

By now, you've all seen the video posted of an argument that occurred between me and Kevin Schmidt.

I don't have an excuse. I want to. I want to tell you that it was a farce, that Kevin and I are fine. Best buddies. That he's not leaving the band. I would love to explain that the pressures of touring for the first time ate at both of us, and that night was a spat brought on by stress.

It was more than that. There are some things friendship can't endure. Times when splits must occur. There are unresolvable differences between Kevin and the band.

I let them happen.

Leaders are people who forge bonds, strengthen ties, and help those in need. I failed both as a leader and Kevin's friend. What I had that night was anger rather than love. Nothing comes from anger but broken bottles and broken ties.

I apologize to all our fans, but most especially, to Kevin for my lack of control.

Anger is a personal fault and one I need to fix. For the love of the band, and all of you, I will, and I promise we'll back on the road, better than ever.

—RAY VAN ZELLER

WELL NOW, THAT WAS AN INTERESTING READ. ZAVIER DEMOS studied his laptop screen and scrolled through Ray Van Zeller's confessional apology one more time.

Ray could *write*. Zavier tapped his keyboard lightly, not enough to type, just enough for that soothing clicking. Then again, even as a freshman and sophomore in high school Ray had worked wonders with words. His poems had been regularly tacked up on the wall outside the English department, and he'd sung a hauntingly sweet song about pining after love for the school talent show Zavier's senior year. Came in first place, too. Lovely melody and elegant lyrics that even Zavier could appreciate, even if the sentiment wasn't anything he understood.

Zavier had sat out of the competition. He'd already gotten a scholarship for percussion to Juilliard. Not like he'd needed to impress anyone, and he'd had senioritis to the limit that year. He was done and he'd let the entire school know it, especially Ray. Turned him down flat when Ray had asked him to join the little garage band he'd been trying to put together.

Better things to do with his time than be a glorified metronome, even if Ray did have a lovely voice.

Zavier snorted. Ah, the righteousness of youth. That had served him well, right up until he'd set foot in New York City, where everyone was young and talented and no one gave a damn.

Oh, but Ray gave a damn, he was sure of that. From the

words on Zavier's screen to the lyrics underneath the driving melody and impressive rhythms found in every song on the Twisted Wishes album. A little rough around the edges, but that only added to the breath-catching charm. He'd followed Ray's career, mostly because he'd never quite gotten over the nerve of that cocky sophomore who'd asked a Juilliard-bound musician to play in his rock band.

The first incarnations of Ray's band were mediocre—Zavier'd watched a few shows from the back of dark bars when he'd been home to visit. But over time, and with the right people, Ray had created something new and different and *special*.

Except now Ray had lost his shit and the band had lost a drummer.

The keys under Zavier's fingers were smooth and warm. He ran his index finger over the little raised bump on the J.

The Twisted Wishes drummer had been getting worse and worse lately, so maybe there was more behind Ray losing his cool than "the pressures of touring for the first time" or any of the other reasons he didn't want to lay claim to.

A touch on the track pad brought up the band's call for auditions for drummers, and Zavier's fingers itched. Hell, his arms—his blood—swam with the need to tap out those delicious rhythms. Embellish them. Improve on them.

He hadn't been on any stage in three months, not since he'd walked away from his position as principal timpani of the Silverton Orchestra.

Damn Maestro Dimitri Ferbran. Regret was an odd thing. It stung and swirled and twisted against Zavier's innards. He should never have tied Dimitri up and fucked him.

Conductors weren't known for letting go of control, so Dimitri's surrender had been entirely too sweet and tempting. Zavier had given in to that, lost his own self-restraint, even though he'd been clear at the start: this was fun and games and fucking. Not a romance. No ties. No future.

Dimitri had planned otherwise, of course. Expected wine and flowers and a long-term commitment. Romantic love. The one thing Zavier *couldn't* give.

Saying no proved disastrous. He didn't even bother to explain to Dimitri that he was aromantic, that he wasn't ever going to fall in love or go out on dates or send him heart-shaped boxes of chocolates or whatever nonsense Dimitri wanted, not when the man was *incapable* of hearing anything he didn't want to hear. They weren't even friends, just bed partners. And while Zavier could master Dimitri in bed, the man was still a maestro outside of it, and he *never* let Zavier forget that. Every rehearsal, every performance had become as much of a battle as their little sexual escapades. Each prac-tice had turned into a fucking lovers' spat where Dimitri shouted criticism over the heads of their colleagues.

Zavier understood stress. He hadn't lobbed a bottle at Dimitri as Ray had at Kevin. He'd merely turned in his resig-nation and walked away.

Three months later, he still hadn't found another orches-tral position. He'd never expected how fast Dimitri would poison the well. All Zavier had found during his job search were shut doors and dead ends.

No one wanted a timpanist who fucked the conductor, then dropped him like a hot potato.

During that time, he'd listened to the Twisted Wishes album, to Ray's voice and clever lyrics, and wondered what would have happened had he said yes to that ballsy sopho-more back in high school.

Zavier stilled. Maybe it was time to find out. He'd kept his hand in drumming on a rock kit, and he did so love the beats underneath Ray's songs. He could do worse than a tour around the country with an up-and-coming rock band, and that would solve both his problem and Ray's.

So. Submit his CV. Type up a statement of intent. And click.

The tumble in his soul was the sheer opposite of regret—giddy anticipation.

They'd call, he knew. They had no choice. Wouldn't find a better drummer, mostly because there weren't any. He leaned back and tabbed to the apology. Above it was a photo as haunting as that little melody all those years ago. Ray, his lovely brown hair all cut and jagged. He didn't wear eyeliner like Domino did—didn't need it. Not with those wide golden eyes of his, like the whiskey he'd thrown at the drummer. His full lips were pressed into a line, and the tension was so bitter and sweet in the set of his shoulders.

No longer the gangly sophomore. Had Ray been older back then—well. Maybe Zavier would have joined the band, at least for the summer. Same amount of years lay between them now, but back then, Ray had been barely sixteen to Zavier's well past eighteen. Too young to fool around with, even for a summer fling.

Once more Zavier's fingers itched, but for very different reasons. Except now he knew better than to lose control and fuck where he worked.

He had no doubt he'd be working with Ray very soon.

CHAPTER
THREE

IF THERE WERE A HELL DESIGNED TO PUNISH RAY FOR KICKING Kevin out of the band, auditioning for his replacement must have been it. He hoped his expression was schooled as the *child* at the kit whaled on the skins like he'd only been playing a few years. Maybe he had—guy couldn't have been that long out of high school.

Then again, not too many years back, Ray'd been the same. Granted, he'd never dreamed of auditioning to go on tour with a band. He hadn't been ready yet. Hell, it took a few years and some singing lessons to settle his voice into a range he could belt out without scraping his vocal cords from his throat.

The kid meant well. In a few years, he might be formidable. Ray gave a little nod to Domino and Mish, and they both struck some final chords.

"How'd I do?" The kid was breathless and glowing. Eager as a puppy, but he also looked like he'd pass out in his food dish if given a chance, which—well, puppy.

"Not bad at all." Ray kept his tone light. "We'll let you know within a week, as we still have some other auditions."

Once the kid was gone, Ray closed his eyes and rubbed

his forehead. No one they'd heard play was up to Kevin's original quality. A few were serviceable drummers who could build up to the tricky rhythms, but they needed someone *now*, not in six months to a year. The kid was the last audition they had booked. "We're screwed."

Domino took a breath before speaking. "Actually, there's one more audition today." For someone dressed in all black, wearing a studded leather collar and two-inch platform boots that could crush skulls, Dom looked *remarkably* sheepish.

"Yeah?" Ray stomped over to the schedule and picked it up. "There's nothing written down." He threw the clipboard on the table.

Mish blew out a breath and backed away, hands in the air. "This is between you boys."

"I should have written it down. Carl approved him this morning, but..." Dom fiddled with the strings of his guitar. "I didn't know how you'd react."

"How I'd—" Except for Kevin, he couldn't think of anyone he'd throw out the door. "Who the hell is auditioning?"

"Me."

Smooth voice, like those images of melted chocolate in commercials. Vaguely familiar, too. Tingles ran down both of Ray's legs, and he rotated toward the door.

There, leaning against the frame, was Zavier Demos. Older, improbably hotter, and still as perfect as ever.

"No."

Fucker flashed a gorgeous smile. "Nice to see you, too, Ray."

No wonder Dom hadn't put him on the list. Ray would have crossed his name right back off due the lingering anger from high school. Zavier had been everything he'd wanted to be. Born with rock-star looks and a rock-star name, and a musical prodigy to boot. Fucking asshole had laughed all those years ago when Ray had asked him to join his first band.

"I thought you went to learn to play *real* music at Juilliard." He let bitterness slip into his voice.

"I did go to Juilliard." Zavier pushed off the doorframe and strode into the room, right up to Ray. Close enough that his black hair glinted in the overhead lighting. "All music is real. Yours especially."

He'd forgotten how blue Zavier's eyes were. They'd hardly crossed paths back in the day—seniors with scholarships didn't hang out with dorky sophomores with garage bands. Zavier's words threw him, though. "I—Thank you."

Zavier smiled, as if Ray had given the correct answer to some unknown question, and every bit of Ray lit up, as if he were still a pining sixteen-year-old. Fuck that to hell. He pushed the giddiness away.

"Shall I play for you? Or do you want to play for me?" Zavier's words stroked over Ray like a lover's fingers.

Holy hell, it was a good thing Carl had gotten bored early in the day. That was a *line*. Would have fallen for it back in school, too. "Well, you're here to play for us." He gestured to Mish and Domino.

"A ménage, then."

Dom had this odd expression, halfway between fear and wonder, but then he had probably had it worse for Zavier back in school. Not by much, though.

Mish was grinning her head off. "Oh, you're fucked up. I *like* you."

Zavier laughed, and even that was bell-like.

How fucking *perfect* can one man be? Guess they'd find out. "You wanna play? Kit's over there." Ray pointed at the drums. "How much of our music do you know?"

No answer until Zavier sat behind the drums, adjusted the stool, and took stock of the equipment. He tapped on the snare with his finger. "All of it." He looked straight at Ray. "Well—all that you've released."

Flutters of hope skimmed through Ray's chest, mixing with the tumult of emotions already churning there. He swallowed. "That's all we need." He'd been working on a few new songs, but without Kevin sober, there'd been no hope of anything beyond lyrics.

Zavier nodded, then picked up a pair of sticks and ran through a round on the kit, testing each instrument. It was stunning. Unlike the puppy before him, Zavier had a calm, determined demeanor, and he played—even for the few minutes it took to drink in the equipment—as if he owned every single inch of the kit.

When he finished, he flicked one stick around in his hand. "What would you like me to play?"

Everything. Anything. God, those hands. "Since you say you know them all, why don't you pick?"

Domino raised an eyebrow. Yeah, unorthodox, but Ray wanted to know—wanted to hear from those lips—which of *his* songs Zavier Demos would choose.

A flicker of a smile, then Zavier spoke. "'White Hot Midnight.'"

That song. Oh *fuck*. Wasn't even on the album. It had been on a demo tape, but had been deemed too challenging for mainstream, whatever that meant. They played it in concert anyway and the fans loved it. There were even some people with lyrics tattooed on them. Blew Ray's mind every time someone showed him in the autograph line.

It also contained some of the most complex drumming Kevin had ever done. They hadn't played it much recently, for obvious reasons.

Ray surveyed Mish and Domino. "You guys okay with that?"

Dom nodded. Mish saluted. "Just give us a moment to tune," she said.

They did, and everyone stared at Ray expectantly. "You going to sing?" Zavier cocked his head.

He hadn't been, not much anyway, because he'd wanted to *hear* the drumming, not his own voice. "Yeah. I'll sing." He took up the mic, tapped it to make sure it was on, and nodded.

It started with the drums—nearly every song did—and after three taps of the sticks, Zavier hit it.

Oh god, it was glorious. Even more so when Dom and Mish joined. Ray threw his voice on top, the words pouring out like they did on stage, in front of hundreds. Thousands. Except now he was only singing for one person. He closed his eyes and let it all go.

Loneliness. Jealousy. Growing up. Letting go. Getting the fuck over things. He'd written the lyrics to "White Hot Midnight" when he'd seen a photo of Zavier in a tux in at his first concert after graduating from Juilliard. The poise. The sophistication. A guy completely out of his league. Ray had been out of high school two years then, in community college and struggling to create a band.

When the solos started, Ray listened, eyes hooded, staring at the floor and the mic cord running against it. Dark against light. A hint of deep orange. Wasn't Kevin playing—the rhythm in his bones told him that. Every beat, every syncopation, was deeper, more right, exquisite. New touches added here and there. Zavier had turned Kevin's drum line into his own—and outstripped it.

Fuck, this was going to work. When the chorus came again, he lifted his gaze to watch Zavier and sang.

All the wilderness
Here in my mind
All I ever wanted
You never knew
The carnage left behind

Alone I lie here
In the white hot midnight

Zavier was lost in a world of his own, playing with a grace and fluidity that made drumming look easy. Lips parted, eyes so bright, body alive.

When Ray started in on the last repeat, their eyes met, and Zavier nodded, as if he were part of the band.

As the last notes faded and silence fell on them, Ray realized he was. There wasn't any other drummer at all. Zavier hadn't auditioned—he'd taken them all on and won.

Even Mish was speechless, which *never* happened.

From behind the drum kit, Zavier still held Ray's stare. No words, but he knew they were a band. That lay in that smile, the triumph written into his shoulders and arms.

You bastard. The thought flitted through Ray's mind, even as his soul melted from the fading echoes of music that he hadn't heard the likes of since Kevin hit the bottle. *You bastard. You knew that song was about you.*

Finally, he spoke. "When can you start?"

That slick grin wanted to turn him inside out. "As soon as you need me."

Now. Ray needed him now.

They had a band again. And he had another hard-on for Zavier Demos. *Shit.*

ONE SONG WASN'T ENOUGH. YES, IT HAD GOTTEN ZAVIER THE job, but he wanted to play on. Burned with the need to drum through every single Twisted Wishes song he could, just to watch Ray Van Zeller sing. The abandon, the way he moved. No wonder fans threw underwear onto the stage. Ray made love to every song with the cant of his hips, the twist of his hands around the mic, the way he rocked through the melody.

"White Hot Midnight" was the most technically challenging song for drumming Twisted Wishes had. It was also an ode to lost years and lost dreams, full of longing and desire —and Zavier had made Ray sing it for him. At him. And god, he'd loved every second. The playing, the agony in that voice. The blending of Domino's and Mish's guitar and bass lines.

He locked gazes with Ray, and power surged through him. Ray wanted him. It was written in the words and drawn in every line of that body. Zavier had always wondered a few things about that particular song, who Ray had written it for.

There was no hiding the bulge in Ray's pants, nor the spark of lust that woke Zavier's own cock.

He took a moment to come down off that high and get his desires under control before dropping the sticks into their holder on the kit. When he could think straight, he peered out past the kit and sought Ray again.

Same smoldering gaze, one that spoke of anger and lust. Ray lifted his chin. "*Now* the asshole says yes to joining the band." He swung away, peering around the room. "Where the fuck is Carl?" A moment later, he set down the mic, grabbed his cell phone, and stomped off, muttering something about their fucking worthless manager.

The bang of the door echoed in the silent room.

Asshole. Zavier swallowed against that lingering taste of regret. Yeah, maybe he was. But he was the asshole who was going to save their band.

God, he wanted a piece of Ray. A chance to tame that anger, or pitch it higher until they were a tangle of limbs and sheets in a bed. The age difference had been too great in high school, but they were both grown men now.

He rose and joined the other two members of the band.

"Don't let Ray's snippiness get to you," Mish said. "He's

had a stick up his ass since Kevin left and the label came down on him for it."

Zavier met her smile with one of his own. "Oh, I won't. Plus there's history there." He gestured at the path Ray had taken. "And he's right. I *am* an asshole."

She laughed. "You'll fit right in, then."

Zavier had already decided he liked Mish, but that quip sealed it. A treat to behold, she was an excellent player. That she'd not even blinked at his off-color comment, had called him fucked up, had welcomed him as an ass—well. She could hold her own.

Then again, he expected nothing less from a woman who could tower over her bandmates and play a mean bass while dancing around the stage in high heels.

He wasn't quite sure what to make of the silent Domino. While both Ray and Mish wore jeans and T-shirts, a far cry from their stage outfits, Domino was in full gear, as if this were a concert. A great guitarist, but no one really knew much about him. "Please don't tell me you always dress like that."

Domino swallowed and ran his fingers over strings and frets. "Whenever I'm in public."

Zavier surveyed the room. "This is hardly public."

Domino gave a shrug. His spiked hair shook and the studded collar around his neck bobbed. "Public enough." He paused, and wonder crept into his voice. "You *do* know our songs."

"That's pretty cool," Mish said. "Are you a fan, or can you just—" she waved a hand "—pick shit up?"

"A little of both. I have your albums, watched a bunch of tour videos people snuck onto YouTube, but I also have a knack for learning by ear."

"Musical prodigy," Domino said.

That comment, the nod, and something about the timbre

of Domino's voice made Zavier take a closer look. He peered behind the eyeliner and makeup. "Do I know you?"

A laugh and Domino looked down, his smile timid and hauntingly familiar. "I doubt you would remember me. I was pretty invisible at school."

Then it clicked. The talent show in high school. That beautiful song. There'd been a guitarist with Ray, the shy nerdy kid. What the hell was his name? "Dominic. Dominic Bradley."

Brown eyes, clever thin lips. Yes. Older now, but weren't they all?

Domino nodded, awe evident. "It's a bit of a secret."

Understanding washed over Zavier. Domino—the persona—was armor. "Safe with me."

That shy smile again. "Thanks."

He was about to say something more when the door banged open. A blond man—trim and built, with a round face that might have been lovely had he not been scowling—strode in. Behind him sulked Ray, a bundle of tension.

The blond stuck out his hand. "You must be Zavier Demos. I'm Carl Roberts, the band manager."

His shake was slightly too firm against Zavier's hand, a sure sign of someone desperate to be in charge. "Nice to meet you," Zavier lied.

"I don't know why someone of your caliber wants to play with this lot. But we appreciate you stepping in."

That comment raised Zavier's hackles. A manager putting down the band? Though he focused on Carl, Zavier spotted Ray's twitch and frown. "I needed a change of pace." He paused. "Do you want to hear me play?"

Carl waved the suggestion away. "Ray said you're the best. He might not know much, but he does know music."

Ouch. Zavier schooled his face. This man was a complete *dick*. "I take it there will be paperwork to sign?"

"Of course." He gestured to the door. "Why don't we go talk about it elsewhere?"

Zavier nodded, but when Carl turned, he stole a glance at Ray. Pale. Shaking. Obviously furious. This wasn't good. He caught Ray's attention and gave a wave he hoped was assuring.

Sign with the prick, then sit down with the band and find out what the deal was. Perhaps he could lend a hand with whatever friction lay between Ray and the manager. He followed Carl out of the room.

Maybe he could help in another way, other than being the replacement drummer. He couldn't be anything more, even if Ray's desire was so obvious Zavier wanted to drink it right in. Wasn't going to happen, which was an astounding pity.

But the debacle with Dimitri had burned too many scars into Zavier's soul. Last thing he wanted was another mistake like that one. Better no sex at all or one-night stands than anything that involved expectations.

Well, at least he'd be able to watch Ray make love to his music. That would be treat enough.

CHAPTER
FOUR

RAY GUESSED THE RECORD COMPANY SIGNING ZAVIER HADN'T taken too long, because the very next day, Carl ordered them back at the same studio space to practice. They were all dressed casually, thank goodness. Dom tended to put away the stage persona for rehearsals. It was weird to play when he was all up in Domino and the rest of them were in ratty T-shirts and jeans. Threw Ray off to see Dom ready for stage when they weren't performing.

Apparently, Dom had told Zavier who he was—or rather Dom claimed Zavier guessed. Of course Mr. Perfect had figured it out. Ray resisted the urge to roll his eyes on the ride over from the hotel when Dom recounted the story.

Mish watched the streets go by out the window. "He's way better than Kevin."

Ray grunted. Yeah, he was. Always had been, even in high school. With any luck, Zavier's playing would get them on the road again, and make the record company happy. Kevin's departure and the aftermath still ate at him—they'd be watching closely. He owed it to Dom and Mish to get the band on track and Carl off their backs.

She leaned back and fixed her gaze on him. "You don't like him."

Dom squirmed on the seat next to Ray, but he ignored that. "It's not that I don't like him, it's..." He waved his hand, because really, he had no reason to hate Zavier Demos.

He just couldn't stand the guy.

Zavier was everything Ray had both wanted and wanted to be back in high school. Beautiful, outgoing, talented, sexy, and smart. Zavier could have had and, if the rumor mill had been anything to go by, did have anyone he wanted back then.

Not that he'd wanted Ray, though. Not as a bandmate or anything else.

Later, when Ray was getting his associate's degree at the local community college and struggling with his music, Zavier was off becoming a professional musician and the toast of the fucking wine, cheese, and tux set.

What galled Ray was that Zavier truly was *that* good. His playing during the audition yesterday had set that in stone—and that was without any rehearsals. With some time practicing together? They'd have a killer sound.

The worst, though, was when they walked into the studio and Zavier was already there, in a tank top and jeans, idly twirling a drumstick. He met Ray's stare and smiled.

Back in high school, Zavier had sported one tattoo—a scene like one from a Greek vase with meandering patterns and a figure of a woman with an owl, but in brilliant colors—on his forearm. Ray had committed every line, color, and swirl to memory. Later, he'd realized the woman had to have been Athena.

Now? Zavier was covered in ink. Sleeves up both arms, and more that disappeared beneath the fabric of the tank. Ray bit down on his tongue to keep from licking his lips. Last thing he wanted was to be caught ogling Zavier, especially with Carl in the room. He headed over to a table where bottles of water had been set out.

Carl, standing over by the door, coughed in that fake way he did whenever he wanted their attention. Ray didn't pay him any mind. Instead, he grabbed a bottle of water and cracked it open. Only when Carl coughed again did he turn.

"Glad to see you're able to be on time for once." Carl's smile was knife-sharp. "Though I bet that has more to do with your bandmates."

Dom flinched and Mish straightened. Ray spoke before they could. "Yeah, everyone knows I'm the slacker." He took a swig of his water, and shrugged. "Drummer's early."

Zavier stilled the stick he'd been twirling. "They say traffic in Los Angeles is horrible, so I gave myself extra time from the hotel."

"You could learn something from him, Ray." Carl tapped his forehead with his finger. "Plan ahead."

Ray shrugged again. "Well, we're all here, aren't we?" They'd even been about five minutes early. Would have been earlier if Dom hadn't forgotten where he'd put his phone. But slip-ups were always Ray's fault. Bandleader, after all.

Honestly, he'd rather Carl pick on him than anyone else.

Ray stole another glance at Zavier to drink in his tattoo-covered glory, and caught Zavier watching him with a furrowed brow. No malice, though. Not like Carl's twisted smirk and glare. At least with Carl, Ray knew exactly where he stood.

He met Zavier's stare. "We should get to work."

"That's the most sensible thing you've said in weeks," Carl muttered. "Guess getting you out of the bottle worked."

This time Dom straightened and Mish stepped forward, her voice ringing out. "Hey, you f—"

Ray spoke first. "How long do we have 'til we're back on the road?"

"Five Asylum starts their tour in less than two months."

Carl strode over to the table Ray had grabbed water, pulled out a swivel chair, and sat his snarky ass down. "You're getting almost equal billing and play time with them, so you damn well better be ready."

Jesus. Five Asylum was a huge band, chart-topping for more than a decade. And Twisted Wishes had six weeks, maybe seven? Brand-new drummer. No pressure there.

Ray swallowed his fear along with a gulp of water. "Let's go, then."

Both Mish and Dom picked up their instruments, and Zavier settled in behind the kit. For a couple of minutes, the three of them tuned, jammed, and warmed up. Ray had given his voice a workout before leaving the house and on the ride over. After the first few times Carl had snickered at him when he went through vowels and pushed his range—well, better to do that shit in private.

"Let's start with 'Haze' and see how that sounds," Ray said. It was the easiest of their repertoire and one of the first pieces they played at shows, partly to get into a grove with each other. He glanced at them all, stopping when he got to Zavier.

A flick of a drumstick and a nod. Felt more like approval than an indication he knew the song. Warmth flared in Ray's belly, but not from embarrassment. Zavier seemed to understand what he intended with this practice.

"Let's see how we sound," Ray said.

Zavier counted out the beat, and they were off. The intro sounded good, and fuck, did Zavier look stunning behind the kit. When Ray threw his voice in, it blended well in and out of Dom's riffs, like it always did. They sounded *damn* good for not playing for several weeks, especially considering Zavier had played exactly one song with them before now.

But something niggled at Ray when they finished. "Mind doing that again without me singing?"

No objections from the band. Carl's chair squeaked and

Ray gritted his teeth. But a moment passed without any comment, so he nodded to Zavier, who set the beat again.

This time, Ray closed his eyes. He needed to see the music, not the performers, and especially not Zavier. The notes and beats washed over him and set bursts of color off in his head. Shapes. Lines. Exactly what he'd seen when he'd written the piece. Good. Very good. Mish's bass sounded exactly right and Dom was his usual controlled chaos. Zavier was perfect. Utterly. When the change-up after the second verse happened—a tricky little twist in the beat he'd written in so long ago—that was when he saw it. A slip in Dom and in Mish—but not in Zavier. A little clash of hues.

He opened his eyes and waved them to stop. "Can you play the transition again?"

"It sounded fine," Carl grumbled.

Everything in Ray tightened. Thank god he had his back to the asshole. He spoke more slowly. "Can you play the transition again?"

"Yes, of course." That from Zavier. "As many times as you need."

Dom nodded.

"There's something hinky going on, isn't there?" Mish ran her fingers over the strings of her bass.

There was, and Ray thought he knew why, but he wanted to make sure. He waved his hand for them to start.

That same clash was there again, and the next time they played, too. Ray blew out a breath and scrubbed the back of his head. "You're too good."

Zavier's sticks clattered as he gripped them in one hand. He grunted, but his smile was back. Approval. Understanding. Every time, it tumbled something deep inside Ray.

Dom stared at Ray like he'd grown two heads, but Mish was laughing. "Oh my god. Of course."

"What the hell are you going on about, Van Zeller?" The chair creaked again.

Ray turned to find Carl standing, hands on his hips. "I'm doing my job, Carl. What do you think?"

"You asinine little—"

Zavier's voice boomed out over the room. "With all due respect, Carl—" His tone said the exact opposite. "Sit down, be quiet, and you might learn a thing or two."

A deep, dark place in Ray's heart flared to life at Carl's shocked expression, at the blush that crept up his neck to his face, and the step backward he took that had him tumbling into the chair.

Maybe he could stand Zavier Demos after all.

Ray put his back to Carl. "It's not that there's a problem," he said. "It's the lack of one."

Mish nodded. "Kevin never got the beat right at the change-up. He always flubbed it."

"And you and Dom covered for that, so it didn't matter." Ray eyed Zavier. "You can't mimic Kevin's mistake."

Zavier took a breath. "I could *try*. But no, not consistently. Not for a performance. I know how the line should sound. I fix it in my head every time I hear the song." He gave Ray a sly grin. "Most people wouldn't have noticed."

Ray straightened, the nerves along his arms tingling. Maybe he hadn't gone to Juilliard or been a fucking prodigy like Zavier. Yeah, he only had an associate's degree in accounting, but these were *his* songs. Every word, note, and beat. "I'm not most people."

"I know." Zavier's sincerity knocked the air from Ray's lungs.

He pulled himself together, though an echo of the teen he'd been wanted to yell, *Took you a fucking long time to figure that out!*

He studied Zavier. "Can you play the drum line alone?"

Zavier got this *distant* look, and it was a hell of a thing to watch—his intensity and scrutiny turned inward. Calculating, thinking, and studying every angle of some invisible chart.

When those blue eyes focused back on Ray, a different heat tumbled inside him, because he swore Zavier gave him an up-and-down look before replying, "Yes."

Ray shoved aside anything beyond Zavier's ability to drum because that was all that mattered now, not how much he wanted to see the rest of Zavier's ink. "Dom, Mish—listen."

Zavier played, never missing a beat, and they all listened, maybe even Carl, too. No squeaks from his chair.

By the time Zavier was done, Dom had his lips pressed thin and he was nodding. "Yeah. I get it."

"Might take a bit to undo," Mish said.

"Wanna try?" Ray knew the answer.

"Hell yes!" A big grin from her. Determination from Dom.

So they did. Ray didn't sing the next time through, but he did after that. By the fifth time, they had it. When they played the song once more, Zavier added some flourishes that were *intense.*

"Fuck, that's good," Dom said. "I can't wait to get on stage."

Neither could Ray. "One down—"

Lots more to go. He scanned the room. Carl was typing on his phone and Zavier—

For once, Zavier wasn't watching Ray. He brushed a lock of his jet-black hair from his forehead and had this shit-eating grin as he took in the drum kit and the room, like he was excited to be here, excited to play. When his gaze finally focused on Ray again, the subtle up-and-down was back and that smile settled into something deeper and so damn sensual it melted Ray's bones.

Fucking hell. The last thing he needed was Zavier having the hots for him, especially after all these years. He turned away. "Okay, let's try 'Dreams Unto You' next."

As the next song started, Ray chewed his tongue. Thing

was, in high school he'd have dropped to his knees if Zavier had asked him to. Wasn't so sure he'd say no now, either.

If he were reading those looks right, they'd probably find out eventually.

Zavier ran a towel over his face, neck, and hands. They'd been practicing all morning and his back, as conditioned as he kept it, was getting annoyed with him. Being principal timpanist and playing concerts had been tiring of course, but that paled to the intensity of *this*. When Ray had laid down his mic and called for a lunch break, Zavier was more than ready. He slipped the sticks into a holder on the kit, popped his ear protection out, stood, and stretched.

At some point, he'd need to talk to Ray or Carl—or whoever did the stage layout—about his setup for concerts. He needed to stand once in a while or his back would bitch and moan.

But now he was grateful for bottles of water and a take-out menu from a local sub shop. He opted for semi-healthy grilled chicken covered in cheese, rather than mounds of pork or beef covered in cheese. He downed one water, cracked open another, and wandered over to the window. Dom was already there and had done what Zavier had intended—opened the damn thing for some air.

Was a bit hard reconciling the image of Domino Grinder with Dominic Bradley. The same tattoos peeked from under the short sleeves of Dom's button-down, but Dom had a far more subdued nature now that he was out of his Domino persona. Shy and thoughtful, except when he played.

God, they were all gorgeous then, the three of them. Mish danced like she loved every note and every inch of the floor had been made to obey her. Dom got lost in riffs and moved like fire. Ray—the things Zavier wanted to do to that man. The fantasies.

He sipped his water and rolled his shoulders. *No.*

"Sore?" Dom shifted to give Zavier room to catch a breeze.

"A little." Not a hard admission—he preferred the truth all around. Soon he'd be living with these three for months and months, in very close quarters. They needed to trust each other. "It's been a while since I've played behind a rock kit. Symphony work is different. More standing. More pauses."

A nod. "I bet. I watched you once when you were playing with Silverton, during that tribute to Prokofiev."

Interesting. "You know, if someone had told me Domino Grinder went to the symphony, I might have laughed...but now that I've met you...again... I get it." Zavier shrugged. "Given your guitar skills, it makes sense."

Dom gave him a shrewd look. "How are we supposed to learn how to shred if we don't listen to *all* the classics?"

Yeah, this band knew music, no doubt about that. "How else, indeed."

"You haven't lost your touch." Dom gestured at the rock kit, then he lowered his voice. "Thanks for putting Carl in his place. He gets...irritating."

"So I'm learning. What's his problem anyway?"

Dom's shoulders dropped as low as his voice. "Who the hell knows?"

Huh. "I thought bands chose their managers?" His voice was as quiet as Dom's—not that Carl would've heard anyway, given he was arguing with Ray.

"He came with the record contract," Dom said. "And the label made it pretty clear everything goes through Carl."

Weird. Zavier glanced at Ray, and the tension in that back vibrated across the room. Zavier slugged back the rest of his water and wandered closer.

"...only have three more days of studio time." Carl shrugged. "You figure out how to make it work. It's not my problem." He glanced at his phone. "I have somewhere to be," he said, then marched away.

Ray said nothing, but once the studio door banged shut, he put his palms on the table. "Fuck."

Zavier schooled his expression. "Did he just tell you we only have this space for three more days?"

Ray's anger was palpable, and entirely appropriate. "That's about the size of it," he ground out. "We can't—" He straightened and turned. Fear. Panic and doubt. So many emotions flickered across that face. "I mean, you're *damn* good. But we can't get it all done in that time. There's too many songs and—"

They needed to run through every one of them. Hard enough in two months. Impossible in three days. "Maybe I can change his mind."

A glance at the door. "I don't think any of us can. Just— don't get yourself fired?"

Zavier chuckled. "Oh, I won't. I have a really good contract lawyer." The record company would be in some pain if they let him go without due cause—and pissing off a self-important shitty manager wasn't due cause.

He headed out the door and down the stairs. By the time he got to the parking lot, Carl's car was pulling out onto the street.

"Fuck." There went that plan.

He needed more information. Probably should have gotten it before he stepped into this gig—but it was *Ray's* band; Zavier couldn't stop himself from auditioning and saying yes. Grown-up Ray was something else, like his music and band. All three plowed through Zavier in a unique way, but none of that helped the Carl situation.

Zavier pulled out his phone, scrolled through his contacts, and hit Call before he had second thoughts.

Three rings, then a familiar lilting voice answered. "My darling Zavier, what can I do for you?"

Always *darling* Zavier. Anyone else, he'd have been mad, but she was older, wiser, and one of the very few to have ever put him in his place without reservation and rightly so. "Hello, Nadia. I've called to ask a favor."

She clicked her tongue. "Your little stint at rock-and-roll not working out?"

Of *course* she'd known about that. Ties everywhere in the music industry. "Yet to be determined, though the band is quite good."

"Rumor says the lead singer has a drinking problem."

That'd been all over the internet. "Pretty certain that rumor is false."

A chuckle. "Darling, of *course* it is." He could almost envision her waving her hand. "A different rumor says it was the old drummer who drank too much."

Which would account for Kevin's downhill playing. "More plausible."

"Mmm. I can't wait until they see *you*. Those rumors should be delicious. Dark, handsome classically-trained drummer with tattoos that make you weak in the knees...if you're lucky."

He couldn't help the laugh. "I'm benign." Though he wouldn't mind seeing Ray kneeling.

"Says the man who can't get a position in any orchestra in North America because he was fucking and flogging his conductor, then didn't have the decency to be a kept boy like a *proper* young musician."

Fuck. *Fuck*. Zavier swallowed a breath, counted to three, then exhaled. "Oh, is that what they're saying?" He shivered, despite the heat of the day, but didn't let an ounce of fear or anger slip into his voice. "How droll."

"He would have showered you with gifts and flowers."

"You know exactly how much that means to me." Not a damn thing. He didn't comprehend that kind of love—or the trappings of it. So much of romance seemed downright *silly*.

Though, had it just been Dimitri falling for him, that wouldn't have been as bad. No, Dimitri had wanted Zavier on *his* knees with declarations of love. Zavier had been so clear about that the first time they'd fucked. Sex without attachments. They hadn't even been friends.

"Oh yes. You're every submissive's dream and every romantic's nightmare." Nadia's laugh was light. "You didn't call to hear about yourself."

No. He hated when she told him the gossip about himself. Ignorance was bliss, and all that. She, of course, told him anyway. A bur under his skin to remind him that he was young and still had much to master. "I was wondering what you could tell me about Carl Roberts. He's Twisted Wishes's band manager."

There was a pause—one that was long enough to mean he'd surprised her. "The band manager? Interesting. Your impressions?"

"I'll keep those to myself for the time being." He'd rather have the information unbiased by his opinion. While Carl seemed to be an unmitigated asshole, Zavier couldn't be certain that Ray hadn't done something to make the situation worse. Though, Ray was too *open* in his pain to be hiding anything.

"It may take me a bit. Managers are so less interesting than musicians."

He kept his chuckle inside. Unlike Nadia, he'd bedded more than musicians. All *sorts* of people were fascinating. "Whenever you can. I don't want to impose."

"Of course you want to impose, darling. It's why you called." She practically purred the words.

He purred right back. "But you adore it when I call." He'd owe her. Not sure what he'd have to give up—that always changed—but it would be worth the trouble.

"True." She paused. "Do take care, darling. The music industry can eat you alive."

It was already chowing down hard on Ray. "After my last misstep, I'm certainly more cautious."

"Good. You were my best student, Zavier. I'd hate to see you fodder for tabloids."

He didn't quite swallow his laugh this time. She'd love to see juicy tidbits about his life spread out for all. They made their goodbyes, and as he hung up, the band's lunch arrived in a beat-up white four-door sedan. He helped the driver carry their order upstairs. Surprisingly, Carl had pre-paid and even given a decent tip.

So being an utter asshole only extended to the band—or maybe to just Ray. Hopefully whatever Nadia dug up would make sense of that.

Once the driver had left and they set about eating, Ray asked the question Zavier had been waiting for. "You talk to Carl?"

"He blew out of here so fast, I didn't even make it to the parking lot before he was gone." He took a bite of his sandwich—and closed his eyes against the flavors. "Shit, this is actually good."

Murmurs of agreement, and for a few minutes, they were content. Food did that—eased pain and frustration.

But as they finished eating, the tension inched back into the air. "What are we going to do about the studio space?" Dom crumpled his wrapper and stuffed it into a bag. "We can't tour on three days of practices."

Ray screwed up his face. "I know. I don't—" He stopped and his expression smoothed out and became distant. Calculating. Beautiful.

Oh, Ray, what do you have up your sleeve?

A sly little smile, then Ray glanced around—and focused on Zavier. "I'm finally going to get you into my garage band."

Delight slithered all the way down to Zavier's core. "How many years have you been waiting to say that?"

Oh, and there was the lovely blush, right on schedule.

"Too many." He didn't look away. "The house we're staying in has a big-ass garage. Not ideal, but it's *space*."

Zavier gave Ray his most charming smile. "You finally have me, Ray."

Mish looked like she was about to choke on her cheesesteak. "You two are going to end up screaming at each other. I know it."

"I don't scream." Not even when Dimitri had thrown a vase at him for not buying roses after their first month together. Raise his voice? Sure. Ordered a man to his knees? Yes. Scream? Nothing so *uncontrolled*.

"I don't, either. It strips my vocal cords." Ray shrugged. "Also, I don't have to like someone to work with them." He stared at Zavier.

Ray didn't like him? Zavier gazed back until Ray turned away, all reddening neck and catching breath. Not true, that. There were, after all, many different *kinds* of like.

Mish was trying not to laugh, and poor Dom looked decidedly uncomfortable when he spoke. "Um. Maybe we should get back to work?"

Ray gave a grunt. "Let's see what we can do until Carl kicks us out tonight."

Despite Ray's mood, once they all got back to their instruments—and Ray to the mic—practice went well. Felt good to play like this again—continuously, passionately, and controlled. Twisted Wishes sometimes spun close to chaos during their songs, with layers upon layers of timing and chords, but Ray had written songs that worked, and his voice carved out sense from the chaos and brought the mess together into a beautiful whole.

Music like this was Zavier's true passion. He didn't understand the hearts of humans, but this he knew and felt. He modified Kevin's lines on the fly, bringing them closer to what he knew as true when he listened to that lovely voice singing.

They managed three more songs before Carl returned and their bodies gave out. Both Dom and Mish were stretching their hands and Ray spoke with gravel between sips of water.

Zavier's back felt like fire. Last time his muscles had complained this much was after he'd spent a night in a club flogging three subs. At least there he'd been able to find an outlet for the buzzing in his blood and the fire in his veins. Tonight he'd have a cold shower and his hand, and Ray Van Zeller's voice in his head.

Fucking *hell*.

But he wouldn't have changed anything at all. This wasn't the symphony, but it was so much closer to a space Zavier might call home. His mind swam with rhythm and his vision with Ray swaying to his music.

Zavier downed another bottle of water and approached Carl. "So why only three days in the studio when you knew there were two months before the tour?"

To Zavier's left, Ray lifted his head. His back was to both Zavier and Carl.

Carl frowned, but that hid something—fear? Anger? Zavier couldn't tell. "The songs aren't *that* complicated."

Yes, they were. Zavier didn't say anything, just stared at Carl. Ray turned slightly, his torso corded with tension.

Finally, Zavier murmured, "You didn't think they'd find a drummer."

Carl lost color. Bingo. Zavier being here, the label signing him, that had thrown things into disarray for Carl. Zavier snorted and turned away.

Maybe Carl thought Zavier could learn the songs in three days, which was possible. He knew the music. But knowing and playing it with the rest of the band were two entirely different situations. They needed to learn to play with *each other*, and that took time.

Zavier clasped Ray on the shoulder. "You're getting your wish."

Those whiskey-colored eyes were wide and his breath as smoky as the drink. "Lucky me." Heat there. A touch of ire, too.

Catnip to his lust. Zavier dropped his hand. Working with Ray was *dangerous*.

Carl cleared his throat. "Better get your bags from the hotel, Demos. You'll be joining them in the house."

Zavier'd figured that. There'd been an itemized receipt for checkout slipped under his door in the middle of the previous night. "They're in my rental." He kept watching Ray, since the view was better.

Ray rolled his eyes and muttered, "Mr. Perfect."

Was that how Ray thought of him? "Not so much."

That only earned him a snort before Ray turned away. "Let's pack up for the night." He rounded and faced Carl. "How early can we get in here tomorrow?"

"Eight a.m."

"Then we'll be here. On time. All of us."

Carl snatched up his phone. "Good to see you finally taking this seriously." With that, he was out of the door once again.

Ray clenched and unclenched his hands, until Mish came over and rubbed his back. "Don't let him get to you, hon. We did good work today."

Some of the tension eased from those shoulders. "Yeah, we did." Once more Zavier found Ray focusing on him. "How do you feel about it?"

Horny and turned on, like he did after any stellar performance. But that wasn't anything he'd say out loud. "Good. Very good. You guys are great to work with and the songs are —" he whistled "—better live than anything else."

The rest of the stress fell off Ray. "You mean that?"

"Every word."

A small smile played over shy Dom's lips. "See?"

Ray shook his head. "Let's get back to the house."

Zavier followed the band down to the parking lot, then tailed the hired car back to a house in the hills. Gated, and yes, it had a big enough garage to play in.

He set his bags down on the bed in the last unoccupied room—the one right next to Ray's. For a moment, he considered that lithe body and sighed.

Off limits. Completely. He didn't want to wind up as gossip for Nadia, after all. Even if he did wonder whether he could make Ray scream.

CHAPTER
FIVE

HAVING ZAVIER IN THE HOUSE WITH THE REST OF THE BAND WAS distracting as fuck. His presence tapped on every last one of Ray's nerves. His voice was like a caress and the sight of him was a constant reminder to Ray's libido that he hadn't gotten any in months and months.

Didn't help that Zavier watched him like he was an item on a menu. Fucking around with the crew was one thing; fucking a bandmate was another. Plus—and he had to remind himself constantly—he didn't like Zavier. Desperation for sex wasn't a good reason to throw yourself at someone. Especially not at Mr. Perfect Zavier Demos, drummer extraordinaire.

While the living arrangements were frustrating as fuck, the practices were incredible. Every piece they worked on, they elevated to a new level and Ray gained a serious appreciation for how talented Zavier was. Wasn't smoke and mirrors. Zavier worked *hard*. Despite the twinges in his features and the shoulder rolls between sessions, he never faltered behind the kit or complained about their marathon practices.

He also quietly backed up all of Ray's musical decisions—or not so quietly when Carl was around.

Yeah, Zavier's playing showed he deserved to have gone to Juilliard. Hell, he should've been in some world-class orchestra or a multi-platinum headlining rock band, but here he was, drumming for Twisted Wishes. Ray didn't understand *why*. What did Zavier get out of the deal? He didn't trust Zavier, even if his body screamed to get closer, especially after Zavier stripped off his tank after one intense session. All that ink on Zavier's back. Saint freaking Michael the archangel descending down to slay demons. More tattoos that dipped below Zavier's waistline. All of it only made him want to stare longer at that unreal body.

Still, they made it halfway through their first album by the middle of the last studio day, thrashing, playing, and meticulously going over every note and beat.

"I don't know why you're bothering with all the songs," Carl grumbled. "It's not like you play them all on tour."

Ray hid his wince by grabbing a bottle of water. "That was with Kevin. I need to know which songs are the best with Zav."

"Zav?" Carl's sneer deepened.

Fuck Carl. Ray'd known Zavier longer than anyone in this room, save Dom. He called back over his shoulder, "You don't mind Zav, do you?"

A laugh. "Zav is absolutely fine." Zavier took a seat at a stool next to the table and grabbed one of the water bottles. "It's what everyone called me at school." The Zavier now was so much more than the Zavier in high school. Same fucking eyes peered back, though. "You can even call me asshole, if you want." Sly-ass smirk.

Fucker. Ray turned back to Carl and shrugged. "You want us at our best, I need to figure out what the new best is."

Mish joined them. "Hey, Carl." Her words and grin were

too bright, but Carl wouldn't know that. He'd never caught on.

He smiled back at her, with that *look* hetero men got when she turned on the charm. "Hey. You sounded outstanding today."

"Thanks," she drawled. She stood over him—all six foot one of her—and there was the hint of discomfort the same hetero men got when they realized Mish could break them in two. "Did you find us another studio space?"

Carl had to crane his neck to answer, his Adam's apple bobbing when he swallowed. "No. There's nothing available."

"In all of L.A.?" Mish tapped her lip with a finger. "Huh."

Carl focused on Ray rather than Mish. "You're something else, Ray."

Ray gave another disinterested shrug, and ignored the burning in the back of his throat. He had as much control over Mish as anyone else—not a damn ounce.

"Don't you worry your pretty little head, darling," Mish said. "We'll be ready for the tour."

"You've only worked through half an album and none of your newest material—you know, the songs that charted?" Carl leaned back and crossed his arms. "And you'll be ready?"

Ray took another swallow of water. "I know what I'm doing."

"That'll be a first," Carl murmured.

The calm Ray had been so desperately trying to hang on to broke suddenly, and he slammed the water bottle down on the table. "Now look here—"

He made to rise, but Zavier clapped a hand on his shoulder and squeezed. Not hard, but enough to zing through every nerve. Ray sank back down onto the chair. "I've gotten us this far." A single in the top five. Sales that were decent. Tours and signing lines that were crowded enough. Fan mail. A gold album.

In the beginning, Carl had been so full of praise, even when he'd offered suggestions and picked at every one of Ray's decisions. Now? The praise was gone. The critique remained, though.

"Oh yes," Carl said. "You're A-plus material. Drive your drummer to drink. Throw a bottle at him. Make the news in such a *stellar* way. Your band's playing on tour has been shit. It's a wonder the label gave you this chance."

Zavier hadn't removed his hand, and that was the only thing that kept Ray from leaning across the table and punching Carl. Thing was—everything Carl said was true. That was the worst thing. Carl was right. Ray'd failed Kevin. Failed the band. The burning turned inward and stabbed like daggers and he ground his teeth, face hot with shame.

Carl had even warned him, back at the start. *Your songs are good, kid. But this isn't like playing bars down at the Shore.* It hadn't been, either. Dude might be an asshole, but he did seem to know the business in a way Ray didn't.

"That's better." Carl rose. "Your lunch will be here soon and you have the studio until eight. After that, they'll be packing up your shit."

"Send the drum kit to the house." Zavier spoke low, but with force.

Carl jerked back. "What?"

"My kit." Zavier slid his hand from Ray's shoulder, and it took every ounce of control not to shudder. "Send it to the house."

"Why?"

A huff that Ray recognized as Zavier's *are you stupid* laugh. "Because I'm a fucking professional drummer."

Carl stared at Zavier. "Right. Okay." He swung around and headed to the door, already punching shit on his phone.

When the door slammed shut, Mish dropped into the seat Carl had occupied. "That man has no right being a manager."

Another grunt from Zavier—this one neutral.

"It'll be fine," Ray said, though his gut told him a different story. Like it or not, Carl was their manager. The first label exec he'd ever talked to had praised Carl up and down. Said that Twisted Wishes couldn't do any better.

"Will it?" Soft, quiet words from Dom. He'd been standing over by the window the entire time. "I mean, Zavier's good—"

"Why thank you." Zavier's cocky attitude was back.

"—but this is shit." Dom gestured around the studio. "They want us to fail."

Zavier rocked back on the stool and rubbed his chin. "The label wouldn't send you on tour with Five Asylum if they wanted you to fail."

Dom finally crossed the room. "But Carl's not giving us what we need."

Ray followed Zavier's hand from his chin to the table. Long fingers. Tats that ended at the wrists. In formal wear, you'd never see the ink.

Zavier gave off a rumble that fit somewhere between a cough and a laugh, and he flattened his hand against the table. "Carl's not the record label."

"He might as well be," Ray said. "He's our only contact with them." Their gateway to the stars, Carl sometimes said.

Zavier arched his eyebrows. "Really? Is that typical?" Not a snide question—honest curiosity.

God, Ray felt like shit—he wasn't smart enough for this gig. Images of Kevin with his bottle of Jack flashed through his mind, and he rubbed his forehead. "Maybe?" They'd gone into this blind, happy to have a contract and a label and some money behind them. "This is so different than when we played in local bars and put out singles, you know?"

But Zavier didn't know. He'd been off getting a music degree and touring the world with symphonies.

Ray pushed himself up. "I'll go wait for lunch. I need some air."

He followed the same path Carl had taken, but unlike Carl, he couldn't jump into a car and drive away. Hell, he was such a fuckup, he didn't know how to drive.

Ray stared up into the clear sky. Dom was right—this was shit, and he had no clue how to fix it.

———

AS THE DAYS WENT BY, ZAVIER WATCHED RAY BECOME MORE unraveled. When they played, Ray was fine, but as soon as music wasn't flowing through the air, he turned moody and snappish, or still and silent—a statue sitting out on the deck, watching the sky.

The few times Carl stopped by to listen to them practice in their makeshift space in the garage, Ray had gone from the Zen, perfect singer to a destructive asshole in no seconds flat.

"Maybe," Zavier murmured at Mish while they cleaned up a broken plate and glass, "we should switch to paper and plastic for a while."

"He's really stressed," she whispered back. "He's a good guy."

"I know he is." Ray was frustrated and scared. Only when he sang did he loosen up and breathe.

The urge to tame that energy and calm those fears gripped Zavier like a vice. Ray was lithe, strong, and responsive to rhythm, exactly the kind of person Zavier loved to fuck. But he had seen how a wild temper could play out between sexual partners who had to work together, and he'd had enough items thrown at him this year.

Maybe if Ray got his shit together...

No. Not a wise option.

"It'll be better when we're on the road. Less time to brood, and Carl's happier if he can see results." Mish dumped a dustpan of shards into the trash.

"If Carl cared enough to pay attention, he'd see the results."

Mish grinned. "You're starting to sound like one of us, Zavier, honey."

"Honey?" He raised an eyebrow at Mish.

"Don't fight me on it. You'll lose. All you boys are honey." She had a smile like Nadia's, though years younger. So he gave in.

"Fine—but only you."

"Somehow I don't think either Dom or Ray would call you that, even if you let them."

"Which I wouldn't." He washed his hands in the utility sink by the laundry and dried them on his shorts. "I'm guessing we're not practicing anymore today."

After a couple of weeks, they'd finally made it to the third album and had been polishing off a fast-paced track that had some heady rhythmic and seductive beats. Ray had sung nearly every repeat, eyes closed to listen, unconsciously moving and thrusting to the song. Zavier would've played that line all day long to watch Ray swing his hips so.

Then Carl had walked in and informed them they had to pack up their gear after tomorrow, because they were heading east a half week early to play a gig they'd known nothing about at some music festival.

They weren't ready—nearly there, but not quite. Not enough to pack up tomorrow and drive across the country.

Ray had held it together well enough until Carl had left...but then the cursing started.

And here Mish and he were, cleaning up. Dom had followed Ray out of the garage, hopefully to try to calm him down.

"We need to at least get through 'Dark Dreams,'" she said.

That'd been the band's breakout song. Moody, angry, and fast. It had a sound that younger fans loved—but also hooked into something nostalgic in people a generation older. Twisted Wishes had tapped into the past and dragged it into the present.

"That would be the smart thing." Zavier studied the door both Ray and then Dom had rushed through. "I guess we ought to see what the damage is." He wasn't talking about glassware.

They found Dom sitting on the couch in the living room, head in his hands. "He's being himself again."

Mish rolled her eyes. "Oh, lord."

That didn't sound good. "Where is he?"

Dom gestured up. Upper deck, then. That had been Ray's sulking spot as of late. Zavier climbed the stairs, and yes, Ray was in his favorite lounge chair, eyes closed, hands curled into fists.

"I'm very sorry to have wasted your time, Zavier." A detachment to those words. "But I don't think we're going to need a drummer much longer."

"Don't fucking start with that shit." Zavier settled into a chair next to Ray. "I'm not in the mood and we have work to do." He put his feet up on the footstool.

Ray stirred. "For what? We can't play that festival."

They really had no choice. Saying no to the label wasn't an option, even if angry, snarky Ray thought it was. "Tough shit. We're playing that festival, so we might as well prepare the best that we can."

Ray practically choked on his laugh. "We don't even have a playlist! I have no idea what songs or—anything!"

The terror of failure was so clear in his expression, in the play of his muscles. The overwhelming fear that they'd step on stage and blow it.

These practices with Twisted Wishes proved that wouldn't happen. Zavier knew the band, and he knew Ray. "Bullshit.

You have a list. You've been crafting it in your head since the day I played 'White Hot Midnight' for you."

Ray let out a sigh and his fists uncurled. "I know what songs sound the best so far, and there's some I think will bleed well into each other and—" He stopped talking.

Zavier huffed a laugh. "You're really fucking good at what you do when you put your mind to it."

"And you're a complete asshole, Zav." Anger there. "Fucking shithead."

"Shithead me or Shithead Carl?" Because there wasn't anyone else he thought Ray would pin that on.

He was quiet for a while, eyes open now. He met Zavier's gaze. "Me. I'm the shithead."

Now there was something Zavier liked: Ray's self-awareness when he calmed down. "Mish thinks we should work on 'Dark Dreams.' We have today and tomorrow." If they got that song worked up, they'd be free to pick and choose from the other albums.

"I guess I could put together a playlist for the festival." Ray took a breath. "They're usually shorter sets, aren't they?"

"I have no idea." Conventional wisdom from having attended a few said yes, but fuck if Zavier'd claim something he didn't know.

Ray rubbed his face. "I'll have to ask Carl."

Ah, now maybe he could help there. "Or I could. Parlay my ignorance into usefulness."

The look Ray gave him seeped into Zavier's bones. A man with that kind of expression deserved to be turned over a knee.

"I wouldn't call you ignorant. Full of yourself? A grade-A fuckwad? Sure." Ray smiled.

Zavier laughed. Couldn't help it. Ray wasn't the first to use him to play *Pin the Tail on the Jerk*. Wasn't wrong, either. He rolled over on his lounge chair and dropped into his most seductive voice. "Why, Ray, if I didn't know better, I'd think you like me!" If only he *could* spank that smirk off his face.

The shudder that ran through Ray was a thing of delight, like a sip of fine liquor, and warmed Zavier the same way.

Ray's arousal was painfully obvious from his sudden flush, the way he licked his lips, and the impressive bulge in his shorts. "I—should go downstairs." With that he rose and tried in vain to get up in such a way as not to show Zavier his hard-on. Failed.

A moment later, Ray was thumping down the stairs and Zavier was alone. He rolled onto his back and stared up at the sky. Ray lusted after him. Probably had for years, but seeing it so close—that was temptation incarnate. Zavier pressed a palm against his hardening shaft. Yeah, he'd be indulging in that fantasy tonight, once he was alone and could jack off in private.

But for now? The band had work to do. Physical lust could be satiated. Musicality took time and energy. Zavier hauled himself up from the chair and headed back down to join the band.

CHAPTER
SIX

MAN, IF THERE WERE ANY DAY RAY COULD'VE USED A BEER, today was that day. It had been a little less than two months since they'd started practicing with Zavier, and tonight, they were performing. Ray hadn't touched any alcohol since Kevin left, and he wasn't about to go near a tall cool one with Carl milling around the band wherever they were in upstate New York.

Plus, it'd fuck up his voice. Instead, he sipped his lemon-honey tea and looked out over the venue. A band was playing on the stage and people were scattered all over the place. Some in the pavilion seating, others on blankets spread out over the lawn. Not too long from now, Twisted Wishes would play right before Five Asylum, the headlining act.

Quite an honor, Carl told them. He'd been all smiles and kindness, kind of like he had been after they'd signed, back when Ray trusted him. One of the bigwigs from the label had shown up, too, and Ray had to admit, it was gratifying to hear praise from the suit. "Carl says you've been working really well with the new drummer. That you're sounding better than ever."

Ray put on his charm and smiled. "Yes, sir. Zavier's

incredibly talented and we're lucky to have him." Mr. Perfect was standing right there, of course, along with the rest of the band. Yeah, they'd come amazingly far.

Zavier shook the suit's hand. "I'm the lucky one. This has been an incredible experience."

Ray almost believed him. Zavier's face was so sincere.

The suit did one of those clapping things bigwigs did when they've run out of things to say to peons. "Well, I should let you gentlemen—" he paused and glanced at Mish "—and lady get ready."

"Of course," Zavier murmured.

They were all smiles until Carl and the suit left. Mish snorted. "Women have been in the music industry how long? Played guitar how long?"

"Since the '30s," Dom said. "Or before." He was dressed as Domino, all makeup, leather, tats, and boots, hair spiked to within an inch of its life. How he got that shit out afterward, Ray never knew. Not enough hot water in the world.

"I should have stomped on his foot for you," Ray said.

Mish rolled her eyes. "Honey, I can take care of myself when it comes to men."

Zavier laughed. "Probably better than the rest of us."

"Oh," Mish said, "somehow I suspect you're more than capable of handling guys."

A flush crept up Zavier's neck. Unusual. "Well, I do have my ways, yes." His smile was devilish and full of light.

Mish nodded. "Had a feeling you weren't straight."

"Me?" Zavier laughed. "Nowhere near."

Ray could've told Mish that.

She and Domino went off to talk to the techs about their guitars, which left Ray with Zavier alone, and he didn't want to deal with Zavier at the moment. So more tea.

The change in climate and the flight across the country had given him a scratchy throat he didn't like. He always brought his own tea and honey, and the green room had hot water—perfect. A moment later, he was sipping the hot brew down.

Mish subtly asking about Zavier's sexuality rolled around in Ray's brain. Zavier had been fearless in high school. First time Ray had seen him in the halls was when one of the football players had shoved Zavier into a locker and called him a fag. Zavier had turned around and punched the dude in the face, hard enough to bloody his nose. "I'm *queer*, you fucking asshole. Get it right."

Second time he'd seen Zavier was about a week later behind the school, mostly hidden by some shrubs. Same football dude was with him, but this time on his knees, sucking Zavier off.

Zavier did most certainly have a way with men. And with women. Pretty much everyone.

While working on his tea, Ray headed outside to a spot between the backstage proper and the concessions area, where the VIP guests were allowed to listen to whatever band was playing currently. They couldn't see much of the stage, but that didn't matter. It was private enough, but gave him a glimpse of the amphitheater lawn.

There, staring out at the crowd through some fencing, he found Zavier. And fuck if he didn't look a little pale. Nerves? Cold feet?

"Hey." He spoke gently, because Zavier's focus on the crowd was intense.

Zavier's features smoothed over. "Hi, Ray." He nodded at the cup. "Your throat okay?"

"Yeah. Little dry from the flight. This is mostly pre-gaming."

"Lemon and honey." Zavier crossed his arms. Behind his smile was something else. Yeah, maybe fear.

"What about you? Are you okay?"

Zavier started and dropped his arms to his side. "Yes. I think so." He took a long look at the crowd before turning toward Ray. "This is different. This type of audience. The size." He shook his head. "I'll be fine when I'm behind the kit."

"Those symphony concert halls have to be pretty big." Last thing they needed was Zavier freaking out. Kevin had done that the first big concert. "You guys even did touring in Europe, right?"

Zavier nodded and leaned back against the fence. Open. Honest. The sunlight shone against his black hair.

It occurred to Ray that Zavier wasn't that much older than him—two years, maybe two and a half. Hell, Ray was nervous, too. This concert might make or break them. "Can't be that different."

Pursed lips, then a smile. "It's—there's more chaos here. The symphony was very organized, even during outdoor performances. The air's different here. The vibe. This is like walking on a live wire."

"Welcome to the rock-and-roll life."

Zavier pushed off the fence and the headed toward backstage. "Can't say I'm in the life until *after* we play."

Ray clapped him on the back, and left his hand there while they walked. "You're the one who's spent days telling me we can do this, that I can." The songs were ready, everything was as done as it got.

Zavier slowed to a stop and Ray's hand fell away. They stood close, inches apart. The air sparked, especially with Zavier looking at him like that. "We can do this," he said. "You're going to walk out onto that stage and blow them away."

Zavier believed in him. *Really* believed in him. The realization was a physical shock. "I—"

"Will blow them away." Zavier's hand clasped Ray's hip, and he spoke each word clearly, like he wouldn't accept any other answer, as if there were no other answer.

Maybe there wasn't. "Yeah. All right."

"Good," Zavier murmured. "Very good." He slid his hand away from Ray. "I need to stretch out my back."

Ray lifted his now-tepid tea. "I should finish this."

Zavier nodded. "And remember what I said, Ray."

He couldn't forget. "I will."

Like walking on a live wire. Every second with Zavier was that. Ray should have been turned on—and he was, in a way. Heat surged through him and yeah, he was hard, but more than anything he wanted to get on stage and do what Zavier had said.

Blow them away.

He finished the tea and hurried backstage to start his vocal warm-ups.

Zavier had been on stage at Carnegie Hall in New York City. He'd played in Geneva, Rome, London, and Berlin. None of those concerts had ever made him as nervous as this one. None of those had been as important.

The festival crowd gave off a strange energy—both excited and apathetic. They weren't headlining, but there were still fans here. He'd seen the T-shirts, heard the cries of Ray's, Domino's, and Mish's names.

He wasn't Kevin. Better? Yes. But not the drummer those fans had known and loved. If Zavier screwed up tonight, he'd take the whole band down with him.

That would *destroy* Ray. Cement in his mind that all those fears were true, that Carl's asshattery was correct.

Zavier wouldn't let that happen. They'd worked too hard in the past two months. Lived on top of one another. Played more music in that time than he'd ever played at once, even at Julliard, even on tour with the symphony. He closed his eyes and focused his breath. Remembered the songs, the rhythms. Ray moving to the music. Yes. *There.* They'd be fine.

When cued, they headed out onto the stage, Domino and Mish first. He followed, climbing onto the platform and behind the kit. Everything was set exactly as he liked. Thank god for competent roadies following instructions.

Domino started, ripping out a low chord and working it upward. Bathed in red light, with his spiked hair, leather pants, and tattooed glory, he looked entirely a rock god. The crowd nearest to the stage cheered and clapped. Then Mish joined in. A sultry and low bass line, blending in with Domino's jamming, lights shining on her now, too. Tall, proud, unbeatable. Their combined notes screamed through the air and floated high, then dropped down and faded as the crowd got louder.

Electricity raced through Zavier. This was it. His turn, his time. One, two, three...

He hit the kit hard and fast, pulsing out the opening to "Diamond Fever." Not their usual opener, but Ray wanted to mix it up. *I want to start with your drumming, if you're up to that,* he'd said. *Let the fans know you're here and good, and that we're back.*

Of course he'd said yes. Now he surged out those rhythms and Domino replied. Mish fell in, complementing perfectly. Glorious. Achingly wonderful. The song was missing one thing.

Ray.

Then he was there, leaping out onto the stage, mic in hand, and his voice soared over them all. Every word, every note like a firework of sound that went on and on and *on* over the crowd. The air changed, the vibe shifted. Zavier couldn't see much beyond the edge of the stage, but energy charged the air and when they finished, the eruption of noise ripped through him like a standing ovation at the end of a concert. Only they'd just started.

Fuck, if he'd known *this* was how it felt, he'd have said yes to Ray all those years ago. The thrill in his body as the music poured through him, the sheer joy of watching Ray sing.

"Hey, Syracuse! How you doing tonight?" Ray's voice boomed out across the amphitheater, and the crowd responded. "Well, we're glad to be here, too. Wanna hear something else?"

More yelling. *Holy shit*, this was wild. Zavier'd been on the other side, but being the focus? His heart slammed against his chest. He grabbed a sip of water from a bottle he'd stashed near his stool. Gotta stay in control.

"I can't hear you!"

They screamed louder.

"All right. Here's a song from our first album..." Ray turned and nodded, a cue to start.

Zavier counted out the beats, this time tapping his sticks so Mish and Domino could hear—and they were off again. The songs seemed to go on and on, some bleeding into one another, some ending on a fucking high that had Zavier panting.

He'd ripped off his shirt after the third song, as had Ray and Domino. Mish was down to a sports bra. Even though the evening was cool, the lights blazed down like fire, and the energy of the crowd... He'd never felt anything like it. Not in the symphony. Not even at the kink parties or clubs. Not when he was wielding a flogger.

Nothing felt better than playing with Twisted Wishes. His back burned and his heart cracked apart from joy. Domino was insane. Mish, an avenging goddess.

Ray was *perfection*. Hips that moved like sin, a voice that never quit, and that *body*.

They were nearing the end of their list. They'd saved two songs for encores: "Dark Dreams" and "White Hot Midnight." So they ended on another fan favorite, "River of Pain." By the time the notes died down and they exited the stage, night had descended fully, and the crowd was stomping and cheering and screaming.

Off to the side of the stage stood Gregor Daye, the lead guitarist and front man for Five Asylum. "You guys are killing it out there. Going to be a hard act to follow."

Ray took a long drag of water and smiled like he was high —which he likely was. They all were. Adrenaline. Joy. Fatigue. "They're here to see you, not us."

Gregor laughed. "Maybe before. But right now?" He paused, and the stomping and cheering vibrated across the stage. "They want you guys." He nodded. "Go give 'em what they want."

When they headed back on stage, the screaming was physically palpable, shearing through the air. Zavier climbed back behind the kit. Ray spoke while Mish and Domino claimed their instruments. "Thank you guys so much. You know we haven't played in a while, and you've been amazing tonight." Whoops and clapping. Over it, Mish started playing out a deep and throbbing line. "On bass, we have the ever-amazing Mish Sullivan. And on guitar, Domino Grinder." Dom played out a riff that was somehow both over the top and utterly him. Cheers and shouts followed. "I'm Ray Van Zeller." Screams this time, going on and on. Ray laughed and held up his hands. "Wait, I'm not done. I want to introduce our drummer!"

Zavier tapped out a simple beat, his heart in his throat. They hadn't talked at all about intros, but he knew that was pretty normal for bands to do.

"You like him?" More shouts and applause. "Yeah, he's pretty fucking awesome. Zavier Demos!" Ray pointed, the pavilion thundered with cheers, and Zavier hit the skins. He had no idea what he was going to play, hadn't planned on a drum solo, but it came as effortlessly as breathing or sex or —drumming. Took the kit, made each piece his, and threw it out into the audience—and to Ray, who danced and shouted and worked the crowd until they were all on their feet.

Slowly, Zavier reined the solo in, Domino and Mish picked up the beat, and they slid into the opening of "Dark Dreams," to the utter delight of the crowd.

Despite all that happened, the reception they'd gotten, Zavier was entirely unprepared for the explosion of screams when they segued into "White Hot Midnight."

He nearly lost it when Ray started singing. That audition, those practices had been nothing compared to now. The words wrapped themselves around Zavier, each verse a reminder of their past, each somehow imbued with a new layer of desire and passion. On the musical bridge, Ray jumped up on the edge of the drum platform and danced and twirled and leveled a stare at Zavier that set off every nerve.

Tease. Fucking sultry little... God, he wanted to kiss that grin off Ray's face and turn those lovely notes into moans. Zavier kept playing, embellishing where he could, adding twists and turns under Domino and Mish's playing until Ray's voice took over again.

When the song ended, Zavier threw back his head and drank in the pounding cheers and screams. He grabbed the sticks he'd used and headed down to join the band. Ray clapped him on the back. "A little payback for your song choice at the audition."

Oh, so that's what it had been about? Heat shot through Zavier—he didn't think it was possible given how much his body burned already. Rather than grab Ray and kiss him to wipe that smirk off, Zavier stepped forward and tossed a drumstick to a girl screaming at him in the front row. Another went a few rows back. The last two he flung as far out as he could manage.

None of that helped quell his desire. When he turned around, Ray still had that devilish grin, so Zavier gave in to half his need and cupped the back of Ray's neck, drawing him close enough to speak into his ear. His thumb pressed gently against Ray's throat, enough to feel him swallow. "You did exactly what I told you to do. I'm very pleased." He pulled away and gave Ray his own evil smile.

Ray's expression was glorious and Zavier's every wet dream. Lust and joy and elation. Ray licked his lips, waved to the crowd, and brought the mic back up. "We're Twisted Wishes. Thank you, Syracuse, and good night!"

They strutted off stage into a pile of high fives from the crew, a ton of water, and the event staff hurrying them out of the way as the lights went up. A moment later, crews streamed onto the stage to tear down their equipment and set up for Five Asylum.

Back in the green room, Zavier finished his water and shoved a hand through his hair. "Is it always like that?"

"Honey," Mish said. "It's *never* been like that!"

He didn't know whether he should be glad or terrified. Maybe a mix of both. He found Ray watching him, wary now. Probably wise, given everything. Zavier winked at him. "So, I did all right for my first time out?"

"Fucking hell," Ray said. "You really are an asshole, you know?" There wasn't any heat behind the words, only that cocky twist to his lips. "Yeah, you did fine. Just fine."

Domino looked more like Dominic. "Holy shit, did that actually happen?"

"Looks like the new drummer made all the difference." Carl's voice cut through their joy like nails scraping across sheet metal. Domino's amazement fell and Ray flinched like an abused man.

Ice descended where heat had been. Zavier straightened. "No."

The room hushed and Zavier rounded on Carl. He and the label executive stood in the doorway. "What made a difference was all those hours of practice, a shit-ton of hard work, and Ray knowing his songs inside and out. He led us to the sound we needed."

He might as well have slapped Carl from that expression. Good. Didn't know what Nadia would dig up, but that man was an absolute fuck.

Ray's chuckle was mild. "You had a huge part in that, Zav." His face was more flushed than before.

He wasn't going to let either man pin the success of the evening on him. "I know who I am. I know what I brought to the table." He shrugged. "But no drummer, no matter how good, will lift a performance like that." He gestured back at the stage. "Takes hard work from everyone. Together."

Mish nodded. "He's good. And smart." She looked at Ray. "I think we should keep him."

The suit coughed and something like humor flickered around his lips and eyes. "We'd be very happy if you'd continue to work with Mr. Demos."

There was nothing Zavier wanted more than to play another show with Twisted Wishes. His gaze strayed to Ray. Well, that wasn't quite true, but tangling with that bundle of nerves and anxiety was asking for trouble, even if Ray was tempting beyond rational thought.

<hr />

THE CLOCK IN RAY'S ROOM READ 3:57. HE CLOSED HIS EYES against the red glow. Fucking *hell*. He should be dead asleep. He'd burned so much energy, his body ached from dancing, jumping, and singing. He'd been higher than a kite after the show.

Zavier had touched him—not just a friendly pat on the back, but an intimate clasp that nearly put him on his knees in front of who knew how many fans. Bet *that* photo was already making the rounds.

He kinda wanted to see it. Did Zavier look like Ray remembered—like he might kiss Ray, like he wanted Ray?

Instead, Zavier had spoken, his breath a caress against Ray's ear. *You did exactly what I told you to do. I'm very pleased.* Very pleased. He'd never heard those words spoken with the same tone as *suck my cock* before.

Ray rolled over and ignored the hardness of his dick. He wouldn't jack off to Zavier. Except he already had once tonight. And had on previous nights. Fucking asshole was stunning and sexy and...not actually an asshole.

Well, maybe a little, but they all had their edges.

Part of him wished he could take the risk and get buzzed on liquor; the other part knew drinking wouldn't help at all. He was too wired from the concert and should have crashed hours ago—everyone else had. Dom was sawing wood in the next room, loud enough Ray was tempted to go in and roll him onto his side to shut him up.

God, the concert. They'd never sounded so good. He'd never felt that alive with the music behind him. Once they'd started playing, Ray hadn't needed to worry. Hadn't had to figure out how to cover for mistakes, bad playing, or anything. The band would nail it, so he'd been free to let go and *sing*.

Trust. He trusted the band again. He'd always known Dom and Mish would play their hearts out, but he'd never known if Kevin would survive the night.

Zavier not only survived, he'd ruled every beat, from the first to the last.

Ray *trusted* Zavier.

Zavier *believed* in Ray.

Ray grunted, and that sharp, painful sound faded in the room. He had no idea why Zavier believed in him. He wasn't anything like Zav. Not as talented, not as skilled. Yes, he worked hard—but he fucked up so often it wasn't funny. Sure, Mish and Dom were on his side, but that was because they'd been together for years and they'd accepted him, warts, foolishness, and all.

But Zavier? He had no reason at all to believe in Ray and every reason not to.

Yet he did. Deferred to Ray. Treated him like an equal. And Ray fucking wanted him, wanted his kiss, his words in his ear and breath on his neck.

Fuck it. He rolled onto his back, stroked himself, and gave into another round of fantasies. Zavier's lips on Ray's, their bodies entangled, Zavier inside him. The orgasm gripped Ray fast and hard, shaking the last bit of tension from his bones. When he could move, he stumbled to the bathroom and cleaned himself up.

This time, when he hit the bed, sleep reached up and dragged him down into nothingness.

CHAPTER
SEVEN

HOW THEY MADE IT THROUGH THE NEXT TWO WEEKS BEFORE THE tour officially started, Ray wasn't sure. He did know, when he climbed onto the bus with Dom, Mish, and Zavier, that he was grateful for the hours they'd be on the road. No Carl, no practices, just the bus and the tour. He could crawl into his berth, close the curtain, and ignore the world.

Practicing with Carl breathing down their necks had been hell. At first, he'd been complimentary after the festival performance, even noting that Ray's song choices had been decent. The label was certainly impressed—Carl had imparted that, too. But after a few days, the jabs returned. Whenever Ray had the rest of the band work on getting the blend just so, Carl called him lazy. If Ray rested his voice, he was weak.

He wasn't...at least he didn't think he was. Maybe he didn't have the blisters and sore muscles the others had, but he still had been focused the entire time.

Nothing meant more to him than Twisted Wishes—he wished he could make Carl see that and get the man off his back. At least Carl wouldn't be here on the bus with them.

Ray eyed the space they'd inhabit for the next couple of months. Thank god.

Touring would be a break from all of Carl's noise. At least Ray hoped.

Dom threw his backpack down on one of the couches and flopped next to it. "Home sweet home, or something."

Mish headed down to the berths and dropped her bag into a lower bunk. "Dibs."

Zavier stopped in the middle of the aisle, eyes a bit too wide. "Wow." He sounded surprised. Amazing—something that stopped Zavier Demos in his tracks.

Ray settled onto the couch across from where Dom sat. "I thought you toured in Europe with the symphony?"

Zavier didn't answer right away. Instead, he sat down next to Ray and placed his bag between his feet. "We did tour in Europe, but not like this." He glanced around the bus too openly and too honestly. "We took buses between cities, but they were regular coaches. This is—" He shook his head. "I knew musicians lived out of their tour buses on the road, but I had no idea."

Yeah, did take some getting used to. A little kitchen and table. The berths for sleeping. A lounge in the back. A bathroom with a shower. All the comforts of home, packed into a vehicle. The first time Ray'd ever walked onto one of these buses, he'd stared at everything too. It was luxurious in its own way, until it became your home for weeks on end.

Mish returned and took the seat by the table. "So what was it like in Europe?"

Great. More Zavier stories. Ray pushed himself off the couch and took the upper bunk across from the one Mish had claimed. Not that Zavier told many stories, but Ray was on Zav overload. That voice, those arms, the way his shoulders and back rippled without a shirt.

This tour was going to be *hell*.

Zavier's chuckle burned into Ray's soul, and despite

wanting to remain annoyed, he leaned against the berths and listened.

"You have to understand that a symphony is about a hundred musicians, plus instruments, plus a crew, plus support staff, plus press. It's nothing like what we're doing."

Ray couldn't help himself. "Shit, how do you even move that many people around?"

The bus rumbled beneath them. Oh. They'd be heading out soon. He reclaimed the spot by Dom, because stumbling when the bus lurched forward would be fucking embarrassing, and that was far worse than being turned on by sitting too close to Zavier.

Zavier leaned back against the leather cushions. "Mostly the support staff did the heavy lifting, along with the host cities. We also spent days in one place, and traveled by bus between close locations, and by plane if the city was farther away."

"So, more like a vacation than living on the road." Dom adjusted his glasses and looked longingly at the coffeepot. "How much you want to bet that thing's on the fritz?"

"It was a lot like a vacation." Zavier rose and headed toward the coffeemaker. Just then, the bus lurched, but goddamn him, he didn't even break his stride, let alone stumble.

Ray hated that man. He also wanted him.

He closed his eyes as the bus pulled out of the lot onto the road. Truth was, he didn't hate Zav. He was growing to like the bastard, and he certainly respected his talent and work ethic. No complaints, no issues, just focus and deference as they perfected their songs.

"This isn't bad coffee." Zavier's voice was soft over the ever-present whine of the engine. He held open a bag of some fancy-label grind and sniffed it.

"Coffee's never bad," Mish said. "Maker is usually a piece of shit, though."

"Let's see." Zavier set about making a pot. He found a case of water and used the bottled stuff, and soon the pot was gurgling away. "So far, so good."

Dom rooted in his backpack. "It's only day one." He pulled out a book and started reading.

Zavier chuckled. "I have a way with machines."

"You have a way with everything," Ray muttered.

No reply, just a knowing twist of the lips, and Zavier reclaimed his seat next to Ray. Mish played with her phone.

Once again, Ray wished Zavier's eyes weren't that blue, because he ended up staring into them too long.

"What will you do?" Zavier's voice curled into Ray's belly and ignited lust and heat.

If he could, he'd do Zav. Any way he wanted. Such a bad idea. "Probably take a nap."

Maybe he could jack off quietly. He'd done that before on tour. Pretty sure they'd all masturbated on the bus, even Mish. Something about the energy of touring and the throbbing rumble beneath them.

"Is that what the kids are calling it these days?" Dom peered at him over the edge of his glasses. Made him look like the somewhat stuffy bookworm he really was.

Ray's cheeks heated. Yeah, maybe he was obvious, but he didn't need his best friend pointing that out.

Zavier raised an eyebrow. "As I recall, you're the kid, kid."

"Two years younger than you isn't that much," Dom said.

"Not anymore, no,"

"Get off my lawn," Mish muttered, and they all laughed, even Zavier.

With the tension broken, the bus picking up speed, and the coffee brewing, Ray made good on his words. He crawled into a berth and closed his eyes. He hadn't planned on sleeping, but his thoughts twisted and jumbled around Zavier's smile, and then slid into nothingness.

Traveling this way wasn't bad. Zavier propped his feet up on the leather couch and watched the world go by. They were heading to Detroit for their next show and would arrive sometime tomorrow. He wasn't sure how the whole driver thing worked. Shifts, he guessed. Like driving across country with friends. There certainly was more than one driver for the two buses—this one and the crew bus.

The coffeemaker had brewed a perfect pot. Even Dom had been pleased, and so had Ray when he'd emerged from behind the berth curtain, blinking and bleary-eyed, some two hours later.

Looked like someone had actually napped and not just slipped away to get off.

Ray clutched his mug and drank, and Zavier watched him in the reflection of the window. While Ray had been out, Dom had claimed the bunk above Mish, which left the one under Ray for Zavier, and didn't that do wicked things to his lust.

He closed his eyes and swallowed the snort. He had more control than this, but Ray was so delightful in so many ways. Even when Ray was at his most stressed and grumpy, there were these buttons Zavier could push, and did. Mostly to direct Ray away from the anger eating at him, but Zavier wasn't entirely altruistic—he got too much of a rush from playing with Ray's obvious submissive side—but at least he could use his own lust to help.

He studied the scenery and then Ray's reflection—and caught Ray watching him. Wasn't unpleasant, that inspection. A little wonder, a little calculation. Ray shook himself, and finished his coffee. When he rose, Zavier readjusted himself on the couch so he could peer across the aisle at him when he settled back with a notebook.

Mish wandered up from the back and scooped Zavier's

legs off the couch. "You're like a freaking cat, taking up all the space."

Accurate. He just smiled and sat back, feet firmly on the bus floor.

Dom put away his book, and that was what keyed Zavier in that something was up. "Is this a meeting?"

"Yes," Ray said.

"More like a ritual." That from Dom.

Mish rolled her eyes. "Ray's gonna figure out the playlist for tomorrow night. He likes our input."

The journal Ray held was worn and scuffed, meaning it probably held all of Twisted Wishes's song lists. Maybe more besides. A little wash of sparks ran up Zavier's back. He *was* part of this band. Playing the festival had been one thing. Rehearsals another. But this...was Ray sharing himself.

Ray slipped the cord off the notebook and flipped through the pages. From what Zavier spied, some had sparse writing on them, others were packed with text. The page Ray stopped at already had writing on it. "I was thinking about a similar list to the festival, though we'll need to add songs, since we'll have about thirty more minutes to play."

They also had several more tracks from the third album down well enough to perform. And wouldn't you know, Dom suggested adding two of them to the middle of the show. "We'll be warmed up, and they'll be expecting newer stuff about then."

Ray nodded.

"Encores?" Mish asked.

"I really liked the way 'Dark Dreams' and 'White Hot Midnight' worked. I say we leave them at the end," Ray said. Both Dom and Mish nodded and he leveled those whiskey eyes at Zavier. "What about you?"

"I wouldn't mess with perfection."

Ray's whole face darkened, his anger sharpening his words. "I'm being serious here."

"So am I." Zavier leaned forward. "They were *perfect*, Ray."

As quickly as Ray's storm came, it lifted and his shoulders relaxed. "You mean that."

Zavier lifted his head. "Yes." He spoke it like a command, and it had the same effect on Ray as it would've had on any of the subs he'd played with. A flush and a melting, that little hint of subspace.

Ah, hell. He shouldn't have done that, because now he wanted more.

Ray shook himself. "Okay, so we'll leave those for the encore." He wrote something down. "And slot those two songs Dom suggested in the middle."

They hashed out bits and pieces of the set, moving songs around and mixing their best known with edgier but fun pieces until they had a good list.

Except Ray had a little frown. Mish must have noticed it too, because she tilted her head. "Honey, what's up?"

"Just—I'm not sure I like 'Diamond Fever' as the opening song."

"Fans loved it," Dom said.

They had. But that didn't change Ray's expression, even though he nodded. "I know. But I think we could do better."

Both Mish and Dom threw out a few other songs they hadn't already listed as openers, but Ray just frowned into his journal. "They're all good options, but..."

Once more, Zavier was staring into Ray's eyes. Need there and fear, all the things that made Zavier's mouth water. "Ray, if you could pick any song, which one would you pick to open with?"

"'Lightning.'" No hesitation. The title bolted out of Ray like a cry of pain. Or pleasure. Beautiful. Both Ray and that song.

Dark and slow at first, 'Lightning,' like its namesake, built and rumbled ominously until it crashed up into a frenzy that left them all playing their loudest and fastest. It wasn't the kind of song anyone used to open a concert.

Then again, why not? So that was exactly what Zavier said. "Why not?"

Ray took a breath and straightened. Mish shrugged, but her smile was splendid. "Yeah, why not?"

Dom seemed taken aback, and not at all his Domino persona. "'Lightning'? First?"

"Yeah." Strength radiated from Ray. "Think about it. No one will expect it. We lowballed with 'Diamond Fever'—it's an easy song. Let's do something different and wake 'em up."

Not that "Diamond Fever" put them to sleep—far from it. But the die-hard fans would go nuts. Hell, Zavier felt a surge of energy thinking about it.

Maybe Dom did too, because he chewed on his thumbnail before a glimpse of Domino slipped out. "Fuck yeah. Let's do it."

Ray beamed and wrote in his book. When he was finished, he closed it reverently, then pulled the attached elastic band around it again. "Thanks, guys."

The bus lumbered on for another hour or so before reaching at a truck stop. They all got out to stretch and mingle with the crew. Ray shared the playlist and that seemed to go over well.

Zavier wandered to the shop, not really needing anything but space. He almost wished he smoked, because that would have given him the excuse he needed to step away and stare at the highway for a while.

He couldn't get Ray's hunger out of his head. Or body. Or cock. He *needed* to, though. Ray was off limits—except that wasn't true. He pushed and played and watched Ray. What did that say about him?

Zavier swallowed a sigh and scanned the shelves. Everything in the store was either something he didn't want or they already had on the bus. There was a selection of alcohol, but it seemed cruel to drink when Ray couldn't.

"There's beer and wine on the bus."

Zavier nearly startled. The surge of adrenaline was there, and he caught his breath, but he'd had plenty of practice controlling his reactions. Still. He glanced at Ray. "Really?"

"Yeah. Dom likes this microbrew stuff, so there's like two cases. Mish drinks what she calls cheap box white wine, but it's not that cheap, and it's damn good." His smile slipped. "I wasn't about to be an asshole to them because Carl's being one to me. Touring is hard enough as it is. I'm not taking away their simple pleasures."

Nadia still hadn't contacted Zavier about dirt on Carl. He studied the case. "I don't drink that much."

"What *do* you do for your simple pleasures?"

People. All kinds of people, in all kinds of ways. He shook his head to rid himself of the image of Ray on his knees. "I guess you'll find out."

Ray got this incredulous look, and Zavier couldn't help patting his cheek. Probably shouldn't have, since it did nothing to quell the heat in his own body and hell did it give Ray a blush you could see from space.

"See you back on the bus." He left without buying a damn thing and took the long way back—enough time to get his cock settled down.

He had to sleep underneath Ray tonight. That would be hell, but one of Zavier's own making.

CHAPTER EIGHT

THE FIRST PERSON RAY SAW UPON STEPPING OFF THE BUS AT THE venue outside Detroit was Carl, who led with an insincere greeting. "How you doing, Ray?"

Ray buried as much of his irritation as he could and managed a noncommittal grunt. Great. Just what he needed.

Carl's smile was fake. "That good, huh? Well, I hope your attitude improves before tonight."

Ray ignored the jibe and followed the crew into the arena. There'd be some kind of green room and dressing rooms. The crew would unpack the equipment and get it sorted and staged. They'd run through a rehearsal, then there'd be the show. Five Asylum had a whole VIP package thing going for their fans. Meet-and-greets, photo ops. Someday, maybe Twisted Wishes would do something similar, but for now they stuck with signing autographs for whoever hung out after the show.

He made it as far as the green room before Carl's voice sounded in his ear, way too close and far too loud. "Have you been drinking?"

Ray whirled around. "What the fuck do you think?" Only then did he notice the guy with the camera and the press pass standing in the room off to the side. Shit, *shit*. He took a breath and stepped back. "No, man. Just coffee, and not enough of that." God, he needed to pay more attention to his surroundings. Fucking thing was, that was one of the first pieces of advice Carl had given him.

The fucker chuckled. "I'm sure." He sounded like he didn't believe a word Ray said, which was pretty normal. "You know the deal."

He damn well did. "Do you need a blood test?" He held out his arm. "'Cause all you're gonna find is caffeine and a shitty truck stop meatball hoagie."

The press guy raised both his eyebrows and Carl looked taken aback. "No, no. Of course not."

Zavier breezed in. "I'd be afraid to know what's in those meatballs."

"Says the man who ate the chili cheese dogs." Domino was in most of his getup, since reporters like the one furiously typing into his phone could be found everywhere behind the scenes at a place like this.

"Eh, cast-iron stomach." Zavier flashed one of his perfect grins at Dom. "Product of my misspent youth."

Mish grabbed a bottle of water. "Next time I'm buying stock in antacids."

The best part of the whole tangent was the look on Carl's face. Ray relaxed. Anything about his "drinking problem" would be buried under the crappy eating habits of rock stars.

The journalist or whatever he was cleared his throat and nodded to Zavier. "You're the new drummer, right?"

Zavier straightened, his movements careful. Calculated. "Yes, I am. And you are...?"

"Gabriel McGinness, from MusicNight Online."

A nod. "I do like knowing who's writing about me," Zavier murmured, and fuck, was it sexy. How the hell did he do that? It also raised quite a blush on the reporter—and that caused a bitter taste in Ray's mouth.

The reporter recovered pretty fast, though the blush lingered. "How does a principal timpanist of a renowned symphony orchestra end up as a rock drummer?"

Less sex in Zavier's voice now. "I answered a call for an audition."

"After you were fired from Silverton?"

Zavier's posture shifted in an instant. He didn't tense up, per se. Ray couldn't say what changed other than his grin dropping, but the temperature in the room fell about twenty degrees, or so it seemed. "I wasn't fired. I resigned."

Oh, there was a story there. Zavier's voice was mild, but concrete—practically daring the reporter to refute him. For his part, Mr. Presspass McGinness or whatever stood his ground. "Dimitri Ferbran said—"

"Maestro Ferbran knows damn well I walked into HR and tenured my resignation before he had his little screaming fit at me." Zavier's smile was back, but unpleasant as hell. "I can give you the number of the Human Resources director, if you wish to corroborate my story." He paused. "And I'm not the only musician to walk out on Ferbran."

Presspass got a curious look. "Really?"

"Mmmhmm. Look it up sometime." Zavier shrugged. "Now if you'll excuse us..."

Carl ushered the press guy out the door. After that, he pulled a can from the fridge, then cracked it open. Of course it was a beer. Ray resisted the urge to look at his watch. He suspected the only reason Carl was drinking was to rub it in that Ray couldn't. Or maybe Zavier's little previous work-place history had been a surprise. Who knew? Interesting that Ray wasn't the only one with a cloud hanging over him.

Once Carl had downed a few gulps, he smacked his lips, which meant the beer was about Ray and not Zavier. At least he was consistent. "So, Ray. Got a set list yet?"

Carl had never been interested in what they planned to

play on tour before. "Of course I have. We worked it out last night." He gestured to the band.

A nod. "Well, I saw a version of it from the crew, but given the opening song, I figured that couldn't be right."

Fuck. Carl was going to give him grief about that? "If the opener is 'Lightning', then yes, it's the correct list."

"Are you mental?"

"Hey!" Mish slammed down her water. "Don't be a fucking ableist—"

"Yeah, Carl, I am. I'm a foolish, ignorant piece of shit." Ray snapped the words out. Carl's attention swung away from Mish and back to him, where it belonged.

Carl stepped forward. "You don't start a concert with—"

The whole room erupted into an argument, Mish and Dom trying to be heard over Carl as Ray agreed with every shit-talking thing that poured from that asshole's mouth.

"Stop." Zavier's voice thundered over them all. And fuck, there was anger in it. Ray's heart ticked up several notches, but Zav wasn't focused on him. No, he was staring daggers at Carl. The room fell silent. "Ray knows music. You even said that."

Carl stammered out something unintelligible.

Zavier shook his head once. "The band agreed on the set. We talked it over. Yes, it's unconventional, but that's what gets people noticed. Ray's idea is a good one."

"You wanna bet on that?" Carl folded his arms.

Zavier laughed. "Yes. But you wouldn't like my price." There was that smoldering, sexy glare again, one that turned the whole conversation into something entirely inappropriate.

Carl paled. "I'm not gay. I'm not touching your dick."

Wow, way for Carl to jump to a conclusion and be the panicked hetero guy. Though even thinking about Carl on his knees in front of Zavier turned Ray's stomach, enough that he looked away. He ended up meeting Dom's wide-eyed gaze.

"You don't need to be gay." Zavier's voice was velvet smooth. "Just heteroflexible enough."

Too much for Carl, apparently. When Ray looked back, he was glowering at Zavier, fists clenched. "Fine. Start with that song, but when it blows up in your face, don't come crying to me." He stormed out.

"Would you really fuck that asshole?" Mish took another swig of water. "I mean—"

Zavier snorted. "No. I have standards."

"Since when?" Ray didn't even know why he said it. Maybe the memory of Zavier face-fucking that quarterback.

"Ray." There was a softness to Zavier's voice. Ray stared back at him. "I didn't mean to upset you."

For a moment, it seemed like they were the only two people in the room, and the years fell away, leaving Ray young and vulnerable. "Yeah, well." He didn't know what was going through the mind behind those blue eyes, but he hated the thought of Zavier fucking Carl or Presspass or *anyone*, because it drove home how little Zavier wanted *him*. "Try to keep your dick in your pants and your mind out of the gutter."

Lo and behold, that earned him a blush, and Zavier actually looked hurt. Would wonders never cease?

"Hey, guys. Let's not snipe at each other." Mish settled down on a couch. "Gotta stick together." Dom nodded and plopped down next to her.

Ray pushed his hands through his hair. Last thing he needed was to alienate Zavier and lose another drummer. Heat rose to his face. "Yeah. Sorry. I didn't mean to get on your case."

Zavier waved his words away. "Part of that was my fault." He focused on the direction Carl and Presspass had gone. "I shouldn't cause you guys trouble with my mouth."

Ray wanted Zavier's mouth...and that was trouble too. "Do you think we should change the set list?"

"No." All three of them answered almost in harmony. That teased happiness from Ray. They might get on each other's nerves, but at least they were on the same page.

Ray sprawled down on another couch, content to relax— until Zavier sat down next to him.

He'd been in the berth above Zavier for hours. In the middle of the night, when Ray had inevitably woken because he could *not* sleep soundly on the road, he'd strained to hear Zavier over the sounds of the road. His breathing, a movement, anything to feel the closeness he'd been denied all those years ago. Now here he was, inches away.

"So what happened with the orchestra?"

Zavier shifted, brushing his leg against Ray's in the process. "Personality differences with the conductor."

"And you walked before he could fire you?"

An affirmative grunt. "Yes. Though, in reality, he couldn't have fired me. He's as much a member of the orchestra as anyone else, even if he's more famous and better paid."

Silence settled between them as the obvious question nagged at Ray's mind—but he'd already told Zavier to get out of the gutter, so he shouldn't be asking about Zavier's sex life. "Why not another orchestra?"

A soft chuckle, one he felt through the shaking of the couch rather than heard. "I was wondering when you'd ask that," Zavier murmured. "Dimitri has better connections than I do, and there are only so many timpanist positions available at any given time."

Dimitri. Ray's turn to shift uncomfortably on the couch. First-name basis. "So you're slumming it with us."

Mish rolled her eyes. "Ray."

Zavier tapped his foot against Ray's. "This is hardly slumming it. So far it's been a pleasure and a challenge. Frankly, I can't wait to get on stage tonight." So much passion in his voice, enough that Ray caught the edge of excitement himself.

He took in Zavier, meeting his gaze and smile. "You have the best seat in the house, you know."

"Oh, believe me, I know that." There was a flicker of motion, and Ray got the distinct impression that Zavier was checking him out, and that only fueled his blood.

Ray closed his eyes. "Soon you'll be in it."

"And Carl will learn you were absolutely right."

God, he hoped so.

———

UNUSUAL TO STILL HAVE SUCH NERVES. ZAVIER PUSHED BACK ON the flutter in his cheek and tingling in his arms. Technically, the festival had been his first show with the band, so he shouldn't have been off-kilter. Yet he was, because *this* concert was personal now. He didn't have to prove himself this time, but with the way Carl had treated Ray, the *band* had a score to settle.

Zavier wanted to ram success, along with his fist, down Carl's throat. He didn't understand why Ray put up with that shit.

When he'd had a free second away from the rest of the band, he'd sent a quick email to Nadia to see if she'd anything to tell him about the manager. Something didn't add up. At all.

And god, that reporter. Gabriel. Pretty enough of a man, but he'd hit a little too close to the mark with his questions. Undoubtedly, something would come out about his time at Silverton and his relationship with its maestro. What the hell would Ray think of that? Did Zavier care?

Yes, of course he did. He'd felt a twinge of embarrassment he hadn't felt in so long when he'd realized Ray was jealous of his sexually charged banter with both Gabriel and Carl. He didn't need to cause Ray issues. Dude was on edge enough.

Now, though, Ray was in his best form: on stage and in

control. They worked through a sound check and a small practice. The songs they played snippets from were ones that everyone expected them to play, off the latest album. Nothing unexpected, and certainly not "Lightning." They kept that under wraps.

Carl frowned at them from the edge of the stage. What *did* that guy expect? They'd blown away the festival. This would be no different. The smattering of VIP folks for Five Asylum seemed pretty happy, even clapping a few times when they worked flawlessly through a song. Another glance over at the edge of the stage, and Carl was gone.

Just as well.

Afterward, the band conferred, and the nervousness Zavier had suppressed was alive in Ray. "It's good. I think it's good." He rocked back and forth on his feet, like someone who'd had too many energy drinks.

The hesitation was alive in Dom, too. "Yeah. I think we sounded fine."

Mish tossed her head. "We're gonna nail it, Ray." Fire there, and determination.

Zavier fed off that rather than his own worries. "They won't know what hit them."

Ray took a breath and settled. "Okay." Another breath and he was nodding. "We'll do this."

They passed through the green room and headed to their dressing rooms when Zavier spotted Carl, lying in wait. Of course. No idea why Carl undermined Ray, but damned if Zavier was going to let that happen.

He grabbed Ray's elbow. "Hey."

Ray nearly jumped out of his skin at the touch, but didn't pull away. Rather, he settled closer to Zavier, like a magnet.

Oh hell. *Yes.* But no as well. They *could not* go on like this. Ray's desire pulled too much against his own.

"Yeah?" Ray's voice was breathless, sweet, and so very tempting.

"I know I was an asshole about the drumming thing in high school. Ray, I love being in your band." Truth. He stepped in closer, their arms skin to skin. "And you're an astounding musician. Don't let anyone—*anyone*—tell you differently." Zavier whispered the words against Ray's neck.

A shiver and a gasp, and then those golden eyes looked into his own. "You mean that?"

"With every fiber of my being." He released Ray's elbow slowly and stepped back, giving them both the space they needed before their asshole manager arrived.

"Ray," Carl snapped.

For a moment Ray didn't respond to the call. He nodded at Zavier, then turned. "Yes?"

"I want to talk to you about the opening song."

Zavier gritted his teeth—but Ray didn't, and that was something.

"No," Ray said, his voice calm. A thrill zipped through Zavier. *Yes.*

"What?" Carl took a step back.

"I'm not changing my mind." Ray put his hands into his pocket. "We're opening with 'Lightning' tonight. If it flops, then we can talk about it, and I'll even give you a shaker of salt to rub into the wound."

So very delightful to see Carl staring back, his ears red and words failing to form on his lips. "Fine." He stepped back. "I'll be watching."

Ray's nod was pretty much a dismissal before he turned back to Zavier. "We should go get changed."

"Yeah." They made their way to the dressing room. For Zavier, it wasn't so much changing as putting on layers he could strip off as the night progressed. By the end, he expected to be bare-chested and drenched in sweat, like every rock drummer on tour.

Dom was already in the room, working on perfecting his messy hair and makeup. Mish sat in her tights and red dress, watching. "I swear, honey, you use more makeup than me."

"I do," Dom said. "And you know it. But here." He tossed her something. "I found this lipstick the other day."

She caught it, and inspected the tube. "Not my color." She studied Ray, then Zavier in turn, and tossed it to Zavier. "It'll go with your eyes and all that black you wear—or don't wear."

The shade was a bright purple. Not maroon or burgundy or one of the purplish reds, but a *true* purple. He stared at it for a moment.

"Ever worn makeup?" Ray's lilt was a touch on the snotty side, as if he expected the answer to be no.

Without replying, Zavier set the lipstick down in front of his dressing station, and slowly stripped off his shirt.

Ray's eyes widened and his gaze flicked all over Zavier's body. The ink, of course. Ray hadn't exactly been subtle in his admiration before, and he wasn't now, not licking his lips like that.

Mish turned away, but her grin was huge. "Should I leave so you can drop trou, too?"

He shrugged and stretched his arms. "I do need to change pants." He had a variety he could wear, from loose and flowing to skintight and leather. "But I haven't decided which yet." He met Ray's lustful look. "Leather?"

The hitched breath was the best. Ray shook himself. "Up to you, dude." With that, he turned to his own wardrobe.

Dom rubbed his chin. "It's probably as cool tonight as it's gonna get on this tour. So if you're serious about the leather, wear them. I think our fans would...appreciate the look."

"What Dom means is that you have a stunning ass and great legs," Mish said.

"Which they're not going to see for most of the show." That from Ray.

He would know what Zavier was wearing. "There's the

three-song acoustical set." They'd set the stage up so he'd be out front for those, standing and playing with the others—like being back in the orchestra, but so much more charged, and close to the audience.

A grunt from Ray, and a sideways look as he pulled his clothes out. "Gonna wear the lipstick?"

"Yes. And the leather pants."

Ray looked like he was trying not to smile.

"Yes, I have worn makeup before. Eyeliner. Lipstick. Contouring. Goth nights were the *best*."

There was Ray's actual smile. "Okay. Let's get dressed and do this."

Zavier's nerves vanished as certainty slipped over him. Ray would win tonight, and Carl would eat his fucking words.

CHAPTER
NINE

FIVE WORDS INTO THE FIRST VERSE OF "LIGHTNING," RAY KNEW he'd been right about opening with this song. The thrum of Mish's bass and the growl of Dom's guitar were a counterpoint to the growing threat of Zavier's drums. The crowd— oh, the crowd. He knew most of them were here to see Five Asylum, but there were Twisted Wishes fans out there, too. A whole hell of a lot of them, because they screamed when they realized which song was being played and sang along. Those in the front strained their arms out to touch Ray's fingers

This was what he'd hoped for, what the band needed. What that fuckass Carl didn't understand. It wasn't about the publicity or the gossip rags or schooling or any of that—it was about the fans. The music. The energy. Give your soul over in words and notes and beats, and the fans gave you their souls right back in tears and screams and outstretched hands yearning for a single touch.

Fucking glorious, every second. Mish moving like sin and Dom grinding across the stage like he owned it. Behind the large kit, Zavier pounded out the rhythm like he was their heart. Might well have been. Where Kevin had been superb while sober, Zavier was magnificent, embellishing on the fly, adding little syncopated beats that made Ray's heart stutter and swell.

He sang all the harder, hitting notes, throwing himself out into the crowd, and running and dancing up the aisles. The fans erupted, but no one was too disrespectful, thank goodness. Getting back up on stage was a trick, but the next few songs were the acoustical ones, so he hoisted himself up and sat on the stage edge until he caught his breath and everyone else in the band switched instruments.

Security handed him water, and he drank before rotating and standing up on the stage. Mish had her upright bass, and Dom looked slightly ridiculous in his spiked collar with his delicate wooden guitar, but so much himself that for a moment Ray glimpsed Dominic behind the Domino persona.

Zavier had come out from behind the kit sans shirt, his tattoos shining from sweat. He was encased in those sinful leather pants, and Ray's breath caught. It caught a second time when Zavier grinned at him. The purple lipstick, those fucking blue eyes, and the way those pants hugged every inch of him.

Unfair.

Ray spun back around to the audience. "How 'bout something more classic?" The fans cheered, and with Zavier tapping out the beat with his sticks, they were off again.

The night seemed to last forever and no time at all. They finished the set, moved back to their normal instruments and soon, too soon, they were bowing after their encore, the crowd, at least under the venue pavilion, on their feet and cheering.

Mish and Dom threw picks and Zavier tossed his drumsticks. Someone in the front row yelled, "What about the pants?"

Zavier laughed and called back, "Want to keep playing, dude! They'd kick me out for that."

Sure, the venue, maybe the label, but right now? Ray really wanted to see what was under those pants, too.

But they were being ushered off and the house lights were flickering on for the intermission before Five Asylum took the stage.

The moments after they stepped off the stage blurred into a kaleidoscope. Slaps on the back. Zavier's sweat-soaked body so close to Ray's, and his grin. Dom's makeup was a mess, as was Mish's. Zavier's purple lipstick was somehow still perfect, and Ray wanted those lips on his. Someone shoved a bottle of water into his hands, and he cracked the cap off and downed half in one gulp.

Gregor from Five Asylum was there, clean and fresh and ready to take the stage. His gaze was shrewd. "Once again, a tough act to follow. You're turning heads, Van Zeller."

"Hope you don't mind." His voice was rough, and he gulped more water. Five Asylum was renowned and Gregor Daye almost a legend—a bona fide rock star. Ray was tickled at the thought of upstaging him.

A chuckle from the star. "God, no. It's good to see someone stepping up." Someone behind Gregor tapped him on the shoulder, and he grunted. "Gotta go." With that, Gregor vanished into a sea of techs and maybe a bodyguard or two.

More water, a protein bar, a change of clothes, some cleaning up, and they were heading out toward the parking lot, where the buses were waiting. One of the security people from the venue strode next to him, ear protection dangling around her neck. "There's a lot of fans waiting for you guys. We set up some lines. I'm not sure how you want to handle it."

Usually they signed everything they could. "How many is —" The words died in his throat.

Apparently, many was a whole fucking lot. The line snaked around the walkway to keep the fans from milling in the lot or around the buses, looping back twice. Way more people than normal. This was only their second concert of the tour. "Holy shit."

She gave him a glance. "You want us to clear them out?"

"No, no." He turned to the rest of the band. "You up for this?" Both Mish and Dom had ear-to-ear grins.

Zavier hung back. "I'm not really part of the band."

Mish grabbed his arm and yanked him forward. "Shut up, Demos. You're coming with us."

Joy bubbled up in Ray. Yeah, he was, and it was perfect.

Turned out, the fans took to Zavier as much, or maybe *more*, than they had to Kevin. Understandable. Talented, stunning—what more could you want, other than a tumble head-long into bed? Not that Ray could have Zavier, but like the fans undoubtedly had, it was a pleasant daydream. Hell, they had more of a shot.

A young woman with short dark hair and that nervous, happy, dazed look fans got was next for an autograph as he worked his way down the line. Ray had already had so many selfies taken, so he was grateful that she only clutched a CD case. It was scratched to hell and back, and who had CDs these days anyway?

Her eyes were wide and dark, even under the bright venue lights. "Mr. Van Zeller?"

"Ray," he said, and held out his hand for the CD case. "What's your name?"

"Mel. Melissa, but everyone calls me Mel."

"What do you want me to call you?" Names were important and personal. He'd learned that from Mish, and a few others.

Her face lightened out of the nerves. "Mel. I like Mel."

"And you have our CD...?"

Mel seemed reluctant to give it up. "Yeah, it's... My mom didn't want me to buy this." Wetness at the corner of her eyes. She offered the case to Ray.

Their very first album, before they signed with the label. They'd sold a bunch at concerts, a few online, and had put the MP3s out there, too. He took it gingerly, because this was a precious item to her. "She doesn't like rock?"

The young woman shook her head. "She likes rock. Her stuff, you know? Her bands. She didn't want me listening to —to—" She hiccupped a laugh. "Gay people."

Yeah, there were people who said they wouldn't listen to Twisted Wishes when the band hadn't kept quiet about their sexualities. But damned if they were going to hide who they were. There were so many people in the industry who were queer. You'd think the critics and the population would be used to it by now. Chances were, her mom listened to queer people without even knowing it. "I'm sorry she's like that."

Another nod. "I had it shipped to a friend's house. My mom was so mad." Her eyes were brimming. "But you understood how I felt. The lyrics. The music. Saved my life."

Oh. A cool wash of gratitude mixed with a touch of wonder flowed over Ray. "I'm so very glad." He paused. "Should I sign the CD? Or the booklet or...?" Sometimes people had very specific ways they wanted items signed.

"The CD," she whispered.

"To you?"

The nod was almost imperceptible, but there.

He signed, leaving space for Mish and Dom, too. "To Mel," he said, and handed it back.

She blinked a few times at the disk, as if not believing it was really there, then she looked up, right at him. "My mom took it from me when she found out. She listened to it...and gave it back." A smile broke out. "Changed her, too."

Then Mel was gone, off to talk to Mish...and Ray was left breathless.

That moment and so many others—that was why he did this. Not for the fame, but for Mel and Bryan and Sami and all the others he'd met so far. He turned and greeted the next fan.

He'd no idea how long it had been by the time the lines finally dwindled down to nothing—only that Five Asylum was playing and his hand hurt, but the post-concert buzz still poured through his body.

Mish gripped him on the shoulder, her expression as exuberant-looking as he was. "That was something!"

Even Zavier looked dazed, and that purple lipstick wasn't so perfect now. Ray still wanted to kiss it off of him. Unfair. "Let's get back to the bus."

"Van Zeller." Carl's sharp voice cut through the night, and they all flinched. Zavier turned toward the asshole, his face a mask, lips pressed thin.

Nope. Ray wasn't going to let Carl ruin Zav's first real show. He strode toward their manager. Better he take whatever licks were coming. "Yup. What's up?"

"A word." Carl had his tablet on hand and gestured back toward the venue's building with the other. Ray dutifully followed him inside and to a small room that looked like it could be an office.

Carl shut the door and leaned against it, neatly trapping Ray.

Shit. This was going to be one of *those* discussions. Carl hadn't imposed on Ray like this before, but Ray knew the intimidation game. It was a high school move. He crossed his arms. "Were you disappointed in the concert?" That would be rich.

Carl snorted. "You know I can't fault your performance. Even your idiotic choice of an opening song was a hit." He shook his head. "Lucky break for you."

The buzz he'd been riding slipped away into anger. "Wasn't luck. I know our fans."

"Your fans aren't enough to pay your way out of debt."

Debt? Wait. "What?" Carl had never fucked around when it came to money.

"Oh, Ray, Ray. Do you have any idea how much you owe the label?"

Owe the...label? Shards of ice crashed into his back. He couldn't think of the words to say, because his brain wasn't wrapping around what Carl was saying. He let his arms drop to his sides.

"That's better," Carl purred. "Now maybe you'll pay attention to me instead of being a fucking shithead."

Had he missed something? Maybe he'd missed something. "I don't understand."

"That's because you're an idiot, Ray. Pretty, talented, but nothing upstairs." Carl tapped his head with a finger, and his grin was lurid.

Jesus, this guy. "Look, I know you hate me. I get it. But what the *fuck* are you talking about?"

"Did you read the contract you signed?"

He had, but so much of it was lawyer speak. He figured the label knew what it was doing. But... He nodded slowly.

"Then you know how it goes." Carl turned on his tablet and showed it to him. "Here's the bottom line."

Ray crept closer to get a look at the spreadsheet. The number at the end was large...and negative. "But we've gone gold, haven't we?" They'd at least hit that with the album before Kevin had crashed and burned. A party. Fanfare in the press.

"Sure you did. But stuff costs, Ray. Your stage clothes. The hotels. The buses."

He thought...he thought the label took care of those. The band was paying for it? What about the concerts? Tickets cost a bundle. He took another look at the spreadsheet, but the numbers blended and shifted before his eyes. Now was *not* the time to be studying this. The buzz was gone, torpedoed by the sickly feeling that he'd screwed up big time somewhere along the line. Carl's cruel grin only confirmed that.

"Can you—send this to me?"

"Sure. Though it *is* a lot of math."

For fuck's sake. He had an associate's degree in accounting. Ray snapped his teeth shut. "Why are you showing this to me now?" Who knew what time it was—late, probably.

"To keep you in line." For once Carl didn't lie. "I'm tired of you mouthing off to me, showing off to your bandmates, especially when they don't know how hard you screwed them over." He shut the tablet off and tucked it under his arm. "Your song choice worked tonight, but I'm your manager, Ray. You're gonna listen to me when I tell you shit and you're going to do it, because I'm the only line you have to the label and the only one who can get you out of the hole you've dug yourself into."

Ray shivered as a deep chill seeped into his bones that had nothing to do with the AC. "Send me the goddamned numbers and I'll take a look at them." Even if he knew in his soul that Carl was telling the truth this time.

Carl's smile fell away. "You better toe the line or the label will drop you and your band, and you'll be stuck explaining why your friends have no money to their name."

Yeah, trapped, and not in the high school bully sense. Ray could almost hear the cell door clicking closed. "I said I'd look at it later. What more do you want?" Oh, he knew. Hated the idea, but what choice did he have? He dropped his shoulders "For now, you're the boss."

"Damn straight I am." Carl pushed off the door and opened it. "Enjoy your night, Ray."

Like hell he would, and given the twist in Carl's voice, he knew Ray wouldn't. Without a word, Ray left and headed toward the bus.

Fucking hell. Yeah, they'd all signed the contract, but they'd looked to him for guidance, and maybe he'd sunk them all. He was supposed to be the leader. Fuck.

Of course, he was the last one to the bus. Dom was already halfway through one of his microbrews. "Hey!

There's the man of the—" His face fell and so did Mish's. Ray didn't want to look at Zavier.

"Honey?" Mish said. "What happened?"

"Nothing." He ground the word out and pushed past them all. "I'm fine." Last thing he needed was Mish mothering him or Dom to pepper him with questions.

"We did good tonight." Zavier's velvet-soft words. "Nothing can take that away."

Ray stared into the back of the bus and let his eyes water. Oh yes, something could. Carl could. Toe the line. Do as told. "Yeah, the crowd loved us. I know." His voice wobbled. "I— need to—" He kicked off his shoes and waved at his berth before crawling in and pulling the curtain shut. Fuck. He jammed his face into the pillow and covered his ears as best he could. He wanted to punch something. Or cry. Or find someone to fuck into oblivion. Anything to get the pain out of his head and chest.

Carl only echoed the voice Ray heard in his own head. He wasn't good enough. He couldn't pull this off. Somehow, this was all a fluke. He'd already burned Kevin out—how long before he took out Dom, Mish, and even fucking perfect Zavier Demos as well?

The pillow, the darkness and the rumble of the bus's engine were all he had to make the agony stop, and they didn't block out the murmur of voices, just muted some words. Dom was angry and Mish concerned. But what got to Ray was Zavier's calm voice. "Endorphin crash. I suspect he had help, too." A hint of deep fury there.

Zavier's breath ghosted across his neck and his praise echoed in Ray's mind. *You're an astounding musician.* Maybe he was, but that didn't mean a damn thing now.

"Fuck. Must have been Carl. That shitbag hell-swine." Mish and her mouth.

Her outburst quieted them all down. "What do we do?"

Dom's voice—not Domino, but the kid Ray had known since that first day of high school.

It was Zavier who answered. "Drink your beer. Enjoy the night. It was incredible." He gave a little laugh, as if he didn't believe how well they'd played. "Like I said, nothing can change that. Ray'll feel better in the morning."

The thing of it was that they *had* fucking rocked it. Played better than even Five Asylum. Ray still vibrated from the audience, those wide eyes staring at him, and the screaming fans with their outstretched arms. There'd been the murmured thanks, tears, and heartfelt happiness in the autograph line. People wanted selfies with him. Mel's story.

Zavier was right—Carl couldn't take that away. But the walking dickbag could make sure it never ever happened again. He could make them destitute. They'd never dig themselves out of the hole he'd put them in by accepting that contract.

That was where Zavier was so very, very wrong—Ray wasn't going to feel better in the morning. He'd never get the rock lodged in his stomach out again. They were beholden to the studio, and Carl held all the cards.

ZAVIER WOKE WHEN RAY SLIPPED OUT OF THE BERTH ABOVE HIS. No idea what time it was...but probably not morning given that they were still on the road and their next stop was outside Chicago. That was only about a five-hour drive, and it had taken Mish, Dom, and him a good hour after the bus pulled away from the venue to chill out—both from the concert and their collective anger at Carl.

Fucking Carl. Before he'd crawled into his bunk, Zavier had shot off another email to Nadia. She preferred phone calls, but there wasn't any good or private time and other than the band, he wasn't sure who he could trust.

As for the band, he didn't exactly want to drop Nadia's name. Not the famous madam from the '70s. No idea how any of them would react to *that* tidbit of news.

Ray's footsteps headed to the back of the bus, toward the bathroom. Zavier waited, but those footsteps never returned, though the soft sounds of water running had filtered to Zavier's ears. He was groggy and tired and should leave Ray to his space, but try as he might, he couldn't slip back into sleep.

He kept seeing Ray's broken expression when he'd climbed into the bus. The hopelessness written into his skin and the desolation in his eyes. Whatever Carl had said to Ray, it had sunk teeth in deep. Too deep.

They needed Ray. Hell, *Ray* needed Ray—not the anxious, strung-out version that was uncontrolled and spiraling, but the thoughtful, creative one who saw solutions and knew the band, the material, and what would light the fans on fire.

Zavier sighed, got up, and followed Ray to the back of the bus. There was a little lounge they'd deemed a quiet zone. Somewhere to go when you wanted to read or rest or otherwise have downtime without someone yapping in your ears.

Ray sat on one of the couches, a small light illuminating the gold of his hair. His head was in his hands, and his naked but inked back heaving like he'd run a marathon. Or was trying very hard not to break down. He looked up when Zavier paused at the threshold and if anything, there was more despair in his eyes than before. "I'm sorry if I woke you." His voice was a mess of husk and gravel.

"It's not a problem. I was worried." Zavier waved at the seat across from Ray. "Do you need a shoulder?"

Ray's laugh was hollow. "I need a fucking brain."

But he nodded, so Zavier slipped in and took a seat. "Whatever Carl said—it's probably not true."

Ray pushed his hair back. "Except that it is." He fisted his locks and yanked, then stood and paced in a very tiny circle, much like a caged animal. "It is."

Oh, the desire to rise up and take Ray's arms, his tense body, and sit it back down on the bench with him. Soothe out his worries and take control of all that energy. But Ray was too far gone, and too volatile. "How?"

That question seemed to suck the wind out of Ray. He sank down. "We owe the label money. More than we'll ever make. The first album with them went gold, and the idea of the tour was to boost our visibility and bring in more funds for the next album with them, but...we're never gonna make enough. Ever. I signed a contract that screws us over and—" He took a long look up the bus. "I've fucked over my friends, 'cause I got them to sign it, too."

Am I your friend? Zavier would like to think that he was. "Record label contracts are pretty much designed to screw the artists over, yeah. But there are ways to survive that. To thrive. There has to be, because others have." He shifted on the couch. "Carl likes playing with your head."

It was almost as if those sentences, that string of words had been the tiny slaps Ray had needed to wake him up out of his shock and fear. "I asked him to send me the spreadsheet he showed me."

A goddamned spreadsheet? "That fucker threw numbers at you after a concert and fan signing?"

Ray nodded slowly. "And told me to toe the line, or he'd make our lives hell with the label. More or less." Another glance up the bus. "Please don't tell the others. They have enough shit to deal with." He sat back. "Hell, I don't even know why I'm talking to you. Carl's *my* problem."

That fucking manager was everyone's problem. But Zavier shrugged. "I'm expendable." A temporary hire.

For the first time since Ray had entered the bus, his expression was clear and collected. "No. You're not." He rose. "I should try to get some sleep."

Yeah, so should he. "Ray?"

Ray paused, but didn't look back. "Yeah?"

"I've never played a concert like I played last night. I want to do it again. Even better."

This time Ray did glance back. "Me too." With that, Ray headed to his berth and crawled inside.

Zavier waited a few minutes, replaying the conversation over in his head. He really needed dirt on Carl, or to find some way to keep Ray from falling apart after every damn show. The fucker had his claws in Ray, that was for sure—probably playing with Ray's sense of responsibility.

Finally, Zavier got up and slipped back into his bunk. He itched to touch Ray in all the ways that might calm that spirit down.

So not a good idea, especially when Ray swung from one emotion to another. So he rolled over, and tried not to think about the naked expanse of Ray's back and just how much he wanted to trace the lines of ink with his fingers. Or a crop. Or his tongue.

One thing he did need to do—find out more about contracts and see what the kernel of truth was that Carl had shoved deep in his shit sandwich of lies.

CHAPTER
TEN

RAY WAITED FOR THE OTHER SHOE TO DROP FROM CARL, BUT IT didn't come. Not at their Chicago show and not today, though he'd finally received the spreadsheet from Carl in his inbox overnight, and he'd spent the better part of the morning on the bus poring over the numbers. Sadly, the information was limited and he had no way of knowing if any of it was correct, especially since the sheet was something of Carl's own making and not an official royalty statement.

Man, he wished he had his contract so he could see when and how he was supposed to get those, but it were tucked into a lockbox back in a storage unit in New Jersey. Stupid not to have it, or at least electronic copies. He wondered if asking for it directly from the label would cause waves.

Probably. He wasn't supposed to be bothering the label with shit like that. He rubbed his forehead and tossed his phone to one side. Trying to make heads or tails of a spreadsheet on a smartphone was an odious task, and he needed to focus on their next concert. He rose to fetch his notebook.

In Chicago, they'd played an amphitheater and had rocked that show harder than they'd played Detroit. Zavier had gotten his wish—another concert, but even better. Same screaming audiences, and a larger line of fans waiting for autographs. So many had wanted selfies, including with the hot new drummer.

The press was pretty jazzed, too. Twisted Wishes had gotten a decent write-up in the Detroit area and the gossip blogs were even being somewhat kind, though too many still wondered when Van Zeller would lose his mind again. Truth was, he always hovered near his breaking point.

Ray sank back down on the couch where Zavier was stretched out. He had to figure out some way to get the band out from under the pile of red numbers in Carl's spreadsheet.

"Meeting time?" Dom looked up from his book, one of his well-worn Oscar Wilde tomes he read over and over.

"Not yet. I wanna look over things. Think about what we've done."

They'd used nearly the same playlists for both shows. Some changeups in the middle, to make sure they kept their hands in all the songs. Different outfits, too. Ray wasn't sure whether Zavier looked better in tight leather or flowing black linen that hung nearly off his hips.

Zavier had kept the purple lipstick. He'd also been keeping quiet when not on stage, though it was pretty darn obvious he was watching Ray when not studying the screen of his tablet. Pity? Concern? Ray had no idea what was behind those looks. Didn't care. *Couldn't* care.

Carl had made every waking moment like walking on cracking ice, so Ray bottled up his feelings. It was the only thing he could do and remain together. But too often there were moments when his stomach rolled and his head hurt and he thought he might hurl if he focused on all the ways Carl could screw the band. The ways Ray had already screwed them.

All Carl had done in Chicago was smile at Ray, and that had been enough to force Ray to hit the bathroom to splash cold water on his face before boarding the bus. He'd stayed up to celebrate with the band—albeit with water—and everyone, including Zavier, seemed to have bought his cheerful demeanor.

Not so much now, from the set of Zavier's lips when his eyes flicked up from the tablet.

They were on their way south to St. Louis, then on to Oklahoma City, then Houston. They'd have a break after the show in Houston, two nights in a hotel before they hit the road again. God, he couldn't wait. Privacy. A shower that wasn't a shoebox. No rumble of an engine. Maybe he could find someone to fuck the tension out of his system and gain a piece of oblivion—at least for a while.

He shivered. Oblivion was what Kevin had sought. At least the occasional tumble wasn't quite as bad as crawling into a bottle...he hoped, anyway.

Ray flipped open the last written pages of his notebook. Tight but messy handwriting. Playlists. Thoughts. Worries. Little snatches of lyrics, most of which were *terrible*. But it got them out of his mind.

When blue shades to violet
And agony encompasses the moon
Will I find my heart or abandon my soul?

He traced a finger over the words and felt the weight of Zavier's stare. Of all the people to become their drummer, it had to have been the one guy he never ever had a shot with. Worse, he was so damn grateful to Zavier for pulling them from disaster.

He looked up and met Zavier's gaze. "Other than 'White Hot Midnight,' what's your favorite song?"

Zavier folded the cover of his tablet over to turn it off and rested his hand on top. "You'll laugh if I tell you."

Was that...embarrassment? "Promise I won't."

Zavier rolled his eyes. "Don't make promises you can't keep."

Ray shrugged. "Come on. I can't think of any song that—"

Oh. *Oh*. He sucked in a breath because he was about to burst out laughing, despite what he'd said.

They'd been joking around one night, Mish, Dom, and him—Kevin had been out somewhere—and they'd written a pop song: "Sprinkles on Top." It was kitschy and came complete with an upbeat but utterly metronomic rhythm and cute lyrics about ice cream. Kevin had *hated* it. Refused to play it, and really Ray couldn't blame him for that.

The rest of the band had only recorded it on a whim and it was one of the infamous session songs that maybe a dozen people had heard before someone—they never found out who—had put it out on the internet.

They'd never played it in public. Hell, they hadn't practiced in *ages*.

"You are *completely* messed up, Demos." Mish shook her head. "Fucking hell. That song?"

Zavier leaned forward. "It's *fun*. And frivolous. And there's so many interesting things you could do with it." He tapped out the bass rhythm. Then another rhythm, then another that wasn't at all 4/4 that somehow *worked*. Then a couple more. "Or slow it down and put a kind of swing beat to it." He hummed the melody to a new time signature. "Would be a fun acoustical piece."

Ray stared at Zavier, his brain already whirling. The fog he'd been carrying around all day lifted, but caution niggled at his wild heart. "We haven't practiced it."

Dom had set aside his book. "That's what sound checks are for." Yeah, he was eager and all smiles. Mish, too.

He could see the notes and the beats Zavier still tapped out like a pulse, or the swing and rhythm of bodies moving together. Dancing. Fucking.

Yeah, he wanted this, but for one problem. "Carl will have a fit."

"Does he need to know?" God, Zavier's voice could make

stone do his bidding. "We can put down TBD for one of the acoustical songs, fuck around at sound check, and go for it."

Carl would still have a fit. It was so not walking the line he wanted Ray to walk. Instinct told Ray that, but his soul told him Zavier's idea would be a fucking massive hit.

"Okay. Let's do it." He'd take the lumps that came with his decision. Guess it had been meeting time after all. He jotted down some notes and the proposed set list—and the words *Zavier Demos is too fucking perfect.* Felt a little like high school. He'd probably written something similar in a spiral-bound notebook back in the day, not his pretentious but well-loved Moleskine.

Zavier stretched out his legs and bumped Ray's thigh with his toes. "I believe in you," he murmured.

Fuck, the sparks and light went up his spine and down into his dick. Nothing like that ever happened back in school, mostly because Zavier was hardly ever within ten feet of Ray, let alone sharing a couch.

Whatever else, it did push away the fear. He pulled out his phone and typed an email to send to the record label requesting a copy of his contract.

Yeah, maybe they'd been screwed by Carl, but contracts went two ways. Perhaps the band could do some screwing of their own—if they had more leverage. If they made a name for themselves and more money for the label, Carl would have less hold over them.

Ray drew a little picture of an ice cream cone with sprinkles right under Zavier's name, then closed his book. Maybe it was also time to open up to everyone, not just Zavier. "I'm sorry I was so out of it last night. Zavier was right—it was Carl, and I want to tell you what he said."

They all looked at him. Mish and Dom wore worry, but Zavier was nodding in encouragement. Well, okay then. Ray took a breath and started talking.

———

ZAVIER COULDN'T HELP WATCHING RAY'S LIPS AS HE EXPLAINED the run-in he'd had with Carl. The news that the band might owe the label a shit-ton of royalties wasn't the most upbeat thing, and both Mish and Dom reacted as Zavier expected them to. They were dismayed, then angry, then skeptical that Carl was even telling the truth. They both reminded Ray that they'd signed too, so he couldn't take all the blame. Of course, Ray did anyway.

"I emailed the label to ask for a copy of our contract." Ray leaned back. "Maybe if we put our heads together, we can figure this out."

Heads. Bodies. His and Ray's. Zavier indulged in those thoughts before setting them aside. No more crawling into bed on the job, even when the job didn't feel like one.

Ray's mouth showed the emotions he so desperately tried to hide. There was a quiver of fear and the angry press of his lips and the way his jaw rocked back and forth when he wasn't talking.

Oh, to take those lips and soothe them with his own. Ray reacted to touch. To heartfelt praise. Most of all, Ray reacted to friendship and trust and that was, admittedly, catnip to Zavier.

There was a bond between Ray, Dom, and Mish. They were a family, that was easy enough to see. They'd embraced Zavier, too—at least Dom and Mish had. Sometimes he wondered if Ray would ever consider him a friend or if he'd always be on his guard against Zavier.

The three of them talked strategy and ideas for a while until Ray looked over. "Your contract's different, isn't it?"

Zavier nodded. "I'm here for the tour, as a session musician. I'm not actually a part of Twisted Wishes."

"Like hell you aren't," Dom muttered.

"Not contractually." Zavier was improving the drumming,

but he hadn't contributed artistically to the group. But he wasn't going to argue with Dom.

"You're part of the band," Ray said. "End of story."

Heat and joy danced along Zavier's nerves. He certainly wasn't going to argue with Ray, either. "Thank you."

Ray clapped him on the leg, and that touch was far too enjoyable. Zavier had been missing that sharp, lovely contact that came with having sex. He didn't particularly understand holding hands or staring dreamily into someone's eyes or whatever people in love were supposed to do. But he liked touching. Holding another. Being held. Curling up on a couch. Watching someone sleep.

Living as close as he had with these three for the weeks of practice and now crammed into a bus—it made him itch for those things again. He craved skin-to-skin contact.

In the end, he even got some. After their meeting, Ray put his journal away and pulled an ereader out of his bag. He shifted again and again on the couch while Zavier had his legs stretched out, his toes occasionally brushing Ray's thighs. Eventually, Ray sighed. "Do you mind if I stretch out?" He waved at the section of couch Zavier's legs occupied.

He shifted his over a bit. "No, of course not."

When Ray was done maneuvering, their legs were practically entwined on the couch.

Delightful. Perfect. Zavier didn't stroke his foot along Ray's calf, though the desire to do so was so very high. He glanced at the ereader. "Anything interesting?"

A little color on Ray's cheeks. "It's a biography of John Adams. I've been meaning to read it for years and years."

"You're into American history?" Not a subject Zavier would have pinned on him.

The color darkened, and Ray tensed. "I do actually have a brain, despite my vapid looks."

Hardly vapid. Sexy as hell, more like it. But he didn't comment on Ray's looks, not with Dom and Mish watching from the *other* couch. "I've never doubted your intelligence. History is so—dry."

Ray stared at him. "Then you've obviously been reading the wrong history books." A grin there and a shrug, then he focused back on his book.

Zavier grunted and shifted, and maybe his toes did graze Ray's leg purely by accident, and maybe he did relish in his slight hiss of breath.

Perhaps Ray was right—Zavier *had* been reading the wrong books. For now, he clicked out of his game, closed his tablet, and enjoyed the tiny bit of contact he had with Ray. Soothing and comforting. He could get used to this.

It wasn't until the tour bus lurched to a stop that Zavier realized he'd fallen asleep. The change in motion startled and had him blinking against the light streaming through the window. "What the fuck?"

"Easy there." Ray patted his shin. "We're just coming into a rest stop. Probably changing drivers. Getting gas. That kind of thing."

Of course. Zavier blew out a breath and then another as he sought to center himself. Didn't help that Ray hadn't moved his hand off his shin. He met Ray's watchful gaze. "How long was I out?"

"An hour, maybe? Not that long." Ray gave him another squeeze. "I'd have woken you up sooner or later."

"Really?"

Dom chuckled. "He knows how awful screwing up your sleep schedule can be on tour."

That seemed a bit much for a bandleader. On the other hand, it was good to see Ray relaxed. And honestly, he didn't mind the physical contact at all. "Hard lesson learned?"

A shrug from Ray. "Mish gets it, but Dom used to sleep every time the bus started moving."

"It's true." Dom stretched out his legs into the aisle. "I'd conk out for hours on end, then be so groggy by showtime.

I'd hop myself up on caffeine and be so damn wired after the show, I'd drive everyone nuts." He paused. "Especially Mish."

"That's because I can't nap to save my life," Mish said. "Not like you gentlemen." She winked at Zavier, and a strange sense of warmth radiated from where Ray still held his leg.

Gentlemen? Maybe. He wore a tux well enough. The image that flitted through his head was not one he needed: him adjusting his cufflinks while Ray knelt before him, naked, eyes upturned in want.

He shook it off. "I can nap, but I wasn't intending to."

The bus pulled into a truck stop. Zavier had no idea where they were. He could check his phone's GPS, but that meant moving and breaking contact with Ray.

"Kevin was the worst." Ray's voice was soft. "He was always sleeping." He looked out the window. "I guess I should have noticed how hard he was struggling a lot sooner."

"Sweetheart," Mish murmured. "You aren't responsible for his drinking."

Ray shrugged again, but it belied his pain. "Maybe not. But I could have helped more."

Zavier was the better drummer. Wasn't hubris, either, to think it. Ray knew it, too. It dawned on Zavier that Ray's remorse had nothing to do with replacing Kevin, but was entirely due to the fact that they had made it to that point. That he hadn't fixed Kevin or changed his personality. "Sometimes all you can do is let go."

Ray swallowed. "I didn't want to. He was my *friend*."

Finally the bus stopped and the engine cut out. They all shifted, and Ray finally let go of Zavier's leg. He missed the touch almost immediately.

I like this man. He'd known that, of course, but there was something more visceral there, deeper than the surface lust he felt for beautiful Ray. Maybe the start of a good friendship, if Ray ever let him in.

Ray was a *mess* and pulled so many ways, and so not the type of person Zavier normally took into his life. But then, Ray had been lurking there on the edges since high school, so why not? Other than the pesky part where they worked together.

So no. Zavier rose off the couch and filed out of the bus with the others. Time to go see what the shop attached to the truck stop had in the way of munchies. As he wandered past the walls of coolers, he checked his email and found a note from Nadia. *Finally*.

He read the message over, then read it again and grunted.

Your rock band manager isn't entirely uninteresting. He used to be a musician. You know what to do, darling!

She wanted a phone call. There was the pull and the push and the resistance. But the carrot had been dangled, as it always had been before.

That night, years ago, she'd held out a length of rope. "Darling boy, everything comes with a price. I'll teach you what you want to know, but you have to decide if you're willing to pay." After pacing in front of her for a good fifteen minutes, he'd held out his hands.

Same resentment now. Same resigned sigh. He tapped her number and headed out of the store.

After a few rings, she picked up. "You're never a disappointment, Zavier."

He fought against both the flare of anger and the one of pride and let both go. "So how is Carl interesting?"

"He was, at one time, the lead singer for a band very much like your own."

Curious, indeed. Zavier paced the length of the hot truck stop lot. "Twisted Wishes is hardly my band, Nadia."

"Mmm, but you're already putting your stamp on it with your bare chest and your leather pants and the way that lovely boy looks at you."

He didn't even have to ask which lovely boy, and if that was what Nadia was seeing, then he really did need to start searching for those stories on the internet. "I didn't call to hear you sing the praises of my ass." He let annoyance seep in, with purpose. Even if he had worn the pants exactly to get a rise out of Ray.

"Your drumming, then. You should read some of these articles, Zavier. 'Demos isn't just another pretty face, though. With his classical training and unlimited energy, his drumming elevates Twisted Wishes to a new level.'"

She was doing this to needle him. "Nadia, I'm standing in the middle of a truck stop somewhere between Chicago and St. Louis. I'm going to have to climb back onto the bus soon. You can email me all the articles you want and I promise to read them and be embarrassed and grumpy. Please tell me about Carl Roberts."

Silence on the other end. "Ah, so this is serious." A change in her voice from the teasing drawl to the other tone he remembered so well: Nadia the instructor.

Thank god.

"Your manager is the failed lead singer of a group called Tenacious Dreams. They had one single that did moderately well, pushing into the Top 100, but after that, they vanished into obscurity. Unlike your Ray, Carl was not a singer/songwriter. Their guitarist wrote most of their material, though the song that went somewhere was penned by Cynthia and Douglas Harndt."

Zavier's fingertips tingled. "They compose blockbuster movie soundtracks now."

"Indeed. Their skill is tremendous. Carl's voice, however, left something to be desired. Even with voice lessons, it never improved enough for the big time. Nor did the lyrical skills of their guitarist. The band dissolved and the members went on to other things. Carl ended up working for the various record labels until he landed where he is now."

Jealousy? But that was such a *petty* motivation. He glanced back at the bus and saw Ray waving at him. Likely it was time to go. "Did Carl manage any bands before Twisted Wishes?"

"Ah, that's an interesting thing, too. No. What I heard—and this is from a friend of a friend—is that Carl had been reasonably successful in the marketing department. Someone over there had the brilliant idea that if the label used a marketing manager as a band manager—rather than the band hiring one themselves—they'd have much less friction with bands. Yours is a trial run on that, since Carl had some practical experience."

Carl was a marketing manager? That explained some things, but not others. "Thank you, Nadia." He headed back toward the bus, at a slightly slower pace than normal.

"You care about him, your Ray."

Not a question, which meant Nadia already had an answer. The question was why. Zavier snorted. "What makes you say that?"

"Oh, darling, those photos show the way you look at him, too."

Zavier stopped walking. He was still far enough away from the bus to speak without being overheard. "That's called lust."

"Mmmhmm. I've seen you in lust, dear. This is something other than that."

Zavier sighed. "I've known him since high school and admire his skills and tenacity. They're all good people, Nadia, not just Ray."

"So your heart's getting all tangled up with them." She chuckled.

He had to laugh. "If you know me as well as you think

you do, you'd know my heart never gets tangled up in anything."

Nadia's voice was velvet. "Darling boy, I know you better than you know yourself."

No, no she didn't. Because he'd kept one thing secret from her. "I suppose we'll see."

Ray appeared in the doorway of the bus. "You coming? 'Cause we gotta move and I'd hate to leave your sorry ass behind."

"Time's up," he said into the phone. "Thank you for your help, Nadia."

"Do keep wearing those pants, Zavier. And I'll be sending you lots of links very shortly."

Wonderful. He pulled the phone away from his ear, disconnected, then bounded up into the bus.

"Talking to your mom?" Ray was nestled back against the couch, exactly as he had been before.

A strange sense of euphoria made Zavier lightheaded. He could stretch out again. Have that fine sense of presence against his skin. It clashed with the absurdity that Nadia could be anything like a mother. He swung down onto the couch as the bus shuddered forward. "No. A mentor."

Ray raised an eyebrow, obviously expecting more.

Zavier toed off his shoes and slid his legs next to Ray's, with delightful effect. A shiver, both eyebrows into his hairline, and Ray repositioned himself.

But not to move away.

Dom snorted. "*You* need a mentor?"

He shrugged. "I did. And the connection is useful." The others stared at him and he remembered Ray's words. *You're part of the band*. "She has a lot of ties in the entertainment world. I'm trying to find out what makes Carl tick."

"You mean other than his hatred of me?" Ray's words were thick.

"Sweetheart," Mish murmured. There was tenderness there. Caring.

Such a contrast from his conversation with Nadia, from her affected "darlings" that were meant to irritate, not soothe. Jealousy was a strange, strange thing, because he rarely got the gut-churning envy that swept through him. So many lovers, not enough friends. Nadia hadn't been a lover—but he wouldn't call her a friend, either.

Ray exhaled and pressed his foot against the outside of Zavier's leg. "You know it's true. You all know it's true."

None of them spoke. Zavier's mind danced around the information he'd been given by Nadia and whether he should share it. Ray's legs were warm against his own. "Carl was in a band." He recounted the rest of what Nadia had told him, and watched their shifting expressions.

Ray closed his eyes. "None of this is on the internet."

That had been another tidbit Nadia had shared with Zavier. "He used the name Clay Rodham while singing."

"And to be fair," Dom said, "the part about him having been in marketing was there, too."

"Yes, but not that he had *no* experience as a band manager!" Ray rubbed his face. "Fuck."

Mish had pulled her red curls back at some point, but now she tugged the clip free and set about pulling her hair back again. "There's nothing wrong with marketing. *I* was in marketing. It can be a successful jumping-off point for a lot of careers. You learn people skills."

All true. "Depends on how good he was. And what his goal is now," Zavier said.

"That's easy. Keeping me under his thumb." Ray opened his eyes. "I do appreciate you digging for intel, though."

Zavier poked him with his toes. "It's the *why* I'm interested in. Jealousy seems so—" he waved his hand "—banal."

"Seems human to me." Ray shrugged, but there was an edge to it. "I want it to stop."

So did Zavier. But how to get Carl to ease up greatly depended on his motivation. However, he knew better than to keep this conversation going, so he let that part drop.

Still, he was curious about Carl's former band. Didn't take that much searching to pull up some videos of Tenacious Dreams in concert. Fuck if the younger version of Carl didn't look slightly like Ray. Long-limbed and blond. Torn jeans with an edge of punk. Ray wore it so much better, though.

"Well, would you look at this?" He held up his tablet. A moment later, they were all crowded around, and he tapped Play.

The clip was almost embarrassing to watch. Yeah, there was a reason Carl's band never made it past one song. The fire, the flare, wasn't there.

When the video ended, Dom leaned back and scratched his head. "That was...okay. I guess."

That pretty much summed it up. Band wasn't horrible. Rhythms were serviceable and they hit most of the notes right. But even in the good videos, there was a tinny quality to Carl's singing, a strain that scraped against the melody he tried to belt out.

They played a few others, and they were the same. Their one song was catchy enough, but in concert it fell flat.

Ray kept staring at the tablet screen. "I'm not... I don't look like that, do I?"

Mish's bark of laughter rang out loud and joyful. "Oh, Ray, honey." She ruffled his hair. "You look nothing like that. Night and day, kiddo."

That seemed to appease Ray, given his chuckle and red cheeks.

After they passed the tablet around again to get their fill of the spectacle, they all settled back down into quiet pursuits, but nothing on his tablet interested Zavier until an email from Nadia appeared in his inbox.

Here you go, darling boy.

Links. Many links that took him to an article about Twisted Wishes and their recent concerts. How there'd been such a huge turnaround in sound. Many people speculated it was Ray sobering up, but many also pointed to the hot new drummer.

Zavier's cheeks warmed. He was well aware of his looks and often used them to his advantage, including to bed people who caught his attention. But praise of those same attributes in the press made him squirm, as if he were walking naked in public.

There was, of course, various speculations about his sexuality, including a mention of his alleged "closeness" with Maestro Ferbran from Gabriel McGinness, the reporter they'd met at the festival. Dimitri, for what it was worth, had no comment about Zavier.

Then again, he had begged and pleaded, then screamed and yelled enough to last Zavier a lifetime.

When he got to the photos of the concerts, they were everything that Nadia had said they were. Tantalizing. Sexy. Almost erotic. The camera seemed to capture every line and passionate expression—and expose expressions he thought were subtle as anything but.

Oh yes, there was no mistaking how he looked at Ray Van Zeller. Nor anything hidden about how Ray watched him.

Damn. Lust trickled down his body and settled in his core, with predictable results. Luckily his clothes were loose and his underwear tight. He could hide his hard-on well enough.

It wasn't just lust—and that made his arousal fade, because he could see it in the photos of himself when he bottled up his emotional reaction. What Nadia had read as *more than lust* was adoration. Ray's talent. His voice and body and movements. He'd admired Ray's career for a while. It was breathtaking to see it up close and personal.

Maybe he needed to admit he was more into Ray than he'd thought, which was highly problematic, given how much he'd like to press against more than Ray's legs. So rather than remain where he felt comfortable and content, he slung his legs out and rose. "Anyone interested in coffee?"

Zavier didn't wait for an answer before fixing a pot. He needed a little more distance from Ray Van Zeller—or they'd both be in a world of hurt.

CHAPTER
ELEVEN

LIFE WAS CHAOS, AND RAY KNEW THAT FOR A FACT. HE'D ALWAYS lived in the whirlwind. The only thing that changed was how fast things moved at any given time. Push one way and things flew off in another direction. He received a copy of their contract from the record label and in return, Carl shoved reporter after shitty reporter at the band in St. Louis. None of them wanted to talk about Twisted Wishes's sound or the tour or any of that—they all wanted to know about Kevin and about Ray's "drinking problem."

By the third reporter, he snapped and slapped a hand down on his thigh. "I don't have a fucking drinking problem!" He rose from his chair in the green room. "I have a fucking   dirt-digging-rats-who-are-only-interested-in-controversy problem."

"Ray." Zavier's voice, low and either soothing or condescending, Ray couldn't tell anymore.

"Back off, Demos." He hadn't known what had happened between them, only that one moment Zavier had been sharing a couch with him all friendly like, and the next, he was giving Ray the cold shoulder and curling up in his berth to play fucking games on that goddamned tablet of his.

"Here, a parting gift for each of you." He flipped both Zavier and the reporter the finger and marched out of the room, his heart in his throat and his stomach a mess.

He shouldn't let any of it get to him. But everything was chip, chip, chipping away at him, and he was done. When he made it to the dressing room, he looked at himself in the mirror. The face of a fool.

He'd spent too many hours overnight reading and rereading their contract, then searching terms on the internet. Panic clawed its way into his soul. He didn't understand everything he'd read, but he did suss out enough to know that the label had them over a barrel. Maybe not in the way Carl had said, but they were beholden to them.

And Carl, who was supposed to be their biggest asset, connection, and promoter to the label, *hated* him. Ray didn't understand any of it, and between the lack of sleep, the fear, the fucking reporters, and Zavier Demos, he couldn't think straight.

Footsteps sounded in the hall, and Ray braced himself for whoever it was. He expected Carl or Zavier, but it was Mish who appeared in the reflection of the vanity. "Honey, what's wrong?"

Everything. He shook his head.

She sighed and walked into the room. "I haven't seen you this upset since Kevin..."

There was the other part he hadn't wanted to think about, but the reporters kept dragging it up. "How do you feel about Kevin Schmidt being destitute while you're touring the US with your new drummer?"

Like fucking shit. He swallowed the lump in his throat. "Did you know about Kevin?" He hadn't heard a damn thing from anyone, and as far as he knew, no one else had, either.

Mish turned him around and pulled him into a hug. "He's not out on the street or anything. He's living with his mom while he gets back on his feet."

Ray tried to keep the anger in, tried to keep the pain from spilling out of his mouth. "You *knew* what happened to Kevin!"

She didn't let him go. Not that he wanted that anyway. Someone caring about him felt nice, and Mish always had his back. She rocked him slightly. "He emailed me back when we were getting ready for the tour. Wanted me to know he was okay and getting help and that he appreciated your letter."

"And you didn't tell me?" His head and heart hurt. Couldn't he trust anyone anymore?

A sigh. "He asked me not to. Knew it would upset you. Wanted you to focus on the band, not him."

He muttered his words into Mish's shoulder. "I'm supposed to be protecting you guys, not the other way around."

A soft chuckle. "Hon, we're here for each other."

Typical wonderful Mish, always watching out for them. When Ray had started fucking members of the crew, Mish had pulled him aside. *"Be good to them, Ray, 'cause they're giving you a lot by saying yes. And for god's sake, tell me you're on PrEP and using condoms."* He was and did, and he had taken her advice to heart.

She opened space between them. "You gotta let this shit roll off you."

He wanted to. Desperately. But every time his head cleared a bit and he could breathe and see, something else came to shove him back into the chaos surrounding him. Too bad the crew was totally different this tour—and as far as he could tell, not a single guy was even the least bit interested in him, or he'd have the stress relief he needed and stop taking it out on everyone else. "That reporter's gonna have quite a story."

"Maybe." There was resignation in her tone. "I'm not worried about the reporter."

He hadn't just flipped off that asshole. Ray leaned his ass against the vanity. "I take it Zavier is pissed."

Mish pulled a chair out and sat down. "Don't know. Sometimes he's hard to read."

Too hard, lately. "What happened after I left?"

She filled him in. His outburst had ended the interview, and the reporter packed up his shit and left. Zavier had sat for a while, then stood and walked out of the room without saying a word.

"He didn't look angry. More...concerned, I guess." She paused. "Is there something going on between you two?"

Other than years of resentment and desire? "No."

Mish was a shrewd, shrewd woman, and that one raised eyebrow told Ray she didn't believe him.

"There's nothing going on. I'm not even sure he likes me."

She shook her head. "You're not even sure he *likes* you? Fucking hell, Ray." She threw up her hands and rose from the chair. "I can't help you with what's right under your nose." With that, she left the dressing room.

Great. Zavier pissed. Mish pissed. Maybe he should hunt down Dom and make sure all of his bandmates were mad at him, just to keep things even. But before he could even push himself off the edge of the vanity, Carl stood in the doorway.

Great. Fucking *stellar*.

"Do we need to have another discussion, Ray?"

Carl's voice scraped along every last one of Ray's nerves. "No."

"Because I'm pretty sure you just told a reporter to go to hell."

"Actually, I gave him the finger." If Carl was going to scold him, he could at least get the details right. "He was a prick and piece of shit."

"He's going to roast you and the band alive."

He'd had enough of Carl's false concern. "Like you give a

fuck. You *want* me to be the drunken asshole singer. Am I not performing well enough for you?"

Carl stormed in, grabbed him by the shirt, and pulled him up. "I want you to be a goddamned professional, you little shit."

Every inch of Ray wanted to punch him in the face. He was too close and reeked of crappy aftershave. It was a struggle not to fight, not to lash out. One thing Ray knew about bullies, though—you hit them, they'll hit you back harder.

"Let me go."

Carl shook him once, rattling Ray's teeth, then let go and stepped back. "You damn well better give this show your all, or I'm pulling the plug." He spun and stormed out.

Ray collapsed back on the vanity, then lowered himself into a nearby chair. They were fucked.

He was still sitting, staring at the floor and trying to remember how to breathe when the rest of the band walked in. None of them said anything to him, just went about getting ready. He should do that too, so he did.

In the end, it was the rhythm and the murmur of preparing and dressing that finally shoved enough of the churning tumult from Ray's head. If Carl wanted their best, they'd give it to them. He'd do it for the fans, since it might well be their last show.

———

THEY BROUGHT THE HOUSE DOWN, AND RAY BREATHED A LITTLE easier. From opening with "Lightning" to their acoustical swing version of "Sprinkles on Top" to yet another ripping version of "White Hot Midnight" as their last encore, they'd whipped the crowd into a frenzy. Zavier had suggested they change how they finished the song, having the instruments drop out until there was only Ray's and the audience's voices belting out the last verse. The screaming and the yelling and clapping kept going, even when the lights went up and the crews ran out to change the stage for Five Asylum. The line for autographs was huge, and they barely made it into the bus in time to have any hope of making it to their next destination when they needed to be there.

Carl pulled Ray aside before he boarded, his grip painfully tight on Ray's arm. "I don't know how you did it." His voice hissed in Ray's ear. "But you did, so you get a reprieve. But one more slipup, and I'm not giving you a second chance. You'll be done, do you understand?"

"Loud and clear." He yanked himself free and climbed into the safety of the bus.

His bandmates were already in their usual places on the front couches. "Maybe we should do one of those VIP experiences." Mish lolled her head against the leather and clutched her half a glass of wine. "Because if we pull off a show like that again, we're never gonna make the bus." Her voice was giddy and higher than normal.

"How do you even book those?" Dom had his beer and had done a crappy job of taking off his makeup, but his face was bright and youthful, a mix of Dominic and Domino. "I mean—" He waved his hand. "We're not Five Asylum."

They were better than Five Asylum. At least tonight.

Ray slipped past Zavier's outstretched legs and grabbed a bottle of water from the fridge. Zavier was lounging on his half of the couch with hot tea, and looked up expectantly at Ray. "You joining us?"

He should crawl into his bunk and sleep. Exhaustion gnawed at him, as well as his actions from earlier in the day, and Carl's cloying aftershave. But he owed it to the band to be better than he'd been. "Yeah. For a little. I'm dead on my feet, though."

He sat down next to Zavier and cracked open his water. "How can you drink something so fucking hot?" He did before concerts when his throat was bothering him, because the heat loosened things up. But afterward? Nope. And Zavier didn't even sing. He didn't need tea.

Zavier's lips twitched, but not in amusement. "My throat's been bugging me."

Ray shifted away. "You get me sick, Demos, and I'll kill you."

"Noted." So neutral. So cool. Zavier shifted his attention away from Ray and spoke. "There are companies that handle those VIP experiences, but I don't know how well your label would react to bringing in someone from the outside."

Your label? "You work for them, too."

"No." Zavier's voice *was* a touch hoarser than normal. "I'm a session musician." He rose and walked to the back of the bus, vanishing behind the privacy curtain they left to separate that quiet space.

Fuck. Guilt rose and wrapped its hands around Ray's throat from the inside. "He's still mad at me."

"Well," Dom said, his voice soft, "you were kind of an ass to him."

Yeah, he had been, but he didn't need Zavier chiding him, especially in front of shitty reporters. "This is why I should have gone to bed." He rose and climbed into his bunk. He'd change and piss once everyone else had turned in.

Texas next. Then New Mexico, Arizona, Utah, California, and Washington. He could do this. They could survive.

Except every inch of Ray hurt, and everything he did or said was wrong. The only right thing was the music.

He had to focus on that. There wasn't anything left he hadn't ruined.

CHAPTER
TWELVE

AFTER THE INTENSITY OF THAT NIGHT'S SHOW, ZAVIER WAS GLAD the band was staying at a hotel tonight. Sleeping on a tour bus had been all right, but the cramped conditions were wearing very thin on him. After yet another incredible concert full of energetic fans and Ray outdoing himself, Zavier was more wired than ever. Yet exhaustion had seeped deep into his bones, along with a growing frustration with the very man making each and every Twisted Wishes concert better than the last.

He hoped a bed that didn't vibrate and shake with the movements of a bus and some downtime off the road would help them all, *especially* Ray. The more Ray pushed himself, the more volatile his emotions became. He was either sullen, an anxious mess, a glorious rock god, or angry as fuck. Zavier missed those few moments when Ray had been relaxed and hopeful and *there* with the rest of the band.

Tonight Ray wasn't there. He'd been moody on the bus, quiet before the concert, astounding on stage, and then snappish after a short conversation with Carl.

Since they'd all opened up about the manager and what they knew, Ray hadn't filled anyone in on what the fuck Carl was saying to him. Zavier saw that wear on both Mish and Dom, and gritted his teeth.

The trip from the outdoor arena to the hotel was uneventful, thank goodness, though Ray fidgeted in the limo, probably still burning off some of the energy that coursed through them all. Tonight's concert had one-upped all the rest. Each time they played, they outdid themselves. Hell, at this rate they'd be headlining by the time they reached California.

Zavier knew his playing was part of that. The band could trust that he'd be there and blend, that they could improvise and still stay together—all the musicality that had fallen by the wayside with Kevin. Twisted Wishes flowed and built on the strengths of each musician.

Wasn't *all* Zavier—far from it. Like with the symphony, a band was a team. He'd replaced a member who hadn't functioned well, and they'd all taken it up a notch in response. *Especially* Ray. God, over the past few concerts, he'd become a firebrand on stage, his voice clearer and sharper, his interactions with the crowd energetic and stunning. Ray was a beautiful sight to behold, half naked by the end, and covered in sweat.

They were all coming down from the high now, but when Ray dropped, he hit bottom fast, as if the concerts were the only time he wasn't full of anxiety and worry.

What had happened? He still didn't know why Ray had flipped him off—was it only a few days ago? Didn't matter. That and Ray's behavior afterward had been for the best. He'd enjoyed Ray's company and the tenuous friendship they'd built. He still admired Ray and thought the man beautiful, but he couldn't become wrapped up in the tumult that was Ray Van Zeller, no matter how temping that thought was.

He'd dealt with Dimitri's violent moods. No more.

When the limo pulled into the hotel, they were each given their own rooms—nice ones, too. An entire floor was dedicated to the band and the crew, though Carl had vanished like he normally did. Zavier didn't know for sure, but he had a suspicion that managers usually stuck with their band. Carl came and went when it served him. Usually after he'd had a word with Ray and crushed his spirits even more.

You know he lies, Ray. Why are you listening to him? Why aren't you talking to us?

Zavier carded himself into his room and tucked the card into his pocket. There was everything he needed—a big-ass bed, a bunch of bottles of water, and a room-service menu. The only thing it lacked was ice; he liked his water cold, not tepid.

Well, that was why there were ice machines in hotels, after all. He grabbed the bucket and headed out to find where they'd stuffed the icemaker in this place. It was, of course, as far away from their rooms as humanly possible. A positive, since he wouldn't hear the contraption dumping ice all night, but he couldn't help being a bit grumpy about the distance. He wanted to toe off his shoes and lie down on that huge bed.

On the way to the machine, he walked by a kid in a hoodie and jean jacket slouching past in the way only youth and attitude could manage. The guy gave him a glance, then folded into himself deeper.

Ah, the righteousness of the young. He'd been there once and had been a complete brat, too.

It wasn't until Zavier was holding a bucket full of ice that his brain pondered what a kid like that would be doing on this floor—the one that was entirely occupied by Twisted Wishes's band and crew.

"Shit." Groupie. Or stalker. Looking a little young, too.

Every muscle tensed. This could be bad—especially if the guy was heading to the obvious place. Mish had her head on straight. Dom was too damn scared of not being Domino. Zavier was too new to the group to have picked up *that* bold a fan and besides, the kid would have stopped.

That left only one person.

Zavier picked up his pace back to his room—he, Mish, Dom, and Ray all had rooms near one another, separate from the crew, who all had rooms on this side of the floor.

When he turned the corner of the hall, the guy was gone.

Damn it, Ray. Don't be doing what I think you're doing. Stress relief or no, this was not the time to be fucking groupies, especially ones who looked too damn young. Even if the guy was of age, the thought of Ray with anyone twisted Zavier's insides. Which said something about his own wants. He tried to ignore that.

Decision time. Zavier knocked on Mish's door. When she answered she glanced at the ice bucket in his hands and gave him a look. "You lost?"

"No. I passed a kid in the hall. Groupie-type, but way too young."

"Well, he ain't here, sunshine."

"Didn't think he would be."

Mish's gaze shifted to Ray's door. "Oh, *hell*."

Okay, yeah, Zavier probably was right. *Shit.* He shoved the ice bucket into Mish's hands and pulled his cell phone out of his pocket.

"Nine-one-one isn't going to do anything," she said.

"I'm not calling anyone." Zavier called up the memo app and hit record, then crossed the room and banged on Ray's door. Better safe than sorry. "Ray."

Nothing.

He pounded on the door again. "I'm not going anywhere, Ray. Open the damn door."

A door opened, but not the one he wanted. Dom stuck his head out of his room. No makeup. Honest-to-god old-guy pajamas. "What's going on?"

Mish answered, "We think Ray's got an underaged groupie."

"Fuck." Dom's eyes widened.

"He's not opening this for me." Zavier thumped the door with his foot.

"I have a keycard," Dom said.

Zavier whipped around. "What?"

"Sometimes Ray sleeps really heavily and wears earplugs. He's terrified of dying in a fire. Used to have nightmares as a kid, so..."

"Dominic," Zavier ground out, and laid his hand flat.

He'd never seen that man move quite that fast. A moment later, the card was on his palm. A second after that, he was in Ray's room. And yup, there was the guy, sans hoodie. Barely any chest hair. At least his pants were on and Ray was fully clothed.

"What the fuck are you doing here?" Ray didn't yell, but there was unmistakable malice in his voice.

"Likely saving your ass from a felony." Zavier pointed at the kid. "How old are you?"

"He's legal," Ray said. "I checked his ID."

"I'm twenty-one!" the guy growled.

Part of Zavier understood the appeal. Guy was broody, with dark hair and pale eyes, and had that whole rebel thing going. Might have been a baby-faced twenty-one-year-old, but he looked like he might be younger than that, too.

Jesus, Ray. What the hell are you doing with this guy? "Let me see this ID."

The guy dove for his jacket and handed over the ID with shaking fingers.

On the surface, it looked legit. And yup, the birthdate placed him a couple months over twenty-one. Zavier stared at it, and the more he looked, the worse he felt. The ID was real. The guy was quite legal, and Zavier'd just blundered into a hookup.

"This is real," he murmured.

"Of course it is." The guy snatched his ID back. "Asshole."

Zavier didn't focus on him—he looked at Ray.

Pale. Angry. "Zavier..." A tremble in his voice.

Fuck. He'd jumped to a conclusion. "He looked young." Had he? Or had that been a convenient excuse?

"*I* look young," Ray said, his voice cold.

Not like his guy did, with his baby face and the scowl that looked more teen than twenty. But best to make a hasty retreat, and try not to think about these two fucking. "Fine. I'm sorry for worrying." Ray could do so much *better*.

"Fucking freak," the guy muttered. He wrenched his jacket off the bed—and a baggie went flying. It landed not two feet from Zavier.

Drugs. Pills and stamp bags and smaller bags of powder. A syringe. A spoon.

"What the fuck?" Ray stared at the bag like it was an alien creature.

Zavier's gut lurched. Ray couldn't possibly be doing drugs. No signs of that at all. Still... "You like to party, Ray?"

The guy grabbed the baggie. "You better turn your pasty ass around and get the fuck out."

Zavier ignored the jerk and stared at Ray. Still pale, still angry, but there was a laser-like clarity when he looked up. "I don't do drugs. Never have. I'm not the fucker Carl keeps saying I am."

Some of the tension in Zavier bled away. "Ray—"

"Get out." Ray's soft voice cut through the room. "Just— get out. Both of you."

The man grabbed his shirt, hoodie, and jacket. "Fuck the both of you."

"Hey." Zavier held up his phone so the guy could see the recording icon. "Don't get any ideas about blabbing to the press."

"Recording someone's illegal." The guy glowered at him.

"So's possession with intent to distribute. You gonna go to the cops?" Guy froze, then shook his head, anger clearly etched into his features. "Neither will I if you get your ass out of here."

Guy did, but not before throwing a snarling look at Ray. "Bet you can't even get it up."

Once the door clicked closed, Zavier stopped the recording. By the bed, Ray stood, his back to Zavier, but hunched over, as if he'd been kicked in the gut.

"What the *fuck* were you thinking?" Zavier ground out the words, anger bubbling up. All those hours and *weeks* of work, all the years Mish and Dom had put in, the progress they'd made each concert. Ray had nearly blown it all up—most of his own fucking life—for what? A moment of oblivion with some drugged up groupie? Alcohol was one thing, weed might be waved away, but harder stuff? Not in a million years.

Ray stiffened. "I wasn't, obviously." He turned, and Zavier read the shame and dread underneath the hard lines of rage. "Get out of my room."

Zavier snorted. "God, is this why Kevin started drinking?" It was cruel thing to say, but Ray was doing everything in his power to be a shitbag. Yes, they were all on edge. Yes, they all needed relief. But with *that* guy? Without even thinking?

"You don't know *anything* about that!" Wild eyes. Clenched hands. "You never even *met* Kevin! He was a fucking good drummer!"

"This isn't about Kevin. It's about *you*. Are you really willing to throw away how *many years*, for a hole to fuck and something to snort?" And yeah, his voice rose, and he waved his arms in frustration. "Jesus, Ray, I know you're smarter than that!"

"Maybe I'm not. I guess I'm the fucking idiot that Carl thinks I am. That *you* think I am." He cast a glance all around the room, then slapped his hands on this thighs. "Fucking hell, maybe you all should just replace me!"

Zavier let silence settle between them. Ray was close to tears of frustration, and not just because of the groupie.

The concert had gone well. *All* their concerts had gone well; even if they were being held over a barrel, the label *had* to like what the band was doing. Yes, Carl was an asshole and a liar, but Ray knew that, didn't he? They'd talked about it. But here he was, stressed beyond belief, dying to slip into nothingness.

When the moment stretched out, Ray turned away again. "I didn't know he had drugs." Soft words. "Shit."

"Weren't looking for a high?" Zavier sure hoped not.

"No!" Ray practically shouted the word. "I said I don't do that shit. I just wanted—" He combed his fingers through his hair. "Jesus, you wouldn't understand. You can have anyone you want." He waved at the door. "Dom would do you in a heartbeat."

Not exactly what he'd expected to come from Ray's mouth, especially given their interactions. "This isn't about Dom or me." Even if he liked Ray. Maybe too much.

"Yeah, it's about me and I'm a fuckup, if you haven't figured that out yet." Ray twitched and paced in a small patch of carpet. "Go ask Carl. He'll tell you all about it." That came with a snarl.

Always back to Carl. Zavier had seen him talking with Ray earlier, but Ray hadn't looked any worse than normal. "You're not a fuckup. You know you're not a fuckup."

"Oh? Who flipped you off the other day?" Ray's bark of laughter was bitter as hell and he gestured to the door. "And then *that*?"

Yeah, sneaking in a random groupie was the wrong tactic for stress relief, especially given the situation. "Okay, the groupie thing was pretty foolish. The rest of us make do with our hand." He mimicked jacking off. Crude, but it would get the point across.

"Not good enough." That was soft and resigned. Ray stared at the carpet.

Excuses, excuses. Zavier hadn't fucked anyone since Dimitri, had to watch Ray every damn night, and yeah, it was hard to jack off on the bus. Anger got the better of Zavier. "Maybe you're doing it wrong, then."

Ray's head shot up, and he pinned Zavier with a look that had fire in it. "You want to show me how it's done, pretty boy?"

Oh, the temptation. The desire to tame Ray's snappish mouth ripped through Zavier. The need to touch his body, to show him exactly how to come. "You wouldn't survive."

"Really?" Ray stepped closer. Desire and lust peeked through the fissures of his deep anger. "Bet I'd thrive."

He should turn away. Leave Ray to his anger and frustration, let him beat one out, but oh, pride was a dangerous thing, and so was Zavier's own lust and frustration. "Take your clothes off." The words came out smooth and silky.

Ray lifted his head. "What?"

Zavier wanted his desire. His submission. His pleasure. "Let's find out which of us is correct."

Zavier was glad he'd thrown on a button-down after the concert. He unbuttoned a cuff and rolled up the sleeve. Habit, really. Something to do with his hands. It also made him imposing. "Take your clothes off."

"You think you're gonna fuck me?" A hint of incredulity, but also of awe.

He started on the other sleeve. "No, Ray. I'm going to tell you precisely how to masturbate."

Ray stared at Zavier for a long moment, and then pulled his T-shirt off, exposing his delectable and well-inked shoulders and his lean, muscular torso. All that dancing on stage and flinging himself into crowds did wonders for Ray's body. "This ought to be good." Mocking smile, and mocking tone. "*You* teaching *me* how to jerk off."

A dark heat settled into Zavier. Ray had no idea what he was getting himself into, but Zavier did. If there was one thing Nadia had taught him, it was the fine art of playing with your catch.

Ray shucked his jeans, and shortly after, his briefs, freeing his already hardening cock. He kicked his clothes away.

Lovely dick. No longer than average, but with good girth. Cut, but so many were here in the States. "Socks, too," Zavier murmured.

"Really?" Annoyance in Ray's voice.

Zavier lifted his gaze and met Ray's. "Really." He wanted Ray entirely naked. Socks were a tiny battle in the grand scheme of things, but he'd win them all tonight.

A lick of his lips, a grunt, and finally Ray pulled one sock off, and then the other.

Good balance. Pity this was as far as they would go, because he could have so much fun with that. Predicament bondage at its finest. "Much better."

Ray pulled on his cock and smirked. "Like what you see?"

"No." From the way Ray started and dropped his dick, that wasn't the response he expected. "Did I say you could touch yourself?" Zavier's veins tingled. Control and obedience. He'd see how far Ray would go under his commands.

Blotches of red marred Ray's features, and he swallowed.

Heat zipped straight through Zavier. This was going to be enjoyable. Ray hot, bothered, and *his*, at least for a moment. "Now, let's get started, shall we?"

RAY HAD BEEN *FURIOUS* WHEN ZAVIER HAD WALKED IN ON HIM and whatever the guy's name was. Then he'd been horrified when the drugs had fallen onto the floor. Jesus. Carl would have had a field day with that. What if the guy had slipped him something?

Now? Now he was cold and embarrassed and too fucking turned on. *Let's get started, shall we?*

Zavier's dark smirk burned through Ray's body, as did the tattoos that circled Zavier's arms from his rolled-up shirtsleeves down to his wrists.

"You not taking anything off?"

"No, I'm not." He inspected Ray, who fought the urge to shiver. "Stay there and don't move." Zavier circled to one side. "This is about you." He laid a hand on Ray's hip. "Turn this way."

Soon Ray stood facing the windows. The shears were drawn, but through them he saw the shimmering lights of Houston. Ray closed his eyes when Zavier's warm hand claimed his other hip. Each finger felt like a brand against his skin. They'd touched before, but not like this, not with Zavier standing so close behind him.

Oh, did Ray's cock like the idea that flashed through his mind—Zavier bending him over and fucking him right there. Or maybe pressing him up against the window. Over a chair. He hadn't bottomed in so long, because everyone expected him to top.

"I thought you'd want to watch me jack off." Zavier was taller, but not by much. Pressing so close to him from behind, he'd not see much at all.

"I told you—" Zavier's hot breath skimmed over Ray's back and shoulders "—this is about you."

Ray blinked his eyes back open, mostly because if he didn't he'd fall over from the dizziness of having Zavier literally a breath away. Bet if he leaned back, he'd meet Zavier's chest. God, he was so fucking hard.

"Stroke yourself, *slowly*." Zavier emphasized the last word, and his breath caressed Ray's neck.

Ray did as told, wrapping his hand around his dick and giving it several much-needed pulls. He bit his lip and stared at the shears. Fuck, this wouldn't take long.

Zavier clicked his tongue. "I said slowly, Ray." Fingers dug into his hips. "Listen to me and do what I say—not what you think I mean." Disapproval dripped from every word.

Ray's heart leapt into his throat. Shit. He couldn't even jerk off right. "Um. I thought that was slow." He took the strokes down a notch.

"Slower."

And again.

"*Slower*, Ray."

And *again*. Fuck! He ran his hand bit by bit up and down his shaft, each inch painfully good. He wanted so much more than this, wanted the quickness and oblivion of orgasm. Not the torture of being aware of every inch of skin, of Zavier's body, and those hands at his hips.

"Yes. Like that. Very good." It might have been Ray's imagination, but he swore he felt Zavier's lips brush his neck. Every nerve tingled, and a grunt slipped out.

A chuckle. "Run your thumb over the head. Slick it with your precome."

Oh god, that felt so fucking good. Ray tipped his neck back and sighed. If he let go enough, he could almost imagine it wasn't his hand around his cock—especially since it wasn't his mind directing. He tried speeding up.

A snort and fingers dug into his hip again. "Ray."

Right, so even without *seeing* Ray's hand, Zavier knew.

"Play with your balls."

That made Ray close his eyes and groan. He had lightning in his veins. This whole thing was too fucking hot. Got even hotter when Zavier made him spit for lube like on some porno and finally—finally—let him pick up the pace. Then it was all listening to that deep voice as Zavier told him what to do. Speed up, slow down, circle the head. Twist. Go fast. Stop. Ease a tight fist down to the root. On and on until Ray couldn't see or think straight.

Every hint of praise from Zavier sang up his spine to his head. Every huff of displeasure singed his soul.

"Fuck." Ray's legs trembled and he rocked his hips into his hand, too aware of Zavier's fingers holding him. "This what you do to someone when you jack them off?" Maybe Zavier was right—he wouldn't survive.

This time Zavier's lips did touch his neck, a press of wet heat, a laugh, and hot words burned against his skin. "No. Most often they're tied down, with my fingers or my cock in their ass."

Oh hell. Now that was an image. Bound and utterly at Zavier's mercy? Being filled by him? Ray's rhythm faltered, his balls tightened, and the world threatened to turn to white and flames. "Oh, shit. I'm close."

Teeth scraped his neck. "Don't come."

Fuck, *fuck*. His veins were on fire. "What?"

"Don't come until I say, Ray." A huff of hot air. "But don't stop, either. Same pace as before."

No way in hell. Not when he was this close. Spots dotted his vision and his body burned for release. "I can't."

"Yes, you can." He couldn't tell if Zavier pulled him back or stepped forward, only that he met Zavier's chest. The hard length of a jeans-covered dick rocked against Ray's ass.

He gasped at the contact. Proof positive that Zavier wanted him. Actually wanted *him*.

Zavier spoke so low, so sexy. "Jack yourself like before, like I taught you. But don't come."

This was going to kill him, but he couldn't stop listening to Zavier. Couldn't stop obeying him. Struggled not to break and shatter against him.

Whispered words followed. Hot and heady. "Faster. Yes. Like that. Now twist. Press the head."

He was dying. So strung out. Each stroke an agony of delight.

"Imagine your thumb is a tongue. Rock your hips like that."

So close to the edge, so aware of Zavier, his heat, his length. But he couldn't—

"Slow down. Roll your balls."

Like being burned and frozen at the same time. Too much.

"Yes, Ray. That's perfect."

He gasped and moaned at the pleasure in Zavier's voice, and didn't know how he was still standing. Everything had gone white. His body shook with the need for release. He wasn't close—he was so far beyond that he barely hung on to sanity by the slimmest of margins. "Please. Please please please."

"You're so beautiful," Zavier murmured. "Come for me, Ray."

He didn't know if he cried out, because the pleasure was so intense it robbed his sight and hearing and took him out of the world. He tumbled and tumbled, hot semen coating his hand and Zavier's teeth scraping against the back of his neck. He fell until there wasn't anything in his head but a haze and silence and blessed relief.

All that remained was him and the man who held him up. Zavier Demos.

Oh *fuck*.

He must have grunted or something because Zavier half carried, half dragged him to the bed and helped him sit on the edge. "Shhh," he murmured. "You're fine."

Ray wanted to bury his face in his hands, but one was covered in jizz. He stared at the drying spunk, as his body shivered against the intensity of his orgasm. He was *not* fine. Not by a long shot. His gaze drifted to Zavier's shoes, a beat-up pair of black Chucks—so incongruous with everything else about Zavier. They should be fine and leather and—

The rest of the night came crashing back in. Carl's reprimand after the concert. They still weren't playing good enough. The press was cooling to them. Then the guy showing up with the promise of one night free of thought. Zavier's fury, his snide remarks, and the utter shame of putting the band on the line.

"Ah hell, Ray." Zavier spoke again, but so soft and gentle it didn't seem like him at all. The shoes vanished from view and there was the sound of a door opening and closing. Soon, a soft, warm, white garment was being draped over his shoulders and back. "Here."

Ray pulled the fabric tighter around him with the hand he hadn't come all over.

And what if that guy had slipped him something? Ray's head swam. *You're such a fuckup, Ray.* Carl's words. *No wonder Kevin drank his days away.* An echo of the words Zavier had said, too.

He deserved the scorn. No wonder Zavier had pulled away from him.

Zavier was back, and this time kneeling at Ray's feet, with a towel. "Give me your hand."

Instinctively, he knew which one. Zavier had wet one end of the hand towel, enough to clean the spunk off. He did so carefully and nearly reverently, as if Ray wasn't some kind of monster. He dried Ray's fingers the same way.

Zavier rose slowly, and vanished once more. When he returned, he had a glass of water. "Drink."

Ray took the glass and sipped. Cool—not cold—and clean. He blinked a few times and focused on the carpet. Zavier finally stopped moving and took a seat on a chair across from him.

"I'm sorry," Ray whispered. "You must think I'm the biggest fucking loser ever."

Silence for a time, then the creak of Zavier shifting on leather, or vinyl, or whatever the hotel furniture was covered in. "Ray, please look at me."

The request flowed through Ray and he obeyed. No thought, only action.

Zavier had crossed his legs and lounged in the chair, looked much the way he normally did, cool and collected. "I don't think you're a loser."

Shame and elation wormed through Ray, clashing and conflicting. He shivered and pulled the robe tighter around his shoulders. Zavier was wrong—except that he was *Zavier*, so he couldn't be wrong.

"I nearly fucked a drug dealer." His stomach churned. "I don't know what might have happened."

Zavier cocked his head. "Why'd you ask him up?"

Ray stared at Zavier. "I didn't. He showed up at my door. I'd never seen him before."

Zavier's brow knitted and he got a faraway look. Then his gaze locked back on Ray. "And *you let him in*?"

Yeah, that had been careless and thoughtless, but the guy had been all dark and pouty and full of praise and—in retrospect—he'd looked like a slightly younger version of the man who sat before him. Plus, it had been months since Ray'd gotten laid.

He put the glass to his lips and swallowed a mouthful before speaking. He'd been *desperate*. "He knocked on the door, and I thought it was Dom or Mish checking in on me. But it was that guy, and he asked if I wanted a blowjob..."

A grunt from Zavier. He rubbed his chin. "And you did."

"Yeah. I did." Shame wrapped him tighter than the robe, but the heat that came with it wasn't comfortable. "Look, I don't do drugs 'cause even over-the-counter stuff fucks me up. If I'd known, I'd have sent him away." He shook his head. "I wish—" Wished the encounter he'd just had with Zavier— the one he'd wanted and needed for two and a half months, the one that had been hotter than fuck and mind-blowing— hadn't come on the heels of *that*.

"Wish what?" Zavier's voice held a kindness Ray didn't understand.

He drank more of the water, mostly to stall for time. "What we did—I wish it hadn't been *now*. I mean—with all that—" He waved at the door.

Zavier uncrossed his legs and sighed. "That's my fault."

"I liked it. If that helps."

A grin. "Oh, I know you *liked* it, Ray."

A shiver up his back, and a dull ache of need followed. But he was too spent and tired for it to go anywhere. "Did you? Like it?"

A deep chuckle. "Ray..."

God, he loved the way Zavier said his name. He swallowed the last of his water. Yeah, not the brightest question, given how hard Zavier had been. "In high school..."

"This isn't high school." Zavier shifted in his chair. "This is *far* from high school."

"You didn't want me then."

"Untrue."

That one word rocked Ray to the core. He stared at Zavier. He'd always assumed that rejecting the band had also included rejecting *him*.

"You were lovely back then and you're fucking amazing now. But you were barely, *barely* sixteen, Ray. I was gonna turn nineteen that summer, and it just didn't seem right."

Ray eyed the hotel room door. "More sense than me."

"Not really. I was a prick and full of myself."

He couldn't help it. "And you're not now?"

Zavier's eyebrows rose and he snorted softly. "Oh, Ray, you're something else."

Heat straight to his cheeks, especially when Zavier's look roamed all over Ray's body, lingering here and there. Despite how he was sitting, Zavier couldn't quite hide his erection.

Ray licked his lips. "Like what you see?"

"Yes." Zavier met his stare and held it until Ray couldn't

help squirming under the burning intensity. No question whatsoever that Zavier spoke the truth. "But I have particular tastes."

"In men?"

"In sex. Dominance. Submission." Zavier shrugged. "It's not everyone's thing."

"You mean... You're talking about BDSM." Just the acronym ignited another spark in Ray's tired and spent body.

Zavier nodded, his smile slight, but so damn sensuous. "That's exactly what I mean. Ever done anything like that before now?"

Cuffs and whips and chains? "Nope. Read about it." He eyed Zavier. "I'm going to guess you're not a submissive."

Zavier chuckled and it was dark. "No, I'm not."

"I'm not, either." Came out suddenly and felt too much like a bald-faced lie. More heat to his face.

Zavier's grin fell away. "No, you're not. You don't have enough self-control."

Like a slap to the face, but as soon as Ray's anger rose, it snuffed out like a candle with no air. He stared at the hotel room door, the one that groupie had come through.

Yeah, Zavier was right. His self-control was nonexistent, especially as of late. Hell, Zavier had borne the brunt of that. Still, he didn't know what control had to do with submission. "But—"

Zavier held a finger up, and every bit of Ray shivered.

"Submission is an exchange of power. It's a gift. You *have* to be in control of yourself to release that to someone else."

Ray's heart thumped against his ribs. "Then what was..." He gestured to the spot where they'd stood, where his semen was drying on the carpeting, where Zavier had told him to come. "What was that?"

A little crack appeared in Zavier's perfection and poise. "Maybe a taste of that type of exchange—for both of us."

What would it take to get Zavier to fuck him? Hell, what

would it be like to kneel and suck him off? Why was he even thinking about that? He couldn't stand the guy!

Except that was another lie. Might've been true the day Zavier had walked into the audition, but it certainly wasn't now. Even when he'd flipped Zavier off, the anger had been superficial, born of hurt and rejection and—whatever it was that flowed between the two of them.

Not only had Zavier saved his ass tonight, he'd listened and cared all the weeks before. Provided solutions when the band had run up against issues. Even gone hunting for information about Carl. He wasn't the arrogant bastard Ray had assumed he was when he'd walked into that audition months ago. "Could we—do this again?" In a different place. At a different time.

"No." A soft word, but final. "You're not in the right space. At all." Zavier deflated into pensiveness. "This was ill-advised of me in the first place."

Who actually talked like that? "Well, it did clear my head."

A huff of laughter. "Then something good came out of the night, at least."

Time stretched a bit, and Ray got the distinct impression Zavier was examining him—for what, he didn't know. "What if—" He took a deep breath. "What if I found self-control?"

Zavier nodded. It was slight, and maybe unconscious, but there it was.

Ray's body flamed.

"I guess we'll see," Zavier murmured. He rose and headed to the door. "Get some sleep, Ray."

"Zav." Another word that came out unbidden.

Zavier stopped, his hand on the door handle.

"Thank you." Tight words. For interrupting Ray. For saving the band. For making him come. God, that orgasm. Even the memory curled his toes.

For a moment, under the glow of the light in the room's

entryway, those blue eyes looked back at him. No smile, but no frown, either. "You're welcome."

Then Zavier was gone and Ray was alone with nothing but the ashen taste of humility and fear in his mouth.

Yeah. He was out of control. Maybe not like the tabloids thought, but yeah. It was a problem with only one solution: stop being a fuckup. Stop letting Carl get to him. Stop pushing away the very people who kept him sane.

Easier said than done. Ray rose and started getting ready for bed.

BOTH MISH AND DOM WERE WAITING FOR ZAVIER IN THE hallway. *Hell.* Too much time had passed since he'd chased the groupie off, time he'd spent playing with Ray and tangling himself into knots.

Who knew what they thought of *that* delay.

He needed to process what had happened, pick apart the whole thing and figure out what the *fuck* had been going through his head when he'd decided to play out that little scene. It was reckless and foolish. Yes, there was the sharp thrill of being obeyed and the deep satisfaction of meting out punishment, something he'd missed so much. Only Ray wasn't his sub. Ray *would not* be his sub. That path was utter madness.

Dom coughed. "Is he okay?"

"I saw the guy come out with a bag of drugs. What the hell was Ray thinking?" Mish's thoughts were closer to his own.

"He's suitably horrified, chastised, and he wasn't thinking at all." Exhaustion was quickly catching up with Zavier. He leaned as casually as he could against the wall and let it hold him up.

"Ray didn't...do anything foolish or get hurt or anything...right?" Dom's face colored, then paled.

For someone in a rock band with albums that had parental advisory warnings on them, Dom could act so...sheltered at times. "No. I got in there before anything happened, Ray didn't know about the drugs, and the guy was of age anyway."

Both of them relaxed. Good.

"Turned out the guy was twenty-one."

Mish grunted. "He didn't look that old."

"Yeah. I felt pretty rash about rushing in there, until the drugs fell out of the shit's pocket." He pushed off the wall. "I don't think Ray'll be letting anyone in his room again." Would likely turn away anyone not associated with the band.

"He takes too much on his shoulders." Dom's quiet voice.

Zavier turned and studied Dom, the words Ray had thrown at him coming back. *Dom would do you in a heartbeat.* There was history between Dom and Ray he didn't know, but he was certain Ray was wrong about Dom. If Zavier propositioned, Dom would say no, in that same heartbeat. "What do you mean?"

"All the criticism, the journalists, the press. All Carl's yelling and Kevin's troubles. He takes it on, blames himself, and then—" Dom gestured at the door. "Goes off the deep end."

"Not the first time he's done this?" God, he didn't want to be staking out Ray's door every night to keep the groupies away. How the fuck had that guy known where to go? *Shit.* They didn't have bodyguards.

"Not *this*," Dom said. "Last tour, he'd find a member of the crew to screw and everything would be fine."

"Carl hired a new crew," Mish said.

Always back to that asshole. Zavier pushed a hand through his hair. "Ray was talking to us, on the bus. He had an outlet, at least for a while." Before the journalist had rattled him. Before he'd flipped Zavier off. Back when they'd shared a couch and leg room.

A little thought niggled at Zavier, one that reminded him he'd pulled away exactly as Ray was reaching out—which meant he was at fault for all this, too. But he couldn't change the past, couldn't go back and undo his actions. His soul roiled. And here he thought himself so careful, so controlled, yet his emotions and fears had gotten the best of him.

"A shared burden is an easier one," Mish said.

Very true. But far too tempting. "Well, this crisis is averted. We should all turn in."

Dom nodded and headed back to his door.

Mish stooped, picked up the ice bucket that had been sitting at her feet, and handed it to Zavier. "It's a little melted."

"I'll manage."

She chuckled and gave him a smile. "I still like you. You're messed up, but you have a heart."

"Gee, thanks." One tired smile later, and he was back at his own door and into his room, shutting out the chaos behind it.

Except he still heard the echo of Ray's moan in his head and felt the heat of that body in his fingertips, even when he plucked some ice out of the bucket to add to his glass of water.

He hadn't lied when he'd told Ray he wasn't a sub. Ray couldn't be Zavier's submissive, for so many reasons, self-control aside.

God, he so wanted to take on that bundle of nerves and desire and need, but Ray made him impulsive and uncovered too many of his own worries. Leaving Dimitri and the orchestra had been easy—not entirely painless, but easy. Leaving Twisted Wishes would gut him completely. He'd already tangled his own hopes and fears, the want to make it big and the terror he'd screw their chances up somehow. He fucking *cared* for Mish and Dom and especially beautiful, fractured Ray Van Zeller. He had no idea how to prove to Ray that he was worthy of every bit of praise, that Ray was the reason the band was skyrocketing in popularity.

Yeah, the media focused on Zavier as the point of change, which was unfair. Ray was the heart and soul of Twisted Wishes. If he was cut out—the terrifying suggestion Ray had made—they'd all wither and die.

Problem was, Ray took the weight of the band onto his back. Zavier could take that weight *off* Ray, if only for a time. He could. He so clearly could. The desire was there, wound so tight around his core. It would be a delight, and honor. And if it went wrong, an act that would tear their whole world apart.

Zavier downed his glass of water, then poured another. He couldn't risk Ray or the band, not even to help in the one way he knew how.

CHAPTER
THIRTEEN

RAY EXPECTED THE NEXT DAY TO BE UTTERLY AWKWARD, PREPARED for it and dreaded it, but when he cracked his hotel door and looked out into the hall, all he saw were the room-cleaning carts. No signs of his bandmates or the crew. No one waiting outside his door with a scowling face. No cops or reporters there to ask him questions about drugs.

He closed the door and tried to still his racing heart.

It was past one in the afternoon. At least he'd managed to show and dress before dinner—that was a plus. Thankfully, Carl wasn't around, or Ray was sure he'd have heard an earful, either by phone or after Carl pounded on his door, even if this *was* a day to recuperate from the past few shows. A few quick texts told him Dom was museum-hopping with Zavier, and that made Ray pause. Hitting every museum Dom could get his hands on wasn't new, but Dom hanging with Zavier was. A twinge of worry wiggled through Ray, but he pushed it down. He shouldn't be jealous of Dom, but that flicker of envy was there. Worse, he was as jealous of Zavier.

Dom had been his best friend from their very first day of high school. They'd been in the same homeroom, Dom in the first desk, Ray in the last. B and V. Not the beginning or the end of the alphabet, but close enough. He missed just hanging out with his friend like Zavier got to do today.

And Zavier? Something told Ray that he wouldn't say much about what had happened. The only thing that might happen was that Zavier would discover Dom was far more in control of himself than Ray when it came to being on tour and keeping his dick in his pants.

Dom was the far better catch. Brighter, more even-keeled. He was the type of guy Zavier should date—not the mess Ray was.

When did I get like this? He stared at his hands. He hadn't always been so fucking afraid of every single action. Hell, he'd done everything he could to get Twisted Wishes going. Bared his soul in lyrics and notes. Threw money and hours and years after a dream. Worked odd hours and some *interesting* jobs to support the band.

Here he was now, afraid even to leave his hotel room. The weight of Carl's words pinned him to the ground. *Not good enough. In debt. Label not amused.* Fuck.

And *Zavier.* Oh god, Ray wanted so much more. Another night with Zavier's hands on him and that voice brushing his back, and those lips on his skin. A moment in time that wasn't fraught with Ray's stupidity and poor choices. Maybe he'd find out if he actually liked being tied up as much as his cock thought he might.

Ray shook himself. It wasn't like Dom and Zavier would be fucking in the middle of an art museum or even contemplating sex.

He texted Mish next. She was closer—down by the pool, enjoying a drink, a snack, and the weather. And yes, of course he could join her. Which was good, because he needed to eat something, and ordering room service and eating alone or sitting at the bar with a soda seemed way the hell too depressing. Despite the need for time away, he *missed* his friends.

Mish was tucked into a nice, shady spot by a cabana with waiter service. Ray slipped into the other chair, and she pushed her sunglasses to the top of her head. "Hi, honey. You doing okay?"

Something about her question made him uneasy. She must have known. "Yeah. Um." He stopped and poked at the drink menu. "How—what do you know?"

She shrugged. "You had a groupie who had a pile of drugs on him, but nothing happened."

Oh. So they knew. His throat tightened. "Yeah." So many of the alcoholic drinks on the card looked good. "Um, Zavier chased him out." He swallowed. "Which was good. I don't know if he would have done anything to me, but..."

"Yeah, Zavier said as much." Sadness there.

"I didn't mean to."

"Oh, sweetheart, I know." She took off her sunglasses entirely and put them on the table. "You just wanted a break."

"Except a story about me being addicted to drugs would have destroyed the band." It came out as a whisper.

She nodded again.

"Zavier says... Zavier thinks I have no self-control."

She huffed. "I'm not sure that's true. I'd have decked Carl about a million times if he treated me like he treats you."

Fair. "I've come close." He paused and flipped the menu over. Nonalcoholic drinks. Yeah, probably the better idea. "Instead I take it out on others. On you guys, and that's not fair."

"It's not fair for you to take it out on *yourself*, either."

"No one else left."

She sighed and patted his arm. "But that hurts *us*, too."

Yeah, it did. Especially when he pulled stupid maneuvers like last night. "I just don't know anymore."

Before Mish could answer, a waitress came over with a glass of water. "Care for anything else?" She smiled brightly at him.

"Um, how about one of these ginger sours?" He tapped the virgin cocktails. "And a bacon cheeseburger, medium rare."

"Fries or coleslaw?"

He ended up choosing the coleslaw. When the waitress left, he played with the condensation on his water glass and didn't look at Mish. "I still don't think Zavier likes me."

Mish burst out laughing and didn't stop until she was hiccupping. It wasn't until after she took a long drink of water to quell those that she spoke. "Oh, hon. Not even you are *that* unobservant."

He must have been beet red because the ice water he swallowed did nothing to cool his face. "There's a difference between lust and actually liking someone, you know."

She waved his words away like cobwebs. "Honey, it ain't just lust. He worries about you, same as Dom and me. Wants to protect you, too, but you won't let him in."

Because fucking your bandmate was asking for trouble. Especially if it got back to Carl. And—it would. "That's because being Zavier's friend is a bad idea."

"Why?"

He wavered. "'Cause... I'm me. And he's him and—" He didn't want to say it out loud. "It's not like when it was someone in the crew."

"No." Mish's tone had dropped to serious levels. "I daresay it isn't. Not with you two."

Ray fought through the tangle of emotions. Zavier wouldn't fuck him until he could control himself, but Ray *could* stop being an ass to his bandmates and let the shit Carl piled on him run off a bit more—talk to them about it—and *that* would fix quite a few things.

He was saved from having to say anything more to Mish when his cocktail and burger arrived. He chowed down on the burger, grateful that he had a distraction. Maybe the *Zavier and him* part of this conversation could die off before he got any more embarrassed, or worse, turned on. Well, turned on more, anyway.

"How long have you had a crush on him?" Mish took a sip of her cocktail.

Ray nearly choked on his hamburger. Well, there went the chance of a change in topic. "I don't have a crush on him! He... I..." He shook his head. "Mish, the best thing for me is to let Zav be."

"Is it? Because what I see is that when you guys are talking, you're a hell of a lot calmer."

Was he? Ray took another bite of his food and pondered. Maybe. Zavier had good thoughts about the band and he seemed to listen to Ray about songs and set lists. He also treated Ray like he actually had talent. "Okay."

Mish snorted. "And he's the last person who will go crying to Carl about anything."

There was that. "Are you suggesting I hook up with Zavier?"

She shrugged. "I'm suggesting you stop flipping him off and stop acting like he hates you. And get over whatever it was that pissed you off *ten years ago* in high school."

Maybe he was holding the high school band stuff a little too hard. He rubbed his temple. Zavier had been so far above him then. "That's fair."

"I hate seeing you miserable, kiddo. And you're not miserable at all when you let Zav in."

Also fair. "Okay. I'll stop being a prick to him." See where that went. He shivered and covered that by picking up his drink and sipping. Wasn't too bad—essentially a whiskey sour with ginger beer rather than whiskey. He didn't really miss the booze that much, probably because he'd never been that much of a drinker in the first place. It was Carl's order itself that chafed, not the lack of a buzz.

"Besides, you could use a friend." Mish sipped her own cocktail.

"I have Dom and you!" They'd been through so much together already.

She rolled her eyes. "Dom and I are like your siblings. You need a *friend*." She paused. "And maybe a fuckbuddy, too."

"Mish!" He plunked the glass down on the table.

She was laughing again, and a moment later he joined her. It felt—good. They hadn't actually talked in a long time, not like this. Not as pseudo-siblings. Yeah, they'd needed a break from the tour, not just to clean and restock and maintain the buses, but to untangle and smooth out their lives, too.

He looked out at the pool. There were children and parents splashing around and a small group of other people —college kids—by the edge. One guy shoved another and the first fell into the pool with a shout and rose above the water with a laugh. His friend cannonballed in to join him.

All at once, it was as if he'd been hit in the gut. Two years ago, he'd horsed around with Dom, Mish, and Kevin at a hotel pool in the Poconos. Splashing. Drinking. Having fun. They'd just signed with the label and decided to road-trip to the mountains for a little celebration.

Fuck. He took a ragged breath. "I miss Kevin. I mean, the guy we knew when we started, back when he was fun and happy and..." A lump took over Ray's throat. "But... I also don't miss Kevin. The shows on *this* tour..." He sat back and focused on Mish. "They've been everything I ever wanted and dreamed about."

"And that has a lot to do with Zavier," Mish said. Her eyes held a similar sadness. "Yeah, hon, I feel that way, too. And the guilt gets you, huh?"

"Yeah. Like—maybe if I'd caught things sooner or done something different, Kevin would be here with us to enjoy this."

She shook her head. "Oh, honey, it wasn't the touring. It wasn't you. Kevin said—" She looked at her drink, grunted, then picked up her water. "When I talked to him last, Kevin said he'd been a functional alcoholic for years. He could hide it from us when we weren't touring." She took a sip. "None of that was your fault, and he doesn't blame you at all. You gotta let that go."

He didn't know if he could. All the thoughts and emotions blended with what Mish was telling him. Words looped and repeated. Notes arrived like splotches of color. Light blue against black. Swaths of red, velvet like rose petals but dark as fine wine.

He stared at where the water lapped along the pool edge and listened to the laughter. "I think... I think..." He'd forgotten his notebook but had his phone, so he opened that to a notepad app and started typing.

He vaguely heard Mish chuckle, but was too busy trying to get what he saw and tasted and heard out. The music would have to wait, but that was easier to snatch back from his head. Words, though, those were like butterflies. A moment of brightness, then gone.

In the heat of a summer day
We were gods with a thousand dreams
But in the night of winter's death
We were nothing but dust and ash
Where did the light we held go
Strands of gold and silver
When can we meet the sun again?

When nothing else came, he sat back, blinked, and looked up.

"Better?"

Much. So much so. The lyrics were rough and there was no music sketched down to go with them, but it was a start. "Yeah." He'd see if he could borrow one of Dom's acoustic guitars later on, and pick out the colors and shapes in his head. A title swam in his head, but he wasn't sure if he wanted to write that down yet. Make it real.

She nodded. "It's good to see you smile, sweetheart."

Was he smiling? Ray laughed. But yeah, his mood was lighter, the lump gone, and the fear that had gripped him held on less tightly. Kevin wasn't here, but Zavier was. Ray could handle both things.

And if he could manage to remain calm, maybe Zavier could handle him—in whatever way that ended up being.

THE CAFÉ IN THE MUSEUM DISTRICT WAS FAR MORE HIP THAN Zavier, and younger, too. However, Dom fit right in, as if he was an early twenty-something student studying art or history or—well, anything, really.

Zavier had dressed pretty casually for their museum-hopping trip: an older pair of jeans and a T-shirt he'd picked up in Budapest during one of the symphony's European tours. Dom, though... Zavier eyed his bandmate for about the fortieth time. Dom looked completely different. He'd seen this side of Dom when they'd rehearsed in private all those weeks ago, but even then, some of his Domino persona bled through.

Not today. Dominic Bradley wore green-framed glasses that matched the forest green in the checkered vest he'd paired with a soft blue button-down. He looked like something out of a freaking twink catalog, despite the muscle Zavier knew lay under the dapper look.

Dominic had shed his rock-god persona entirely—and was positively vibrating with joy. Who knew Dom was such an art and science geek? At every stop, he had regaled Zavier with some interesting tidbit of information about pretty much everything they looked at.

It was, in some ways, intimidating. That was a strange experience, not being the know-it-all for a change. At least Dom had rolled up the sleeves and worn a pair of jeans, or

Zavier would have felt underdressed for their jaunt out to as many museums as they could stuff into a couple hours.

They'd managed to see art and dinosaurs and walk through part of the nearby park. There was still the zoo, about a dozen other smaller places, plus galleries, the park itself, and the university district.

The coffee in the café was good, as was the southern food. And, honestly, so was the company, even if Zavier's brain was ever so slightly overloaded with information. They'd been at this since nine in the morning.

Dom tapped a map of the local area. "Did you know there's an amphitheater nearby?"

"That's one thing I do know," Zavier said. "I performed there with the symphony. A year ago? Two years?" He shook his head. "It all blends together sometimes."

Dom looked up. "Do you miss it? Playing with them?"

The question caught Zavier off guard, mostly because the answer came so quickly, he had to sit back and figure out *why*. "No." He spoke slowly, more to taste the words than for any other reason. "No, I don't."

Dom cocked his head, obviously expecting more.

"I did enjoy playing. There's a lot more to being a timpanist than kettledrums and triangles, which is what most people think the position is like. But I don't miss the symphony." He certainly didn't miss Dimitri, who had been a demanding asshole of a conductor, even before they'd hooked up.

A quirk of a smile on Dom's lips. Made him look even more like a college student. No wonder he got carded sometimes—he *did* look young. "Rock gets into your soul."

It did. It had. "So does classical." He still found himself humming snatches of music only aficionados would know, or tapping out complex rhythms that would befuddle a whole host of rock musicians, though he doubted there'd be a time signature or beat he could throw at Dom that would confuse him. Or, for that matter, would confuse Ray or Mish. Twisted Wishes used some interesting rhythms indeed.

Dom chuckled, then sobered. "Ray applied to Juilliard, you know."

Zavier choked on his coffee. "He what?" The words shot through him, like an unexpected clap of thunder.

The reply came softer. "He did. But with his GPA..." Dom shrugged. "And he had no formal musical training. Besides, even if he'd somehow gotten in, he'd never have been able to afford it."

That was something to chew on. He'd never paid attention to Ray's financial situation back then. Didn't know it now. "His family couldn't have helped?"

Dom shook his head. "I mean, they did okay, but he's the youngest of five, and his parents were taking care of his grandmother who had Alzheimer's, and between all of that..."

Yeah, tuition to an expensive music school would be the last thing on anyone's list. "So he never went to college?"

"Oh, he did. Got an associate's from the local community college. Took some voice and music lessons when the band started getting more gigs after we graduated. Enough so he could read music."

Ray hadn't been able to read music in high school? Holy shit. Zavier leaned forward. "Are you telling me that Ray had *no musical training* at all as a kid?" And put together *this* band? Wrote *those* songs?

"Just the music appreciation stuff we all got in school."

Which had been crap. "And they said I was a prodigy." He shook his head.

"You were." Dom toyed with the remains of his meal. "But he's *really* good, Zav."

"I know." He'd seen it. Felt it. Played with them all.

"This shit with Carl..." Dom sighed. "It's killing him. He's always been self-conscious about his lack of training and schooling. All of that. He thinks his skill is all a fluke, as if someone's gonna realize he's faking and take it all away."

And Zavier had walked in as a reminder and an example of a "true" musician. He winced. "No wonder Ray was so pissed when I showed up to audition."

Another expression pulled at Dom's lips, this one much more rueful. "Yeah." His featured smoothed out. "But here's the thing—you treat him like an equal."

"He is." Ray was astounding as a musician. As a man.

Dom nodded again. "It makes an impression, though. I think it's one of the reasons everything has fallen into place when we're on stage. He doesn't have to worry about you, and he knows you don't worry about *him*. You trust him."

But offstage Ray was a different story, as they all found out last night. "You said he carries it all on him."

"Yeah." Dom leaned back, and looked wistfully at the map. "Do you think we could walk and talk?"

"Dude, I can play four different beats at the same time."

Dom's grin made him look like even more of a twink, and it occurred to Zavier that this was a completely cultivated look, just like Domino.

They paid and headed out toward yet another museum. Zavier fell into step next to Dom. "Thanks for inviting me along today. I hope I didn't step on your plans to go cruising."

Dom's cackle of laughter was unexpected. "Oh my god. You're the only one who's ever figured that out."

So there was a method to Dom's madness besides being a museum freak. He couldn't help the smile. "I lived and breathed the wine, cheese, and finger sandwich crowd for years."

"Mmm." There was almost something wistful in Dom's voice. "On the one hand, it sounds lovely. On the other, I'd probably go insane after a few weeks."

Zavier glanced at him. "Because rock gets into your soul?"

A nod. "But Domino is untouchable. And I mean that literally."

Too intimidating. "Not if you're into that sort of thing." Dom's stage persona would probably fit right into some of the dungeons he'd been to.

"But *I'm* not into that sort of thing." Dom's voice was quiet. "Not all the time."

Which gave Zavier a pretty good idea what Dom wanted, and yeah, he could have filled that role. If there was any spark whatsoever between them. There wasn't. A friendship, yes. But Dom didn't scratch any of Zavier's itches—and he suspected the other way around was true, too.

"So, what? You put on the real you and scour the museum set for a hookup?"

A wry chuckle. "Pretty much."

Well, how about that? "Does it work?" He had to know. He really had to.

Dom's smile was devilish. "All the time."

Zavier's turn to laugh. "Man, if I'd known..." He hated stepping on someone's plans.

Dom waved his arm. "No, I've enjoyed hanging out with you. You were the impossible kid to befriend in high school. This has been fun." His voice dropped a little. "And I feel better about you helping Ray out."

Something about the way Dom spoke made Zavier's skin heat. He glanced over. "What?"

There was that smile again, the one he never saw on Domino but seemed to live on Dom.

Instinct told Zavier he wouldn't get an answer, even when pressed, and he was pretty sure he understood what Dom was hinting at. He shrugged. "I like Ray." Needed him as a friend. Wanted even more. The thoughts settled onto Zavier, ill-fitting and scratchy, but he pushed them aside. No time to ruminate. No space.

"Good." Dom rotated his map. "There's a place up here I want to check out..."

Turned out to be a used bookstore. Or rather, an antique-book dealer. This was a little higher than the wine-and-cheese set. Nice literature, but not really Zavier's thing.

He eyed Dom talking to the shop's proprietor, a tall, broad man with dark hair and tan skin, who was practically eating Dom whole as they conversed. It was like watching a master at work. The way Dom laughed and moved and spoke—all quite real, but also quite enticing to the shop's owner.

Time to leave him to his conquest. Zavier coughed. "Hey. I'm gonna head back. I'll catch up with you later."

Dom grinned like a kid at Christmas. "All right. You know the way back?"

Zavier rolled his eyes. "I'm quite capable of finding my way to the hotel, yes." He pushed the door open, and headed out, leaving Dom to his prey.

The only problem was that the walk back gave him far too much time to contemplate Ray Van Zeller and all the details he now knew.

Zavier *had* been a musical prodigy. But...so had Ray. Only Zavier had been the one with money, lessons, and the asshole chip on his shoulder from being told how good he was. Ray hadn't had any of that, and he'd climbed his way toward stardom anyway.

Fucking hell, where would Ray be if he'd been in Zavier's shoes? He shook his head. One thing he'd learned, both in school and outside of it, playing *what-if* games with the past didn't get anyone anywhere at all.

So the real question was how could Zavier help Ray now? He had no idea. Well, that wasn't true—he had many, *many* ideas. Every single one of them heated his blood.

Zavier sighed. Those were the ones that were out of the question, even if a little voice in the back of his head kept asking, *Why not?*

CHAPTER
FOURTEEN

THEIR DAY OF FREEDOM WAS OVER AND CARL WAS BACK. THAT smooth, fake voice grated up Ray's spine to his skull as he stood by the tour buses. They were nearly packed—just the final check to make sure they had everything and no equipment had wandered away.

There was a nasal quality to Carl's voice Ray'd heard when they'd found videos of Tenacious Dreams, and now he couldn't unhear it. Wasn't horrible, a gray dagger across Ray's vision, but it also wasn't surprising that Carl ended up in management. Maybe vocal training could have fixed it, but who knew?

When Carl strode up to him, Ray almost didn't flinch. "You're on time," Carl said.

Ray rolled his eyes. The early-morning summer sun was heating up the humid Texas air. "It's a fucking Christmas miracle." He stared back as Carl's face darkened.

"Well, I guess you didn't get any action last night, huh?" Carl gestured at Mish and Zavier, who were laughing at something on Zavier's tablet. Dom was already on the bus reading.

Those two, together? No way. Zavier wasn't Mish's type. And if Mish was Zavier's, Ray had seen no signs of that.

He had felt exactly how much Zavier had wanted him, though. And the memory burned through him with both shame and desire. He shouldn't get on Carl's nerves, but at least that man knew he was a fuckup. Ray turned around and looked Carl up and down. "You offering?"

From the murderous look on Carl's face and the way his right hand curled into a fist, Ray guessed he'd said the wrong thing. *Fuck*. He stepped back out of instinct and held up his hands.

An instant later, Zavier was next to them both. "There a problem?" His sudden presence and deep voice was like that of a hulking bodyguard.

Must have had the same effect, because Carl shook his head. "Just complimenting Ray on his punctuality." He broke away and headed toward the crew bus. "Where's the equipment manager?"

Ray let out a breath. Wow. Okay. No joking like that around Carl, especially not in anger. Zavier had teased along the same lines earlier, but Carl hadn't reacted like *that*.

Zavier raised an eyebrow.

"Um—he was insinuating you and Mish had fucked and made fun of me for not getting any. So I asked him if he was offering."

Mish must have heard the tail end of that when he came over, since she snorted. "Nice."

Except it hadn't been. They hadn't seen the fury in Carl's eyes. "He's either really homophobic or—"

"—really in the closet," Zavier finished. "Or his dislike for you is deeper than we thought."

"Tell me something I don't know." Ray checked himself when Zavier frowned and blew out a breath. "Sorry. The snark comes out too fast when I haven't had any coffee."

Zavier pointed at the bus. "Then by all means, let's get you caffeinated."

Those words should have bothered Ray, except Zavier said them without any malice or judgment, like he *actually* wanted to get Ray coffee.

He watched Zavier board the bus. "I don't understand him," he said to Mish.

"Honey, you don't have to. All you have to do is trust him." A wink and a smile, then she was following Zavier's path into the bus.

Well, guess coffee it was. Ray boarded and got himself settled. Everything was stowed where he wanted it, including his notebook. Memories of the day before trickled through and he took out his phone.

Yup. The lyrics—such as they were—were still there. "Hey, Dom?"

"Yeah?"

"You got your acoustic guitar handy?"

Dom dropped his book and shuffled off the couch. "No. I'll pull it from the hold." In a flash, he was gone.

Zavier had another one of his questioning looks as he put together the coffee, but Mish answered, "Songwriting. Ray fiddles with the melody on the guitar."

"Saves your voice?" Zavier said. He set the pot and pressed a button. A couple moments later, it glugged to life.

"Yeah, basically. And lets me see—hear the notes. I don't nearly as well when I'm singing."

"I didn't know you could play." A hint of surprise in his words. It was echoed in his face—but it wasn't an unpleasant expression. Read as happy, even.

"Not anything like Dom can."

Speaking of which—Dom bounded back onto the bus with a guitar case in hand. "Here you go."

Ray took the case and nodded to Dom. "He taught me to play."

He rolled his eyes and flopped back down onto the couch. "Don't let him fool you. He's not bad, and he mostly taught himself. I just helped out here and there." He picked up his book. "Plays piano, too. But he'll never tell you that."

Zavier chuckled. "You have to keep some secrets, Dominic."

Dom...blushed. A lot, and glanced up at Zavier. Ray thought the bus might have started moving for the lurching in his stomach. He had no right to feel jealous, but Dom and Zav?

He turned away. "Guess someone did get lucky last night." He ground the words out.

Zavier caught him by the shoulder. His grip wasn't hard, but it was utterly firm and commanding. Ray found himself looking straight into his eyes. "Not with me." He let go of Ray, then stepped away, heading for his berth. "Coffee's almost done."

Ray sank down onto the couch, because it was more graceful an option than teetering over. He hazarded a glance at Dom, who shook his head and smiled. "Not my type."

Mish rolled her eyes. "Oh, lord. Zav, honey, I'm going to need a cup of that, too."

Zavier laughed.

Ray stared at Dom. "But—" He'd known the way Dom had looked at Zavier back in high school.

A mug of coffee descended into Ray's view. "Drink this before you hurt yourself," Zavier said. He passed between Ray and Dom and handed Mish a mug as well, then returned to get his own cup. "Dom?"

"Please. Ray's gonna be the death of me."

Ray wrapped his hands tighter around the mug, despite the heat. "But—"

Zavier handed Dom a mug, then sat down next to Ray on the couch. "I'm not *everyone's* type, Ray."

No one was. Ray knew that. But Zavier was as close to perfection as they came. "Still."

Mish snorted and Zavier toed his shoes off before stretching out his legs in that annoying way he had before, back when Ray wasn't so pissed. Back before Ray'd flipped him off, and before he had kissed Ray's neck and made him come.

The memory brought the heat of desire and the flush of shame. He sipped his coffee. It was, like Zavier, perfect—dark, strong, and hot.

The bus rumbled to life under them and shuddered forward, temporarily pausing everything as they all found their balance. On the road again.

Zavier's foot brushed against Ray's thigh when he shifted. "Dom likes tall antiquarian book dealers with broad shoulders and interesting accents," he said. "I'm commonplace next to that."

"I—uh—" Dom coughed. "Well."

"Wait, you fucked a book dealer last night?"

Dom shrugged and smiled. "He was cute."

So was Zavier. Ray shook his head.

"Dom's the smart one," Mish said. "He can slip off and get laid, and no one knows he's Domino."

His grin got a little wider and he shrugged again before sipping his coffee.

Ray couldn't do that, though. Not in a million years. He was himself pretty much all the time. Unfortunately, sometimes he was an asshole and he couldn't strip that off and shove it into a drawer. "Hey, look." Ray glanced around at all of them. "I'm sorry I've been such a jerk lately." He focused on Zavier. "Especially to you."

"I wasn't entirely fair to you, either." Zavier poked Ray's thigh with his toes. "All is forgiven."

The tightness in Ray's chest lessened. *Forgiven*. That was good, because wow, he'd fucked up. Yeah, maybe Zavier could have been less of an ass, but he still had to stop flying off the handle at everything, stop being out of control.

He leaned back and pulled his legs up until he sat cross-legged. More of Zavier's foot now touched him. That soothed as much as the coffee. "I gotta figure out how not to get strung out when reporters dig for shit." Hell, he had no idea how bad the news about the band was. "I'm guessing my outburst the other day went over *so* well."

Mish blew out a breath. "You know, maybe we should look at those rags, see what they're saying so we can be ready for the questions they ask."

Wasn't a bad idea at all, except for one problem. "You know I'll blow up if I look."

Zavier sipped his coffee, but it didn't hide the smirk.

Ray glared at him. "Look, I will. I'm not saying anything that isn't true."

"I know." Zavier's voice was gentle. "I'm not making fun of you at all. You're sometimes so self-aware, that's all."

Sometimes, but not always. Ray gulped down more coffee. Zavier's toes were still pressed against his thigh. "It took Mish and Dom a long time to get me to stop searching for our name on the web."

Dom nodded. "I mean, the good stuff's uplifting, but the bad stuff—"

"It's demoralizing." Mish stretched out her legs. "So we swore a pact to not look. Carl was *supposed* to let us know about good press and all that, and he does, sometimes."

"Sometimes," Zavier repeated. He huffed out a breath. "That man..."

She shrugged. "Yeah. Pretty much."

"I'll look," Zavier said. "I don't mind, and I've seen some of it already."

"Vanity-searching yourself?" Ray couldn't help it, even if it *was* snark.

Zavier's smile was wide and lovely, and not what Ray

expected at all. "God, no. I try very hard not to, because that shit kills." His expression melted into seriousness. "The mentor I mentioned? Sent some articles."

"Good or bad?" Ray had to know.

"The ones I read? Generally very positive. Praising the sound, the tightness, the energy..."

"The drumming?" Mish said.

Zavier blushed. Ray had seen that before, but this time he looked downright uncomfortable. "Yeah."

"Hon, you *do* make us sound better."

Dom nodded, and Ray had to agree, too. "Look, none of us are *mad* about that."

Zavier looked out the window and grunted. "I know. I mean, I know I'm good, but I'm not *the* reason Twisted Wishes resonates with fans. It's you guys, and they don't know how fucking *hard* you worked to bring me in, to *make* that sound happen. It's frustrating to see praise that's true—but only a little part of the story."

"They're not going to understand the other part of that, though," Mish said.

Zavier nodded. "Know that, too. Frustrating as hell, though."

Ray knew knowledge didn't always change emotions. "Why'd your mentor send them to you?"

A chuckle, and Zavier met Ray's stare. "Because she likes to try to embarrass me. It's a game."

"Did she embarrass you?" Dom's voice.

Zavier pursed his lips and nodded to Dom. "A little. I was surprised at how I looked in the photos."

"How do you look in the photos?" Ray's mug was empty, but he really didn't want to move away from the couch, even if he did want more coffee.

"I looked—" Zavier shook his head and leaned over to unzip his messenger bag. He pulled his tablet out, and with a skill that Ray marveled at, somehow flipped the thing open and unlocked it without putting down or even spilling a drop of his coffee. He handed Ray the tablet. "Here."

Ray took it, even as his stomach flinched. Last time he'd stared at a tablet, it had been Carl's, and it had been the video of him yelling at Kevin. This, though...

He glanced down, then stared. Holy shit. It was a photo of him and Zavier from one of the acoustical sets when they were both out at the stage edge, taken from below. Zavier was lit perfectly, his black hair slick, his body glowing.

And he was looking at Ray with such open passion Ray felt the heat of both stares—the one in the photo, and of Zavier watching him now. Both went to his head and to his balls. Fuck, Zavier was hot.

He wet his suddenly dry lips. "You look like a rock god."

"He is a rock god," Dom said. "We all are."

"It's only been ten weeks," Zavier murmured.

"You were always a rock god," Ray shot back. They'd been living nonstop with each other since the audition. He damn well knew how good Zavier looked and played. He handed the tablet back, glad that his hands weren't trembling like his heart was. "You willing to dig into the bad, too?"

Zavier nodded. "Paradoxically, it's easier for me to read than the good."

"Why?" The question came from Mish, but Ray had been about to ask it.

"Because I can ignore the bullshit, especially when I know it's bullshit." Zavier laid the tablet between the back of the couch and his legs. "With the good, I can't tell if it's smoke or fire."

Ray didn't say a word. Because when it came to Zavier, it was most certainly *always* fire.

THE DRIVE BETWEEN HOUSTON AND DALLAS WAS SHORT, WHICH Zavier found to be both a relief and an annoyance. He enjoyed not moving, but he also was getting very fond of the way Ray stretched out with him on the couch. Two cats, Mish called them.

As they traveled, Ray plucked out notes on Dom's guitar —snatches of intriguing melodies and phrases—and jotted notes down in his journal. Not musical ones, but cryptic symbols nonetheless. Shapes. Letters. His own system.

Zavier itched to learn more about that, but Ray was absorbed, so he didn't ask. He did tap out rhythms as Ray played, though. Simple and complex ones, which Ray took and wove into the melody.

"That gonna be something when it grows up?" Dom glanced up from his book. "Sounds damn good."

"Maybe."

Despite his cagey reply, Zavier felt the true answer. Ray was composing. Couldn't be anything else. "Does the song have a name?"

"Not that I want to say yet." Ray shifted on the seat, and put the guitar away. "But yes." Amber eyes met Zavier's, but no more words. Just a smile.

That was enough. Their little session of submission, as bad an idea as it had been, also seemed to have unlocked something in Ray. Or maybe taking the day off had. Hard to say. Whatever the reason, the outcome was a move back toward the rough-hewn friendship they'd carved. As an added bonus, Ray was regaining control of himself and shedding his anger and annoyance.

Though Zavier wanted to throat-punch Carl, especially after having skimmed through the good—and the bad— about the band on the internet. Generally, the press was as he'd seen in the articles Nadia had sent: positive, even glowing in places. Their shows were seen as rising to or even surpassing Five Asylum's. They were becoming one of the season's hottest, must-see groups. There were comments speculating about how an album with Zavier behind the drums might sound, how he'd elevated Twisted Wishes, and there was also praise for Ray's energetic and outstanding vocals. Accolades rained down for Mish and Domino, too.

The photos were *amazing* and Nadia was going to have a field day, because Zavier had become a new sexy catch, or something like that. The press dug back into the past and pulled out photos of him in a tux. Black tie and tails or nearly naked, Zavier Demos cut a stunning figure. He'd rolled his eyes at that.

The bad was—interesting. Mostly it revolved, as everyone knew, around Kevin and that one night where Ray had lobbed a bottle at him. There was an article about Ray's "violent" outburst in St. Louis, including how Ray had flipped off Zavier. Perhaps offstage Van Zeller and Demos are not as in sync as on, but that didn't mar their performance, nor their onstage chemistry.

Onstage chemistry. Those were powerful words.

No one had dirt on Domino, thanks to Dom's night and day personas. For Mish, they speculated about her sexuality —gay or straight? As if those were the only choices. As if it were anyone's business but *hers*. The press was horrid in that respect.

The dirt around Zavier focused on his departure from Silverton, but since he seemed to be enjoying the rock-and-roll life, no one had really dug any deeper than Dimitri throwing a tantrum. There was also quite a bit of speculation about his sexuality, too, which also made him roll his eyes.

The questions people wanted Ray to answer, though, did all revolve around Kevin. Had they been lovers? Did Ray regret drinking? Was he doing a twelve-step or some other program? Had he talked to Kevin? On and on.

Zavier started a list. Any of the questions were bound to bother Ray, but all of them would put him over the edge.

There was also the question of whether Ray and Zavier were fucking—and that one hit a little too close for comfort.

He'd rubbed his eyes and turned off his tablet after about two hours of that nonsense.

An hour later, they arrived in Dallas. Zavier had to hand it to Ray—he always seemed to know what city they were near. To Zavier, all the venues were blending together. One outdoor amphitheater looked a lot like another. The accommodations, while slightly different, were similar enough. Déjà vu wasn't just a feeling—it was a piece of his life now.

They'd huddled in the bus before they'd arrived and had changed up a few things, but left the show pretty much the same as they'd played in Houston, since that still buzzed in their veins. Good thing, too.

When they stepped off the bus in Dallas, it wasn't just Carl waiting for them, but one of the label bigwigs, as well. Carl wore his usual twisted and displeased look, deeper than normal.

But the exec, he was downright excited. "Here's the band everyone's talking about!" A corporate smile followed.

For his part, Ray stepped forward and offered a hand. "Not bad for an opening act, huh?"

Zavier flinched internally. They were more than an opening act and Ray needed to believe that.

"Not tonight." Where the exec's grin widened, Carl's mouth only became more pinched. "You're headlining this concert."

Ray seemed to stop moving. Stop breathing. Hell, Zavier's blood went cold and hot. Headlining?

"What?" Ray let go of the exec's hand.

Carl spoke, and his tone made Zavier want to punch him. Too dismissive, too snide. "Gregor Daye has laryngitis, so Five Asylum canceled. Should have canceled the whole thing, but the promotion company seems to think you guys can step up."

"We agree," the exec said. "Given your most recent performances and the number of fans coming to see just you, there's no reason you can't play the full show yourself."

"We can." Ray's voice was soft, but the certainty behind those two words took Zavier's breath away.

Carl started to speak, but it was as if Ray didn't even hear him. His focus was on the suited man with the power tie and slick smile. "We can do this. We've got enough material. We're ready." He turned and looked at them in turn. "Right?" No doubts at all. It was if a switch had been flipped and Ray *believed*.

Zavier could only nod with Dom and Mish. *Oh, Ray. Go. Do this*. There was the strength and conviction—and control.

There wasn't even any time for Carl to cut into them, because they were off into a whirlwind of resetting play lists, performing sound checks, doing warm-ups, then plunked right down into pre-concert interviews.

Of course, the reporters tried to dig into Ray. But Zavier damn well wouldn't let them take this night from Ray.

This journalist was named Samantha Galloway. "How do you feel about Twisted Wishes doing so well after you replaced your drummer? Don't you think that's a little unfair?"

Ray's color changed, paling, the flushing red as embarrassment and ire rose.

Zavier beat him there. "Oh, come on, what kind of question is that? And with me sitting here?"

She paled herself, and turned a little toward him. "I meant no disrespect."

"Of course you did."

Silence.

"No one—not Ray, not me, not Domino or Mish—could have predicted how we'd play together. Or that I'd even be available or interested. And asking Ray that—" He shook his head.

She had the decency to look taken aback. Everyone around the table shifted, especially Carl, who sat next to Samantha. Interesting.

Ray's gaze flicked to his momentarily, then focused on Samantha. He straightened in his chair. "Look, I miss Kevin. I wish he could be here. He made those albums what they were, too." His gaze shifted to Zavier. "I mean, I love your playing, but..."

"Hey, I know I'm filling shoes."

Samantha swallowed and glanced at her phone, which was recording the interview. Carl stared down at his hands.

"I'd say you should ask Kevin how he feels, but..." Ray shook his head. "Leave him alone. He's been through enough."

After that, the interview shifted away from Kevin and on to other topics like recording a new album and whether Zavier would remain. They answered those honestly, and the whole process felt a damn sight better than it had before. Afterward, once the journalist and Carl had left, Ray focused on him.

A sense of calm flew through Zavier. *Yes.* There was the trust he craved. The understanding and spark of friendship.

"Oh god." Ray leaned back in his chair. "Are they ever gonna stop asking about Kevin? It's not okay talking about him like that."

"Hon, it'll be okay." Mish rubbed his back. "You did fine. Zavier, too."

He only wanted to take some of the burden off Ray, let him run with this night. Lead them into a show that would win over the label.

Ray rose. "Yeah." He met Zavier's gaze. "Thank you. I'm really grateful."

So was Zavier. He nodded, because it seemed the best response.

A smile flitted across Ray's face—first one Zavier had seen pre-concert in a while. "Let's go get dressed."

They did, and when they took the stage, the whole audience was theirs.

Zavier drank in the energy and excitement, the glory that was Twisted Wishes, and the singular excellence that Ray brought to the stage.

He rained his sticks down on the kit and wanted to live in that moment forever.

CHAPTER
FIFTEEN

RAY WAS STILL HIGH AS A KITE AFTER THE AUTOGRAPH LINES. They'd headlined their very own show and had their first VIP encounter. Those had been in the works for a while, though Carl had neglected to tell them. Still, the whole thing had been an unbelievable experience, so he couldn't even be mad about that, especially since the VIP packages would continue. The label executive had praised the band afterward for their energetic and fan-inspiring performance and complimented them for stepping up when Five Asylum had to back out.

They were heading to the buses—band and crew—for a little celebration when Ray stopped in his tracks, the realization hitting him like a hammer in the head. Zavier bumped his shoulder and gave him a questioning look.

"I left my notebook in the dressing room." He had to get it. Its potential loss was like a punch to his chest.

Zavier nodded. "Want company?"

"Nah. Should only take a second." With that, he turned and jogged back into the building.

Thankfully, the Moleskine was exactly where he'd left it, sitting on the vanity. The rest of the things in the room—the clothes and makeup and other items—were packed up.

One of the crew, Sasha, smiled at him. "Thought you might be back for that," she said.

He gave a laugh. "Yeah. It's like my security blanket." He gave the crew a wave.

"Hey," she said. "You joining us for movie night?"

The whole band had been invited. Mish thought it was a great idea, and so did Dom. *They're working their asses off, too,* he'd said.

Ray agreed, except he didn't know if he'd make it to the party. "Really depends on when I start to crash." He bounced up and down. "Right now I'm fine, but—"

Sasha gave him a little look he interpreted as interest. "Well, I hope to see you, if you don't crash."

Oh, honey. You'd be better off trying that on Mish than me. He smiled and headed out—and ran straight into Carl. Almost literally.

"What the *fuck*, Ray?"

"I—" He held up the notebook, but the rest of the sentence died in his mouth. Carl was furious, red-faced and glaring. Ray took a step back.

"I've been all over this fucking venue looking for you." Carl pointed down the hall, like a schoolmaster, and the bottom dropped out of Ray's life.

What had he done? Why was Carl so mad? Jesus, the label guy had *loved* them! Still, he went the way Carl pointed. *Don't make waves. Stay calm. Stay collected. Controlled.* Like he should be. Like Zavier wanted. God, he should have stayed with the band. Or taken Zavier up on his offer to come with him. His head swam like he was drowning in the booze Carl always accused him of drinking.

At the end of the hall was a tiny room, a closet of an office. He followed Carl inside and flinched when he closed the door. Ray swallowed a breath and turned.

Carl shook his head. "That—" he pointed in the vague direction of the stage "—was not good enough."

Ray gripped his notebook, the cover biting into his palm. "But—everyone loved it." His voice wavered. *Hold it together.*

"Is that what you think?" Carl's lips curled into a smile that was anything but kind.

"The label—"

"Mr. Collinger was being kind. Reality is that your performance out there was barely adequate as a headlining band. It was mediocre, and barely up to an opening act's form." He shook his head. "You're lucky you have such enthusiastic fans. They pulled the weight for you tonight."

That wasn't right. It couldn't be right...could it? Ray played the night over in his head again. Tried to remember exactly what the exec had said, what he'd looked like. Had his smile been too wide? Shit, *shit.*

He wanted to slam past Carl, tell him he was full of it, and flee back to the bus. But that was the act of the fool Carl said he was. Probably what the asshole thought he'd do. Instead, he took another breath. "Okay, what do we need to do better?"

Carl blinked at him, and for a moment looked dumbfounded. Then he snorted.

"No, I'm serious. If there's a problem, how do we fix it?"

"Stop being so goddamned condescending." Carl turned away.

Condesc—"I'm not!" Ray's voice rose, along with his anger. Both he tried to catch and tamp down. He would not explode. Not here, not tonight. "I'm not trying to cause trouble, Carl. I'm asking for your opinion as our manager. What are we doing wrong?"

"More like what are *you* doing wrong, Ray."

"Me?" His voice crept up. He was giving each and every night all that he had.

"You've got to be better. Get more vocal training. Stop hitting the notes sharp. You're not giving your all out there. It's lucky your bandmates have talent."

Oh. Ray's heart turned to stone. Had he sung sharp? He couldn't really remember the night clearly now. It all came in bits and pieces—visions of light and sound and tastes. He tried to piece together what he could, but his heart rammed in his chest. The video of Carl's singing flitted through his mind. So much easier to critique a performance from the outside. Maybe he *had* been off tune. Probably. Yeah.

"I—" He met Carl's cold gaze.

"Get your fucking act together, Ray, That's your only choice." Carl spun, wrenched open the door, and walked out.

All the while, Ray struggled to breathe, to think, to not throw his notebook—the one possession he cared about—against the wall. Screaming would feel good, but probably fuck up his voice even more. They'd just headlined their first show, and it wasn't fucking good enough for Carl. He could track down the exec, but what would that look like? A sniveling kid looking for approval?

What good was a notebook full of songs if the singer was crap? Was he fucking up?

He didn't know. *Shit.* What was he going to do?

ZAVIER WAS STANDING OUTSIDE THE CREW BUS, LISTENING WITH one ear, but paying attention to the walkway from the venue. Ray had been gone too fucking long. A few more minutes and he'd grab one of the security staff that still hung out by the gates, and go hunting for him. It didn't take *that* long to grab a notebook. So far, the only people coming down that path had been the crew with the last of their things, along with Carl, who'd stalked off to his hired car. Zavier's blood chilled as watched him leave.

Finally, a lone figure appeared, silhouetted by the lights, moving slowly, as if the world had crashed down on their shoulders.

Fuck. When the person came closer, he knew it was Ray. "I'll be right back," he muttered to no one in particular.

As he hurried up the path, Ray stopped. He was still too backlit by the venues lights to make out his features, but the way he held his body made Zavier's chest ache. It was all wrong and so different from before. Where Ray had been tall and energetic, he was now slumped and curled into himself.

Oh, he had a very good idea why—and man, did he want to wrap his fingers around Carl's throat and squeeze so tight.

When he finally reached Ray, those once lively amber eyes were staring at the ground. "You didn't need to come up here. I was gonna go to the bus."

But he did need to come. Every movement Ray made skated across Zavier's nerves like metal on glass. "I wanted to see how you were doing." He spoke softly, and buried the urge to reach out to Ray. He had to give Ray room to move or stay or reach out—whatever he needed.

Ray's barked-out laugh contained so much pain, Zavier's lungs ached in sympathy. "I don't think I'm gonna make the movie night. I'm—done." He ran a hand through his hair.

"That's okay."

Ray shook his head. "It's not okay. I should be there for people, but—" He finally looked up at Zavier. Shattered. Ray was *shattered*. The only way to describe it.

Zavier took a step forward.

"I'm tired and a mess and out of control." Ray's voice wavered. "I don't want to ruin anyone's fun."

Zavier flinched a little. Because there was the seed of doubt he'd sewn, with intent even. "You're not out of control."

Ray's Adam's apple bobbed. "Maybe not now, but I'm hanging by a thread, Zav. Give me ten minutes and—" fear and humiliation cascaded through Ray's voice "—call a reporter. I'm sure Carl would love that."

God, he wanted to pull Ray to him. Or put him on his

knees. Zavier studied Ray's bleak face. "I'm not calling anyone. You know that."

Ray nodded. "You're a good friend, even if I'm a shitty one."

Friend. The word blazed through Zavier. *Finally.* "Maybe I can help you."

"What, be a better friend?"

"You're a fine friend, Ray. I like you the way you are. I was thinking more along the lines of me taking control for a time." He watched Ray's expression shift from confusion to under-standing and back to confusion. "If that's something you're interested in."

Ray wavered on the path, looking past Zavier, then focusing on him like a laser beam. "You—I—" He licked his lips. "You're talking sex. With me."

"Yes. But I'm also asking you to trust me and listen to me and obey me, for a little while."

Ray shivered. But he'd also straightened, and the weight that had pressed him down wasn't evident anymore. "I—are you sure?" Shock there.

Zavier chuckled. "Oh, Ray. I wouldn't be asking if I wasn't."

His shoulders relaxed. And after a few swallows, he whispered two words. "Yes, please."

Desire, need, and elation chased through Zavier. He shoved his hands in his pockets, lest he put Ray on his knees right there, out in the open. "Why don't you go to the bus and wait for me, and I'll tell the others you've hit the wall and are crashing. We'll have a few hours to ourselves."

Ray shuffled his feet. "What about you?"

"What about me, what?"

"What are you gonna tell them?" Ray rubbed the back of his neck with his free hand, and Zavier bet if the light were better, he'd see a nice blush on Ray's neck and cheeks.

Ah, yes. "Well, I warned them I wasn't that into movies and, quite honestly, I need some downtime, too."

"Downtime," Ray murmured. "Fucking me."

Zavier closed the gap between them, but didn't touch him. "We'll see about the fucking once we see about the obeying."

Ray's normally light eyes were as dark as the night sky above them. "Okay." His voice had shifted from heartbroken to gravelly with lust.

Good. Zavier'd lift a little bit of the stress Ray carried. "You should go get on the bus and wait for me, Ray."

"Okay—I—yes." He nodded once.

Zavier turned and let him pass, then followed him down the path back to the lot. Once they hit tarmac, their paths diverged. He found Mish talking with one of the crew members, a fine-looking woman with dark brown skin and short, curly hair. God, he hated to interrupt them.

Thankfully, Mish looked up. "Hey, was that Ray?"

"Yeah. He's crashing. Hit the wall."

She grunted. "Similar to other concerts?"

Mish wasn't a fool, and Zavier bet she was just as observant as he was. He nodded. "You know how it goes."

"You gonna watch over him?"

Something about the glint in her smile made that question not so innocent. "Was thinking about that. Movie nights aren't my thing."

The crew member—he racked his memory until he pulled out Sasha as her name—grinned. "You seem more of a people person than a watch-people person."

That, strangely, did sum him up well. He liked to watch, sure. But hands-on was so much better, and he had a willing Ray waiting for him in the bus. He chuckled. "I also need a little quiet. Even with ear protection—it gets a bit much in the kit."

Mish patted him on the shoulder. "Go take care of Ray. We'll see you guys in a couple hours."

He nodded, and detangled himself from the crowd around one of the buses to board the other. He waved at the driver, then passed behind the privacy screen.

Ray looked up from the couch, all nerves and beauty. The stress still hung on him like an ill-fitting shirt. "I didn't know what to do, so I waited."

Perfect. "That's exactly what I told you to do." He gestured toward the back of the bus. "Let's go have a chat where it's a little quieter, before the buses start moving."

It was also far more private back there. No chance they'd be overheard by the driver.

Ray rose, and Zavier followed him past the berths and into the lounge at the back. He pulled the curtain closed, then turned. Ray was breath and lust and jangling tension. Not exactly where Zavier wanted him to be, but they would work on that. There was time. Right now, though?

"Ray, may I kiss you?"

Shock washed across Ray's features. He stammered out a reply. "Yes."

Good. Zavier stepped close, enough to see the wild beating of Ray's pulse.

"But...why ask?"

"Consent," Zavier murmured. He cupped Ray's face with one hand. "Everything tonight has to be something you want." He slid his hand against the other side of Ray's head. "You can say no. You can tell me to stop." He tilted Ray's head up and their lips touched.

Ray whimpered.

"Trust that I'll heed your wishes." He held Ray's head firmly between his hands. Brushed a thumb against a flushed cheek.

"I—do trust you." Ray's words were warm breath against Zavier's lip.

"Good. Will you listen to me tonight? Will you obey me?"

Ray was trembling against him. "Yes."

Zavier kissed Ray, gently at first, letting him stiffen and moan, then relax. Lips moved gently, coaxing, opening, claiming, until Ray's mouth was his and that hard, lithe body was molded to Zavier's. That taste, the press of Ray against him put fire into Zavier's blood. He'd needed this. Wanted it since he'd auditioned. They'd danced and danced for months. Countless days of living with each other. It was time already.

The second time he kissed Ray, it was to claim his mouth. A kiss that pulled whimpers and sighs from him, had him digging his fingers into Zavier's arms. But it also had him tipping his head back and thrusting his hips against Zavier. Savoring Ray's desire was a joy. Finally, his hands were where they belonged, playing a different kind of music.

Zavier held Ray's head with one hand and slid the other down to his ass to pull them tightly together. He drank in Ray's gasp and groan when Zavier ground their dicks against each other so there'd be no doubt about Zavier's intent.

They weren't in high school anymore, and Zavier would have every inch of Ray that was offered to him.

When he broke the kiss, it was only to bite and lick and suck at Ray's neck until he was twisting and thrusting and shaking in Zavier's arms. "Oh fuck. Oh god, yes."

There. Each word cascaded down Zavier. Ray's pleasure, his need.

The engine turned over, then the bus lurched, sending them both off balance and breaking them apart for a moment.

Zavier laughed. Not the most ideal conditions. But a little space would keep him from getting too far ahead with Ray.

Ray groaned in exasperation. "Cock-blocked by a bus."

"If you think you're frustrated now, just you wait." Zavier grinned.

Ray caught his breath. "I remember. I remember that night."

So did Zavier. Ray was glorious in obedience and breathtaking to watch come. "This time, we need to set some ground rules."

A nod and a curious expression. "Like—safewords and stuff?"

So, Ray did know a little bit about BDSM. Zavier sat on the lounge's couch and patted the cushion next to him. "That's part of it. Come, sit."

No hesitation. A good sign. Ray didn't lean back, so the nerves were still there.

But then, Zavier was nervous, too. This was the hardest part...the beginning. "I want to set some expectations."

"Okay."

"This isn't going to be a love affair. I don't do relationships."

Ray's brows knitted. "But I thought...dominance and submission was a kind of relationship?"

"You've been doing internet searches, haven't you?" Ray's blush told Zavier everything. Thing was, Ray had a point. "Yes...yes, it is a kind of relationship, one built on consent and trust and caring. On surrender and control." He couldn't fault Ray for shivering. He trembled a little himself.

"But you don't do relationships," Ray said.

Yeah, that sounded contradictory, but explaining that he was aromantic and didn't fall in love wasn't a conversation he wanted to have at the moment. Besides, chances were that Ray wouldn't believe him, or that he'd think Zavier was broken or some of the other shit former partners had said. "I do kink relationships, but I don't do romantic relationships."

Ray studied his hands. "So this is...friends with benefits?" He looked up and met Zavier's gaze. Lovely amber eyes with such a yearning in them.

"Are we finally friends?" Zavier murmured the question. "Or are you still pissed at me?"

Ray grunted a laugh. "Touché." But his smile was bright.

"We're friends. I may always be a little pissed at you. And I'd *really* like to know more about these benefits, please."

If they'd already had this conversation, Zavier would've hauled Ray over his knees and spanked his ass for that. But they hadn't, and he didn't even know what Ray enjoyed. Hell, he didn't know if Ray knew what Ray enjoyed.

He patted Ray's thigh. *Friends*. They were friends. Thank god. "Tell me what you know from your internet reading."

Ray did, and it was about what Zavier expected, plus a few deeper topics. Information about safewords, consent, and subspace. But he'd also learned about the differences between sane, safe, consensual play and risk-aware consensual kink play. He'd looked into types of domination and bondage. Slavery. Pain and edge play.

"I'm not so sure about knives and things like that," Ray said.

That Zavier understood. "I'm somewhat squeamish when it comes to blood, so you needn't worry about that." Aside from the whole man-loving-man thing that barred him from donating blood, he'd also fainted every fucking time. Not from giving his own, but seeing all those bags of other people's blood. He shuddered.

"And yet, all your tattoos."

Zavier grunted and rubbed his arms. Painful in their way, but so worth it. "Most of the time, I don't see any, and it's *my* blood. There's a difference."

Ray nodded absently.

"What turns you on?" That was what he really wanted to know. What fantasies could Zavier make come true for Ray—or torture him with?

Wants and desires apparently took a little more to pry out of Ray. He stammered, shifted in his seat, then got up and paced, his neck red and his body in motion.

The answer was, however, fairly close to what Zavier

thought Ray might enjoy. Being tied up in various ways. A number of sex acts. Toys. Gags. Cuffs. Submission. Everything he loved to do to a willing partner, a willing submissive.

"But none of that humiliation shit. I get enough of that from Carl."

"I will *never* treat you like that pile of assholes does." That came out a little harsher than he intended, but the look in Ray's face was priceless, full of thankfulness and hope.

Ray breathed out. "Can we—just—" He waved his hand. "Start?" All that energy, both the good and bad, had returned and was ramping him up.

"Very soon." Zavier watched as Ray moved back and forth again. "How do you feel about spanking?"

A blush to high heaven. Excellent. Fire for Zavier's blood.

"I'd—like to try that. Maybe more."

"Flogging?"

Ray nodded. "I want to know what it feels like—if nothing else."

"We can work up to it." Zavier made a mental list of items he'd need to order and have shipped to their next hotel. They'd both enjoy their next day of downtime. So many ways to torment Ray zipped through Zavier's mind. What he could do with a nice bed and some lengths of rope.

He pried out a few more details before Ray was too keyed up to continue—apparently descriptions and photos of cock-and-ball torture had made him both curious and horrified—that was also something they could see about trying, should the *benefits* part of their friendship work out well, but that was far too much to start with.

"Do you have a safeword in mind?"

Ray shook his head. "Linguini?" He laughed. "But no, I don't know. What about red and yellow? I read about those, and I like the idea of a word that means slow down."

"Perfect." Everything was falling into place.

"Now what?" Ray stood still at last, and seemed to be holding his breath.

Zavier relaxed into the leather and crossed his arms. Time to take control. "Now we start."

CHAPTER
SIXTEEN

RAY STARED AT ZAVIER. "NOW?" GOD, HE HOPED SO. HE'D BEEN high and low and strung out, then Zavier had kissed him and the world had fallen away. But then he'd had to tell Zavier his desires. It was almost too much.

Zavier nodded. "As I said."

"What do I do?" Anything. All Ray wanted was for Zavier to touch him or give him an order or—fuck him. He needed to be fucked. Wanted that so badly. He didn't want to think anymore.

"You do whatever I tell you to."

"This is bullshit." He turned, pushed aside the privacy curtain and marched into the main part of the bus. He understood the whole submission idea, didn't need Zavier coddling him.

He heard Zavier grunt, then rise. "Do you want this?" No accusations, no anger. So typically Zavier.

"Yes!" He whirled around and found Zavier standing at the entrance to the lounge. "Yes—just—" He ran his hands through his hair. "Tell me what to do!"

Zavier returned to his seat on the couch in the lounge. From there, he uttered one word. "Strip."

The order was smooth and gentle and exactly what Ray had wanted, yet he struggled against it. He needed what Zavier offered. Craved it. But both the high from one of their best performances and the low of Carl's dismissive and cruel words swam through his blood. Every bit of his body tingled and tensed. He stood in the middle of the space, staring but not seeing the bunks in front of him. The palms of his hands hurt from where his nails dug into his flesh.

"Ray." Zavier relaxed on the couch, arms outstretched on the couch back and his long legs open enough that Ray could kneel between them. God, he was so beautiful. "Stop."

He sucked in a breath through his teeth. "I'm trying."

"You're failing." No malice, only simple fact.

He gritted his teeth. "What the hell do you want from me?"

A cock of the head and a raised eyebrow. "I'm not sure how 'strip' is in any way ambiguous."

It wasn't. Not at all. Ray unclenched his hands and forced himself to do what he so wanted to do: he toed off his shoes and pulled his shirt over his head. The AC of the bus cooled his overheated skin and he tossed the shirt onto his bunk. His hands shook, but he managed his belt, and the button and zipper on his jeans. Each move felt like fire and heaven.

He'd no idea why Zavier made him feel this way, made him want so much more than the friendship they'd finally managed. Control and surrender. He couldn't stop thinking about Carl's words. The energy of the crowd. Ray bit his lip and pushed both his jeans and underwear down. They pooled around his ankles and he kicked them out of the way, then removed his socks.

"That's better."

Zavier's approval washed over him, etching into his bones and calming his nerves. Maybe if he did as told, his life might be better. Make more sense. At least for a little while. He was *tired* of the chaos that flowed around him.

"Come here." Zavier pointed to a spot in front of him. "And kneel."

Too far away for a blowjob. Still, Ray did as told, shedding the part of him that chafed, that wanted to rebel. He walked back into the lounge area and dropped to his knees exactly where Zavier had pointed.

"Have you ever done yoga?"

Odd question, but he answered, "Yeah. Not seriously, but yeah."

"Do you remember child's pose?"

He did. It was simple and relaxing. "Of course."

"Put your forehead on my shoes, and stretch your arms behind you." Zavier closed his legs.

God. Humiliation flooded Ray. This wasn't sex. It was subservience. He searched Zavier's face.

He found laughter dancing in Zavier's eyes, and an emotion he couldn't identify. "Do you trust me, Ray?" he asked.

Yes. No. He nodded slowly. In the end, the answer was yes.

Zavier leaned forward and cupped Ray's face, his palm warm. "Then do as I ask."

He closed his eyes and did as told, folding forward and pressing his forehead against the leather of Zavier's shoes. It was exactly as humiliating as he thought it would be. Naked and prone. There was nothing sexy or hot about Zavier's order.

The bus lumbered on and the rumble of the wheels on tarmac vibrated through every inch of Ray's bones. His muscles clenched and unclenched, and seconds dragged by. Zavier said nothing, though beneath Ray's forehead and the leather on which he rested, toes moved, enough to remind him exactly where he was.

On a bus, stripped and bowing to Zavier Demos.

He *hated* it, but not enough to move. *Do you trust me?* Yes.

Plus, he wanted to see where this friendship with benefits went. What Zavier meant to do with him and to him. His flesh warmed at that thought even as he squirmed against it.

But the seconds and minutes ticked by without so much as a word from on high. Hell, he couldn't even hear Zavier breathe over the deep throb of the bus on the road. Infuriating. This was so damn dumb. What the hell did Zavier want? What was Ray supposed to do? Just bow here forever? He shifted and flexed. He should sit up, tell Zavier to fuck off, and go curl up in his berth.

Do you trust me?

No. He didn't. Zavier wasn't any different than that asshole dickwad Carl, always on his back, always griping about something. Not good enough? Hell, the concert tonight had been perfect. Their best yet! He hadn't been out of tune. He *knew* he hadn't. And the fans had responded, screaming and dancing and singing along with Ray. The light in their eyes when he ran into the crowd. The signs. Mish leaping and twirling across the stage. Dom shredding every chord. Zavier—

Ray's breath caught.

Zavier had played as if his very soul were in the music, his arms flying, his body soaked in sweat, ecstasy in his face. He'd played exactly like they all had, with love and passion and an intensity that made Ray ache to reclaim. They'd been a *band*. Twisted Wishes at their finest.

Afterward, Zavier had clapped Ray on the back, and his grin and the shine in his eyes speaking the words they could hear over the thunder of the audience clapping and screaming. They'd all done so fucking well. That had carried straight to backstage. The rest of the night had been a whirlwind of autographs and slaps on the back. Then Carl had pulled Ray aside and dumped a verbal bucket of ice water all over everything.

Ray needed to up his game.

Except he didn't know how. If tonight hadn't been good enough for Carl and if the execs had been lying like Carl said...then they were *fucked*.

He sighed down into Zavier's shoes. Maybe what the band needed was a different vocalist, because obviously he wasn't cutting it despite doing his best. But that would mean leaving behind the very thing he'd spent years creating. God, he was so tired. He pressed his forehead against Zavier's shoes and let the rest of his body melt toward the floor until his skin hummed with the sound of the motor and his tears slid down onto the leather.

They *were* fucked. He didn't know how to fix it. He couldn't fix it. They were done.

The couch creaked and fingers stroked his hair. "Oh, Ray." Zavier's voice was a murmur of warmth and kindness. "What did that shitbag *say* to you?"

Carl's words flittered to the surface of Ray's thoughts, and he spoke into the floor of the bus. "That our performance tonight was barely adequate. That I needed to do better. I'm barely pulling my own weight in the band." He paused. "My singing was sharp."

Zavier stiffened, even to his toes. Those pressed up against Ray's forehead. A moment later, his hand cupped Ray's neck. "Sit up, please."

Ray did, moving slowly. The tiny world of the tour bus swam like he'd been drinking Kevin's Jack Daniels. When he settled onto his heels, Zavier was before him, kneeling on the same floor. For a second time, Ray's breath caught.

Zavier cupped each side of Ray's face with his warm, rough hands. His beautiful drummer's hands. Ray closed his eyes.

A thumb swept over his cheek, and coolness followed. His tears. God, what did Zavier think of *that*? Weak. Pathetic.

"Look at me." Soft, soft words, but a command nonetheless.

Ray peeled open his eyes and met Zavier's earnest gaze.

"Where did I go to school?"

"Juilliard."

Zavier nodded. "That makes me a Juilliard-trained professional musician, right?"

Fucking asshole. Ray ground his teeth and tried to nod.

A faint, sad smile, and Zavier's thumb brushed Ray's cheek again. "I'm not saying this out of hubris. I want you to understand—I've spent years having music theory crammed into my skull. I've been trained by the best in the world and I've played with the best in the world, Ray."

"Yeah?" He couldn't keep the cocky snarl out of his voice. "Must be nice."

"Sometimes it was. Other times it was absolute hell." He paused. "You're the most talented musician I've ever known. You're certainly one of the hardest working. And you have never, ever sung sharp in any of our concerts."

The bus swam around Ray and his lungs burned. "Fuck you." He threw the words out like a shield, something to block the openness in Zavier's expression, the honesty.

Those damn thumbs again, smoothing over flesh. Soothing his pain away along with his tears. "You know I'm not lying."

Ray pressed his lips closed. He wanted to shake his head, but Zavier held him, like a soft, velvet vise. Hands, words, and looks. He was, both literally and figuratively, naked before the man.

"This was supposed to be sex," Ray croaked.

Zavier chucked. "Oh, we'll get to that, but I need to know you're okay first."

"I'm okay."

Another chuckle. "There's something else I know, besides the fact that you're a damned excellent vocalist and songwriter. Do you know what it is?"

Couldn't shake his head, so he glared at Zavier. "No."

"Carl Roberts is a fucking liar. Just about every sentence that waste of space utters is false and designed to undermine you, cut you down, and make you second guess yourself."

A shudder ran through Ray, like a chill, but so much deeper. Ice in his bones. "Why?" The question burst out of his soul.

Once more, Zavier's thumbs eased the pain erupting in Ray. A simple motion. Intimate. "I don't know. I can't figure him out. But he lies, Ray. He *lies*. Don't trust anything he says." Finally, Zavier slipped his hands from Ray's face. "When we stood on stage, after the encore, how did you think the concert went?"

"It was the best we've ever done." His throat was so dry, but he didn't want to move, didn't want to break whatever spell had Zavier kneeling here with him. "Absolutely amazing."

A slow nod from Zavier. "Yeah. I felt it, too. We clicked and everything went higher. And the fans..." He got a distant, haunted look, before focusing back on Ray. "I bet you anything the press will contradict Carl."

"The label exec seemed happy, but Carl..."

"Lies."

Maybe. Yeah. The knot Ray had been carrying in his stomach since his talk with Carl eased. If the press loved them and the fans loved them, then that would impress the label, too. "Do you think we can play a show like that again?"

"Yes." That one word was absolute, and it slid over Ray like he wanted Zavier's hand to.

He shivered. "I trust you."

"Now you do." Zavier's tone had shifted to something deeper. Rich and dark. His smile matched, and a spark of lust flamed in Ray.

He swallowed. "What now?"

"Now?" Zavier cocked his head. "Now you undo the first button on my shirt."

Ray's pulse ticked up and his cheeks warmed. Even more when Zavier lifted an eyebrow. He leaned forward, too aware of the motion of the bus and the huff of Zavier's breath. He did as he'd been told.

Before he could sit back, Zavier whispered, "And the next."

When he'd undone the second button, lips grazed his neck. "Keep going."

Oh god. Every part of Ray heated and his cock was hardening with Zavier's every breath against his skin. He kept going until Zavier's shirt was open in front.

"Push it off."

He did, and the skin beneath his hands was hot and smooth. Fabric slipped off those shoulders, revealing all of Zavier's ink. Every line, figure, color, and swirl. Ray wanted to mouth those shoulders, kiss the knotwork on Zavier's pecs.

Zavier shrugged the shirt off his wrists. "Sit back on your heels."

The pulse in Ray's ears sounded louder when Zavier rose and towered over him. He was eye level with the impressive bulge in Zavier's pants.

Fingers brushed Ray's hair. "Yes, you can unbutton my jeans." Amusement in that voice.

Ray really wanted to see what Zavier looked like naked. Where those tattoos led, what else was inked. His length and girth. The muscles of his thighs. How much hair he had. Everything. Ray undid the button and nearly went for the zipper—but stopped.

"Very good." Zavier's murmur felt like a kiss on Ray's back, and every hair stood up in pleasure. "Now the zipper."

He pulled the tab down, and waited. Zavier's underwear was black and cotton, but whether briefs or some other style, he couldn't tell. Nor did he find out, because Zavier pushed both down, freeing his dick and exposing the rest of his body.

Tattoos snaked down onto his hips and across his lower

abs, and jutting from a thick bed of curls was Zavier's cock. Not overly long, not overly thick. Like every other inch of Zavier's body, it was too fucking perfect. "You're unreal."

A chuckle, and Zavier stroked himself. "I could say the same." He slipped two fingers under Ray's chin and lifted until Ray was staring up at him. "Have you bottomed, Ray? Sucked cock?"

He shivered, and not from the AC. Hell, this close to Zavier naked, close enough to take that dick into his mouth, Ray was blazing with heat. "Yes. Both. Though—it's been a while since I've bottomed."

"You prefer topping?" Curiosity there.

"No."

Zavier's smile deepened at that.

That made Ray's pulse rocket up. "But...people expect rock stars to be a certain way."

A chuckle from Zavier. "I don't."

"That's because you've been a rock star all your life."

His smile slipped away. He touched Ray's cheek. "No, I haven't. I was lucky and privileged, that's all."

"Yet here I am, on my knees for you." For Zavier. He closed his eyes.

Fingers danced over his cheek. "We can stop. If you need to, we can stop."

Emotions tripped over inside Ray. The need for Zavier. All those years of wanting the man. His brashness and now his tenderness. None of it made sense, and at the same time— it did.

"I don't want to stop." He didn't know why there were tears in his voice or eyes. He wanted the world to make sense.

"Ray, look at me."

He forced his eyes open, made himself look up, up that glorious body and into those blue eyes.

"Do you trust me?"

That question again. "Yes."

Oh, the grin. Part sweet, part devil. "Then suck my cock."

He didn't even hesitate, because this, *this* was what he wanted. He wrapped his lips around the tip and tasted the salt and musk of him. Slid his tongue around that shaft and took as much as he could inside, sucking and licking and mouthing the thickness.

Fingers curled into his hair. "Oh fuck, that's good." Zavier rocked back slightly.

Yeah, it was. So damn good. Zavier's heat, the way he filled Ray's mouth. The desire that sped down Ray's body straight to his balls as he sucked and tasted him. The burn of his scalp from his hair being held. He slid his hands up Zavier's thighs, wanting more, wanting to be claimed and fucked. He tried to take more in—once he'd been able to deep-throat just about any guy—but Zavier pulled back. Ray moaned in frustration.

A click of Zavier's tongue was all it took to spiral worry down the same path need had taken just moments before. "As much as I would love to face-fuck you until I come down your throat—you do actually need that for other things."

Like singing tomorrow night. Damn Zavier for being...*responsible*. Still didn't stop Ray from trying and being stymied over and over again. He grabbed Zavier's ass—

—and was rewarded by Zavier stepping away. Fuck! He met Zavier's gaze. There wasn't anger there, nor disappointment. But Zavier wasn't exactly pleased with him.

"Do you understand what submission is, Ray?"

He shivered. He was supposed to do what Zavier said. Except he was also kind of doing what he wanted. Fighting with Zavier for control, trying to make him—*Oh*. Oh shit. He'd been trying to make Zavier face-fuck him anyway.

"I expect an answer."

"I—I do. But—I'm not really doing a good job, am I?"

"No, no, you're not. You need to let go, Ray. Let me give you what you need."

He chewed on his tongue. "So what happens when I don't obey?"

The corner of Zavier's mouth quirked up. "You're about to find out."

Ray couldn't help the swallow of fear, or the blaze of heat that followed. What the hell? But he kind of did want to know what Zavier would do.

"Wait here." With that, Zavier stepped around him, and out into the main part of the bus.

Ray went stone cold. Was Zavier leaving? Was he—what was he doing? Ray nearly twisted, nearly stood, but Zavier's question—the one he kept asking—flitted through Ray's mind. *Do you trust me?*

Everything in him melted. *Yes.* He did. He needed to start acting like it.

Zavier touched Ray's hair, and those warm fingers trailed down to his neck and back. "I know this is hard for you."

"It shouldn't be." The weird tears were back in his voice. "Should be easy." Sex usually was. He'd turn off his brain and fuck and everything would be fine.

A soft laugh. "Ray, you've been fighting for years. For your music, for respect, for your bandmates. I'm not surprised you're fighting me."

He'd been fighting Zavier since his audition.

Zavier slipped past and took a seat on the couch again, dropping a few objects next to him. He was still hard, which shocked Ray.

Ray wasn't anymore. The desire he'd had before had slipped away. "I don't want to fight you, Zav."

"I know." He gestured for Ray to stand. "Come here and turn around."

Took a little to get up, both from his legs being numb and the rocking of the bus, but he did as told. He gasped when Zavier's hands closed on his hips, when leather creaked and Zavier's hot mouth pressed into the small of his back. Fire flooded him, and his flagging cock revived. Every nerve tingled when Zavier nipped his teeth and traced tongue and lips over Ray's ass. His legs wanted to give out from under him.

"Oh fuck, that's—" He lost all words when Zavier bit him hard. Really fucking hard.

He let out a long moan. Fuck, that hurt, but also felt so damn good. He'd probably bruise.

"Like that?"

"Yeah," he whispered. "It's hot."

"Mmm." Zavier captured one of his wrists, then the other, and pulled them both behind Ray's back. He kissed each pulse point. "I'm going to bind your hands together."

Heat flashed everywhere and Ray wavered, his lungs light. Fear of being in someone else's power, and delight for the same damn reason. *Zavier's gonna tie me up.* How many times had he come in the dark, quiet hum of the bus fantasizing about that with Zavier sleeping below him? "Okay."

Another kiss to Ray's back. "I promise I'll take care of you." Zavier crossed one wrist over the other, and held them in a tight grip.

Movement, then Zavier was wrapping his wrists with something. Not rope, not fabric.

Ray couldn't help the moan. He'd watched enough porn where men got tied up. Wondered what it felt like. Sometimes even wrapped a wrist with whatever was handy to try to see, but nothing prepared him for the way he wanted to melt to his knees, nor the heat of being held by Zavier—or the sheer sense of *security.* Holy fuck, he didn't understand that.

Another kiss. Words murmured against Ray's skin. "It's okay."

Whatever Zavier was using stretched a bit, but after a couple more winds, Ray's hands were well and truly tied behind his back, and everything seemed light and wavy. "Zav." His speech was weird.

"Yes?" Strong arms held him. Zavier's hand pressed against his stomach.

"Can I—kneel again? 'Cause I'm gonna fall over."

A small laugh. "And here I was going to tie you up and spank you—but seems that's not punishment at all, is it?" Zavier pulled Ray down against him. Moving and rotating him until he was, in fact, lying across Zavier's lap.

Couch was real leather, too. This close, his nose pressed against the cushion, there was no doubt. "I'm sorry I'm not what you want." He'd never been what Zavier wanted. "I just wanted you to like me. Join my band."

Fingers skimmed over his ass. "Ray, you're exactly what I want."

The shock and the sting of the first swat against his ass drove breath from Ray's lungs.

"And I like you quite a lot."

Another blow, harder than the first. The pain spread up his spine, then turned into heat and light, and Ray bit back a moan.

"And I'm *in* your damn band." There was an edge to Zavier's voice now, and when his hand landed, Ray cried out. Fuck, that *hurt*.

"I'm *really* tired of hearing about high school, so we're not going to talk about that anymore."

Zavier kept spanking him, and Ray squirmed and slid and cursed. Because each blow was fire that stung and made him shake, and each piece of that pain melted and shifted and made him want more. "Please," he said between gasps for air, "Oh god, please." His cock rocked against Zavier's thigh with each blow.

"You know how to make me stop." There was such a coolness to Zavier's voice. So much command.

Ray whimpered. He did know. Problem was, he didn't want Zavier to stop—he didn't know what he wanted—but stopping wasn't even on the list.

But after more blows—Ray didn't even know how many —Zavier did stop. Ray gasped and sobbed. "Fuck, no. Don't stop!"

"Shhh." The pinch Zavier gave his ass cheek made Ray see spots and flooded his senses with that heady mix of pain that melted to pleasure. "I have you. And we're not done."

He tried to move his arms, failed, and remembered they were bound behind his back. He was in the back of a tour bus with Zavier Demos, who'd just spanked the hell out of him. "What the fuck are we doing?"

Zavier tapped his ass, and even that gentle touch sent shivers of pain-pleasure all through him. He groaned.

"Something we probably should have done a lot sooner, in retrospect." A click-snap punctuated Zavier's sentence and cool, slick liquid spread down Ray's crack.

Lube. Oh god. He squirmed. He was already damn hard from the spanking, but this—even the anticipation had him losing his head and nearly his load.

As if reading his thoughts, Zavier spoke. "Don't you *dare* come yet." There was a growl to it. "Not until my cock is nice and deep inside you."

Ray bit his tongue and fought every urge to come unglued right there and then. "Better fuck me soon, then."

Three sharp blows to his ass had Ray gasping. "I'll fuck you when I'm damn well ready." Zavier teased a finger against Ray's hole. "And you're not ready at all." He pressed a digit in.

Ray's mind blurred and slipped away at the familiar pain and then the sweetness of being breached and filled. His breaths were closer to a long string of moans. "Please. Please please please." God, oblivion was right there. He could taste the science and heat and light. Hell, he was already floating.

Zavier finger-fucked him, gently at first, then harder, hitting his prostate with each thrust until Ray couldn't help seeking friction for his cock. He was so close. He wanted to let go and vanish into that heat. Would have, but for one little command. "Zav!"

A devilish chuckle. "You're so damn beautiful, strung out. Almost makes me want to tease you for the rest of the night. Keep you right here—on edge until you can't stand it. Until you're begging me to let you come."

He was already. "Zav, *please*."

Zavier manhandled him, swinging him around until he was sitting on that lap again. Zavier's hair was disheveled and the skin under those amazing tattoos was flush. And his eyes—oh god, they seemed to peer into Ray's soul. Zavier moved them again, the muscles in his arms flexing, and he sat up and on the edge of the couch. Ray wrapped his legs around Zavier's back and leaned in. His ass hurt from the spanking. No doubt it would hurt more when Zavier fucked him.

He'd never felt more vulnerable with anyone. Or more *safe*. Naked. Bound. In Zavier's arms. He pressed his forehead against Zavier's shoulder. "Please make the world go away."

Teeth scraped against Ray's skin. "I will. For you, I will."

A wrapper ripped, Zavier rolled the condom down over his dick. More lube, then Zavier was lifting him up—fuck, he was strong. Drummer's arms. Shoulders that Ray could lick and suck and bite.

Zavier lowered Ray slowly, and his cock was there, pressing against Ray's hole, then stretching and burning. Ray groaned as Zavier entered him. The fullness, the pain that turned to sparks and heat in his blood.

"Oh," Zavier breathed out. "Yes. Like that."

Ray didn't know what he was doing. He held on with his legs and cried out every time Zavier thrust up into him. This was going to kill him. The decadence, the sheer overload. Zavier pounding up, hard, fast, each stroke a perfection of light and sound and rhythm. Ray rocked in time, finding

Zavier's beat, and added his own melody of grunts and pleas and moans on top.

He wanted so badly to come. If his hands had been free, he'd have been beating himself off to get there. But Zavier had taken that away, and given him so much.

"Look at me," Zavier murmured against his ear.

Their gazes met, and there was fire in those eyes as they tracked over Ray's face. "That's it, Ray, let go. Let it all go for me." He held Ray's hips in a bruising grip and thrust up hard. Again and again and again. "Give all of it to me."

Ray was consumed by both ecstasy and agony. The concert. The high of fans screaming his name, the low of Carl's snarl and his words. The fear he'd never be good enough. His rage at Zavier for saying no all those years ago. All those moments became the sobs, the cries, and the moans he threw at Zavier. He didn't know what he was saying or if anything made sense, but Zavier didn't stop moving inside him, didn't stop the sweet and agonizing beat.

Zavier seemed to drink all of Ray's words down with moans and cries of his own, until at last he wrapped a hand around Ray's dick and pumped.

Different rhythm, faster and tighter. Ray wouldn't last another second, no matter what command. "Zav, I can't, I can't..."

"Come for me, Ray. For *me*."

The world split into light and the shattering music of sparks and colors, and his whole body burned. Ray was vaguely aware of Zavier's surprised curse and his rhythm falling to pieces as he thrust into Ray's body. At the end, Zavier held Ray, his cock buried inside, and his breath coming in huffs on Ray's shoulder.

Everything was perfect. No noise, no chaos. Just the rumble of a motor, Zavier's kiss on his shoulder, and Ray's gloriously aching body. He held on to the oblivion until the colors faded and his leg told him this wasn't the most comfortable arrangement.

But even then, some of the peace remained, so he closed his eyes and leaned into Zavier.

"That's some benefits," he murmured.

Zavier laughed, and that was heaven, too.

ZAVIER EASED OUT OF RAY, THOUGH HE WISHED HE COULD HAVE remained buried longer. Wanted to hold on to the compliant and relaxed man in his arms for a few more minutes. But practicality won out over desire.

Besides, he needed to free Ray's wrists. Took a bit to unwind the wrap—cuffs would have been easier, but he hadn't thought of packing those. Or rather, he had, but decided against it because he wasn't going to get involved with Ray.

He had absolutely no regrets about tonight. None. Ray had needed him, had needed *this*.

And so had he.

Once his arms were free, Ray wrapped them around Zavier's neck. "Thank you." It was a whisper of words. "You have no idea."

Zavier rubbed his back. He knew, probably more than Ray realized. "Your ass is going to hurt tomorrow."

"Don't care. Will remind me of you."

Admittedly, he enjoyed the hell out of that thought—Ray aching and cursing, then remembering Zavier's hands and cock. "Good."

A chuckle from Ray.

"I need to get up," Zavier said. "Lose the condom."

Ray muttered something but relaxed, so Zavier shifted him over and poured him onto the leather cushions, grateful there was enough space to lay him out. Zavier stood and pulled off the rubber. In the adjoining tiny bathroom, he wrapped it in tissues and stuffed it in the trash.

When he stepped back into the lounge, Ray wiggled on the couch and winced. "Fuck, you're brutal."

"That was *hardly* brutal." A little spanking and some fucking? He shook his head and chuckled. "But the real question is...did you enjoy it?"

Ray stilled. *"Yes."* So much emotion was balled up into that one word. Ray reached for him...

...and Zavier went. Because after was just as important as before and during. Maybe more so. He lay down and wrapped himself around Ray, spooning against his back.

Ray settled in, relaxing against him. "I loved it," he said. "Is that weird?"

"Not one bit."

Ray trembled, the night catching up with him. The adrenaline slipping away. "You won't use it against me, will you?"

"Never." Zavier stroked his hair.

"Because I know I'm not—I'm not—" He gave a helpless grunt.

Oh, Ray. You're far more than you believe. "Do you trust me?" Zavier whispered the question against Ray's neck, and he shivered in Zavier's arms, his body still trembling from orgasm, pleasure, and exhaustion.

"Yes." Same answer as before. "God, yes. After tonight, I'll never not trust you, Zav."

He kissed the back of Ray's neck. "Good. Because I want to tell you something. It's not speculation, it's not belief or opinion, it's goddamned fact. You're an astounding musician. And you work fucking hard. You love the fans."

There was a catch to Ray's breathing.

"Twisted Wishes...this band you've allowed me to join, to be a part of...is something so brilliant, I don't know why the whole world isn't falling at your feet, where it belongs."

Ray huffed a laugh. "Now *that's* an opinion."

Zavier nipped the skin on his neck. "Hush. I'm not blowing smoke up your ass."

"Just plowing your cock there." Laughter and joy.

Yeah, he had, and he would again. As often as Ray liked and their schedule allowed. "*Listen*, Ray."

He settled down and melted against Zavier.

"Carl's gonna come at you again. Bastard like that can't help it. He'll look for that opening and jam in the blade, and it's gonna hurt. And when it does, I want you to remember this moment, right now, with me."

"Okay..." A whisper of breath warmed Zavier's arm.

"There's nowhere I'd rather be in this world, no job I'd rather have than in your band as your drummer. It's a fucking *honor* to be here."

Ray shook, then gulped a breath and something close to a sob burst out of him. "You...you..." Then he was crying. Silently, but unmistakably.

Good. If there was anyone who deserved to be cracked apart by truth and joy, it was Ray Van Zeller.

They stayed like that for a while, until Ray murmured and turned. "We gotta be close to wherever they're stopping by now."

Probably. Zavier gave Ray's neck one more kiss, then let him go. They both rose.

For the amount of pleasure they'd had, there was surprisingly little debris. A condom wrapper. The bottle of lube. The length of sports tape he'd used to tie Ray up. Clothes. There were a few drops of lube or maybe semen on the leather, but that would wipe up easily.

"Why don't you crawl into your bunk? I'll clean up."

"You sure?" Ray's voice was still full of weight, with a touch of slurring. Either exhaustion or subspace. Didn't matter, really.

Zavier hooked his arm in Ray's. "Yeah. Let's get you to bed." Didn't take much coaxing to clean the spunk off Ray or get him in his sweats. Ray even drank a bottle of water for him.

"I like this." Ray slipped into the upper bunk.

"Being fucked?" He pulled the privacy curtain closed until just Ray's head and shoulders were visible.

A sleepy, happy chuckle. "That too. So good."

If that wasn't it... "What do you like, Ray?"

Those whiskey-gold eyes looked up at him. "You taking care of me."

Words as warm as Ray's gaze, and they cascaded through Zavier, heating him in a way sex never did. This was joy—taking care of Ray, easing his burdens.

He leaned over and kissed Ray on the forehead. "It was my pleasure."

Ray closed his eyes and murmured something Zavier didn't catch—then fell asleep. He turned off the light in the bunk and carefully pulled the curtain the rest of the way shut.

A pleasure indeed, and an honor. He truly enjoyed Ray's company and his friendship. Mish and Dom were good people, too, but Ray—he understood Ray. The drive and passion, and even the fear, too.

He hummed a few quiet bars from "White Hot Midnight," found his own sweatpants to put on, and headed back into the lounge.

Cleaning up was easy. He wiped himself and the leather cushion, and shoved his clothes away, along with the tape, the condoms, and the lube. Ray's things he folded and left on the couch in the lounge. Wouldn't be out of place, since Ray had a habit of forgetting to pick up bits of his clothing.

But rather than crawl into his berth, he grabbed his tablet and settled into the seating area up front. The bus would be stopping soon. Plus, he was still high from Ray and his moans and cries—that on top of the warmth of pouring a happy Ray into bed.

His mailbox was hell—why the hell had he signed up for

so many mailing lists? He needed another account just for spam and ten-percent-off coupons. He kept deleting mail until he reached a familiar name.

Nadia. Zavier hovered his finger over the message box. The preview read: *Darling, be careful.* There was an attachment.

His good humor fled and apprehension took up its nest. No choice, really. He tapped the screen.

A photo, dark and a little grainy, but unmistakably him and Ray, on the path between the venue and the buses. Taken with a telephoto, if he had to guess—because no one had been that close to them.

They weren't touching, but that didn't matter, since both of their expressions were clear. Two men, either about to fight or fuck.

Shit. He didn't hide his sexuality, never had. Neither had Ray. But the press was *horrible* about queer men who were having enjoyable sex lives—and this was exactly the kind of stress Ray didn't need. Especially not after tonight. Especially not with Carl breathing down his neck.

Zavier turned off the tablet. There was nothing he could do. Tomorrow, he'd see what the damage online was, then talk to Ray.

Tonight, he'd keep enjoying the time he'd spend giving Ray exactly what he'd needed.

CHAPTER
SEVENTEEN

THE MURMUR OF CONVERSATION OVER THE RUMBLE OF THE BUS woke Ray. He was sore in a way he hadn't been in so long, and that was damn good. Zavier had fucked him. Spanked *and* fucked him. Made him cry with pain, pleasure, and understanding, then taken him out of this world.

Wasn't love—Zavier had been pretty darn clear about that —but it was something strong. Friendship. Caring. Ray trusted Zavier, and Zavier liked him. Behind the weight of that utter truth, all the shit Carl had said slid into the background.

"You should show him." Dom's voice.

"I will." Zavier did one of his bitter chuckle things. "I didn't realize what the pictures of us onstage looked like to everyone."

Mish snorted. "Oh, hon. For how observant you are, you have a huge fucking blind spot, don't you?"

"You're not the first to say that."

The coffee machine gurgled. Oh, thank god. Ray flipped over onto his back and every nerve fired at once. "Ow, fuck!" He clamped a hand over his mouth, but the damage was done. They knew he was awake now.

Mish was laughing. By the time Ray crawled out of his bunk and flopped into his usual spot on the couch—wincing as he did—Dom was blushing, probably because he'd seen Ray too many times the morning after a good round of sex. Plus Zavier had that *smirk*.

"So you *did* fuck last night." Dom looked right at Ray, but reading his expression was impossible, because it looked a little like relief and that couldn't be right.

Zavier held up the carafe. "Coffee, Ray?"

"Please." He cleared his throat and met Dom's gaze. "Yeah. We fucked last night."

"Took you long enough." Dom looked longingly at the coffeepot.

What? "Umm..." He stared at Dom.

"Jesus, you guys have wanted into each other's pants since the audition." Dom rolled his eyes. "Then you were such shits to each other with the taunting and teasing. It was getting damn annoying."

Ray didn't know what to say. Zavier was blatantly not looking his way at all as he poured two mugs, though his smile was that fucking know-it-all number he wore sometimes. Ray settled on watching Mish.

She shrugged. "I'm with Dom on this. You guys got it out of your system?"

It was Zavier who answered. "No." A simple word. He handed Ray coffee and sat next to him with his own. "Not at all."

Now Dom had that fucking smirk. "Yeah, didn't think it would be that easy for either of you."

Well—yeah, Ray wasn't satisfied with only one night with Zav. Didn't expect it to be just one night, either. Especially not when it came to the whole spanking and ordering part. He wanted more of that—and more of Zavier screwing him into mindless pleasure. But also more of that singular understanding. The way Zav had tucked him in.

Shit. Because he hadn't expected Zavier to take care of him like that. His cheeks heated and he sipped his coffee. "Um, what were you guys talking about before I got up?"

They all moved cagily. Well, not Zavier—he pulled out his tablet, woke it up, and handed it to Ray. "Tell me what you see."

Shit. *Shit*. It was a photo of him and Zav, standing outside the concert venue, when he'd been so fucking upset at Carl. You could see both their faces. His was full of anger and pain, and Zavier was a picture of sex and determination. They looked exactly like two men about to go fuck.

Which they had been.

"We're...this is right before we came back to the bus."

Zavier nodded, took a sip of coffee, and scrolled the photo up so the headline appeared.

ENEMIES OR LOVERS?

Oh. Ray scrolled the photo back and took another look. Yeah, okay. They might have also been about ready to scream at each other. "I—what do we do about it?"

Zavier grunted. "Let me show you a few other things."

More photos, this time from a couple concerts. All of Ray or Zavier or both. And their expressions when they looked at each other—holy shit. No wonder Dom wasn't surprised.

"I didn't realize I was so—" Ray waved a hand "—obvious." He sipped his coffee to steady him.

"Same, actually. Usually I'm more opaque."

Mish rose and got her own coffee, and one for Dom. "Both of you are so open when we're onstage." She settled back down onto the couch and lifted an eyebrow at Zavier. "I'm guessing you were a lot less expressive when playing in an orchestra."

Zavier seemed to think about that for a while. "It was *different*. There was passion, but it was more personal, more contained. Shorter bursts."

Mish nodded. "Well, there you go."

Ray eyed the tablet. "You have another tab open."

"Ah. Yes. That one." Zavier waved at the tablet. "Open it."

Ray clicked on it and stared. "This is a fanfic site." Then he read and his stomach dropped straight through the floor of the bus. It was a fanfic page for Twisted Wishes. Real person fanfic. And he was staring at the category list for Ray/Zav. The number of fics was impressive, given that Zavier had been in the band all of two and a half months. "Fuck."

Part of him was really creeped out. He wasn't a fictional character to play around with. Flesh and blood. Real feelings. But another part of him was a very curious. "Have you read any of these?"

A pause while Zavier drank some coffee. Then he shrugged. "I skimmed a few. You're not you and I'm not me and some of the acts—well. I think we'd need to be made of something a bit more bendable than bone."

Dom snorted.

"Yeah, but they got any good ideas? Should we be taking notes?"

Zavier pinned Ray with a gaze that made the rest of the world drop away. "I have a much better set of notes for that, Ray."

"TMI," Dom practically squeaked.

And hell, Ray's dick went all nice and hard for Zavier's voice and the way it played along his nerves. Notes. Zavier had *notes* on how to fuck him. He shivered and gulped down another couple swallows of coffee. "Okay. But what do we do about all of it?"

Zavier waved a hand. "Own it."

"You mean, tell people?" God, Carl would flip. On the other hand... Carl would *flip* and there was a certain delight in *that*.

Mish cleared her throat. "Honey, the interesting thing is that by and large, the fans love the thought of you and Zav."

"You wouldn't actually have to say anything," Dom said.

"Just keep doing what you're doing. I mean, it's not like you guys stare goo-goo eyes at each other. Or that you're all over each other, touching and kissing."

Zavier shook his head. "Not at all my thing."

Because Zavier didn't do relationships.

"Yeah, so if you stare at each other like you want to set each other on fire, that's like...normal." Dom blushed. "Well, for you two."

Because it was all about the benefits of being friends. The heat and the sex and kneeling at Zavier's feet. Man, Ray's dick really was into that, too. And his pulse and his blood.

"Makes sense," he murmured. He finished his coffee, then rose. "I should go shower. We gotta be close to the venue, and if I'm sitting here in sweatpants and nothing else, that's just one more thing for Carl to dig into about."

He set the mug on the counter. "Thanks for the coffee, Zav." And last night. And taking care of him. But he couldn't say those, so he scooped up his toiletry bag and a set of clean clothes, and headed to the back of the bus.

Ray showered using cooler water than he generally did, and dressed quickly. He had a good deal of stubble, but there'd be time before the show to shave. Or maybe he wouldn't.

When he stepped out of the bathroom, he wasn't all that surprised to find Zavier sitting in the little lounge, and the privacy curtain drawn shut. "Hey."

Zavier smiled and cocked his finger, beckoning Ray to him.

With a start, Ray realized Zavier was sitting exactly where he had been last night. He crossed what little distance that divided them and knelt. No idea why, but it seemed the perfect thing to do. The effects of his cooler-than-normal shower evaporated as heat and need took over.

"Oh, very good." Soft words. Zavier cupped Ray's face

and stroked his cheeks. "Close your eyes and breathe. Listen. Wait."

Ray did as told, and everything turned sublime. The rumble of the bus. Zavier's warm hands. His own breath, in and out. No idea how long they sat there.

"Don't open your eyes." Another brush of Zavier's thumb. "I want you to tell me the truth—are you fine with us not hiding this? Being—not obvious, but not concealing, either."

"Yeah." The answer was simple, and it startled Ray a little. "Doesn't change much, does it?"

"For the people out there? No. For us? Maybe. It's an acknowledgment, Dom and Mish knowing."

"Just means they'll give us space."

Zavier's chuckle was low. "Like now."

Ray tried to nod. "Do you want—I mean—" He sighed. "I was trying not to be turned on by you. Took a cold shower and everything."

"And here you are, all nice and hard for me again." Zavier grinned. "I could get you off. Probably quicker than you'd like, but we *are* in a time crunch."

Ray swayed as the bus slowed down and pulled around a curve.

"Or," Zavier continued, "you can hold on to that need until later, and I can draw it out of you slowly and in ways you may not have experienced before."

Ray shivered. "The second option sounds like it might kill me. I want that."

Zavier stroked his thumb over Ray's lips. "Give me your hand."

He did, and Zavier brought it to his own thick erection, housed in his jeans. "You're not the only one waiting for later."

"Good." Ray licked his lips and tasted traces of salt and Zavier. "If we're gonna do this, I want you as invested."

Zavier sat back and chuckled. "I am. Believe me." He rose and pulled Ray up. "Come on, let's go look bored and tired for Carl. I think we're nearly there."

Yeah, the bus was moving a lot slower now. Ray grabbed his shower gear while Zavier opened the curtain and headed up front. After Ray shoved his shit into his bunk, he joined the others. "We didn't figure out the set list."

Mish pursed her lips. "Let's talk it out over catered donuts and a shit-ton more coffee."

Zavier lounged like he hadn't a care in the world. "We should shake it up a bit."

Yeah. And judging from Dom's and Mish's nods, they were all for that plan, too. He'd have to grab his notebook before they got off the bus. But right now, there were too many stops and turns. He closed his eyes.

Mish and Dom were fine with him screwing Zavier—or rather Zavier screwing *him*. The fans wanted it. They worked well on stage and provided speculation for the press. He grunted. "Carl's gonna be so pissed."

"Good." Zavier's voice, but it was echoed by Mish and Dom, and that warmed Ray's heart. If nothing else, he had the band. His band. His *friends*.

And one with some really amazing benefits.

THERE WAS NOTHING BETTER THAN THE ANTICIPATION OF waiting. Or, Zavier mused, watching others wait. He enjoyed both thoroughly. Pleasure was always more intense when denied before. That explained why he was still reeling from his night with Ray—they had been dancing around each other for so long. And no, one night wasn't enough for either of them. Not nearly.

Ray had knelt without hesitation. God, that alone played along Zavier's nerves and sweetened what was to come. But there were pleasures he could indulge in sooner, too. Like a little touch of sadism, not from caring but from the exact opposite. This time, his target was Carl, the lying, scheming, utterly contemptible band manager.

All of the members of Twisted Wishes were dressed—Domino had made his reappearance—and mostly caffeinated by the time the bus pulled into their next venue, another outdoor amphitheater.

Unsurprisingly, Carl was waiting once the bus parked. He climbed into the bus and snarled, "What the *fuck* is this?" He was holding a tablet with that photo of Zavier and Ray from the previous night.

Enemies or lovers? Kill or fuck? Zavier knew the answer to that one. In his blood and written on the skin of Ray's ass. He cocked his head at Carl. "Why, it's a picture of me and Ray." He turned to Ray. "Doesn't that look like a picture of me and you?"

Ray leaned forward for a better look. "It does, yeah. Isn't that when we were talking last night?"

"Think so. Damn, they've got a good lens." Zavier shook his head. "Gotta give 'em credit for that."

Carl stared at them. Mish was trying not to laugh, and Dom had his nose in a book.

"This isn't a joke." Carl tucked the tablet under his arm. "What the hell were you two doing?"

"Talking." Zavier crossed his arms. "Funny thing. We'd just finished a killer concert as a headlining act, one that had fans on their feet the whole night and which was critically acclaimed by the press—" he held up his own tablet to an article by a well-respected music critic "—and yet, someone read Ray the riot act for not being good enough. Weird, huh?"

Carl stared at him. "Demos, you better remember that you're not part of this band."

A cold chill wormed through Zavier's chest. "It's true. I'm an outsider who knows music at an echelon most people don't even know exists. And I rather agree with her." He tapped the case of his tablet, still open to the music critic. "Even if I was also in the middle of that amazing moment."

"Carl." Ray's voice was soft. "Can we please cut the crap? What do you want from us, from me? I checked the charts, and we're on them. Spotify's featuring us. We're charting on iTunes." He shook his head. "If you just want to see me bleed, there's a knife in a drawer over there. You're welcome to go at me with it."

Well, that wasn't Ray's style at all. Zavier rocked on the balls of his feet. It was fucking fantastic, and about time, but he worried about the sudden shift.

"Or me," Dom said. "I'm quiet and all, but I bleed just the same."

Mish snorted. "Me? I'll tear your arm off."

Zavier clicked his tongue. "Mish, violence is not the answer."

Carl's face turned red, then white. Oh, there was rage—but also fear peeking out from behind. Uncertainty. He didn't know how to handle this united, outspoken front. "Yeah, well. I don't want to see anymore headlines about fighting." He paused, and a little curl of distaste took up residence in his voice. "Or being lovers."

"But the fans love that part!" Mish stood and looked down at Carl. "Two beautiful men eying each other? Gets the blood moving."

Carl shook his head. "There's DJs from the local radio station here. You're scheduled for a live interview in an hour. Hope you're better behaved with them." Carl spun and fled the bus.

Silence descended for a minute or two, then Mish blew out a breath. "Fuckin' A, that felt good."

It had. Zavier eyed Ray. Small smile and a bright look. "Yeah. But I'm sure he'll make us pay. It's just a matter of when."

"But now maybe he'll fuck with all of us, and not you." Dom tossed his book aside. "Did he really slam you down after the concert yesterday?" The smile fell away, and Ray nodded. "That man's an asshole."

"Which is more or less what Zav said." Ray rose and grabbed his notebook. "Let's go find donuts and hammer out the set list before we have to go answer embarrassing questions from radio personalities."

They found the donuts in a well-appointed lounge. Their crew was already unloading equipment and shit, and the catering coffee for both the band and the crew was top-notch.

Once they got their sugar fix, Ray cleaned his fingers of cinnamon sugar and locked eyes with Zavier. "You suggested shaking things up."

"I did." His pulse beat a little faster. What did Ray have up his sleeve? Hell, Mish and Dom leaned in, too.

"What if we open with 'White Hot Midnight'?" Ray's grin was toothy and excited and *stunning*. Somehow, Zavier would get a piece of that tonight. He wasn't sure how, given the close quarters they shared, but he'd figure it out.

"And close with?" Mish asked. "Gotta be something damn good."

"Let's figure it out," Ray said.

They tossed song ideas around until they came up with a lineup that was different but still as exciting. "Lightning" became an encore and "Bleeding Roses," a slower, ballad-like song got thrown into their little acoustic set.

"We should do some covers." Dom rubbed his chin. "Like that punk version of 'Born in the USA' we played around with a couple years ago."

"Hmm. A homage to the Boss and home." Zavier peered at Mish. "Well, maybe for three of us at least?" He had no idea where Mish had grown up, but he, Dom, and Ray were all from New Jersey.

"Oh, I'm a heathen from the other side of the river in

Pennsylvania, from around Windgap." She leaned back. "We kinda love Springsteen, too, you know."

Zavier laughed. Of course. "Bet you even went to the Shore, huh?"

"Don't make me hit you with a donut, Zavier, honey." Her words were as sweet as her smile.

He held up his hands in surrender. Because Mish? She had good aim. He'd seen her nail Dom with a sock, and bop Ray in the back with an empty water bottle. He had no desire to get powdered sugar all over him...unless it was so he could order Ray to lick it off. He added that to his mental checklist, then shoved all those thoughts away.

It was interview time.

Despite Ray's crack about the types of questions, the band interview went well, even if a little odd. It was live on the radio and being fucking played over the outside speakers. Couldn't exactly hear their own words, but the cadence was there, on a few-second delay, filtering into the room from an open door down a hallway.

Of course, the DJs started in on the questions about Kevin, but Ray handled it gracefully.

"Look, I know everyone wants to know all the details. But man, I don't want to keep dragging him out with this. The press has been hounding on him, too, and that's not fair." He paused. "Kevin's a good guy. Can we cut him a break?"

After that, they did. Then came the question Zavier had been wondering about himself.

"So, what's next for you guys?" The DJ looked honestly curious.

"Well..." Ray scratched the back of his head, which was a nervous tic.

If Zavier had been closer, he'd have pressed his calf against Ray's. *There's no wrong answer here.*

"I've got some new songs stirring in my brain, and I know

the band's ready to start working on another album once the tour is finished."

Both Mish and Dom agreed, their voices blending together.

"Yes."

"Hell yeah."

"Does that include Zavier?"

Ray's whiskey eyes met Zavier's, and there was a little hope and a little fear there. "I'd—we'd like it to, but that's up to Zav."

Zavier couldn't look away from Ray. "Are you asking me to join your band, Ray Van Zeller?" Maybe his voice was a little too playful, but fuck it. *This* he'd tease Ray about until they were old and gray.

Ray got his lovely blush. "Seems like I'm always asking you that question, rock star. What'll it be?"

He huffed a laugh. "Best times I've had in my musical career have been touring with you guys. Yes, I'll join your band."

There must have been enough fans in the venue—or maybe that was the crew—but a cheer went up outside a few seconds after the echo of them talking. Zavier straightened out in his chair. "That's not for us, is it?"

The noise got a little louder.

"Yeah, I think it's for us," Dom said.

Which meant the press would have fun with that. But hey, it was good news, not more *Has Van Zeller Lost It?* shit.

The DJs finished the interview and the band got ready for sound check. Somehow they managed to pull together a version of the Boss's anthem that was also very Twisted Wishes. It was challenging to do and they read each other so well as a band. The VIP guests loved it. Ray was shining in his element and the day was bright.

In the back of his mind, Zavier knew Carl was lurking, but

until the asshole struck, they'd revel in their sound and the crowd and *everything*.

With the world lifted off his shoulders and music in his veins, Ray was a sight to behold. Zavier would certainly do his part to keep him like that—and relish every moment, breath, and moan doing so.

After the sound check, they headed back to the lounge and dressing rooms. Dom ducked out to the bus for his book and Mish was hanging out with the crew, which left him and Ray alone as they made their way to the dressing rooms. Ray gave him a look that was sly and full of teeth, and slipped into one of the rooms. Well now, someone wanted a little action. Zavier followed and shut the door.

Ray leaned up against the vanity on the far side of the room. "I figured we had a few moments by ourselves."

"So we do. Which makes me wonder why you're over there and not kneeling at my feet." Zavier pointed to the floor in front of him.

A lovely blush crept up Ray's neck, and he was across the room and on his knees in an instant.

Good. While they'd set ground rules, they hadn't talked about how they'd start scenes, especially given the limited time and privacy they had. Zavier ran his fingers through Ray's hair. "You can always kneel if you want to play, Ray. Or ask me to fuck you, or however you wish. But if you don't want to, simply say 'red' and I'll back off."

"Safeword for even starting?" He looked up. "I'm saying yes now."

Indeed, he was. Large pupils. Slight trembles. All that lovely tension. "I don't want to be manhandling you and pressing you against a wall if that's not your thing. Consent is sexy."

Ray smiled. "That—I want that. Yeah, maybe not always, but I promise I'll tell you if it's too much. Or the wrong time.

But please, please, surprise me. I need—" He took a breath. "I want to surrender. Make me."

Oh, that was just too good to pass up. He tightened his hand in Ray's hair. "You remember how I taught you to touch yourself?"

No nodding—his hand was too tight in Ray's hair. "Yeah. I remember."

"Get your dick out and show me. *Slowly*."

He didn't loosen his hold in Ray's hair, but Ray obeyed—and nearly perfectly, too. Took that hard cock out of his pants and into his hand and stroked its length so slowly. Teased the head. Pressed into the slit. Twisted and slid.

He panted. "Can I touch my balls?"

"Yes."

Such a show at his feet. Ray, his eyes closed, his mouth open, jacking himself off. Fondling his nuts. If they didn't have a show in a few hours, Zavier would have whipped out his own dick and fucked Ray's mouth.

Ray hissed. "Fuck." Oh, he was close. Tempting to let him come, but even more to let him dance on stage and sing unsatisfied.

"Stop."

Ray flicked his eyes opened and sighed, but he stopped. And that was lovely, too. The obedience. "You're gonna make me wait."

"As I said before." Zavier stepped in and pressed his hard length against Ray's face. "And you're still not alone in that."

Ray nuzzled Zavier's jeans-covered shaft with his lips and nose. "You should wear leather tonight."

Zavier pulled back on Ray's hair. "Up, please."

Ray rose, his jeans hanging open, and Zavier spun him around. "Hands on the vanity." He spoke the order into Ray's ear.

A little moan, and Ray obeyed. A few taps of Zavier's

hands against the inside of Ray's thighs had him spreading his legs so nicely. All the tension fled from Ray's body. "Zav..."

"You like this?" He stroked down Ray's sides. So much clothing between them, but Ray still moved under his touch. Liquid and needy.

"Yeah. Can't think when you do this. Don't wanna..."

That was part of the point. Zavier chuckled and peeled Ray's pants and underwear down, exposing his ass. "Oh, that's nice." He ran his fingers over the bite mark he'd left. Not a deep bruise, but enough for both of them to know what it was. There was also a smattering of light bruising from the spanking. "I can't wait to lay a crop on you. Or a flogger."

"I—want that." Ray was breathless. "At least try."

Deep thrumming sounded through the room. Five Asylum's sound checks. Zavier pressed a hand against Ray's back. "Oh, we will." He stroked one side of Ray's ass, then slapped it. Hard.

Ray yelped, and Zavier held him in place. A bass refrain cut through the air and before Ray could settle, Zavier spanked the other cheek. "So here's a little rule when we're playing like this: you don't tell me what I should do."

"Oh fuck. Zav—I—"

Another blow, then another. And more until he'd laid down ten blows to each cheek.

Ray groaned, but through it all, he hadn't moved much. Hadn't tried to cover his ass. Which said something.

Zavier ran his hand over Ray's ass cheeks. "Was that too much?"

A hiccupped laugh, then a whisper. "No." Ray bowed his head. "I liked it. I hated it too, but I *liked* it." He chuckled again. "Which I guess kind of defeats the purpose of punishing me."

"Not at all." Zavier skimmed his fingers between the

cheeks and brushed Ray's hole, which earned him a deeper moan. "It leaves you hot and bothered and wanting me, which is its own punishment."

Ray sighed. "Yeah. I'll give you that."

Zavier tapped his ass lightly. "Get dressed. As much as I'm enjoying this, we're pushing our luck."

Ray moved slowly and carefully, but in a short time was relatively decent again, albeit with an impressive bulge in his pants. Not that Zavier could fault him. His own erection bordered on painful.

When Ray was done, he met Zavier's gaze. "Can I at least ask for a kiss?" That sly smile was back.

Zavier grabbed the back of Ray's neck and kissed that grin right off him. They moaned and melted and ground against each other—not so much a scene anymore, but two men desperate to tangle into each other until they both got what they wanted.

Ray broke the kiss. "Okay, maybe that was a bad idea."

Zavier dug his fingers into Ray's tender ass and savored the way they moved against each other. He could get off just on that. "I don't know. I like your mouth, Ray."

"And you haven't even fucked it yet." A murmur of words in his ear.

They eased apart. "Don't tempt me. You need that instrument of yours."

Ray scrubbed the back of his neck. "Yeah, I know. I should probably go pre-game with tea."

Yeah, that would be wise. Zavier stepped forward and claimed another kiss. "Go. I'll start getting changed."

Man, that smile was really everything. It looked so good on Ray, so easy. He gave a little salute and slipped out the dressing room door.

Zavier sank down into the nearest chair and cast a look around. He hadn't been planning on leather tonight—it was hotter than hell out—but maybe he could compromise with something on the tighter side. Or really loose.

This is different, his mind whispered. And it was. It had been a long time, and if he were being truthful, the first time he'd enjoyed a partner both in and *out* of bed.

CHAPTER
EIGHTEEN

ANOTHER SHOW THAT BLEW THE PREVIOUS ONES AWAY. RAY didn't comprehend how they'd done it, only that they had. Top of their game. Every note perfect. The songs, the crowd, the way Dom stalked across the stage. Mish's stellar solo that had both men and women tossing their underwear on the stage. Hell, he wanted to whip his out, too, if only because of her playing.

Zavier wasn't wearing his fucking sexy-ass leather pants, but he'd lined one wrist and arm with leather bands and a stylish cuff. The pants he wore were flowing and slit from the cuff up the sides, high enough you could almost see his package.

Almost. A shame Ray couldn't—though he'd tasted that dick on his tongue. Felt it inside him.

God, his ass hurt, and maybe that was why he'd danced so hard. The moment he stopped, it stung like fuck, but if he moved, the burn was good.

He'd never thought he'd like being ordered around, or spanked, or any of that. But with Zav, it seemed so...natural. Right.

The signing line was kind of hell with a burning ass and a dick that wanted nothing more than to be fondled and stroked by the drummer next to him.

Zavier's attention was currently on the young woman before him. "Classical is a superb way to learn rhythms beyond the standard 4/4 or the outrageous 6/8." He winked at the girl and signed her poster. "Seriously, though, don't give up on orchestra. Use what you know for rock." She nodded and moved on.

Fuck, Zavier really was too much. Part of Ray figured he was in way over his head, but the other part kept repeating what Zavier had said—that Ray was a fine musician. Dom said it, and Mish, too. Carl said the opposite.

Ray shook himself and smiled up at the next fan. "Hey, how ya doing?"

The young dark-skinned man stammered, "Fine." Then continued with "Oh my god, that was the best concert I've ever been to." Which got mashed into "This is my boyfriend and I just came out to my parents and they were okay with it and I'll stop now." The kid blinked. "Thank you."

Indeed, he was holding hands with another kid, who blushed and waved. "Hi."

"Hey, you guys. Congrats! That's all wonderful." They had Twisted Wishes T-shirts, and he scrawled his signature on them. "You two keep being yourselves, no matter what the world tells you, okay?"

They beamed and moved away so the next person could talk to him.

Yeah, he needed to listen to Zav. And himself.

The signings took forever, but they weren't leaving until the last person came through the line. After that, they piled back on the bus and collapsed as they took off for yet another city. Phoenix this time. They'd get another break when they got to Utah and a longer one in California. Ray couldn't fucking wait. Yeah, the concerts were phenomenal, but they did wear on the body and mind after a while. How did Gregor Daye do it in his fifties? Ray was twenty-six and could barely manage.

He glanced over at Zavier, who was back in jeans and a T-shirt, but those leather bracelets and cuff were still on his arm. Ray stared at Zavier's wrist. What it would be like to have cuffs of a very different sort on *his* wrists?

Zavier raised an eyebrow and smiled, as if he knew.

But the bus was moving, and Mish and Dom were here, so it wasn't like anything was going to happen. Didn't keep his mind and dick from wanting Zavier's hands and mouth on him. That cock in his ass.

They chatted for a while, going over the best bits of the concert. Mish had loved opening with "White Hot Midnight," while Dom had loved the acoustical set.

"What about you?" Dom lounged on the couch and looked about ready to fall asleep.

"It's hard to choose just one," Ray said. And it was true. His mind flitted between the fans and the music and the fucking colors in his head. All of it sang in his blood, but the cries of the fans and their smiles and wide eyes in the signing lines stood out most of all.

"That seems unfair," Zavier murmured. He was stretched out like always, feet against Ray. "You made everyone else pick."

"Not you." He met those very blue eyes. "What was your favorite moment?"

Zavier took a deep breath and held Ray enwrapped with his stare. "When you dashed out into the crowd and sang 'Bleeding Roses' with the woman who had tears in her eyes."

Heat to Ray's cheeks. Her name had been Charlie, and she'd thanked him in such a husky voice when they'd finished. Her favorite song. He'd no idea why it had moved her so, but it didn't matter. "The fans are always my favorite moments."

The smile that danced over Zavier's lips was heat and light and wrapped itself into Ray's soul.

Eventually, they all crawled into their bunks, murmuring their good-nights. Ray considered jerking off, but somehow he got the feeling that would disappoint Zavier, especially after the band's conversation. Besides, there was something sensual and edgy about the tension in his body and mind. *Good* tension for a change, not anxiety.

He should have pulled out his notebook, because little snippets of the song he was starting to think of as "Dare to Be" flitted in his mind. More words. Burgundy hues and blue like Zavier's eyes all slipped and floated behind his eyelids until they twisted and slipped away into nothing at all. Later, awareness crept back in, along with his bladder screaming at him. *Fuck.* All that water during the show. The bus was quiet but for the rumble of the road and Dom's quiet snores. Hopefully Ray wouldn't wake anyone.

He slipped out of his bunk and headed to the back of the bus. When he was finished and he'd washed his hands, he stared at his reflection in the mirror. This part of touring wasn't exactly what he'd dreamed of when he'd imagined being a rock star. Hell, he wasn't even sure he *was* a star. Everything seemed elusive, but that might have been the hour and the haze of sleep that still clung to him. He shut off the light and headed out into the lounge.

The privacy curtain was drawn across the entry to the rest of the bus and a small reading light had been turned on over the couch, illuminating Zavier's black hair, his naked chest, and his gray sweatpants. Ray let out a breath, and every part of his body rejoiced.

Like before, he crossed the space between them and knelt down, clasping his hands behind his back. Zavier didn't utter a word, just slid a hand into Ray's hair and tightened his grip.

The sweet, sharp tugging against his scalp sent lust straight to his balls. He'd always loved his hair pulled and Zav seemed to have homed right in on that.

Zavier still didn't speak, but his smile melted Ray's bones. With his free hand, he pulled out the hard dick tenting his sweatpants and stroked. In the reading light, precome beaded in the slit. His abs quivered and his sweats slid down when he shifted.

Even though instinct screamed to bend forward and take that taste, Ray didn't. He relished the tight hold on his head, and gave into that. Whatever happened, Zav would make it good. Maybe painful, definitely pleasurable, and hopefully Ray would feel every bit in the morning.

Zavier's grunt was one of satisfaction. He pulled Ray toward his dick and whispered, "Just the tip."

Ray closed his mouth around the head of the cock he so desperately wanted and licked every bit of salt he could from the slit. He sucked and mouthed what he'd been given, throwing his entire being into pleasing Zavier.

The grip in his hair loosened. "You're fucking unreal, Ray." Satisfaction and pleasure in his voice. "You're making it very hard for me not to fuck your throat."

God, he wanted to give Zavier that. Worship him fully from his knees. Taste Zav's come in his mouth. He moaned.

"I know you'd like that." Zavier tugged him off. "You love being on your knees for me, don't you?"

"Yeah." Ray met that hot stare. "So much." Reminded him of the days when he was first putting Twisted Wishes together. Money was tight, and he'd found several very enjoyable ways to earn some cash. No shame in trading his body for payment. Hell, in a way he still did that with the singing. With Zav, giving a blowjob was better. More intense. Personal. Pleasing him? God, that was a fucking high.

Zavier pulled at his hair. "Stand up and strip." He let go.

The bus might have swayed, or maybe that was his heart and brain, but Ray did as told, kicking his own pants away and waited for the next order.

Zavier stood and shucked his sweats, and pulled Ray to him until they were chest to chest with a warm hand firmly around the back of Ray's neck. Their cocks brushed, and Ray couldn't help thrusting just a little.

The way Zavier's smile sharpened only made him moan.

A click of his tongue. "You were doing so well, too." He pressed a finger to Ray's lips and whispered, "Not a sound. You don't want to wake the others." Those clever fingers drifted down to tease Ray's nipple. The other had stayed clamped around his neck.

He had a pretty good idea what would happen, but it still took all of his energy not to cry out when Zavier pinched and pulled and rolled the nub mercilessly. God, the pain and the ecstasy. He melted against Zavier, who pressed his thigh between Ray's legs.

Hot words in Ray's ears. "Fuck yourself on me."

He did, gripping Zavier and rutting against him, abandoning all sense of propriety, control, decency. All the while, Zavier abused his nipple and ghosted kisses over his shoulder.

"Should I mark you, Ray? Let the press know I'm fucking you?"

Oh god, yes. *Yes.* The desire to answer clashed with the order not to speak. He chanced it anyway. "If that's what you want, Zav. I—yeah."

Zavier let up on his one nipple and switched hands so he could toy with the other, untouched one. "What I want is every bit of you screaming for me." He kissed Ray's shoulder. "Now, no sounds."

Zavier bit Ray's shoulder and clamped fingers around his nipple, yanking hard. The agony was amazing and wonderful, and Ray couldn't breathe. He could barely stand. Wanted to slide down Zavier's body and do whatever the hell he commanded. Everything existed only in that moment between the white heat of pain and the glory of pleasure beating through his blood.

Ray didn't come. Kind of felt like that, but he was still hard and panting and pressing against Zavier, even as he was being held upright because his legs were jelly.

"You're so incredible like this, Ray. You should see yourself." Zavier kissed his neck. "Over to the couch. Kneeling. Hands behind your back and head down."

Zavier guided him, which was good. The words made sense, and he wanted to obey, but he was so fucking high he wasn't sure he was moving right or doing what he needed to. Zavier's tugging and pressing and stroking got him into the right position.

Ray's rasping breath sounded in his ears as he pressed his forehead against the leather of the couch. He needed this. Every ounce of him needed to be grabbed and fucked and given over to Zavier.

Zavier pressed his lips to Ray's ass, licking and biting until Ray couldn't help squirming. He clamped his lips closed, but still couldn't keep from groaning.

A deep chuckle. "Quiet now." Zavier spread Ray's cheeks and mouthed his hole.

Ray rocked and gasped and shoved his fist into his mouth to keep from crying out. It had been *years* since he'd been rimmed. Zavier's tongue pressing into him was like a live wire straight to his balls. He moaned around his hand. Despite the sounds—or maybe because of them—Zavier didn't let up, and *fuck*, was he good. Ray rocked back, wanting and needing more. He was on fire, his whole body aching to come.

"Zav..." He whispered the name like a plea and a prayer and a curse all wrapped into one.

Finally Zavier let up, but only to spit and slide a digit—from the stretch, his thumb—inside Ray. "Shh." He worked Ray's ass, stroking and pressing until Ray was gnawing at his fist again, trying to remain silent. But the grunts and groans slipped out anyway. "So needy, aren't you?" Zavier purred the words, soft and low.

Eventually, he quit finger—or thumb—fucking him, and the sound of a condom wrapper ripping filtered over the thrum of the bus's motor. He spread cool lube into Ray's crack and ass, igniting pinpricks over his back. The thick head of Zavier's cock nudged against his entrance.

Please. Please fuck me already. Screaming it out was out of the question, so he pressed his forehead into the seat cushion and mouthed his knuckle. He was so far gone, he'd probably shoot the moment Zavier stroked him. Or hit his prostate.

"Give me your hands, Ray." Murmured words. Zavier took hold of the one still behind Ray's back—and waited.

He was loath to give it up, but did, offering it at the small of his back. Zavier took the other and brought the wrists together.

"Very good." He thrust forward, driving his cock into Ray.

The burn. The stretch, then the utter joy of being filled. He did groan, not loudly, but enough to elicit a pleased grunt from Zavier, who pulled out and plunged in again.

Being split by Zavier's dick was even better now than the first time. Sharp, rapid thrusts drove breath from Ray's lungs and burned against the bruises from Zavier's spankings. He squirmed with the sharp bursts of heat against his flesh, and torment turned to color and light in his vision.

Oh yeah, he'd feel this in the morning. Love it, too. Loved it right now. He pressed back into Zavier's thrusts, meeting his rhythm until they were one quick beat. Synchronized and perfect, just like on stage.

"Fuck, Ray," Zavier murmured, his voice tight. He shifted

his grip on Ray's wrists, catching them with one hand. The other Zavier wrapped around Ray's dick.

Sparks of bliss and agony burst in Ray's blood. He whimpered. Didn't mean to, but his balls ached and his spine was on fire and he was going to come in an instant. Took every bit he had not to spill over Zavier's hand then and there.

Zavier leaned over him, weighing him down, whispering into his ear. "You wanna come so bad, don't you? But you won't. Not yet."

He stroked Ray harder, and Ray squeezed his eyes closed. Red and white halos flashed in his vision. He was gonna die here. Burst something. He couldn't even plead. It was all he could do to suck down air and rock back on Zavier's cock.

The thrusts ramped up, as did Zavier's hand, and it was fucking perfect—brutal and yet tender. Ray spun between the poles of desire and agony and his whole world tunneled down to color and sound and light.

"Now, Ray."

His orgasm raked through him. Someone gasped—maybe him. Probably him. Then everything hazed and sparked until he couldn't see or hear. Zavier thrust deep, groaning as he came, then stilled and lay over him. He wanted to stay that way forever, but a moment later, Zavier pulled out and let go of Ray's wrists.

"Hey." Zavier whispered the word into his ear.

Ray tried to reply, but it came out as a croak. His head swam in light and darkness and pleasure. Buzzed like being drunk. He swam though the overwhelming feelings, trying to find his way back to coherency.

Hard, especially since he liked being here—fucked into oblivion.

Hands on his body again, this time to turn him to his side and straighten his body out. Zavier crouched in front of him. "Green, yellow, or red?" Concern there.

"Green," Ray murmured. So much so. "That was...incredible."

"Not too much?" Zavier stroked his hair.

"No." His voice was breath. "Never too much. Perfect." He licked his lips. "You fuck me like no one else ever has."

He couldn't tell if it was delight or sadness that flickered over Zavier's face. He leaned in and kissed Ray's forehead. "Man, you've had shitty lovers."

He shrugged. "Not shitty. Just not you. No one's ever pushed me like that. Or asked me what I wanted before we even started. Most just want me to get them off, you know? Or maybe I was the shitty lover, only out for myself." Yeah, that could've been it, too. God, he was an asshole.

Zavier murmured against his forehead, "I'll take care of you, Ray. Fuck you nice and good. Teach you how to please me."

He relaxed into Zavier's embrace. "I don't want to be a burden. I'm such a burden."

"You're no such thing." Zavier chuckled. "And it's not like I'm being entirely altruistic by upending you and ramming your ass until I come."

Okay, there was that. "Will you—will you tie me down someday?"

Zavier exhaled and nibbled at Ray's ear. "Just wait until we get to our next hotel and you see what I ordered off of Amazon."

He never thought those particular words would make him shiver. "Fuck." But of course they'd sell sex toys. They sold *everything*.

Zavier stood and offered him a hand. "Time to sleep, I think."

Ray took it and let Zavier pull him up. Oh yeah, he'd be reminded of this night as soon as he woke in the morning. Zavier turned off the reading light, and they both slipped back into their bunks, as quietly as they could. Dom was still snoring softly. No telling if Mish was awake or not.

Though, if the slight throb on his shoulder was anything to go by, they'd be able to tell something had happened as soon as Ray crawled out of bed. Of *course* Zavier had bitten the shoulder with hardly any ink.

Zavier had marked him. Claimed him. No strings attached but those Ray put there himself. He stared up into the darkness. One thing was for sure: it was nice to be wanted and a relief to be looked after—even only in this manner. He closed his eyes and let the hum of the road and the ache of his body lull him to sleep.

ZAVIER KEPT THE LEATHER BRACELETS AND CUFF ON EVEN WHEN they weren't performing, because Ray couldn't stop looking at them. He'd already ordered several items, including restraints, from Amazon and had them shipped to their next hotel. Yes, the cost of having the box held would be astronomical, but undoubtedly worth it, given the way Ray reacted to every single touch, smile, and suggestion.

The memory of Ray melting into submission at Zavier's feet stirred both need and peace in him. He'd had compliant subs before and bratty ones, too. He'd fucked and played with a great many people in his life, but the way Ray reacted moved Zavier on a deeper level. Toping Ray was *fulfilling*— and not only in the sexual sense.

They *complemented* each other with their friendship, with Ray's brashness, sexuality, kink, and that inherent neediness to be taken from the world.

Unexpected, yes. But like syncopated beats, they might not share the same exact rhythm, but they merged and found each other, over and over. Zavier had wanted that kind of meeting of minds with someone for so long. That he could help Ray as well? Keep him steady and relaxed? Even better.

In Phoenix, Zavier managed to get Ray alone for a few minutes in the hours before they went on stage. Enough time to pull back the collar of his T-shirt and kiss the bruise on his shoulder. The one that looked exactly like the sexy bite mark it was. He'd no doubt when Ray tore off his shirt, every camera would focus on that.

"Carl will have words," Zavier murmured against Ray's skin.

Ray relaxed in Zavier's arms and said, "Let him. Don't care anymore."

At some level, Zavier didn't care, either, but a voice in the back of his brain reminded him that Carl hadn't fucked with Ray—or the band—in a while. Which was unusual and troubling, but he set the worry aside.

"I have something for you." He let Ray's T-shirt cover up the bite mark. "To keep you grounded."

"It's not something like a butt plug, is it?"

Zavier laughed. "I don't think you'd be able to move like you do onstage with even the smallest plug." He paused. "Have you been plugged in the past?"

Red touched Ray's cheeks. "No."

"Played with toys?"

He shook his head.

Oh, good. So some of the other items would be a new experience for Ray, too. "It's not a butt plug." He pulled a thin, tightly woven rainbow-colored cotton bracelet out of his pocket. Ray studied it and held out his wrist.

"No. That's not where it's going." Zavier smiled at Ray. Oh, the confusion, then realization. That blush grew deeper and he shifted from foot to foot. "If you're willing."

"On my dick." Ray licked his lips. "You want to tie it around my dick."

Zavier nodded and waited.

"Yeah. God, yeah. Do it."

So Zavier did. Even dropped to his knees to unzip Ray's pants, which got him a moan. Ray was already semi-hard by the time Zavier freed his dick. Precome and everything. He stole a taste of salt from the tip and savored Ray's gasp and tremble. Then he tied the bracelet around the base, tucked Ray back in the best he could, and zipped him up.

Huge pupils, flushed face. "I can feel it."

"That's the point. I *want* you to feel it. I want you to know who owns your ass, at least in bed."

Ray swallowed. "I thought this was just a sex thing. Not that you *own me* own me."

Yeah, they were walking close to that line. "It's a game. You're still your own. You can take that off if you want and nothing will come of it, I promise." Zavier cocked his head. "You can always, *always* say no to me."

"Green," Ray murmured.

This man was too much. Zavier took that mouth until Ray moaned, then broke the kiss. "Let's go kill 'em tonight."

THEY DID EXACTLY THAT UNTIL THEY WERE DRENCHED IN SWEAT and exhausted. Zavier's back burned and Ray looked like he might fall over, though his smile was so bright they could use it as a spotlight. Carl lurked in the wings, frowning, and once the encores were over he marched into the green room, where the band had collapsed, and pointed at Ray. "What the hell is that?"

Ray followed the path of Carl's pointing finger to his shoulder. "It's a hickey. A bite mark." Carl stared. Ray stared back before lifting an eyebrow. "Yeah, I got it during sex. You got a problem with that?"

Rather than reply, Carl stomped out of the room.

Dom shook his head, finally not blushing at the mention of sex. "You'd think he'd never met rock stars before."

"He's probably going to try to figure out who gave it to Ray." Mish rubbed her feet. "Which is idiotic, 'cause Zav's right here."

Zavier couldn't help laughing. If Carl didn't want to put two and two together, well, he wasn't about to help him.

They cleaned up for the signing lines—Ray back in a T-shirt—and managed to get through everyone before midnight. Then it was back onto the bus and off to Utah. Long trip, but one with a hotel room at the end and a day off from playing. Even with Ray giving him those long, hooded looks, Zavier didn't have much energy left, either to dominate or fuck. Still, when Ray headed toward the back of the bus, he followed.

Mish and Dom both had smirks. Zavier rolled his eyes at them, but smiled anyway. He pulled the privacy curtain closed.

Ray stood in the space, swaying with the bus, and staring at the couch on which they'd taken so much pleasure. "I had to ditch the bracelet. It was pretty disgusting by the time the concert was over."

"That's fine." Zavier swept a hand over Ray's back. He felt the shudder when he cupped Ray's neck. "Figured that might happen."

"Hence string and not leather?" Ray met his gaze. There was a hunger there, a deep, deep hunger. But none of the other signs that meant Ray was a live wire of lust.

"Exactly." He let his hand fall away. "Is there something you want?"

Ray nodded slowly. "It's—not sex, though. I'm beat."

"Ditto."

"But my mind won't stop. I—god. Do you ever get music and words and everything just—tangled up in there?"

"No, but other things, yes." He pulled Ray toward the couch. "Tell me about it."

Ray sat and dropped his hands into his head. "The words are easy to get out. I write them down, even if they're shitty. But the music—the colors and the shapes and the lines—I can't stop seeing them. Feeling them in my blood." He lifted his head. "I bet that makes no sense. I've tried to tell Mish and Dom, but they don't get it."

"Don't worry about it making sense to me." Zavier focused on Ray, whose gaze shifted from object to object in the room. "Tell me anyway. I want to know."

"I...see music, Zav. Like *see* it. Shapes and colors and..." He shrugged. "Been that way forever. I put hues and forms together on the guitar until they look right."

Fuck, Ray really had been a musical prodigy. *Hell.* Someone should have noticed. "Synesthesia," he said.

Ray nodded. "Yeah. I found out there was a name for it on the internet." He laughed. "Was kind of a relief."

One Zavier knew well, for different reasons.

"I do note things down with colored pens and stuff. But sometimes my brain gets so fucking *full*." Ray sighed and collapsed against the back of the couch. "Would it be weird if I—knelt at your feet? Like the first time? Not for sex. Not even to submit or whatever it is I do when I get all out of my head to obey you—but just to be here? With you?"

The worry there. Warmth spread through Zavier, and his chest ached. "Ray, you can always kneel like that if you need to. Or we can sit. Whatever you need from me." He dropped his hand on Ray's knee. Kept it there.

Ray relaxed under his touch. "Told you I was a burden. Just ask Dom."

"Shush. I bet Dom would disagree."

"Oh, he would, just to spite me." Ray rolled his head and met Zavier's gaze. "He's put up with my antics for years, but we're not like this." He gestured between the two of them. "He's not touchy-feely. You like touching me."

"Like I said, not entirely altruistic on my part."

Ray laughed. "But it's not always sexual."

That was true, too. He pulled Ray's head down into his lap. "This okay, or do you really want to kneel on the floor with your forehead on my shoes?"

"Wanna do both. But this is fine." Ray's words were soft, and his body relaxed.

Zavier stroked his hair. "Tell me what you see."

"I'm calling it 'Dare to Be.'" Then Ray whispered words and colors. Shapes. Sometimes he spoke so low, Zavier couldn't hear. He also tapped out a beat on Zavier's thigh, one Zavier echoed and improvised with on his back, until Ray was humming and singing and then slipping into sleep. A continuation of the song Ray'd been working on before. And now Zavier had the name—one even Mish and Dom didn't know. He held on to that like a talisman.

How many years had it been since he'd had a friend like Ray? One he could sit and be with? He couldn't remember. Once sex came into the picture, everyone had always expected *more* from him. Some great romantic connection. Dinners and presents and declarations. But Ray didn't seem to need that and it was a fucking miracle.

He fell asleep at some point, too, and woke when Mish pulled back the privacy curtain. She smiled at them and pointed to the bathroom.

Zavier waved his hand. He could stay like his forever, but Ray would probably be more comfortable in his bunk. He stroked his fingers through Ray's hair. "Hey..."

Ray stirred. "Fuck—uh. What time is it?"

"No idea. Mish needed the bathroom and that woke me up."

Ray gripped Zavier's knee. "Guess we should sleep in real beds, huh?"

"That's not until Utah. But you're gonna get a huge knot in your neck if you sleep on me all night."

Ray moaned and sat up. "Yeah. Probably."

When Mish cleared the bathroom, they all headed up and crawled into their respective berths.

"Zav?" Ray's voice filtered down from above.

"Yeah?"

"Thank you for listening."

Yeah, there was that warm content feeling again. Like sitting in the sun or lying on a beach. A perfect moment. "Always."

Nothing more, just the rumble of the bus and the soft sounds of his bandmates falling asleep.

CHAPTER
NINETEEN

THE CONCERT AT THE VENUE NEAR SALT LAKE CITY NEARLY LEFT Ray naked. He'd jumped into the crowd and bodysurfed, but it had gotten pretty damn rowdy and he'd lost a good part of his pants and had been felt up more in those few minutes than all his times cruising bars.

By the time he'd make it back on stage, he'd been laughing and high with adrenaline, but after the show, he'd realized just how lucky he'd been not to be dropped. Still, he loved running out into the crowd.

Carl, predictably, was furious. "You so eager to show your dick, Ray?"

"Not particularly." He was also too damn tired to get upset with Carl or get down on himself. Plus, there'd be a hotel bed tonight. Two. One for him and one for Zavier. Which one he'd end up in, he didn't care, as long as Zavier was there.

"Seems like it to me." Carl crossed his arms.

Ray shrugged. "I'll admit stage diving was probably not the best plan, but it seemed like a good idea at the time."

"Every singer does it once in their career," Mish said.

Carl threw up his hands. "You don't even fucking care

about your image, do you? They think you're a slut, Van Zeller. A—"

"Drunk? That hasn't been in the news for a while. And they don't think I'm a slut, they think I'm fucking Zavier."

Carl stared at him.

Ray rolled his eyes. "I've been keeping track of the scandal sites. It's all about sex and rock and roll now, not about drunk, mean Ray beating up on his poor ex-drummer. Or about my uncontrolled temper, or any of that."

Hell, even Kevin had issued a statement that pretty much debunked Ray's violent personality and outed himself as being in rehab. Ray had gotten an email from him. *Couldn't stand them saying that about you. I know we had our differences, but for what it's worth, I'm sorry. You were a jerk sometimes, but I was more of one.*

Yeah, maybe they were in debt to the record company, but they were also screaming up the charts and a name on many, *many* people's lips.

Ray sighed. "Look, I don't plan on crowd surfing again. That was a little *too* intense."

Carl grunted and almost looked satisfied with that answer. "I guess you do have a brain after all."

Ray didn't even bother answering that, just grabbed a bottle of water and chugged it back. "We gotta go do the signings." With that, and completely unrehearsed, the whole band rose and walked out of the room.

Zavier hooked an arm over Ray's shoulder. "I guess I don't need to ask if you lost your balls out in the crowd."

Mish's laughter echoed down the hallway. "If anything, he's grown them back."

"I don't need to hear about Ray's balls." Dom tugged at his studded collar. "But the look on Carl's face during that whole convo was priceless!"

God, Ray loved this band. Loved them all. Zavier's

warmth seeped into his skin and a cheer went up when they walked out near the crowd like that.

The signings went well. So many people had stories or hopes and dreams they wanted to share. The delight of the fans bolstered and carried Ray through the night and straight to the hotel. More press and fans as they entered, then they were on the elevator and to their rooms. Once more, they had a good portion of the floor for the band and crew. Or maybe all of it, he wasn't sure.

When the band got to their rooms, Mish held up her hand. "Wait a minute, who's in which rooms?"

Turned out Ray and Zavier were across from each other.

"Nuh-uh." She snatched Zavier's keycards. "You're next to Ray. I'm not putting up with listening to you guys going at it all night."

Dom was trying not to smile. Zav, for his part, took her keycards. His smile threatened to melt Ray's bones. "I'll try not to be too loud."

"It's not you I'm worried about, hon." Mish winked at Ray, then vanished into her room.

Shit, he didn't need to blush that hard. But with the way Zavier looked at him, and Dom smiling at the floor...yeah. His cheeks were hot.

"You guys have fun," Dom said, then entered his room.

That left Ray and Zavier in the hall. "Go in and relax." Zavier nodded at the room. "I need to call down to see about getting my package anyway."

And that sent heat to other parts of Ray's body. Zavier's Amazon order. Fuck. Just the *thought* of being tied down to a bed had him tripping over his feet to get into his room. Relax? *Yeah, right.*

The room was nice. Big bed. Good space. Lots of bottles of water and some fruit. He dropped his bag on the floor in the closet and looked around. About the time he spotted the door that joined their two rooms, he heard the gentle knock from the other side. Took no time at all to unlock the door, and there was Zavier.

"Well, this will make things much easier." Zavier grinned.

Oh yeah. No slamming doors. No keycards needed.

Zavier peered inside. "I think my room might work better." He motioned for Ray to join him.

After stepping inside, Ray agreed with Zav. This room was larger and the layout a little better. Same big bed. A chaise lounge. Even a padded bench by the foot of the bed. "How come I got the smaller room?"

Zavier shrugged. "This was gonna be Mish's."

"She missed out."

A chuckle. "I'm sure she'll make do, somehow." Zavier stepped close. "As will we."

Ray swallowed. "This is not going to help me relax."

Zavier gripped Ray's chin. "The question is, do you want to relax, or start now?"

"I want both." The answer came out before he could even stop to think.

Zavier smiled. "I can work with that." He snaked a hand around Ray's back and pulled them together. He was hard—harder than Ray, but not for long. "Go shower, and when you're finished, kneel at the foot of my bed."

"Okay."

Zavier nipped Ray's neck, then whispered into his ear, "I'm gonna make you scream tonight."

He trembled and thrust against Zavier. "You can try."

A pat on his ass, and Zavier stepped back. "Go."

Ray went. A shower didn't take too long, but he took his time, easing out some of the aches from performing and trying to calm his dick down, though every minute closer to kneeling for Zavier only fired his blood. He shut the water off and dried himself. He hesitated in his room, but no. Clothing would be pointless. He did crack a bottle of water and drink some, though.

God, he was nervous. Maybe because this was *real*, not them playing around in the bus. The water bottle in his hand was cool against his overheated skin.

"Ray." Zavier's voice filtered in from the other room. "Come here, please."

Right. Ray put down the water and entered the other room. He stopped halfway to the bed. The bench had been moved, and laid out on the white bedspread were a selection of items he'd only seen in porn. Cuffs. A collar. A flogger and a crop. A gag? Yeah, that was a ball gag. *Holy shit*. Rope. And yes, a butt plug. There was also a dildo that was quite a bit thicker than Zavier's cock. *Shit*. Ray took a step closer. Oh god, there were nipple clamps, too.

Something close to a whimper came out of his lips.

"Green, yellow, or red?" Zavier's calm voice.

"Green. I think. I—uh. You're not gonna use all of those on me?"

A huff of laughter. "No. Certainly not. I wanted to show you the option, though." He stepped behind Ray, still fully clothed, and kissed his neck. "What interests you? What scares you? What makes you say red?"

He studied the toys. "There's nothing I'd say no to. The dildo frightens me more than the plug. It's massive."

"Mmmhmm," Zavier purred into his ear. "It is. It's something to work toward—a goal, if you'd like."

He nodded, though the words *something to work toward* both delighted and worried him. "I want the cuffs. I want tied down. I'm not sure about the collar."

"It does have implications. It came with the cuffs. We don't ever have to use it." Zavier slid his hands down Ray's sides.

Okay. "I'm really curious about the flogger. It's not gonna be like you spanking me."

"No." Zavier gasped Ray's hips and pressed his bulge into his ass. "Not at all."

Yeah, he wanted to try that. "Can I ask you something?"

Zavier kissed along his shoulder, licking at the bruise he'd made. "Of course."

"If I said 'do anything to me,' what would you do tonight?"

Zavier stopped moving for a moment, then he breathed along Ray's skin like he'd just won a jackpot. "You absolutely amazing man. You have no idea." Another press of lips to Ray's neck. "I'd cuff each of your limbs, tie you to the bed facedown, and flog your ass. Spank you afterward—so you know the difference—then plug your hole and watch you for a while. Your struggles. Your need. How you move and want and breathe. And when you're ready, I'd fuck you into that rather nice mattress until you scream my name."

Shit—*shit*. Ray couldn't breathe. His whole body flamed with want and desire, and he wasn't quite sure how he was still standing, except that Zavier had his arms around him. "Yes."

"Yes?"

"Please do that. Everything you said. Do it to me."

Zavier nipped at his skin. "Get on your knees."

Ray dropped to the floor.

"Head down, Ray. Hands at the small of your back."

Not the child's pose they'd used earlier. *This* was subservient. But this time he didn't mind. He was Zav's to use and pleasure tonight.

Footsteps, and then the sounds of items being moved and the bed cleared. "The best thing about watching you on stage tonight was knowing I'd be fucking you later. All those fans screaming at you. Ripping your clothes off. Feeling you up." Zavier laughed. "I don't generally think of myself as possessive, but there was something succulent about knowing that my cock would be in your ass and my name on your lips while they pawed over you."

Ray moaned. Fucking hot, hearing that from Zavier's

mouth. A fleeting thought ran through his head. *This is a little more than benefits.* He quashed that. Later. Maybe he'd bring it up later.

Zavier fell silent as he worked. The bed frame creaked. "There," he said. "Ties to bind." Fingers brushed Ray's hair. "Sit up. Slowly."

He did, and blinked. Everything was brighter. Heady. "How do you do that? Make me feel so—" He shook his head.

"Out of it? I don't, exactly. That's you reacting to me. Look up subspace sometime." Zavier held a pair of cuffs in his hand. "Your wrists, Ray."

He offered them over and groaned when Zavier buckled the cuffs on tight. "Shit. I—fuck, this is hot."

A chuckle. "Wait until I have you spread-eagle on the bed."

That didn't take too long. Zavier had him stand, then lie down on the comforter—and the next thing Ray knew, his arms were tied down, one to each corner. The cuffs weren't too tight, and while his arms were extended and there wasn't much room to move, there was some. He rocked his cock into the bed.

Zavier swatted his ass. "I didn't say you could get yourself off."

"This whole thing is getting me off."

Another blow to his behind. It stung, but there wasn't enough force to even call it punishment. "If you come, I'm still gonna fuck you."

Yeah, Ray figured. "Might get me off twice."

A grunt. "Some night, when we have time, I'll see just how many times I can."

That would be fun and torture all rolled into one. "Okay."

Zavier cuffed Ray's ankle, then tied it down. "You really are magnificent."

Embarrassment crept up Ray's spine. "Just horny. That's all."

"No, that's not all." Zavier kissed his ass, then cuffed and tied the other leg.

He had no idea what Zavier meant, and the impulse to ask fled as soon as Zavier caressed his back and sides. He wiggled, but nope. He really was tied down to the bed. A spike of panic, followed by delight ran up to his head and pinpricks rose on his arms.

"Mmm." Zavier patted his ass. "I could drink you down when you move like that."

"This is intense."

Soft leather trailed against Ray's right arm. He turned his head and watched the end of the flogger slide over his skin. Zavier smiled at him. "It's only going to get more so."

God. He shivered at the words, at the leather slipping over his heated skin. Zavier moved out of his line of sight. "I'll start slow."

That was all the warning Ray had before those leather strips fell on his ass.

He jumped, even though it didn't hurt. Not one bit. Just a thud of softness on one cheek. Then repeated on the other. He pulled at his bindings and settled into the mattress. No way it would stay that painless.

It didn't. Each blow came harder and a little faster and warmth radiated up from his ass—then pain. Sharp stings as the leather hit the same spots over and over and over.

"Fuck." His whole body tensed.

"Let go, Ray."

He couldn't. Not right away. It wasn't until the pain made him cry out that he hit that amazing spot where the heat and the sharpness slid into pleasure and light.

"There you go." Pure joy in Zavier's voice. "Dance for me, Ray."

The blows became harder, and Ray moaned and swayed

as much as he could with the rhythm Zavier had laid down. Each time, agony blended to heat into warmth that radiated up his bones and made him fly. He didn't know where he started or ended, only that he *was*.

When Zavier stopped, Ray groaned—and fell a little out of that high. But Zavier's hands were on him, smoothing, calming, and inflaming. God. He'd never really thought about liking pain before, and he wondered if it was that or Zav or the surrender.

"Want to feel the difference between that and a spanking?"

Yes. No. *Shit*. "Yellow."

Zavier trailed fingers over Ray's burning ass. "That's fine. It's a lot to take in at once, I know. Being bound. Being flogged. I'm grateful that you've allowed me this much."

Tears leaked out of Ray's eyes. He wasn't crying. Not really. It was relief and joy and fear and...love. He was in love with Zavier—with his patience and his voice and his kindness. With the kink and the admiration. His snarky replies to Carl. Everything.

Fuck. He wasn't supposed to fall in love.

"Shh. We can stop. I'll untie you."

"No," he rasped. "I—give me a minute. I'm okay. It's just overwhelming." And it was. The pain and the ecstasy. The way he loved being held down. Zavier's ministration. "You can spank me." He wanted to give Zavier that—whatever it was that he got out of this—Ray wanted him to have all of it.

Zavier took a breath and blew it over the heated skin of Ray's ass.

Ray squirmed. The coolness hurt and soothed and made him want to fuck the bedspread until he spent himself. He was already hovering in that perfect buzz of pleasure.

"Four blows, then. And I want you to count them." There was an edge to Zavier's voice. Not anger, but something hard and hot. Lust?

"Okay."

The first took his breath away, and he barely got "one" out before the second landed. Oh fuck, they burned. More than the flogging, More than before. Needles up his back. The third put tears back into his eyes and the fourth had him screaming the number out.

In the silence that followed, Zavier appeared in his vision. He'd stripped off his shirt somewhere along the line and his ink-covered chest was ruddy with exertion.

Zavier brushed some tears from Ray's face. "Thank you for letting me do that." More than lust in his voice, but Ray couldn't say what. "Thank you for trusting me—though I don't think you enjoyed it. Not like the flogging."

Ray closed his eyes. "I—maybe. I don't know. It *hurt*, but now...'s not too bad." It wasn't. With the sharpness and immediacy gone, the ache that spread out was delightful and calming. He relaxed into the bed. "Feels like you should fuck me."

A finger brushed his lips. "I will. But I want to plug you first. Stretch you. Watch you. Can I do that?"

Warmth in Zavier's voice. Ray flicked his eyes open, his cock suddenly very eager about all those things. "Yeah. Green, Zav."

His heart melted when Zavier smiled. He wanted to see that expression every day. That joy.

He closed his eyes again. The bed dipped slightly, and this time it was Zavier's lips that brushed his. He opened and gave himself over to Zavier's kiss, those fingers in his hair. When Zavier pulled back, he kissed Ray's cheek. "Promise I'll make it good for you."

Understatement of the year, mostly because Zavier started by rimming him again, to the same effect as before—Ray went out of his mind. Might as well have scooped out his brains because he couldn't think beyond what Zavier's mouth and fingers were doing to open him and pleasure him. He thrust against the mattress, too aware of how close he was.

Every limb tingled, and doubly so because they were bound down and stretched and he was entirely Zavier's.

Lube followed, then the cool, hard tip of the plug. He thrust back on it, taking it, even as it burned and stretched his ass. When he'd seen it on the bed, the plug hadn't looked any larger in girth than Zavier's dick. In practice, though, it was larger—harder—and oh god, did it feel good.

And yeah, after it was seated he squirmed and squirmed and thrust and moved. Couldn't help it. Every shift rubbed the damn thing against his prostate, and pleasure exploded in his body. He was going to come like this, bound and flogged and plugged.

He pushed his cock against the roughness of the comforter and panted. "Fuck, Zav..."

"Oh, Ray." Zavier's words were a sigh and a caress all rolled into one. "You're so fucking beautiful."

Ray moaned and searched for him, but wherever Zavier was, it was out of his line of sight. Turning this way or that only stretched his arms and legs and shifted the plug more. Lightning shot up his veins, and he shuddered.

"You're close, aren't you?" A rustle of clothing, then a sound he knew very well—Zavier was jacking off. "On edge without me even touching you."

The thought of Zavier watching him, of masturbating to his bound form, only made Ray thrust harder against the bed.

"Yeah, that's it, Ray. Show me how much you enjoy being tied down, being plugged for me. I want to hear it. See it."

He moaned and squirmed and gasped. So close. "Zav. Fuck, Zav. I don't know what to do."

A chuckle. "Fuck yourself, Ray. Nice and hard. Pound that bed until you come all over it."

Fuck. Ray pulled at the binding, let go, and did exactly what Zavier said. It hurt a little—the fabric was rough and not slick, but the friction was incredible. Thrusting as Zavier had ordered drove the plug against his sweet spot over and over until the bursts of lights in his vision turned too bright. He groaned out as his orgasm overtook his body.

"Fuck, yeah, Ray. Keep going." Gravel in Zavier's words. The bed dipped.

Ray shuddered and twisted because the plug wouldn't stop shifting, wouldn't stop driving him high even when his balls emptied. Too much, not enough.

Then Zavier's hand was on his back, stilling him. "I'm taking it out," he whispered.

The loss was both relief and agony. Ray missed being full. "Don't—no. Need..."

"Mmm. I'm not finished with you yet." Pressure against his ass again—then Zavier's dick was sliding in, replacing the plug.

Lights and sparks and heat. Wasn't going to come again, and everything ached as Zavier thrust in and out, but he was there inside him, on him. Weighing him down. Zavier felt like nothing else in the world. "Fuck—yes."

A sigh, and maybe it was the yes that did it, because Zavier was ramming into him. As if their bodies needed to be one, as if this was the last thing they'd ever do together. Felt so fucking good, Ray couldn't help the moans or the shouts or babbling Zav's name over and over.

Somehow Zavier found that spot on his shoulder and bit it again before he groaned and pumped hard into Ray, chasing his own pleasure until neither of them was moving.

Zavier's huffs as he caught his breath tickled Ray's ear.

"Fuck yeah. Yeah." Ray kept repeating that until Zavier slid out, caught his head and kissed him, over and over until Ray couldn't speak anymore.

After that, Zavier rose and released him, taking off the cuffs so reverently, Ray couldn't help blushing. "It's like you're worshiping me."

Zavier laughed. "I am, in a very small way. You gifted yourself to me. Let me do this for you." He kissed Ray's wrists and ankles, had him roll onto his stomach again and applied some kind of salve to his ass, then drew him up to standing. "We've made a mess of this bed."

Good thing they had another. Zavier helped Ray into the other room and made him drink a bottle of water before they slipped under the covers together. Ray's head swam with the ache of his body, his heart, and the swirl of confusion in his head. "Zav?"

"Yeah?"

"What do you get out of this?" Surrendering let him out of his mind, but god, the work it must take for Zavier to get him there.

Zavier kissed his forehead. "Everything."

"Not good enough."

He felt Zavier chuckle. "It's too late to explain psychology. I enjoy your pain and your pleasure and your surrender and making you struggle and watching you overcome. I adore being inside you. Biting your skin. Tasting you. Everything, Ray."

Oh. Well, that didn't sound so bad. He liked all those things too, but in reverse. "We match."

Another huff of laughter. "In a way, yeah." Another kiss, like the last. "Go to sleep, Ray. I'll watch over you."

He sighed, relaxed into Zavier's arms, and obeyed that order, too.

ZAVIER HAD TO ADMIT THAT IT WAS NICE TO WAKE UP NEXT TO Ray in a hotel bed. The games and sex they could squeeze in on the bus or at the venue kept him going, as did their chats and their connection with each other. He'd never felt so satisfied by any kinky relationship before. Such a joy to get Ray off and have him obey, even when the orders made him uncomfortable. He'd at least try, like with the spanking last night.

In some way, their games had helped Ray and given him an outlet—and given him strength to push back at Carl. If it was something as simple and intimate as wearing that bracelet tied around the base of his cock—tight enough to stay and remind him of Zavier—they were both happy enough to command and comply.

Compatible. Comfortable. That was what they were.

But a morning like this, where Ray was quiet and sprawled out next to him and sleeping soundly, was a goddamned *gift*. Zavier resisted the urge to stroke his relaxed features. Beautiful and carefree. While he also enjoyed tense, passionate Ray, there was something about the trusting and vulnerable version that stirred a deep satisfaction in him.

He'd never tire of this sight.

So he watched, still heavy with his own waking, as Ray moved from sleep into wakefulness, then finally opened his lovely eyes. His smile was like gold, as was his sleep-rough voice. "Hey."

"Good morning." Now Zavier did reach out and touch Ray's cheek, tracing the lines of that smile.

"Wake long?" Happy muttered words. Ray moved closer to him.

"No. Not too long."

"Mmm." Didn't take long for Ray to curl up around him, or for Ray to ghost kisses over his shoulder. There were better places for those lips to be, though. He tipped Ray's chin up, and claimed his mouth.

Oh, that sweet moan in the back of Ray's throat. Zavier deepened the kiss, and lingered until Ray was pressed hard against him and trembling with need.

When he relented, Ray was breathless. "And here I was gonna go lower."

He did love Ray's mouth on his cock, but being on tour made Zavier hyper-aware of Ray's throat and voice. How sensitive it was to overuse, or to a cold, or deep-throating a cock. "As soon as we're off tour, I'm going to face-fuck you properly." He kissed Ray's neck.

Ray shuddered, but the stillness after that felt wrong. Zavier pulled back.

A little line between Ray's brows, and that inward turn. He wasn't frowning, but concern had stolen Ray's smile. He met Zavier's gaze. "Zav, what are we doing?"

Pinpricks—the bad, cold kind—traced down Zavier's legs. Oh god, no. Not this conversation.

"We're waking up next to each other in bed." He tried to keep his voice soft. *We were enjoying ourselves. Can't we just enjoy ourselves?*

Ray opened up space between them and propped his head up on his hand. "I mean—overall. What are we doing?"

Breaking up, because that was how these conversations always ended, with his partner wanting more than Zavier could ever give. He rolled onto his back and stared up at the ceiling. "What do you mean?"

"Wanting to face-fuck me after the tour is over implies you're gonna stick around. All the plans you have for me later. Yeah, once this tour is over, you'll be with the band, but seems like you think we'll still be doing—whatever the hell this is that we're doing."

Zavier swallowed around the lump in his throat. "I like being in the band. I want to hear the rest of 'Dare to Be' and all the other music you see, want to add my beat to your songs. Play with Dom and Mish. Make something together." He paused "And us? I'm...happy. You're happy. I don't see why we wouldn't just—keep doing what we're doing."

Did this have to have a label? Why couldn't they just be friends? Bed partners? Dominant and submissive. He rubbed his face. *Shit*. He wasn't ready for things to end.

Ray said nothing for a long time, and Zavier studied the texture of the hotel ceiling.

Finally, Ray shifted, rocking the mattress slightly.

"Zavier." His voice was so tender. "Can I ask you something personal?"

Not the normal question he got in this situation. He risked turning his head and looking into those eyes. "Sure." He owed Ray that, at least.

"Did someone hurt you?"

"What?" He sat up slowly, and took a better look at Ray. There was so much worry in his face, and Zavier didn't know what to make of it, because what lay there wasn't disappointment or sadness. "No. What do you mean?"

"I mean, did someone break your heart? Use you or—" He waved his free hand. "I just want to understand."

"No." If anything, Zavier had been the one to break hearts and use people—not intentionally. "What exactly do you want to understand?" Because suddenly it felt like they were having two different conversations.

Ray scooted himself up to sitting, and leaned back against the headboard. "I know you said, when we started fucking, not to expect romance or a long-term commitment or anything like that."

Zavier nodded, though part of him cringed at the words *when we started fucking*. Yes, that was what they'd been doing, but it sounded so—cold. And the part about long-term a little foolish. He'd never managed more than a few months with any given partner, unless they were people he occasionally ran into at clubs. But that wasn't a relationship.

"Seems like we're beyond 'no strings' now, especially if you're talking about the future."

He had been, hadn't he? "It's—we're friends." He wasn't sure what they'd been when they'd started, other than bandmates. "I enjoy your company. I think you like mine, so I don't see why anything would have to change when the tour's over."

Ray chewed his lip. "So, this is still friends with benefits? With kink on top?" His brow remained furrowed.

"Yeah." Was that so wrong? Why was that always so wrong?

"But you're not in love with me. Nothing beyond a friendship."

And there it was. Very much two statements, rather than questions. Zavier pressed the heels of his hands against his eyes. "I'm not in love with you. I've never been in love with *anyone*, Ray. I don't fall in love. I don't *get* love. I—" He shook his head. "I can't explain it. All the romance shit—doesn't make *sense* to me."

Of all the bedmates he'd had, he'd never felt as fucking torn up as he did now. People came and went in his life. Most of the people he'd fucked were exactly that—someone to fuck. Ray, though...they'd become *friends*. Good ones. He was comfortable with Ray. Enjoyed his presence and everything about him. They were compatible in *so many* ways.

"I'm aromantic." He wasn't *broken*—he knew that, even during moments like this, when he felt shattered, everything was *wrong*. Why was the world this way? He'd never understand. "You probably don't even know what that means."

That strange silence again. He expected hate or anger or *something*, but when Zavier lowered his hands and watched Ray, none of those emotions were there. Concern, and that worry from before, yes. But no resentment.

Ray spoke carefully. "I know what *aromantic* means, Zav." He nodded. "Yeah, okay. That makes sense."

Heat and cold danced across Zavier's skin in waves. Ray *knew*. He knew? He fucking *knew*?

Zavier was breathless, and all his control vanished in a tumult of emotions he couldn't channel. "*What* makes sense?" His lungs tightened and he fought back the tears, because what damn Dominant ever cried in bed? "Fuck."

"It's okay." God, Ray's voice was even beautiful when he murmured. "Everything now. I get it—as much as I can."

"Get what?" Zavier repeated. "Me being an emotional mess right now or me being aromantic?"

"Both," Ray said. "Though the emotional mess is kinda freaking me out a little. That's usually my thing."

Zavier laughed. He couldn't help it. Their roles had switched up a little. "Yeah, well. Call it shock. No one's even known the word before."

"I do, though." Ray was so damn serious.

"How?"

He shrugged, and his embarrassment blush crept up from his chest. "We have a lot of queer fans. Get mail and tweets and stuff. Sometimes people used words I didn't know and I realized I didn't think that much beyond 'gay' and that was pretty shitty of me. So I did research and learned what I could about other identities."

That was completely consistent with what Zavier knew about Ray. Everything came back to the band and everything with the band came back to the fans.

"You're not disappointed?" If Ray knew what *aro* meant, he'd know that the chances Zavier would ever fall in love with him were very, *very* low. Especially since he wasn't demi or gray or...well, attracted to Ray in any romantic way. Sex, sure. Friendship? Yes, please. But hold the roses and the candlelit dinners and all that.

"Disappointed? With you? Fuck no. Last night you tied me up, beat me, then fucked me until I couldn't think. I'll never be disappointed with you."

"Really?" He didn't quite believe that.

Ray's smile had returned. "You aren't romantic. I mean— you just *aren't*. But you like me and you care—"

"I'm your *friend*, you asshole, of course I care." He didn't know how many times he'd have to say that to get it into Ray's skull.

"I *know*. Point is, you're not pining after the one true love of your life who broke your heart or some such shit I couldn't ever compete with." Ray shrugged. "I've dated guys like that. Don't want to do it again. I was *never* good enough for them. They always wanted the one that got away—and that wasn't me."

Zavier struggled to wrap his brain around what he thought Ray was saying. He ought to get up and make coffee, but his skin was still in that weird prickly stage after surprise and fear. "So what now?"

Ray pulled his knees up to his chest, tenting the sheet. "I like *this*. Being in bed with you. The kink. Being your friend. You've helped me so much, and I don't know if you know that." He rested his head on his knees. His eyes were soft, and so was his smile. "I just needed to understand what was going on. Best friends with benefits is fine."

A second wash of pinpricks cascaded over Zavier, and he scrubbed his arms. They were remaining friends. They weren't changing anything. Holy fuck. "Best friend? I thought that was Dominic."

"Yeah, and Mish, too. I can have more than one best friend, you know." A little snarky smile with that.

"Yes, but you're not fucking them." Zavier paused. "Why *aren't* you fucking Dominic?" They were obviously close and had been since high school. That was a hell of a lot longer than Zavier had known Ray—*really* known Ray.

Ray barked out a laugh. "You know, I'd been wondering when you'd ask me that." He sobered. "Dom was the first person I came out to. And when I did, he came out to me." A little shake of the head. "We were like fourteen at the time, I think? Anyway, we tried kissing and it was *horrible*."

Zavier chewed on his tongue to keep from laughing. "Horrible?" Kissing Ray was nearly as good as being inside him.

"Yeah. Felt like we were siblings. Which in some ways we were. And are. Neither of us has a brother, so...we kind of filled that role. Including driving each other nuts."

Zavier had seen that enough times on tour. Both of them irritated the other, but in a way that was kind of like siblings did. "Makes sense."

Ray had his serious look on again.

"Please don't tell me you have another personal question." Zavier couldn't cope with being out of his element a second time this morning.

"No, it's just that all the aromantic people I've ever met or talked to were asexual, too."

"And I'm very much sexually attracted to people."

"Understatement of the year."

Okay, that was enough snark from Ray. Zavier pulled him over, exposing his bruised ass, and slapped him hard. Ray's yelp was rich and hot and tinged with a moan. So very good, that. He landed several more blows, enough to make Ray's cheeks red and his body tremble.

"So, business as usual, then?" Zavier said. Ray was as hard as he.

"Ohgodyes," Ray said. "*Please.*"

How could he refuse when Ray asked so nicely? "Condom," he said. "And lube." Another swat to that lovely ass sent Ray scrambling.

Ray's whole body was flush by the time he returned. "Cuffs again?" A little hope in that voice.

"No, I think this time we'll try something a little different." He wanted to be the ropes and cuffs that held Ray. Be his pleasure and punishment. "Here's what I want you to do."

RAY'D FUCKED PLENTY OF TIMES BEFORE, BEEN ON BOTH THE giving and receiving ends, but never like this.

"I wish there were mirrors so you could see yourself."

Zavier's words were hot in his ear and his cock deep inside Ray.

The thrusting, the movement, wasn't what brought him close to breaking, it was that thought, that image, the one he could nearly see against the white ceiling. The decadence of him splayed on top of Zavier, held tightly, one hand gripping his hip, the other on his shoulder. Arms like ropes, those muscles corded. Ray's own hands gripped Zavier's limbs, body writhing with each hard thrust. Open mouth, loud moans, wide eyes. "Fuck, Zav."

Incessant and hard, Zavier drove into him as if they could be one person, one soul. Ray's ass burned from the flogging, the spanking, and now this. The sharpness was like fire, driving him out of his mind. He arched as much as he could against Zavier, wanting more, needing the bliss and light that came when Zav slid deeper into him.

"Don't you ever think that I don't want you." A whisper of air and a caress of lips. Zavier pumped Ray's dick, stroking and pulling in time with his relentless fucking.

Ray shuddered, that peak too close, too near. "Can't. I'm gonna—"

Hot words and teeth against his neck. "I want to feel you come around me."

After those words, it was all light and heat and pleasure as Ray came hard, spilling himself over Zavier's hand.

Didn't take much longer for Zavier to follow, crying out his own release with such abandonment that Ray wanted those mirrors, so he could see controlled, calculated Zavier Demos wild and shattered because of *him*. That would be almost enough to get Ray off again, had such a thing been possible. Still, he moaned and shifted against Zavier, and then they were both still.

"God, Ray. You're such a fucking miracle." There was still the edge of abandonment in Zavier's voice.

Ray had no idea what to make of that statement.

Zavier pulled out and Ray shifted. "I should—" Get up, or at least get off of Zavier. Couldn't be comfortable for him, though he enjoyed the confinement and the burn against his ass.

"No. Stay." Wasn't so much a command as a plea. "I like you here, like this." There was a softness in Zavier's voice Ray'd not heard before. He relaxed against the hard, warm body beneath him. Somewhere along the line, Zavier tossed the condom off the side of the bed.

"Poor rug," Ray said.

"I'm sure its seen worse, or the same. Hotels are liminal spaces."

He snorted. Couldn't help it. "You say the strangest things sometimes."

"No more than you." A press of lips and enough admiration that heat rose to Ray's cheeks. "Singer and songwriter."

"I'm—"

"Shush, Ray. Just let me hold you."

Both their breathing evened out. The morning and the night before tumbled through Ray, heavy but comforting. Zavier's arms were loose around him, one warm hand near his cock and the other idly stroking near his nipple. Pleasant little shocks cascaded down Ray's limbs. Heat and light. Splinters of color. He hummed the notes and felt Zavier inhale.

"Will you sing for me, Ray?" A rough whisper, full of those emotions Ray still couldn't name.

"What song?"

Zavier stilled. "A new one. Something no one has heard before."

Ray shivered in his strong arms. "You've heard pieces." Helped puzzle out the beats in his head. Listened when he needed an outlet.

Zavier kissed the back of Ray's neck. A request without words.

So Ray sang the lyrics that had been dancing in his mind for days. Chased the colors and movement and sounds.

In the heat of summer
We were gods of a thousand dreams
In the night of winter
We were dust and ash
Where did the light we held go
Strands of silver and gold
When will we meet the sun again?
Stretch out your arms toward the moon
Sing to your soul to find the room
Dare to dream
Scream out loud
Dare to be
Who you are

When the last note faded, his voice was as rough as Zavier's had been. "That's all I have."

"Oh, Ray." Those hands drew them tighter together. "That's glorious."

"It's 'Dare to Be.'"

"I know." Zavier's breath ghosted across the back of his neck. "Ray, what do you see when the music's in your head?"

He found Zavier's hand on his hip, and twined their fingers. "Colors. Shapes. If I close my eyes, I see the music dancing."

"And what do you see when you sing 'Dare to Be'?"

He shivered against Zavier and felt more than heard the soft moan in response. Wasn't sexual, but so intimate. They could stay like this forever, the two of them. "Red. Deep red, like good wine. And blue, like the sky in summer, dotted among the red. They move and twist and everything turns to crystal and light."

Zavier kissed his neck. "Thank you." Such reverence and joy.

Ray closed his eyes and tried to etch this perfection into his mind before it slipped away. Because of course, it would.

That happened when the alarm on Zavier's phone chirped. A sigh from beneath him. "Time to get up. We need to be washed, packed, dressed, and back on the bus in an hour."

Ray groaned in frustration. But they both moved and separated as they hurried to get ready.

Still, the warmth in Ray's soul didn't abate, and burgundy and bright blue danced in his head.

CHAPTER
TWENTY

R<small>AY'S ASS WAS SORE ENOUGH THAT DANCING TONIGHT WAS GOING</small> to be *interesting*, but it was the Hollywood Bowl and fuck if he wouldn't give it his all. Still, he had to survive the bus ride there, enduring Zavier's placid and knowing smile, Mish's smirk, and Dom's blush. Guess sound traveled. Well, *oops*. A large part of him didn't care because he'd enjoyed himself. The other part was still absorbing what Zavier had told him— that he was aromantic.

So much of their relationship snapped into focus, and lingering doubts about the future drifted away. Zavier didn't want this to end. If anything, he wanted to extend their partnership longer.

Hope slipped into Ray, soothing away fear. They could be together, be friends, make music, have sex and play. He could kneel for Zavier and sleep next to him. Ray could love Zav and...

Since Zavier's legs were tangled in his, Ray felt the exact moment when he tensed. "Shit," Zavier muttered while staring at his tablet. He tapped and swiped and his frown deepened, then swung his legs around to sit up, and Ray lost that warmth and connection. "Fuck!"

"What?" They all said the word—him, Dom, and Mish—at nearly the same time.

Zavier was trembling, and given his expression, it was from anger. He silently handed his tablet over to Ray.

He braced himself mentally, then looked. Another photo, this one taken through sheers of a window. It took Ray several seconds to puzzle out what he was looking at—a man in the throes of passion. Naked, though the photo was blurry enough to keep it from being explicit. Another figure lurking behind. Cold terror shot through him, because *Ray* was the man in the photo. That was Zavier behind him.

They could deny it, he guessed, but, fuck he was shitty at lying. "This—this is from Houston."

"Yes." Zavier's answer was clipped and precise.

"But we were twenty floors up!"

"Maybe a drone. Maybe a photographer in another room." Zavier stood and paced to the berths, then back. "Someone knew exactly where your room was."

"That's creepy," Dom said, voicing the thought running through Ray's mind.

He checked the caption. Yeah, the gossip site knew it was him. His room, after all. Right hair color. All that shit, but the identity of the person behind Ray was unclear. He read on, then nearly dropped the tablet. The story mentioned seeing a young-looking fan entering the elevators.

Zavier took the tablet out of Ray's hands and passed it to Dom. Mish read over her shoulder. "Fuck," she murmured.

Ray looked up at Zavier. "How'd you find that?"

Zavier sighed. "A friend sent it to me. She—looks out for me."

"Your elusive mentor?" Dom again.

Zavier nodded. "Nadia Rudd."

That should have come as a shock. Maybe would have, had Ray's mind not been fixated on that photo and the article. But it also made some kind of sense that the woman best known for escorts and sex parties would have been a mentor to Zavier.

That she was helping Zav—warning him—also spoke volumes.

"Who's the other guy?" Mish asked.

Zavier sat down. "Thankfully, that's me." He ran a hand through his hair. "This is not what you—what we need right now."

"No kidding." Finally Ray's anger rose. "Why *now*? It's been weeks!"

Zavier shook his head. "Doesn't make sense. No one sits on something like that."

Ray could only blow out a breath and stare up at the ceiling of the bus. No use asking what he should do—there really wasn't anything to do. "At least we know. I'd hate to be blindsided by this from Carl."

"Oh god, that shitfucker's gonna have a field day." Mish handed the tablet back to Zavier.

Yeah, he would. "I don't understand why no one's contacted us. I mean, yeah, Carl's an asshole, but the rest of the label?" This wasn't the sort of shit you fooled around with. "Companies usually get these things pulled down right away."

Ray shook his head. "I don't know. They've never done a damn thing about any of the shit that's out there about us. Hell, they wanted me to lie about abusing alcohol, and I'm still paying for that."

Fucking hell. This was going to get interesting.

———

IN FACT, THE FIRST WORDS OUT OF CARL'S MOUTH WHEN HE strode onto the bus were, "You fucking perverted fuck."

Ray's stomach lurched and he stood, but Zavier slipped between them. Carl shoved him aside. "You fucking druggies,

Ray?"

He froze. No one but the band—and of course, the guy—knew the guy had been carrying drugs. "No, I'm not."

Carl held up the tablet. "Photo says otherwise."

"No, it doesn't," Zavier said. "That's me behind Ray, and yes, I'd swear that in a court of law." He paused. "I'm nearly three years older than Ray and haven't touched drugs since pot in high school."

A little color dripped from Carl's face. "They saw the dealer go up."

Oh *shit*. Tension visibly coursed through Zavier, then there was none. "You little fucking—" He raised his fist.

Ray *moved*, pushing past Carl and banging Zavier up against the wall of the bus. "No. Nope. Zav. Not worth it." He wouldn't let Zavier end up with an assault charge, not to protect him.

"That piece of shit set you up." Zavier snarled the words, his face red, his body shaking. "Tried to destroy your career and the band and—"

Ray gave him a little shake. "You still have the recording?"

Zavier blinked and the fight in him fled, or maybe he wrestled it under control. Hard to tell. He took a deep breath. "Yeah, I do."

When Ray faced Carl again, Carl was white and red. Terror and anger. "It was you who told that guy to go up, wasn't it?"

"You have no proof at all." Carl practically spat the words.

Ray nodded. "It's true. But we do have a recording of Zavier confronting the man before anything happened, my reaction to the drugs, and telling him to get out." He shrugged. "So you can figure out how to get those gossip sites off my case, unless you want them speculating about your involvement, too."

The fight left Carl, too. "I should have never signed you, Demos."

"You shouldn't even have a job, you washed-up, out-of-tune has-been." Rage made Zavier's words sharp.

Mish cleared her throat and rose. "I think you should go, Carl, before I decide to stick my boot up your ass. You fuck with these guys again, and I won't be so kind."

Where Carl had been furious at Zavier, that slipped to fear as Mish loomed over him. He managed to squeeze around Ray and flee the bus.

"Well, fuck." Dom exhaled. "I thought we were gonna see blood."

Zavier scratched the back of his head. "Sorry. I shouldn't have lost my cool."

Ray gripped his shoulder for a moment. "Role reversal again."

Zavier dropped to the couch. "I knew he'd come at you again. Didn't know he was such a shit to set you up with a drug dealer."

Yeah, that had been unexpected. Completely. He should have been as upset at Zavier, but he clung to the bubble of calm that enveloped him. "I think I need to talk to the label. Get a new manager. Find out what they're doing about this, since Carl is of no use." He dug his notebook out of his bag. "But right now, we've got a set list to finalize and whatever shit they're feeding us here to eat. Come on." Better to focus on here and now. He ushered them out of the bus.

RAY SEEMED UNAFFECTED BY THE REALIZATION CARL HAD NEARLY ruined his carrier. Unfortunately, Zavier couldn't shake the desire to wring every bone from Carl's neck. He took another breath and followed Ray into the venue. A strange reversal of roles, indeed. He wasn't usually given to violence. The kink was completely different—that was a shared desire and entirely consensual, and while he might hurt people who wanted that, he'd never *harm* them.

He wanted to harm Carl. Wanted justice. His body ached with anger and hatred rolled through his brain, lacing his blood with pain, enough so that he still shook as they walked.

Dom clapped him on the shoulder. "Yeah, I know. I wanna kill him, too."

Zavier let the laugh be bitter. "I don't get why he's so calm."

"Ray?" Dom peered ahead. "Because you have his back. We have his back. Carl can't prove jack shit. You can. We can corroborate. Nothing will come of it all."

"Fucker is slimier than pond scum." Zavier hated the burning in his gut, his need to lash out. Dom was right, they had all the cards, but the thought of Carl harming Ray...

That set Zavier off completely.

"Pond scum at least serves a purpose. That man?" Dom shook his head.

The green room was full of fruit and yogurt, donuts, and coffee. Zavier made a beeline for the table and snagged a chocolate donut. Maybe if he stuffed his face, he'd feel better.

Ray met his gaze and gave him a little smile. "It's okay."

It wasn't, but Zavier nodded.

They hashed out a stellar set list, building on their experiences from the past shows, then got ready for sound check. Right before they headed onstage for that, Carl arrived again, looking all kinds of worried, angry, and unhappy. But he was trailing a man in an expensive suit who was smiling like a used car salesman.

He introduced himself to Ray and the "rest of the band" as Anthony Vea, a vice president from the label. "I have some fantastic news for you." He paused, his grin widening. "Your latest album has officially gone platinum."

Holy shit. Now that *was* good news. Ray seemed startled,

then ecstatic. He pumped the bigwig's hand, then grabbed Dom and hugged Mish.

When Ray turned his way, Zavier shrugged. "I wasn't on the album."

That earned him a punch in the arm. "Shut up. If it weren't for this tour—"

"Ray is quite right," Mr. Vea said. "Sales have shot up tremendously since you joined the band. We expect we'll be seeing more sales milestones from Twisted Wishes in the future." He cleared his throat. "The band has some time off here in Los Angeles and we're hosting a party to celebrate."

Ray nodded. "Yeah. I mean, that's fantastic." He was beaming.

Here was proof that Carl's actions hadn't entirely fucked Ray over, so he wouldn't have to murder the bastard after all. For now. Something still needed to be done about the man, but there wasn't any time to pull the exec aside to talk about him, mostly because Carl never left his side. Typical. Still, Zavier had one question to ask. "What's going on with the photos of me and Ray?"

The VP's smile evaporated. "There's no conclusive proof that they are of Mr. Van Zeller, as blurry as they are." He paused. "But I suppose you've just confirmed that to us."

"I supposed I have," Zavier said. "Carl was sure they were of Ray, though."

The exec glanced at Carl, whose face was rapidly turning red.

"There was also some rather litigious insinuations in the article I read." Zavier shrugged. "Seems like something you'd be on top of, you know?"

"Zav." Ray's voice was soft. "If they can't prove it's us..."

"They can't." The exec shifted uncomfortably, focus sliding between the two of them. "However, I'll double-check that the legal department is working on it."

A touch on Zavier's arm. "Let's celebrate our successes

and let them handle it?" Ray's look was a pleading one, and the band was being called for sound checks anyway.

When they stepped out to run through a few of the songs, Zavier shuddered. The sheer amount of energy in the air—the historic view from the Bowl. It was too much to put into words.

Gregor from Five Asylum gave them a wave from the side of the stage while they played, and called Ray over when they finished, probably about the platinum record thing. Ray shook Gregor's hand and slipped what looked like a business card into his pocket.

Connections. Good. Ray needed support outside the label, too.

After they retreated to the dressing rooms, Ray collapsed into Zavier's arms. "We're going to shatter this place tonight."

He held Ray—vibrating, ecstatic, lovely Ray—and kissed his forehead. "Yeah. You earned that right. You deserve to be here."

Ray pulled back. "So do you."

He couldn't help grinning—Ray's joy was always infectious. "Should I wear the leather pants?"

"You better." Ray's eyes were as glowing as his smile.

Zavier did just that, and as predicted, they completely shredded the audience with their performance. Even before they got back to the hotel, the reviews online were calling it a show of a lifetime. The photos? Those were gone, as was the article. All-around good news.

They didn't bother with any elaborate play that night, though Ray begged for the cuffs and to be fucked hard.

That was a different type of music to Zavier's ears, as were Ray's grunts, moans, curses, and ultimately, Zavier's name on his sweet lips. As he held Ray afterward, everything was perfect, except for the unsettled knot that had taken up in his soul.

His own words came back to haunt him, ones he'd said to

Ray. *Carl's gonna come at you again. Bastards like that can't help it.* A bastard like Carl had something else up his sleeve. He'd not lose Ray to that. Or lose the band. *This* was his life now, and he'd do anything to protect it.

DESPITE THE PRESENCE OF PRESS AND CARL, THE TWISTED Wishes platinum-record party turned out to be a pretty sweet shindig, especially since Ray got to see Zavier strutting around in a tux. Granted, he'd seen Zav's outfit up close and personal in the hotel room before they'd all piled into the limo to the ostentatious restaurant the label had booked. He'd even been on his knees at the time, naked with his hands cuffed behind his back.

They'd spent a lot of time naked over the past two days. Sleeping. Fucking. Playing. They'd also spent time with the band, horsing around at the pool, going out to eat. Had been so good to connect with all of them, but being with Zavier was like nothing else. His touches, his glances. They could inflame or be friendly or drop Ray straight to his knees. He loved every single minute of his time with Zavier. The benefits were *outstanding*.

The paparazzi did have quite the time photographing them, including shots of some very intense looks Zavier had given Ray—his *I'm going to fuck you so hard later* gaze. But there weren't any photos—yet—that anyone could point to and identify them as a couple. They didn't hold hands, and, as Dom had pointed out, didn't stare into each other's eyes, or any other couple-like activity.

Had to confuse the hell out of the press. Didn't bother Ray, though. Zavier was *Zavier*. Ray loved him for who he was, even if that meant the reciprocal wasn't quite the same. Zav cared for him—Ray knew that in his bones. He also knew it from the bright cotton bracelet Zavier had tied around his wrist under his shirt before they'd left the hotel room. *So you remember who you are.*

His own person. But also the man Zavier had promised to tie down and fuck later that night.

Mish might have been wearing an elegant black dress, but she still kicked him from her seat across his in the limo. Even in sleek heels, she could pack a wallop. "You're off in lala land...nervous?"

"Nah. I'm thinking about the last couple of days, that's all. Gonna be weird to get back on the road." They still had a concert in Seattle, and they'd added a stop before that in Oregon.

"I'm kinda looking forward to being done," Dom said. He was the only one not *quite* in fancy duds. Domino wore the tux jacket, but a black pair of jeans, a bright red T-shirt, and his studded collar. His usual makeup, too. "I want to be myself for a while, and get some sweet, sweet loving, like Ray's been lucky enough to get."

He flipped Dom off, but laughed. Couldn't fault Dom for playing up the persona or wanting out of it, either. Dominic Bradley in a tux looked very different than Domino Grinder. People expected Domino to be outrageous, but apparently Dom-the-twink got more action in bed.

When they arrived at the restaurant, there were photos and handshakes and fans wanting autographs. Took them forever to get into the place. The venue was all glitter and chrome that sparkled and pulsed like a glass full of jewels. A little glitzier than Twisted Wishes themselves, but it was a nice change of pace, even if Ray did feel like he was playing dress-up. Out of all of them, Zavier looked the most natural in his clothes—but then, he was used to wearing a tux from his orchestra days. Plus he moved like sin in any clothing. Hell, he moved like that naked.

Ray worked his way to the bar and ordered a tonic water

with a lime wedge speared with a cocktail sword. "I'm not drinking," he told the bartender.

A moment after he got his drink, he was dragged off by some marketing guy who wasn't Carl to chat with one of the VPs of the label he'd yet to meet. Well, chat really meant shake hands, listen to praise, and nod and smile while the press took countless pictures.

A few journalists asked him some pretty easy questions about his feelings on the success of the band, what was next, and how Zavier Demos fit into the picture. He set his drink down and answered their questions, including the one he expected.

"Are you and Zavier lovers?"

Ray laughed. "That's kind of a personal question, isn't it? I know people are saying there's photos of us, but—" He let the reporter squirm a bit, then shrugged. "Zav's become a very good friend. He's a phenomenal musician, and hell yeah, I look forward to working with him on our next album."

No one asked about the hazy photo that had been taken through the sheers. No mentions of young fans. The rumor that it was Zavier standing behind Ray had taken hold. The fact that it wasn't a rumor at all? Not his problem.

Given the paparazzi and what had already happened, at some point photos would come out of him and Zavier that would solidify all the speculation, but for now, he wouldn't give them anything to go by. Besides, the label's lawyers had gotten the blurry shots taken down. Maybe that would make the gossip sites and the photogs think twice about taking very personal photos.

Still, someone was bound to catch them kissing, even though they weren't all over each other in public. Zavier might not be romantic, but he obviously still enjoyed physical contact of *all* sorts.

Someone tapped him on the shoulder, and he turned to

find Carl leering at him. Ray didn't put his fist in his face, but did twist away from his touch. "Yeah?"

"Photo time with the record." Carl marched away.

Well, okay then. Ray grabbed his drink, took a quick sip, and coughed. *Damn*. Bitter. Lime must have been strong and bled in a bit more. He set it down again near the staged shoot.

The platinum record and certificate looked stellar, even if their album had never been released on anything resembling the shining large disk above the certificate. His head swam a little as he held the plaque with Dom, Mish, and some label exec. Zavier stood off to the side, grinning. After about fifteen minutes of being maneuvered and primped for the best shots and then posing with the execs, too, they eventually got a few shots with Zavier as well. Even if he wasn't on the album, he was part of why they were here tonight. It was only fair to include him.

Ray rubbed his eyes—all the flashes from the photographs left after images, and his head felt weird. Probably too much heat and not enough liquid. He extracted himself from the crowd and found his drink again. Still on the bitter side, but wet and cool.

Another reporter cornered him, and he answered more questions and sipped his drink. Wasn't helping. His brain swam and his eyes felt wrong. Everything was bright, and he couldn't clear his throat.

He excused himself once the questions petered out to get some water, but got lost along the way. Too many mirrored columns and twinkling lights. People everywhere. The room swam. *Shit*. He took a breath and wheezed.

Okay—there was definitely something wrong with him. His throat itched all the way down and it felt tight. Tighter by the second. What the hell? He put down his drink and grabbed the little cocktail table to steady himself.

Oh *fuck*. Oh god. His throat. He tried to gasp for air and only managed a little. Someone grabbed his arm.

"Are you drunk already, Ray?" Carl's face swam in Ray's vision.

No. No. He tore away. Not drunk. Couldn't breathe. He needed Zavier. Where the hell was Zavier? He pushed through the crowd, trying to find those broad shoulders and dark hair. There...!

Noise all around now, though none of it made sense. He tripped over something and stumbled.

"Ray?" Warm hands caught him and Zavier's voice sounded in his ears, frantic and worried. "Ray!"

He tried to speak, but nothing came out. Or in. You needed breath, a throat that worked, to get words out.

I'm dying. He clawed at Zavier. *I'm gonna die.* He wasn't ready. Not at all. *Please don't let me die!*

The last thing he heard was Zavier shouting his name.

Ray collapsed into Zavier's arms, and his emotions shut down. They had to, he didn't have time to contemplate worry or fear or anything.

"Call nine-one-one!" he shouted over the suddenly panicking crowd. He laid Ray on the floor and racked his brain for what to do next as people crowded around and a fucking flash went off. "Get back!" His voice was a growl in his own ears. "Get a doctor!"

Blotchy skin. Swollen lips. Breath coming in tiny wheezes. Fuck. *Fuck.* Allergic reaction? Anaphylaxis maybe. Probably. *Shit.*

"Zav!" Mish was next to him in an instant, a bright yellow tube in her hand. "EpiPen."

"I don't know how—"

She popped a blue cap off and jammed it against Ray's thigh. Held it there. Counted. Pulled it away. "I'm allergic to bees and wasps."

And they'd been playing outdoors all summer. "What's Ray allergic to?"

She shook her head. "I didn't know he had any."

Neither had he.

Zavier's head swam with every awful outcome as they waited for what seemed like hours for the first responders to arrive. It was probably minutes, eight or ten or something like that. Ray was breathing, though, and the crowd wasn't pressing too close.

Lots of clicks of phone cameras. Zavier wavered between anger and nausea. Thankfully movement and commotion swarmed around them again, then a woman in a uniform was kneeling with them. A paramedic, with more following. The band answered her questions as best they could and Mish handed over the EpiPen.

"Food allergies?" The paramedic took Ray's vitals.

"None that I know of," Zavier said.

Mish shook her head. "Same. He never mentioned any."

"Where's Dom?"

"Here." A quiet voice behind Zavier. "He doesn't have any food allergies. He's allergic to penicillin and derivatives." He fidgeted. "I have power of attorney for his healthcare."

Of course he did. Made sense—best friends since high school, and Dom had been by Ray's side the entire time. Didn't stop the punch to Zavier's gut, because he couldn't do *anything*. Ray had come to him for aid—and he'd failed. Utterly.

"You should be here." Zavier rose.

Security and other paramedics were shooing people out of the way as they pulled in a stretcher.

"Zav..." Dom's eyes were wide, and his face too pale, even with the makeup. Dominic peering out from underneath Domino. "You should go with them."

He wanted to. God, he *wanted* to. But he was useless to Ray, and Dom was not. He gripped Dom's shoulder. "You have power of attorney. I don't. He trusts you." The fear in Dom's eyes mirrored the terror lurking behind the locked-down, rational part of Zavier's mind. "*I* trust you."

Maybe that was what Dom needed to hear, because he took a breath and nodded.

"He was drinking." Carl's sharp voice.

They both flinched, and Zavier rounded on Carl. "He was *not*."

"You sure about that?" Carl nodded back at a tumbler that looked to be a half-drunk gin and tonic sitting on a high-top cocktail table.

Zavier knew, without a doubt, Ray wouldn't have touched alcohol. Not tonight, not when so much was on the line.

"Did he have a drinking problem?" That was from the paramedic.

"Yes." Carl's smile was horrific.

"No," all three of them—Dom, Mish, and Zavier—answered, in echo of each other.

Zavier continued, "He never did. That was the spin the label decided on." He glared at Carl. "You know Kevin admitted to being in rehab, right?"

When they lifted Ray onto the stretcher, Zavier put his back to Carl and clasped Dom's shoulder again. "Go with him. We'll handle things here."

Because this—being here to counteract Carl—was how Zavier could help Ray.

Dom nodded, then was jogging after the paramedics.

Zavier turned to Carl. "You know he's never had an issue with drinking." He strode toward the other man. "And yet, every fucking time, you blame it on Ray boozing it up, as if he were some out-of-control drunk." He went straight past Carl to the glass he'd pointed out. "When in reality he hasn't touched a drop since Kevin left the band." Zavier leaned over and sniffed. Tonic. Lime. That was all. "This is tonic water."

"Must not be his glass." Carl glared at him, seething.

A flash went off—cameras. Phones. Recording. Good.

"It's his glass." A man in the simple black slacks, apron, and vest of the bartenders tonight stepped forward. "I watched him put it there before he stumbled. And I served him tonic and lime, like he asked." His gaze flicked from Carl to Zavier. "That's all Mr. Van Zeller has had to drink tonight." He paused and focused on Carl. "You even heard him order that one. Watched me make it."

From the corner of his eye, Zavier caught the edge of another uniform—this one not a paramedic's. Not security, either. He met the police officer's gaze. Cop stared back. "Did you touch the glass?"

"No. I just leaned over the table and sniffed it."

He nodded once. "You, and you, and you." He pointed to the bartender, Carl, and Zavier in turn. "Stay here. Don't touch a damn thing."

"You should pull the security tapes," Zavier murmured. A hideous, horrible inkling formed in the back of his mind. Carl wanted Ray to act drunk. There were ways to do that. Drugs you could use. He'd already set Ray up once.

The cop eyed him. "Already being done." He glanced around. "You three stay here. Everyone else needs to leave this area." He paused. "Now." That word was ground out with enough authority that the gawkers finally moved, taking their phones with them. They were directed by some additional police to another area of the venue, away from them, presumably to get statements.

Zavier stared at Carl, that smug bastard. And watched as the smugness melted to worry and fear. *Oh, you fucking asshole of a man. If you hurt him, I will kill you.*

Zavier pulled out his phone and texted Dom.

> R may have been drugged. Roofie or something. Still figuring it out.

Across the room, Mish waved as she was ushered out. "Go to the hospital. I'll meet you there," Zavier called.

Carl snorted. "Since when did you become the leader of the band?"

"I'm not." Zavier tucked away his phone. "Ray's our leader. Has been all this time." He cocked his head. "Right now? I'm playing band manager, since ours is an incompetent fool."

Carl started toward him.

"Don't." Zavier's command rang out, momentarily silencing the entire room and stopping Carl in his tracks. "Don't even *think* it. I won't touch you, but if you lay a hand on me, I will rip it off and shove it down your throat."

Three police officers descended upon them, and the rest of the night became another blur of questions and answers and anger checked and choked back and checked again. His phone buzzed multiple times, but he didn't answer. Didn't look.

Probably shouldn't have talked to the cops, either, but the worry and fear crept in enough to cloud common sense. Yes, he had threatened to rip Carl's hand off—but Carl *had* been storming toward him. Yes, there was a history of animosity between Carl and Ray and the band. No, he didn't know why.

Thankfully, the bartender corroborated everything he'd said about Ray and drinking. Told the cops what Zavier already knew—Ray hadn't touched alcohol that night. They noticed some kind of white substance at the bottom of Ray's glass, but in the end, it was the security recordings that told the whole story. Ray getting his tonic and lime. Chatting his way through the crowd. Putting his drink down for a second while talking to someone...and Carl dropping something in while no one was watching.

Fucking *Carl*. Again. Carl, of course, had clammed up as soon as the officers read him his rights. Wouldn't even tell them what the drug was. Said he wanted to speak to a lawyer.

Eventually, the cops cut Zavier and the bartender loose, with thanks and business cards. They'd be in touch. By the time Zavier stumbled out into fresh air, his mind was a mess of emotions and his body buzzed and ached in ways he didn't know were possible. Chest tight. Pounding headache. Heart racing. He was both cold and sweating. Zavier pulled out his cell and read the first two texts that were visible.

> When will you be here?

That was from Dom.
Mish, too.

> Honey, where are you?

There were more. Details about Ray. The hospital name. They scrolled off screen and his vision blurred.

He wasn't religious, but he threw a prayer up into the universe anyway. *Ray. Fuck. Ray, please be okay!* He closed his eyes, and forced his stomach to quell, tried to take enough deep breaths to get his pulse under control. In, out. Control. Find a center and latch on to that.

From behind his eyelids, he saw a flash of bright light. Cameras. Press. Paparazzi. He opened his eyes. *Of course.*

They descended on him like locusts to wheat. He'd been Nadia's student, so he drew himself up, pocketed his phone, and found the restaurant's taxi stand. "Get me a cab."

The attendant was wide-eyed. Zavier watched him flick a glance at the reporters, then he ducked his head. "Right away, sir."

He tucked his fear for Ray deep down and schooled his features, then faced the cameras. They called his name, asking questions on top of one another. A miasma of sound that screeched across Zavier's brain.

What happened to Ray Van Zeller? Was it true he was drunk? Were he and Ray lovers? Why had they taken away Carl Roberts in cuffs? Why wasn't he at his boyfriend's side? How did he feel?

He felt like knives were stabbing through every part of his body. That was how he *felt*. Ray had needed him—and he'd been helpless. Zavier swallowed the pain and held his ground. "I have no statement at this time." He spoke low, but with force, like the deep boom of a bass drum.

Didn't matter. The questions went on. Recorders and cameras were shoved in his face. He couldn't duck them, couldn't make them stop. Trapped and enclosed by bodies, Zavier's every nerve said to fight, to escape.

Once—only once—in his life, he'd been bound. Held by ropes and cuffs and completely at the mercy and will of another. He'd submitted freely then, and had hated every second of that loss of control, but he'd endured, because that too was a type of self-mastery.

If you keep your head, Nadia had purred that night, nothing will ever faze you again.

She'd been so very wrong about that. He could be unnerved. There were some things—some people—that threw him off. Situations that cut to his bone. Ray did more than *faze* him.

But he'd never let this pile of camera-laden, ethically challenged humans know that. When his taxi pulled up, he pushed through the crowd and slipped into the cool, dark interior, and shut the shitshow out. They rapped on the window and yelled at him.

Only a thin strip of the driver's face was visible in the rearview mirror. "Where to?"

"Whatever the nearest hospital is. Wait—" There had been

a text with the name. He dug his phone out and read the name of hospital off.

The driver pulled away, and the flashes of cameras and tapping on the window were gone. "You okay?" Concern in the driver's voice.

"I'm trying to get to my friend." Zavier held on to his phone, focused on breathing, and read the rest of the texts. That helped, somewhat. Ray was all right. Not well—but he wouldn't die. Didn't die. Would recover. That was all that mattered.

Except relief unlocked a faucet of emotions that churned through Zavier and roiled him with nausea. He clutched his phone to keep his hands from shaking. The bitter, bitter taste of helplessness. Gratitude that Dom and Mish had been there to do what he couldn't. The awful *what-if* that lingered—what if he never saw Ray again?

He swallowed. Ray was alive. Repeating that took the nausea away.

Zavier sent a message to both Mish and Dom via a group text.

> I'm on my way. Had to talk to the cops for a while.

Mish texted back with a room number in the emergency department. They want to keep him overnight for observation, but they're waiting for a room to open up in the hospital.

Good. Bad. He couldn't tell. He just wanted to get there and *see* Ray. Touch his hand. Verify what his logical brain knew was true. Ray was *alive*.

Zavier needed to see the rise and fall of his chest, feel the warmth of his skin. Wanted to know beyond a doubt that everything was all right. He cared for Ray more than he'd ever cared for any other friend. Didn't know what that meant, needed to examine it further, but there was no time, because the taxi pulled up to the hospital.

Thank goodness he'd shoved his driver's license and a credit card into the pocket on his phone case, because he had no cash whatsoever. His wallet was packed in some bag at the hotel, but he refused to be without some means, even at fancy dress parties. He handed the credit card over. When the receipt came back, he left a sizable tip and signed. Then he was out of the cab and heading toward the door of the emergency department.

There was a metal detector to get through at the emergency room, then an information desk. He explained who he was, filled out some paperwork while they checked out his license, then led him back.

"My daughter really likes you guys," the nurse murmured. He was a thin black man with a hard-to-place accent. "You're a bit too punk for my tastes, but I'm glad you care for each other." He slowed as they neared one room. "He's in here."

Zavier stopped at the threshold and sucked in a breath. Beyond the wooden door lay Ray, in a hospital bed, unconscious, pale, and in a hospital gown. There was an IV drip and wires running from underneath the sheets. One of those pulse monitors had been clipped to his finger.

Mish and Dom sat nearby, both looking as exhausted as Zavier felt.

"Hey, hon." Mish rose from a nearby chair, still in her black dress, strangely somber and out of place against white linoleum and the green bed curtains. She pulled him into a hug.

The bubble of pain rose closer to the surface, and he pushed it back down. He *didn't* cry. He *couldn't*. Not now. But he did sag into her embrace and press his forehead into her shoulder.

"He's gonna be okay," Mish crooned into his hair.

He drew back and took in Ray and the equipment connected to him. Many of the numbers on the machines meant nothing to Zavier, but his pulse seemed good. Blood pressure, too.

Alive. Ray was alive. "I'm so, so..." Happy? That wasn't the right word at all. "Glad." Grateful. Relieved. "I wish I could have done more." Done *something*.

Dom rose slowly from his seat, still decked out as Domino, makeup and all. Garish in the dim light and surrounded by the sterile environment of the hospital. "You kept your cool. Made me go with him."

"Was the right thing to do." The jealous part of Zavier thought it should have been *him* by Ray's side. But Dom had the legal means where Zavier didn't. That Zavier *wanted* that level of connection to Ray, that responsibility, meant something, too.

He shook his head and pushed the churn of questions in his soul back down. "You're his friend, too."

Dom nodded. "Still."

Yeah. Still. But Zavier was here now. Ray's chest rose and fell. The monitor showed his heartbeats. Zavier crossed the small distance to the bed and laid two fingers on Ray's hand, the one that didn't have the IV catheter in it.

And yes, he was warm. So warm.

He didn't realize he was trembling until Mish steered him to the seat she'd vacated and pushed him down into it. "You're gonna fall over. Where would you be then?"

He shrugged. "You and Dom do fine on your own."

"Bullshit," Dom said. "And you know it."

Mish tousled Zavier's hair, which he generally hated with a passion, but from her it felt fine. "You're starting to sound like Ray when you say things like that."

He did sound like Ray at the moment. He stared at his unconscious form. "What did the doctors have to say?"

Dom spoke. "What we thought—a severe allergic reaction.

They got him under control, though. The EpiPen was a good idea." He sounded bone-tired, and far closer to being Dominic than Domino, despite his state of dress. "They're running blood tests to figure out what was in his system, but he should be back to normal in a few days."

Zavier propped his elbows on his knees and dropped his head into his hands. Ray would be *fine*. If only his mind would catch up. In his mind, Ray collapsed into his arms. Over and over again. Carl's sneer.

Fuck. Rage was a volcano inside him. He hissed out a breath and sat up. "That fucking asshole *Carl* drugged him."

"What?" Both Mish and Dom spoke, both twitched away, as if Zavier had struck them.

"It was on the security video. He dropped something in Ray's drink, probably trying to start an incident for the rumor mill, only it nearly *killed* Ray."

Nearly. How much of a misstep would it have taken for Ray to have died? He didn't want to think about it. Couldn't help running each scenario through his head.

Mish's hand was in Zavier's hair again, and she drew his head against her side. "Honey, it's okay. He's alive. He's here."

That was what he saw, yes. Ray alive in the hospital. All the machines read the right things. No alarms. But in his mind, Ray was falling again. And again. Zavier could only catch him and watch, helpless and ineffective, while everyone around him did what he so wanted to do—take care of Ray. The tears he hated, that he fought against, slipped down his cheeks.

Mish pulled a chair over next to Zavier's and took his hand. "It's gonna be okay."

"I know." He did. But he wasn't so foolish to think that this night hadn't changed anything. Everything inside Zavier had been flipped sideways and nearly crushed into bits.

He never wanted to lose Ray. Never wanted to come close to losing Ray again.

CHAPTER
TWENTY-ONE

WAKING UP WAS LIKE FIGHTING TOWARD LIGHT AND SOUND. RAY didn't want to scrape and push anymore, but he kept crawling until he could blink open his eyes and taste antiseptic, too-cold air. There was weird shit on him, and this wasn't a hotel or the tour bus. He was alone in a tiny bed with metal bars as sides, and there were way too many pieces of equipment hooked up to him.

Hospital. He was in a hospital.

Damned if he knew why—he couldn't remember. *Shit.* What had happened? Why couldn't he remember? Had they been in an accident? Where was everyone else? He tried to push himself up, but every movement felt like swimming through mud.

"Fuck." It came out as a croak.

Movement in the room, then Zavier's cracked voice. "Ray? Hey, hey."

God, Zavier looked horrible. Hair every which way. Dark circles under his eyes and his fancy dress clothes all wrinkled and askew. He brushed fingers against Ray's forehead. "It's okay. You're okay."

"What?" That came out as a bark. God, his throat was dry. He tried to push himself up again.

Zavier pressed against Ray's temple. "Shh. Relax. Wait."

The pressure was comforting. Known. Like when he prostrated himself on Zavier's shoes. Ray closed his eyes. *Wait.* He could do that. Zavier was here and he trusted him.

"I'm going to get you some water." The fingers remained. "Be good and stay put."

An order. Relief flooded through Ray. He might not remember what had happened, but this was normal. Zavier was taking care of him.

When he closed his eyes, Zavier removed his fingers. More movement in the room. Water being poured.

"Here." Zavier was close again. "Please drink."

Might have been couched as a request, but Ray knew better. Opening his eyes was still painful, but he took the plastic cup with the straw, sipped down some water, and swallowed.

Bliss. Pure, utter bliss. Practically felt the liquid flowing into his body and down his veins. Another sip felt better, and another. He stopped after that, because man, he was *dizzy*.

He tried speaking again. "What—" So far so good. "What happened?"

Zavier, or a disheveled version of him, pulled a chair closer to his bed and perched himself on the edge. "What's the last thing you remember?"

Ray scoured his mind. They'd been getting ready for a party. Some of it came back. Zavier's lips on his neck and the braid of thread he'd tied tight around Ray's wrist. *So you remember who you are.* He raised his wrist, but the braid was gone and an IV catheter was stuck into the back of his hand and taped down.

"We were getting ready for—there was a party. The album went platinum."

"Yes, it did. And yes, we went."

"I don't remember being there." He searched and searched, turning the water cup in his hand. "You'd promised to tie me down when we got back. I remember we got into the limo at the hotel and all I could think about was kneeling naked before you in your tux...then there's nothing."

Zavier shifted on the chair, a tinge of color in his cheeks. "And see—I forgot that promise." He shook his head, looking far, far too tired. "I was so worried about you."

"Zavier, what happened?"

Silence and a very grave face. Zavier closed his eyes for a moment, then met Ray's gaze. "Carl drugged you. He dropped two crushed-up pills in your drink while your back was turned."

Suddenly, Ray was colder than the water had been. The trembles started next when he realized exactly what that meant.

Zavier stood and reclaimed the cup. Stroked his hair. "Shh, Ray."

The trembling went on. He didn't remember *anything*. Not one moment. "What...what did he *do* to me after that?" It came out rough and tight.

"Nothing." Zavier cupped his face. "He didn't touch you. No one did."

"Then why am I here?" In a hospital bed with wires and an IV and machines all stuck to him.

"Turns out you have a severe allergy to whatever it was. You had an anaphylactic reaction."

Oh *shit*. He must have looked shocked or disturbed, because Zavier stroked his cheek. "You're fine now."

Which meant he hadn't been then. Fuck. He leaned into Zavier's touch and listened as he spilled out the rest of the story. Mish's EpiPen. Dom riding with him to the hospital to direct treatment. Zavier speaking to the cops. There were lawyers and law enforcement involved now, from the local to the state and even the record label. Everything jumbled in his head.

It was only the next day. Dom and Mish had left to clean up and change, leaving Zavier on watch. Ray had a sinking suspicion that Zavier chose to stay because he would not leave.

It was a Zavier thing to do.

But overall, the whole situation was a *mess*. The rest of the tour—well, their part of it as the opening band for Five Asylum—had been canceled. The press was full of photos and rumors.

Tears came to Ray's eyes, and that was horrible and unexpected, but he couldn't help them. He'd known Carl hated him, but hadn't thought that hate was enough to make Carl want to *kill* him. That one fact played over and over in his mind.

Zavier wiped the salt trails away, murmuring words that didn't make sense.

Finally, Ray whispered, "I'm sorry."

"You have absolutely nothing to be sorry for. None of this was your fault."

On the surface, he knew that. But deep inside? He didn't understand how it had even come to be. "But *why*?" Why did Carl hate him so much? What had Ray *done*?

"Carl Roberts is a vindictive asshole who can't cope with anyone he sees as inferior climbing above him. Didn't matter that you worked hard. Didn't matter that you're insanely talented. He only saw class and status."

"The dumbass slacker succeeding." Made a twisted sense. "Shit, that's a hell of a way to live, with that much poison."

A soft, sad laugh. Zavier tipped Ray's chin until he gazed up. A position of trust and surrender. "Ray Van Zeller, you're an amazing man, and I'm honored to be your friend."

He fucking loved Zavier. Down to his toes. With every piece of his body.

"Always?" It was all he could push out. The only word.

Emotions played over Zavier's face, and for a moment, Ray saw fear there, but then it was gone and Zavier nodded. "Always. As long as you're true to yourself."

Ray closed his eyes. He wanted to be honest and true, but this wasn't a love affair—it was a friendship. A deep and abiding one. He'd just happened to have fallen in love with Zavier, which...he'd deal with that later. Figure out how they could be themselves together.

Right now? He wanted out of this damn bed and gown. Needed to be free of all this machinery. "You think they're gonna let me out of here anytime soon?"

Zavier let him go. "Let me go find a nurse and see what I can do."

If there was anyone who could spring him from a hospital, it was Zavier.

Took far longer than Ray had hoped to get him the fuck out of the hospital. Long enough that he endured breakfast and lunch in bed. Food wasn't that bad, but it was still hospital food.

He spoke to both Mish and Dom on the phone, thanking the latter for everything he'd done. "I know I put you on the spot."

Dom chuckled. "You know I'll be there for you, but maybe you should add Zav to your health power of attorney?"

Yeah, he should. Wanted to, if Zavier was willing. Something they needed to talk about once they got out of here. If he ever got out of here. Damn, he itched to be free of this bed!

What really annoyed the hell out of him was that they wouldn't remove the IV from his hand until the discharge papers were ready. By mid-afternoon, he was about ready to rip the thing out himself. The only reason he didn't was

Zavier's presence by his side and the fact that Zavier's hand was wrapped around his ankle. The occasionally tightened grip felt gloriously like a cuff and relaxed Ray in an instant.

It also made him harder than he liked, given that he was only wearing a hospital gown. Zavier's sly smile didn't help. Ray cleared his throat. "I'd say you're awful, but—"

That smile didn't falter. "You want it." Zavier spoke low, in that entirely too sexy voice of his.

"I need it." Ray glanced at the IV in his hand for the umpteenth time and every nerve itched to get up, get dressed, and get out. He *hated* hospitals. The feel, the vibe, the way they never, ever let him sleep. Granted, he'd been unconscious for most of this stay, but *still*.

Zavier tightened his grip yet again. "Lean back and relax."

Ray tried. He *tried*. But he wasn't kneeling at Zavier's feet, so the tension didn't leak away like it should, at least not at first.

"Don't move." Zavier's order was sharp, even as it was low volume.

Every nerve in Ray's body jumped.

"Ray..." That was Zavier's one warning.

Breathe. He had to breathe. Inhale. Count to three. Exhale. He willed himself into jelly and sank into the bed.

"Yes, very nice."

The murmur of approval played along those same nerves, warming them and softening Ray's muscles. He was totally unprepared when Zavier ran the back of a fingernail up his instep. Electricity to every limb. He twitched and shook and hissed.

"No moving." Amusement in Zavier's voice. Bastard knew exactly what he was doing. But after a few minutes, the touch, the command put him elsewhere, to that heady, thinky place he ended up in whenever he and Zavier played.

Felt like home. They could have been anywhere—a hotel room, in the back of a tour bus, in a *hospital* room—and it would've felt like home. All he needed was Zavier's touch and his voice. After a while, the lovely torment stopped, and Ray floated, happy and relaxed until a doctor knocked on the open door and breezed into the room.

Zavier let go of his leg, and Ray missed his touch immediately.

The doctor was on the younger side and black. Fit, with short hair and a deep voice. There were the perfunctory introductions and the doc performed all those simple tests that had already been done to him a thousand times that day—he listened to Ray's heart, took his blood pressure, and looked over his chart. "Well, Mr. Van Zeller, you seem to be past your scare and everything checks out. Your system has had quite the shock, though, so feel free to relax for a few days. I'll have your discharge papers written up shortly."

So, still not free. "Do you think I could get this fucking thing out of my hand?" He waved his hand with the IV.

The doctor didn't even blink. "I'll have a nurse come and take care of it." He breezed out with the same speed he'd come in.

Of course. Which meant it would take another fifteen hours. Ray closed his eyes. "I'm never getting out of here."

"You will," Zavier said. He patted Ray's leg again.

"God, I like that. You touching me. Feels like I can take on the world when I know you're there."

Zavier grunted. "Here." He picked at one of the leather bracelets that always seemed to be tied around his wrist lately, except in the shower, and freed it. Next thing Ray knew, it was tied around his ankle. "A little reminder of me for when I can't touch you."

Like the string that was gone, but better. Fire was chased by calm, and Ray settled back against the bed. "I like that."

"Like a tiny cuff."

"Exactly."

Didn't take fifteen hours, but it did take nearly forty-five minutes before a nurse came to remove the IV catheter from his hand, and then another forty-five before Ray was handed his discharge papers. He'd also been prescribed a medicine to take to help counterbalance the shit Carl had given him. Getting that took time, too. But eventually he was allowed to leave.

Thank *god*.

By the time they got a cab and drove back to the hotel, the medicine had taken effect and Ray could barely keep his eyes open. "Not fair," he murmured as he leaned against Zavier as they rode up the elevator. "I spent most of the day in bed."

"But it'll be a giant hotel bed with no machines and no IV."

"You won't stick any needles in me."

A laugh. "No needles. No. Not at all my kink."

"Good." Ray couldn't be happier about that. That kind of pain wasn't his thing. "Join me in bed?" He missed Zavier. Wanted him near. Needed to feel his warmth.

"It's still pretty early. I'd be a mess in bed. Tossing and turning."

True. It had been after five when they'd left the hospital, far too early for most people to sleep, unless they were hopped up on drugs.

When they reached their floor, Zavier maneuvered him— really half carried him—to their joined rooms. Ray had trouble seeing straight enough to walk. His head was mush and all he wanted to do was close his eyes. "Holy shit, this stuff is strong."

"Well, they gave you something pretty powerful. I bet Benadryl knocks you on your ass, doesn't it? This is worse." Zavier keyed them in.

"Yeah. I just don't want to sleep."

"Best thing to get your system back in shape."

When they made it into the room, rather than being alone, both Mish and Dom were there.

Surprisingly, Dom was dressed down, even for him. Shorts and a T-shirt. "Dude, did you spring him and go to a bar to celebrate or something?"

Ray groaned. "Fuck you. I'm not drunk."

"They doped him up with some powerful stuff to counteract anything left in his system." Zavier sounded like he was laughing.

"Bastard," Ray murmured. "Why is everyone here?"

"Mmmhmm. I *am* a bastard." A moment later, Zavier deposited Ray on the end of the bed. "And they wanted to see you. Same as me, last night."

"Hey, kiddo. You look better." Mish patted his knee.

Dom snickered. "Except for that goofy smile."

"'S not goofy. I'm happy. I'm here." Ray flopped his arms out, and man, the bed felt good. Cool. Soft. "With everyone I love."

He did love them all. Especially Zavier. Head over heels. Hard enough that it scared him and if it scared him, it would probably terrify Zavier. Still, he should tell him, explain that he didn't expect anything in return—but Zavier should know how he felt.

That was only fair. Tell the truth. They'd said they would.

Mish and Dom both said their good-nights. The next few minutes—hours? Whatever. They were a blur of movement and commands and getting undressed and under the covers. So perfect. Crisp. Clean. The bed was heaven.

He cracked his eyes open and found Zavier watching him. "Stay?"

Zavier cupped his face. "I'm not leaving you."

Good. That was enough. Ray closed his eyes and fell into blessed darkness.

Zavier had watched Ray fall asleep, then peeled off his dress wear and taken a long, hot shower before finding more comfortable clothes. A T-shirt. Jeans. Once dressed, he stepped into the other hotel room and left the joining door cracked for when Ray woke up, because chances were he'd come looking for someone once the drugs wore off.

But right now, both Mish and Dom were sitting on the bed, waiting for him.

Mish spoke first. "How is he really?"

"The doctor said he'd be fine. The stuff Carl used should be more or less out of his system, but the drugs the hospital gave him will make sure there's nothing lingering that will cause issues. Kind of a precaution."

"He could use the rest," Dom said. There was a thoughtfulness to his look, and that sharpened the longer he stared at Zavier. "What about you?"

"Me?" Zavier worked to school his features, even as his brain tried to turn the past twenty-four hours over in his head.

Dom straightened and suddenly looked nothing like either the shy musician or the imposing rock star. He didn't even look like a twink on the prowl. No, he had the posture of an equal. A friend—a very concerned friend. "This whole thing hasn't been easy on you, either. How are you holding up?"

"I don't know yet." That was the most truthful answer. "I haven't had time to sit down and think."

Mish rose from the bed and crossed the room. She held out her arms in invitation, and Zavier gave in, letting her hug him—welcoming the touch. If they could see he was out of sorts, he really did need to get away for a little bit and churn though all the thoughts in his head.

She brushed her hand against his hair. "You're a good man, Zav. And Ray cares a great deal for you."

He took the compliment, and it warmed him. "I know he does." He pulled back. "And thank you."

She patted him on the cheek. "Take care of yourself, too, kiddo."

Dom chuckled. "She means that. Or you won't hear the end of it."

That also warmed him. Their camaraderie. Many of the musicians he'd worked with in the symphony had found him somewhat cold as he fought to prove himself as a young and talented musician in a sea of talent—and that had put up barriers, which meant that he'd never really formed friendships there.

Here, they'd had to stick together, from day one. Mish and Dom were his friends. Ray, too, of course, but in a different way.

How different? God, his whole body itched. That was exactly the question, wasn't it? How different was Ray from everyone else, and *why*? His head was a fucking mess. Part of him wanted to ignore the spinning of his mind, push on, and be here for everyone.

You can't. You're useless like this.

"Zav?" Mish interrupted his thoughts. "What do you need from us?"

Nothing. Wait. "Give me a minute." He rummaged through the desk and found hotel stationery. No one sent letters anymore, but hell, they always left this stuff anyway in nice places. He scrawled out a short, simple note, put it in an envelope with Ray's name on it and sealed it up. "Can you give this to Ray if he wakes before I come back? I need to get some fresh air."

Mish took the note. "Of course."

He made sure he had a keycard and his wallet, nodded at the two of them, and took off out the door.

I'm not running. Okay, so he *was* running, but not away. He'd return. He just needed to wander for a while.

Rather than the elevator, he took the stairs all the way to the ground floor, then followed a corridor in the opposite direction of the arrow pointed toward the lobby, until he found himself at a loading dock. He let the door slam closed and lock behind him.

The alley led to a main street, and he chose the direction at random and walked. And walked some more. He turned corners on a whim. Stopped and studied window displays without really even seeing what was in them.

Ray. He couldn't get that singular moment out of his head. Ray stumbling to him, terrified. Unable to speak. Falling into his arms. The swirl of people. Time standing still.

Zavier hadn't been able to help. Only that wasn't *entirely* true. He'd made space for the people who had helped. For Mish and for Dom. For the paramedics and the police. He blinked at the store window—stationery—and turned away.

Keep walking. Don't think. Except he couldn't stop thinking, and that struggle led him straight to a car rental place below a garage.

Zavier slowed and stared. Driving did clear his head, or at least gave him the space he needed to puzzle things out. So much of his high school years had been filled with drives once he'd gotten his license. His parents had been understanding about that, in retrospect.

So he went in and rented a car. They took no notice of his name, and the paperwork was quick. The rental guy pulled around the compact car that would be Zavier's, and within fifteen minutes, he was on the road. Didn't take him long to find an interstate. Then he drove and drove as his mind replayed Ray falling into his arms. The ambulance pulling away. Carl's red face.

He'd been there for Ray but unable to help, and that bore into him like fire. If Ray had been anyone else, maybe it wouldn't have caused such terror. Maybe that dark pit in his gut wouldn't be there.

But Ray wasn't like anyone else to Zavier. That was a *problem*.

Zavier knew who he was, knew his own tastes and needs and desires, or lack thereof. But Ray *threw* him. There was so much about Ray he enjoyed, and not only the sex and the kink. The friendship. The music. His smile. Every damn thing. Watching him closing in on death's door? That had been too much. Far too much.

He needed Ray. Didn't want to be without Ray.

Zavier couldn't find answers to calm the turmoil in his head, nor were there any brilliant insights on the road, so he just kept driving.

CHAPTER
TWENTY-TWO

Waking up in a hotel room was far easier than it had been in the hospital. Awareness seeped into Ray like it normally did. The sound of a minifridge and an air conditioner. The soft sheets and too many pillows. No lights being turned on at odd hours or that strange antiseptic hospital smell.

He stretched and opened his eyes. The room was dim, but the brightness of the light around the curtains told him it was day—which meant he'd slept through the night.

He was also alone in bed. Alone in the room, too. Worry gnawed at him like hunger. He'd expected Zavier to be here. Maybe...maybe that wasn't right. Except they'd not been too far apart since the start of the tour and rarely out of sight since they'd started their kinky relationship.

Then again, had the situation been reversed, he'd probably have given Zav space to sleep and recover. He threw back the sheets, and stumbled out of bed and into the bathroom.

There was nothing but hotel shampoo, lotion, and soap on the counter—Zavier's toiletry bag was missing. The shower was dry. Hell, the toilet paper roll still had those folds the cleaning staff put into them. The gnawing inside Ray turned sharp and painful.

Zavier wasn't here.

He could, however, be in the next room. No need to panic. Once Ray'd washed his hands, he made his way back into the bedroom, found his own luggage, and pulled out a pair of sweatpants. The door to the adjoining hotel room was open, and the other door cracked—an invitation. He pushed it open, hoping to find Zav.

But it was Mish curled up on the bed with her laptop. When she looked up, Ray's heart dropped to the floor and he gripped the doorframe. Words didn't come, not with that mixture of relief and worry and sadness flowing through Mish's expression.

Oh god.

"Hey, hon." Soft words. "How are you feeling?"

"Where's Zav?" His voice was a mess. Too dry, too full of agony. He watched her like a hawk.

Shoulders dropped. "He went out for a while." Same concerned voice. "He left a note."

Fuck. Ray's legs wobbled and the world wanted to crash down. "A *note*?"

Mish could move fast when she wanted to, because she was off the bed in a heartbeat and wrapping Ray into a warm hug before he could even turn and flee into the room behind him.

"Sweetheart, no. No. It's not like that." She drew him into the adjoining room, and there were Zavier's bags. Seemingly untouched, but there. "He was really shaken up by you—" She cut herself off.

He sat when Mish pulled him down to the bed next to her, and memories came back. Not of that night, but of waking up in the hospital and of Zavier's explanation of what had happened. "He was shaken up by me nearly dying."

A nod.

Ray closed his eyes. Yeah, that made sense. Couldn't have been easy—and imagining himself in Zavier's position only drove his pulse higher. He'd have been a fucking *wreck*. Zav, at least, had control and poise.

Ray flicked his eyes back open. "I don't even know what time it is. How long has he been gone?"

That was when Mish bit her lip and flushed, and all his fears poured back into him.

"Mish." He didn't quite recognize his own voice, because there was an edge he'd never managed before. "Don't you fucking coddle me."

She took his hands. "I'm not. I'm just as worried about him as I am you. You take the world on your shoulders, but you have us, and Zav. He... I don't think he has anyone."

"Except me."

She nodded. "And he'd fight the world to keep you safe."

Ray struggled with his heart and mind and soul. "How long, Mish?"

"Since just after he brought you here. He grabbed a shower and said he needed to think and he might be a while. He left you a note in case he wasn't back before you woke."

That was awfully like Zavier. Thinking ahead. Knowing how Ray might react. Ray rubbed his temples and glanced over at the clock next to the bed. Nearly three-thirty in the afternoon. Which meant Zavier had been gone almost an entire day. "I should check my phone. See if he called."

Mish shook her head. "We turned it off because it was ringing off the hook. And if yours is anything like mine and Dom's, your voicemail is full." She rose, picked up an envelope, and handed it to him.

Too much to take in at once. He turned the envelope over in his hands. It was obviously the hotel stationery, and bore his name, written in precise, beautiful cursive. Who the heck wrote in cursive anymore?

Zavier, of course. Ray set the letter next to him on the bed.

"Why...wait. Who's been calling?" Then it hit him—the memories. The information Zavier had told him the day before in the hospital. Carl had drugged him. Their *band manager* had nearly killed him. "Oh my god. The press."

"Yeah. The press. The record company. Lawyers. Your family. The cops—they came in person, and security let them in. But you were still asleep."

Ray rubbed his shaking fingers over his arms. "I—I don't know what help I'll be to the cops."

She patted his thigh. "You don't have to talk to them. And you probably should get a lawyer first. We all should, I think."

Yeah. Yeah. And this was when he really needed Zav, because his mind was rocking and his body burned and all the chaos threatened to close in around him again.

He swallowed. "Where's Dom?" Because he needed to know where everyone in his little musical family was, especially now.

"Sleeping. He spent the night here, in case you woke up."

Because everyone bent over backward to take care of Ray when he screwed up. "Fuck. I'm so sorry I've put this all on you."

Mish rolled her eyes. "Ray, honey, none of this is your fault, so you just stop that shit now."

He was already so tired and he'd just gotten up. Cops. Lawyers. How was he supposed to deal with all this? He pulled at his hair. "I know."

He did. Logically. He nearly started in on the rebuttal anyway, but his gaze landed on his ankle and the leather bracelet—Zavier's leather bracelet—tied around it. That brought different memories: Zavier's touch and voice. The press of his fingers against Ray's lips.

Shh. Stop. Breathe.

He did. Inhale, exhale. By the fourth time, his head quieted enough that he let go of his hair. "Yeah. Okay." He didn't know if he was talking to Mish or himself or both. "I should get dressed and figure all this out."

She bumped his shoulder. "You do have us, you know. You're not alone."

Yeah, he wasn't. He stared at the leather around his ankle, picked up Zavier's envelope, and opened it.

The note inside was brief, and written in that same beautiful hand.

I'm not leaving. I'm not. Read those words again. Call me when you're ready.
—Zavier

Beneath that was Zavier's cell number. He hadn't had it— they'd never exchanged numbers. Hadn't needed to. Ray brushed a thumb over Zavier's name.

"'When you're ready,'" he muttered. "That's so fucking Zavier."

Mish chuckled. "He loves you."

"He *cares* about me."

"What's the difference?" She rose and kissed him on the top of the head. "He's not a robot, Ray. He's a lot like you in a way—so damn passionate it overflows onto everything he touches."

"He's got more self-control."

"Or more fear." She smirked. "You boys are something else, you know?"

He had no idea what she meant "What?"

But Mish only laughed again. "How 'bout I get you coffee that's not the hotel room stuff?"

His stomach grumbled. "Um. And a bagel? With cream cheese?"

"Anything your heart desires, sweetheart." She headed for the door.

When it clicked closed, Ray rose. Mish couldn't give him

his heart's desire, not really. What he wanted most was Zavier.

He fingered the note, then set it on the dresser when he crossed back into his room. *When you're ready*. That was a double-edge command. Ray wanted to call Zavier now—but he also knew he wasn't ready. Not in the way Zavier meant.

He had shit to dig through before he would be ready to call. Best to get started now.

———

RAY TOOK OFF ZAVIER'S LEATHER BRACELET BEFORE SHOWERING, but tied it right back onto his ankle when he was done. He liked it there and he needed the reminder that Zavier wasn't *gone* gone, even if he wasn't here at the moment.

The A/C in the hotel room cooled his damp skin when he plodded out of the bathroom. The shower had helped clear his head, but not enough. Too many questions and fears swam like sharks around him. Problem was, he didn't have nearly enough information to even start to chart a course. So, first things first.

He got dressed. Comfortable clothes. Loose jeans and an old T-shirt from the Wildwood Boardwalk—a little memory of home.

Mish had left coffee and a bagel on the dresser, next to his phone and a business card. He took his time eating and letting the coffee work his magic. Next, he turned on his cell. The business card was from the police, and had a case number scrawled on the back.

Yeah, he'd have to talk to them, since he'd been the victim of a crime.

Ray shivered. Why why why *why* did Carl hate him? He couldn't work it out. Even jealousy didn't make sense and not having a reason—a legitimate reason—baffled him more than anything else. He could have *died* that night.

Mish had suggested getting a lawyer, but who knew how the *fuck* he was going to find one of those? He wasn't about to trust any who called him, since he had an inkling of what this whole series of events could mean.

He wasn't sure he wanted to go through the pain and drama of suing the record label. Yeah, it might mean big bucks, but what would it do to him and the band?

Shit.

Once he turned on his phone and sifted through the messages—text and voicemail and email—he didn't have many more answers, either. The label wanted to talk; there were several messages, both from execs and label lawyers. The underlying theme—the unwritten thought—was that they wanted to work things out *without* lawsuits.

How complicit had they been, though? Did he want to keep making albums and money for the company that had given him *Carl Roberts* as an advocate?

Yeah, he needed a lawyer of his own, and to figure out what *he* wanted, which was whatever was best for the band. He'd need their input for that—including Zav's thoughts.

'Cause Zav was as much a part of this as everyone else.

When you're ready. He nearly heard the words in Zavier's smooth voice, and nodded absently. He had a good idea when that was. Hopefully Zavier would be ready by then, too.

That time wasn't yet, though. Lawyer first. He rubbed his eyes and paced the room. If Zavier were here, he'd ask him about Nadia Rudd. Surely she'd know a good entertainment lawyer. But he had to do this without Zav. Problem was, he didn't know anyone else, really. Just the band, the crew and—

Five Asylum. He sucked in a breath. Gregor had given him his business card. *If you ever need to talk shop*.

Well, this was shop, wasn't it? Ray dug out his notebook and fished the business card out of the little pouch in the back. He dialed the number before he changed his mind and listened to the ringing while his breath caught in his chest.

"Hello?" Given the deep voice, it absolutely was Gregor Daye on the other side.

"Hey, it's Ray Van Zeller."

A pause. "Hello, Ray. I suppose I shouldn't be entirely surprised to hear from you, given everything."

He couldn't help the bitter laugh. "To be honest, I have no idea what's out in the public right now. It really doesn't matter."

"It never does." Spoken like Gregor knew and felt that. But then, he had fifteen years of stardom, so Ray bet he did. "Are you healthy?"

"Yeah, I am. I'm—lucky."

"Good. And yes, I gathered that." Another long silence. "What can I do for you?"

"I was hoping you could recommend a lawyer. Or knew someone who could."

A laugh. "You're a smart kid. And yes, I can. She's worked very hard for us over the years, and I'm sure her firm can help you with what you need."

Ray scribbled down the name, Tara Gonfaus, and the number into his notebook. Everything about the band was there—and this wouldn't be any different. "Thank you. I don't know how to repay you."

"Shit, there's no need. Just be yourself and do good for someone down the line. That's all."

"Yeah, I can do that."

Another chuckle from Gregor. "Take it easy, Ray."

"You, too."

And that was that. Ray put the phone on the bed and walked back and forth to burn off energy and anxiety.

Breathe. There was Zavier's voice again. He obeyed, too. Because it helped. Those little tricks and the leather around his ankle. Being naked at Zavier's feet.

Yeah, that wasn't happening, not now. He wasn't ready. But he could do something similar. Ray stopped pacing and pulled his T-shirt off. Everything else followed. Then he knelt on the floor, in front of the chair Zavier would have sat in, and folded himself into child's pose.

In an instant, he was alive and so aware of himself, of how naked he was, how vulnerable. And yeah, he got hard. But he also let go. Let all of the shit vanish and slip away, except for his heartbeat and his breath. He even let Zavier go—and the fleeting wonder if he'd be proud of Ray right now. Inhale, exhale, melt.

The noise in his head softened and vanished, and he melted, letting the floor support him. Letting himself be. Just as slowly, a quiet voice spoke, the assured one in the back of his head, the one so often drowned out by worry and the world. *What do you want?*

If he could have anything, if the world were fair, the best option for the band would be to cancel the contract with their label without penalty. He had no trust in them; he doubted anyone in the band did. Their playing and his composition would suffer if they stayed. He didn't want to give the label any more—especially since he'd nearly given his life because of their ineptitude. Carl worked for the label and fought against Twisted Wishes and Ray at every turn.

Twisted Wishes would be better off elsewhere, either on their own or with another label—they could figure out which later.

Ray wanted Carl in jail. A deeply vindictive part really wanted him behind bars *and* suffering. More than anything, he wanted to know the reason behind all the shit he'd been through.

If the band was truly in debt to the label, he wanted that gone. Erased. And then some, because the label didn't get to put them all through hell only to walk away with clean hands and no damage.

Yeah. That was a decent start. Ray pushed himself up to sitting and peered around the room. Everything seemed a little brighter and the tumult in his head was gone.

He dressed, grabbed his phone again, and made another call.

It went straight to the lawyer's voicemail. He left a coherent message, and not five minutes later, got a call back.

"Mr. Van Zeller." Ms. Gonfaus's voice was clear, with a faint accent he couldn't place. "I'm pleased you've reached out and I do hope we can help you."

They spoke for quite some time, long enough that both Mish and Dom poked their heads in, and he waved them off. He took three pages of notes and gave the contact information for the police and the case number to her.

"I don't think your wishes are unreasonable," Ms. Gonfaus said. "Though I don't think we'll see Mr. Roberts in jail, given what we discussed."

Yes, attempted murder was a serious charge, but the best they could hope for was attempted manslaughter, given the fact that Carl hadn't meant to kill him. That severe an allergy to what had turned out to be a common sleep medication was pretty rare. No, Carl had wanted to embarrass Ray and destroy his career—not kill him. Plea bargaining would likely take that down more, especially since Ray didn't want to be dragged through a long and protracted court case.

"More's the pity."

She grunted. "Your bandmate is correct, as well. Someone from your legal team should be there when you speak to the police, even though you're the victim."

God, he hated that word, even if it was true. "I think Zav talked to the police that night."

"Very likely." She sighed. "We'll also want to talk to your partner and the rest of the band if we're to represent Twisted Wishes as a whole."

"We can set something up." He paused. "I haven't even looked at the press."

"Don't if you don't want to. Do if you do. But *do not* respond to any of it. There are two words you need to start using: no comment."

He repeated them back to her, tasting them in his mouth. Yeah. "I can do that."

"Good." Something in Ms. Gonfaus's voice softened. "You've been through quite a time, Mr. Van Zeller. Let us take it from here. I'll call you tomorrow with an update."

They said professional goodbyes and hung up. Ray stared at the time on the phone: 8:22. Holy shit. He wondered if lawyers charged time and a half. But then, he was pretty sure he wasn't going to be the one paying for Ms. Gonfaus's services once all this was over.

He shuffled to the adjoining room and found both Mish and Dom there. "Hey."

Both of them wore worry in their own way. Dom stood. "Hey, man." His voice was a mess.

God. Ray was a fool to think he was the only one affected by all this. He crossed the room and pulled his oldest friend into a hug. "Dude, I'm fine."

"Obviously." That came out broken. "But you weren't. Yesterday, you weren't."

He pulled back and gripped Dom's shoulders. "Yeah, but it's today, and I'm here and fine. And I've just spent god knows how long talking to a lawyer to get all this shit figured out."

Dom blinked. "You—found a lawyer?"

Ray flopped into the chair Dom had vacated, and filled his bandmates in on what he'd been up to, leaving out the whole meditating-while-naked part. They didn't need to know that.

He'd tell Zav later.

"So, now what?" Dom chewed on his nail.

Ray shrugged. "We wait. Lawyer said she'd call back

tomorrow." His gaze drifted to Mish's tablet. "I also kinda want to see how this is all being spun."

She grunted. "What I want is dinner."

That would probably be a good idea. "I'm guessing that heading down to the hotel restaurant or going out would be a very bad plan."

Dom's laugh was bitter. "Oh yeah. I went down just to see what was up, and the place is crawling with paparazzi. I hightailed it out of there, just in case someone did recognize me."

"The label hired some security. I think mainly to appease the hotel, since this shit is hitting them, too. Though I bet their bar receipts will be good," Mish said.

"Fuck their receipts. And the label." Ray sighed. "Guess it's room service, then."

She pushed a menu over. "We were waiting for you."

He had to laugh. Then he had to keep from crying. Everything was so out of hand, but they'd get through it. "You guys are the best."

Dom fidgeted. "What about Zav?"

Oh. Ray's heart flipped at the thought of Zavier. His voice. Filling him in on all that had happened. Hearing what was in Zavier's head, because he was damn well gonna pry that out. If nothing else, Zavier owed Ray *that*. "I'll give him a call after dinner."

"You're not mad?" There was confusion in Dom's voice.

He wasn't. God, he missed Zavier so fucking much...but he was kind of glad for his absence, because it had proved something to Ray. He could be in control of himself and solve his own problems.

"He's done so much for me. If he needs space to figure shit out, it's the least I can give him."

When you're ready.

He was. All he needed was some food in his stomach.

CHAPTER
TWENTY-THREE

Zavier bought a small roll of antacids, a toothbrush, and some toothpaste from the truck stop across the street from a motel somewhere outside of someplace. He had no idea where he was, only that he might need to stop eating hot dogs from disreputable establishments and maybe he should have had the forethought to take a bag with him when he'd gone for a "walk."

He jogged back across the road and to his room. Place looked like a shithole, but the rooms were clean enough. Not even bed bugs, thank goodness.

He should have anticipated that he'd do this, wander far and wide. He'd left that note for Ray, after all, knowing that there'd be a decent possibility he'd not be back right away.

But it was easier to think that he was just going out to clear his head. To ponder. Not that he would hunt down a rental place, plunk down money for a compact car, and hit the highway. He wasn't about to admit to himself that he'd gotten in over his head and that large questions about what exactly he was doing loomed over him.

It was—as Nadia had once said when he'd first realized he

liked tying people up, beating them, and then fucking them—existential crisis time.

He wasn't running from Ray. He was running from *himself*, which was a futile and foolish exercise. And yet here he was, in a tiny concrete room off some state route, who knew how far from the posh hotel Ray was holed up in.

He missed Ray with every fiber of his being. They hadn't been out of each other's orbit since that first practice. They'd eked out a friendship and a kinky relationship and now they had something—something Zavier didn't want to name and didn't want to face and never *ever* wanted to let go of.

He stripped the comforter off the bed and lay down. It wasn't the most comfortable bed, but no worse than the bunks in the tour bus.

He'd known for most of his life that he was a little off center of normal. First he realized he had no gender preference when it came to bed partners. He'd found a word for that fairly fast—pansexual. The kink was easy enough to quantify, too. He loved dominating. Enjoyed the tears and moans of his partners. He was, as Nadia put it, on the mild side as a sadist, closer to a service top, since he so enjoyed giving his partners what they desired most. He had a passion for making his subs fly or go out of their heads or whatever they needed most from their kink.

But his aromanticism? That had been harder to find words to describe. He'd never particularly understood the trappings of romance, from the diamond engagement commercials to why people found giving flowers some holy romantic gesture. The whole concept of starry eyes and falling so in love that your whole being was consumed with the thoughts of another scared the shit out of him. People actually lost their whole sense of self to *love*? That sounded like some kind of *nightmare*, like love was a zombie that ate your brain. He'd seen it, too, people changing their whole selves to be with someone. Even politics and interests and religion. Atheists becoming born-again. Liberals turning right wing simply because they'd fallen in *love* with someone.

Being completely uninterested in romance had made sex in high school and college a lesson in how he absolutely had to set expectations *early*. Because, man, did his bed partners expect him to fall head over heels for them. God, even that expression *sounded* painful. Like, how was ramming your face into the ground a fun experience at all?

People seem to obsess over romantic love and the constant declarations and gifts. He'd been raked over coals when he hadn't met whatever romantic standards his partners expected, even when he'd worked so damn hard not to lead anyone on, and set expectations. The worst was when his partners had claimed they would die if he didn't return their love in the way they expected. Guilt wasn't caring.

He did care for friends and family. Hell, he'd go out of his way to help them, care for them. Be there to support and cheer and listen. Provide a shoulder when needed. *That* was the "love" he understood, his definition of what *friend* and *family* meant. The sense the word made to him.

Everything else seemed like play-acting.

It had been such a fucking relief to discover that he wasn't screwed in the head when he'd finally stumbled across the aro community. A breath of fresh air. He could finally be who he was: Zavier Demos, the guy who utterly enjoyed sex and kink and didn't do romance.

He rubbed a hand over his face, unwrapped the antacids, and popped two in his mouth. Mint. Would go well with the toothpaste later. His stomach roiled. *Fuck.* Usually he could stomach questionable rest-stop meals.

The ceiling had water stains in a corner. Lovely. Zavier closed his eyes. He'd been in worse.

He couldn't say he was in love with Ray, because he *wasn't* in love with Ray. He'd never felt any of the things society said he should feel when someone fell in love. He hadn't lost his sense of self. His heart didn't flip over and over when he thought about Ray—at least not when Ray wasn't in the middle of anaphylaxis. He'd contributed the latter to being terrified he was about to watch his best friend die.

He had been so very afraid and angry and desperate to do something—anything—to help. That was a moment Zavier never wanted to live through again. Ray collapsing into his arms. Watching Ray struggle to breathe. Not knowing if he'd see Ray again. That had hurt so fucking much.

The worst part had been watching Dom leave with Ray. Oh, he didn't begrudge Dominic at all—Ray had been smart to give someone in the band medical power of attorney. Hell, they all should do that.

But it hurt that it hadn't been *him*, that they hadn't reached that point yet in their relationship.

And there—right there—was the twist that left Zavier breathless.

Whether he liked it or not, whether he acknowledged it or not, he was *in a relationship* with Ray Van Zeller. They were kink partners. They thoroughly enjoyed each other's bodies. They were bandmates. They were *friends*. Best friends.

Zavier pried his eyes open and stared back up at the ceiling.

Maybe that was the difference. Ray had become a friend on top of everything else—or rather, they'd been friends *first*. He didn't become friends with the people he fucked, because that only led to expectations he couldn't fulfill, and even then he still had issues, like with Dimitri.

And he'd never fucked with anyone he'd become friends with. He'd made some friendships at Juilliard, but they'd been based around music and nothing else, and he'd never bedded one of them. His strange friendship with Nadia had been all about kink and not at all about sex. Aside from the one time she'd tied him up and flogged him, they hadn't even touched but for chaste hugs. Neither of them had ever been interested in the other sexually. Sure, Nadia liked to tease about his sexiness, but that was born from her sadism—it made Zavier uncomfortable.

Since Juilliard, he hadn't made many friends. Dom and Mish were both good friends now since they were also a *band*. They'd lived on top of each other for almost three months. You didn't go through that without forming bonds.

Ray was *everything*, though. He fit into Zavier's life so damn comfortably. Ray was his best friend and a man who understood him. A sweet submissive who listened, and *didn't*, in equal, intoxicating measure. Someone who enjoyed sex as much as Zavier did. Ray was also an exquisite musician in his own right. That Zavier could help Ray relax and lift the world off for a while—well. That was also a turn-on and a kink.

Service top, indeed. Nadia had pinned that on him early on.

That would explain why not being able to help Ray had been so fucking *devastating*. Coupled with everything else? Yeah, he had needed to run away, or at least run until he found the space to process it all.

Why that space had to be a shitty motel room, he didn't know.

Note to self: next time, run off to a five-star place. Order a rare steak and a bottle of fine wine. Skip the antacids.

Next time, he'd take Ray with him.

Zavier shivered. He hoped the note had been enough to keep Ray calm. He owed Ray an explanation, but at least, for now, he had one other than "need to work shit out."

One thing he did know—Ray was capable. He was strong. He'd be *fine*. And Mish and Dom would watch out for him. Zavier would go back. He was going back. First thing tomorrow. He'd take a look at his GPS and figure out where the hell he was, and chart a course home to Ray.

Zavier rose, grabbed the toothbrush and toothpaste, and headed into the bathroom. The best thing he could do now would be to sleep until Ray called him. He had no doubt his phone would ring eventually.

THE RINGING OF HIS CELL WOKE ZAVIER UP. PHONE SAID IT WAS just past eleven-thirty and the screen blurred when he tried to blink sleep away. His vision sharpened when he realized the caller was Ray. *Thank goodness.* He would've headed back in the morning regardless, but he wanted to hear Ray's voice.

He answered. "Hey."

"Zav? You okay?" Ray's voice was so clear. Full of wonder and worry, too.

Reasonable question. Zavier toyed with the answer, the edge of sleep making his emotions—and everything else—sluggish. "I am now, yeah." All the tension was gone, whether from being asleep or having screwed his head back on, he wasn't sure. "What about you?"

A laugh. "I'm fine. I miss you, but I'm fine."

"I miss you, too." Because he did, but the phrase—even in his own voice—made him groan. "I think that's the single sappiest thing I've ever uttered in my *life*. Please don't take it the wrong way."

A long pause from the other end, then a whisper of words. "You're allowed to miss your friends, you know."

The little bit of hurt woven into Ray's voice tugged at Zavier's conscience. "I do know. And I do mean it. I just wonder how many people actually do, you know? Or if it's just one of those things people say." He rubbed his face. "Fuck, I'm sorry. I just woke up. I'm...more jumbled than normal."

"You're *never* jumbled. It's interesting to hear you like this." There was that little twist of amusement on the other end. "Keep going. I wanna hear more."

He could almost see Ray's smirk. "If you were here, I'd turn you over my knee for that tone."

The response became far more grave and deep. "If you were here, I'd gladly take the beating and love every second of it. But you're *not* here, Zav." An exhale. "There's so much I want to tell you."

Heat in his blood, both at spanking Ray and listening to him. Seeing him. "I'm coming home, Ray. Tomorrow."

There was a crinkle on the other end. "Never doubted. I figured you needed space and you said you weren't leaving. You've never lied to me."

It was so damn good to be connected again. He *had* missed Ray, more than he wanted to ever say. His *partner*. Zavier's body sang with warmth. "Tell me about your day."

"You mean the part after I freaked out because you weren't here?"

"I'm betting you're exaggerating about freaking out. You're incapable of that before your first cup of coffee."

A cough and a laugh. "Okay, yeah, might be stretching the freak-out part. I was worried, but fine, once Mish said you'd left a note and—never mind."

That was interesting. "She said *what*, Ray?"

"She said that you love me."

Oh. The coolness of the shitty hotel room settled down over Zavier.

Ray babbled through the phone, his pitch higher, and breathless. "But that's not right, is it? You don't love me, not like hearts and flowers love and—"

"Ray, stop." Ray was getting perilously close to explaining aromanticism, and Zavier *really* didn't need that right now. "I do care deeply for you."

"That's what I told her. She said there's all kinds of love."

God, he really did wish he were next to Ray, who was undoubtedly a nice shade of embarrassed-as-all-fuck, and Zavier could so play with that. But who knew how many miles and hours of driving separated them? "There are all kinds of love, yes. But I have a very difficult time with the word *love* because it's been soaked by society with so many things I don't understand or feel."

"I know. I—"

"Shush. Please." Silence on the other end. Good. "I drove out here to wherever the hell I am because I needed time in my head. I've had that, I've figured my shit out, and I'm coming back. But it's too fucking much right now to explain over the phone." His voice cracked a little, which he hated.

"Okay." Ray was breathless.

"You know I care, Ray. We're incredibly tangled up in each other's lives, and I don't want that to end."

Ray gave a little bark of a laugh. "Can I say something now?"

Maybe there was a touch of heat rising to Zavier's cheeks at the Ray's rueful voice. "Sure."

"I'm not worried. You said to call when I was ready. Well, I'm ready."

He had scrawled that onto his note. "What are you ready for?"

"You. Us. The band. Whatever the future holds." There was a pause and more rustling—Ray was either getting up or sitting down. "I talked to a lawyer today."

Oh. That was good. Calm settled into Zavier's bones. Ray was fine. He'd come through and out the other side of this crisis and taken charge. While he so enjoyed taking care of Ray, there were limits—both for Ray's good and for Zavier's. Twisted Wishes was *Ray's* band. What Carl did, he'd done to *Ray*. The person to solve all of that couldn't be Zavier.

He ran a hand through his hair. "Do you have a plan?"

"Yeah. Or at least I know what I want and we've talked about what's most likely and what to aim for." There was a thump, and Zavier was pretty sure Ray was pacing. "I gave my statement to the police, too. Now it's just a matter of waiting for wheels to turn and legal people to talk to each other. But we do have them over a barrel, in many ways."

Well, yes. Carl's malicious actions had threatened Ray's life. "Sounds like you have everything in hand."

A chuckle. "Or at least have found other capable hands to put the problem into." There was a pause. "Zav, I need you, though. I can do this shit, sure. But having you here—just here in the room—would make all of this so much easier."

"Moral support."

"More than moral support. You believe in me. You have since you walked into that audition, even when I was being a little shit to you."

Zavier rolled onto his side. "Yeah, I do, and I did even back then." He studied the wrinkles in the sheets. "I wish I were there, Ray, because I'd lay you out on that big hotel bed and show you *exactly* how proud I am of you. How much I believe in you." Wouldn't that be a treat? He stroked his hardening length.

There was a groan on the other end of the line. "Shit. How am I supposed to go to bed now?"

"Well, there are a bunch of toys in my bag."

A laugh. "Is this gonna turn into a phone sex thing? You telling me what to do to get myself off?"

"No." He kept his voice soft. "I'm really tired. I only slept a couple hours at a truck stop last night." He'd driven until hunger and exhaustion had taken him off the road. A few hours later, his brain—and a couple of eighteen-wheelers lumbering past—had put him back on the road. "And the sooner I wake up tomorrow, the sooner I can come home."

There was a catch in Ray's breathing. "That's twice you've said *home*."

"Yes. You're home, Ray. Wherever you are."

Another hitch in Ray's breathing. "I—feel similar."

Zavier heard the other words, the ones Ray was trying *so*

hard not to say for Zavier's benefit. It was endearing and a kindness. "You know what I want to fall asleep to?"

"What?"

"The thought of you pulling that dildo out of my bag and banging yourself with it until you come with my name on your lips."

"Oh fuck." That came out as a moan.

Zavier chuckled and ran his thumb over the head of his dick. "Can you do that for me?"

"Yeah. I can."

"Good." He paused. "Good night, Ray. I'll see you tomorrow."

Ray exhaled. "Good night, Zav. You're evil, you know?"

He just laughed and disconnected the call. Yeah, he was. But for all that he was tormenting Ray, he was tormenting himself as well. He set his phone on the nightstand, then delved into the fantasy he'd set for Ray, knowing that in that large hotel room, Ray would be fucking himself senseless.

Zavier came faster than he wanted, pumping his jizz out all over his chest. The orgasm was entirely unfulfilling, except to help exhaust him more. Too tired to get up, he wiped himself off with the bed sheet. Sleep would be an indulgence, and tomorrow?

Tomorrow he'd join Ray in that big hotel bed of his...of *theirs*.

RAY WOKE THE NEXT MORNING FAR TOO EARLY TO BOTHER MISH or Dom. Living in what amounted to two hotel rooms without Zavier and without being able to leave was weird and getting uncomfortable. He didn't venture over to Mish's or Dom's rooms, because he didn't want to intrude on their privacy. They'd had to deal with all of this shit, too—it was the least he could do. He expected they would wander over when they were up and dressed, and they'd all order room service.

Apparently there were less paparazzi hanging around the hotel, but some still lingered. His lawyer had suggested they lay low, as had the cops. So they had.

But the hotel life was wearing thin. He hoped they could figure out what the next steps were soon so they all could move on. At least the label was still paying for the hotel, though Ms. Gonfaus said their firm would pick up costs if the label decided not to pay, and then tack that on to their demands.

He killed some time with a long, hot shower to ease away his aches, both from stress and from his activities last night.

After Ray had hung up with Zavier, he'd done exactly what Zavier had requested. He'd gone into Zav's bag and pulled out a dildo—one Zavier hadn't used on him yet—a condom and lube. Then he'd fucked himself to exhaustion. And yeah, he'd cried out Zavier's name while shooting his load.

Intense and primal, the orgasm had left him both fulfilled and gutted. He wanted Zavier, wanted his touch and his hands. He was so fucking in love with Zav that it *hurt* when he thought about him. There were times when he absolutely wanted to fall at Zav's feet and blather on about what Zav meant to him. Except Zavier would be confused and perplexed at best. At worst, he'd be horrified at Ray and his over-the-top emotions.

He couldn't fault Zavier. From a certain point of view, falling in love did seem like a kind of temporary madness that either evened out into something solid, steady, and calm. Or it shattered, leaving behind a trail of pain and pieces to gather and start again.

But he couldn't help what he felt any more than Zavier could. It was absolutely enough that Zavier cared about him and wanted to be with him. They *were* friends, and the sex, with the added bonus of Ray's newfound kink, was incredible. Plus, he got to see Zavier play drums all the damn time, and that was its own glory.

Content, Zav had said at one point. Yeah, that summed it up nicely. Maybe more than content. Happy. He'd let Zavier set the pace. After all, he *liked* Zavier in charge—at least in some circumstances.

He appreciated the headspace Zavier had given him with the kink and the sex and the friendship, but in the end, Twisted Wishes was his to lead. He'd built the band from high school. It was only fitting that he take them into whatever lay in the future. He'd also taken the brunt of Carl's shit. Yes, he'd consult Dom, Mish, and Zav, but he would be the leader—and a better one than before.

Sadly, showering, dressing, and ruminating didn't take *that* much time, even when done leisurely. Still no sign of Mish or Dom, and he wasn't about to text either of them. They deserved their sleep. None of this, especially his medical crisis, had been kind to them, and he'd be a fool to think that it hadn't affected or stressed them out.

Which left him alone in two big rooms with very little to do. He glanced around his room until his gaze lingered on his tablet. Shit, well, he was kind of curious about how the media was spinning this. Hell, he had no idea if Zav had managed to slink out of town unnoticed, and if he hadn't, how was *that* being talked about?

With trepidation in his soul, he approached the device and picked it up. Only one way to know for sure. Ray flopped down in the nearest chair, turned the thing on, and started the rounds on the usual sites.

In the end, the press wasn't that bad. Interesting in places, too. Lots of confusion and speculation. No mention of Zavier leaving, so he must have managed to avoid the reporters and the paparazzi.

Ray was gonna grill Zav about how to do that. Fucking *magical*. He wanted that skill.

Of course, there were the awful photos of him unconscious on a stretcher being worked on and moved to the ambulance, and ones of Domino climbing in, in his full persona. Speculation as to why it wasn't Zavier, ranging from them having broken up—which very few people believed—to Zavier being held for questioning by the police—which was closer to the truth.

There were also photos of Zavier, from when he left the club to head to the hospital. Fuck, he looked tired in those. And grim, his mouth pulled into a tight line. Worry carving deep fissures around his eyes. Anger when he spotted the press photographing him.

But he hadn't said a thing, only gotten into a cab bound for the hospital.

The pictures of Carl getting hauled away in handcuffs were something *else*. Ray was glad he hadn't put anything in his stomach yet because his gut fucking rebelled. Sick and hot and angry—it hit him all at once, leaving him breathless and heaving.

There was the man who'd nearly killed him. The man who'd been supposedly shepherding them through stardom, and working for their best interests. Carl looked wild and desperate and utterly guilty in those photos, and once the initial shock had worn off, the only thing in Ray's heart for that bastard was contempt.

The speculation about why Carl was arrested was all over the map, everything from gay-bashing to being enamored with Ray or Zavier or both, to being some kind of spy for another band.

What bothered Ray the most was that *he still didn't know* the reasons behind Carl's actions. He shook his head and searched on. And rammed up against pages upon pages of text and photos and tweets that made his eyes water and his throat tighten. He set the tablet down and got up to pace.

Get-well messages. Outpourings of love and concern. Photos of signs and cards and little vigils with candles and lights, entire Instagrams worth of messages. It was *everything* and far more than he deserved.

I'm just a guy who sings.

He could almost hear Zavier's laugh and the words he'd probably say. *You're so much more than that, Ray.*

On the one hand, his lawyer said to lay low. On the other hand, he probably should say something to the fans. They did have an official Twitter account for the band, but Dom managed that. Ray headed back to the tablet and called it up.

Nope. No statement at all.

Well, something to talk to Ms. Gonfaus about. He was about to flip over to his personal email when his phone buzzed with a text. He scrambled for it. Could be Mish or Dom, but it could be Zavier, too, now that he had Ray's number.

Dom's name was blazoned across the top of the phone.

Yo. You up?

Ray let out a sigh of disappointment.

Yeah, come on over.

He sent the message, then headed into the adjoining room.

Wasn't just Dom, but Mish, too. They ordered breakfast, two pots of honest-to-god coffee and not the room brew stuff, and more breakfast food than three people could probably eat. But when it came, they all dug in as if they hadn't eaten in weeks, sitting at a round table that barely held all the dishes.

Once Ray'd stuffed his face with enough pancakes, he sat back. "I got online to check out the spin."

Dom gulped his coffee. "Some of it's really weird, huh? Like the theories and all."

"Yeah." Ray soaked a piece of bacon in syrup. "But the fans are amazing. Did you see all the messages?"

Mish chuckled. "The fans have always been there for us, and for you." She had her *well, duh* look on.

He nearly told them he didn't deserve it, but Zavier's voice loomed in his head, as did his touch in a simple leather strip around his ankle. "We should probably make an announcement on official social media or something."

Dom scratched at the stubble on his neck. "I've been thinking about that. Wanna talk to your lawyer about it."

"She's the band's lawyer, Dom. All of ours. Whatever we do, I want you guys to be comfortable with it, you know?"

Mish nodded slowly. "You call the shots, Ray. We'll back you up."

"What about Zavier?" Dom was chewing on his thumb-nail again, and Ray wondered how he managed to have any nail at all sometimes.

"I called him last night. He'll be back today. And yes, he's part of the band, no matter what the contracts actually say." Ray wanted Zavier in his bed and life and in the band. He suspected both Mish and Dom understood that, too. But he wasn't gonna voice it out loud.

They both were, as he figured, completely down with that idea. They loved Zavier just as much as Ray did, albeit differently.

Polishing off the remnants of breakfast killed a little more time until the next phone call—and this one still wasn't Zavier. It was Ms. Gonfaus.

He answered. "Hey, I have Mish and Dom here, can I put you on speaker?"

"Of course."

That talk went well. A couple of key things had happened, the largest of which was that Carl had confessed to trying to drug Ray. But he'd wanted Ray out of control, like the drunkard they'd originally painted him as. He hadn't expected Ray to have a severe allergic reaction.

Ray had been pacing, but he found the nearest flat surface, the bed, and sank down onto it. "But why?" The question tore out of him painfully, taking a bit of his throat and the sound of anger with it.

"I can send you the files," she murmured. "Part of it was he thought you'd unfairly gotten ahead somehow, but most of it was, according to Carl, at least, that the label had an idea to market Twisted Wishes as a bad boy—and girl—rock band, and your fight with your former drummer played well into that idea."

Ray was glad he was sitting, because he was shaking too hard to stand and his fury was burning a hole in the top of his head. "They...*what*?" His voice was too loud, too angry. Both Mish and Dom flinched.

Ms. Gonfaus was diplomatically quiet.

He reached down to his ankle and pressed Zavier's bracelet into his flesh, and counted to five. "Shit. Sorry. It doesn't matter going forward, but I'm *livid*." He ground the word out.

"As well you should be," Ms. Gonfaus said.

"They could have at least told us," Dom said. "I mean, if that was their angle, we could have worked with them to use it? Rather than getting used by them?" He got up and took Ray's place, pacing. "What a half-baked marketing plan!"

A chuckle from the phone. "But one that gives us quite a bit of leverage. I believe we'll be able to negotiate with the label in a very beneficial way."

They went over those details again, and both Mish and Dom agreed.

"What about Mr. Demos?"

This time Ray stood. "Well, Zav's not here at the moment...and he's technically a session musician with a separate contract with the label." He paused. "But he's joining the band. Has joined, for all practical purposes."

"I see." The sound of pen scratches. "That's good, since I suspect now that you're not touring, Mr. Demos would have found himself cut loose from the label."

Ray stopped moving. "I don't care about the legal tangles. He's part of Twisted Wishes."

"Understood. But I will need to speak with him about his contract and how he wishes to deal with that."

Made sense. "Okay. I'll ask him to call you when he's back."

A few more scribbling noises. "Good."

They wrapped up a few more items, including drafting several simple social media statements for Dom to post, which he did.

"Hey, is that stuff about Carl in a police report?" Dom asked.

"Yes," Ms. Gonfaus said.

"I want to see it," Ray said. "As soon as possible."

Dom made a sour face. "Bet they'll be on some website, soon."

"That'll be a media field day." Mish poured herself the remaining coffee.

So they drafted a statement about that, too, so Dom could post it later.

When they finished the call, Ray didn't really want to think about Carl, but he couldn't stop doing exactly that. "Fuck. That asshole."

"Fuck the label to hell." Mish stood. "And they smiled at us and praised us and got on our case for stepping one foot out of line."

Yeah, that was the short and long of it. Ray scratched his head and dropped his gaze to his ankle, to that little strip of leather. He took a breath and straightened. "Doesn't matter anymore. I mean, it *does*—but we gotta look forward. This is an opportunity."

To decide their own fate. To be wiser about partnering with labels.

Mish chuckled, came over, and wrapped her arms around him. "Hey, hon, when did you get to be the levelheaded one?"

He laughed. "I had help."

Over Mish's shoulder, Ray caught Dom rolling his eyes. "Hey, he's a good man!"

Dom held up his hands. "No argument with me. He's good for you, but you're way the hell sappy for him."

Mish pressed a kiss to Ray's forehead. "Let him be. Zavier knocked some sense into him. I'll take that with sappy any day."

Heat rose to Ray's cheeks. "I'm standing in the room with you guys."

"But drummer boy isn't." She stepped back. "Where is he, anyway?"

There was a tightness in Ray's chest, half from the unknown, and half from anticipation. "I don't know. I think his walk turned into a drive."

"He was pretty strung out about the whole hospitalization thing." Dom picked up the book he'd been reading and flopped onto the bed. "You really need to add him to all the power of attorney stuff, I mean, if you two are gonna keep..." Color touched Dom's face.

"Fucking." Mish's smile was wide. "If you and that boy are gonna keep fucking so damn hard as to wake the neighbors, and if you're gonna run through life together like nothing in the world can stop the two of you...you really should look into the paperwork."

Like nothing could stop... Ray laughed. "Sorry if we kept you up."

Dom was more than red-cheeked now. "Anyway, I'm gonna read."

Mish's turn to roll her eyes. "What I really want to do is lounge by the pool, but I guess here is still the safest place to be."

After reading and talking and getting annoyed with each other, they eventually ended up playing gin rummy on the bed until Ray's phone buzzed. This time it was a text from Zavier:

I'm 30 minutes out.

Ray read the text out loud for Dom and Mish, and Mish tapped Dom's arm. "Come on. That's our cue to get out before we get run over by Zavier's libido."

"Jesus," Dom muttered, and his blush sprang back, but his smile was warm. "Enjoy."

Oh, in the end, Ray would. He was sure of that. But right now? He was nervous as hell, which didn't make sense. Except it was Zavier, so that tingle in his blood and quickness in his pulse did make sense in a way. A good kind of nervous? Maybe.

He headed back into the adjoining room. Another shower would help. As he peeled off his clothes and glanced around the room, a plan formed in his head. Something Zavier would understand, an action that had meaning. A way for Ray to show Zavier that he understood.

CHAPTER
TWENTY-FOUR

DROPPING THE CAR OFF WAS AS EASY AS PICKING IT UP HAD BEEN. The person behind the counter, an older gentleman this time, didn't blink at his name. He processed the paperwork, took payment, and off Zavier went.

Getting back into the hotel, however, was another thing entirely.

While it had been easy enough to sneak out via a fire exit and an alley behind the hotel, getting back in required him entering through the lobby. Zavier tried to play it cool, tried to breeze into the hotel and to the elevators, but the press and paparazzi were there and they were on him in a heartbeat.

He was glad he'd added ten minutes to the estimate he'd given Ray, because the phones and recorders shoved into his face seemed as dangerous as knives. He backed away, hands held up defensively. "I don't have anything to say."

The questions that came were pretty much what he expected: What happened? How was Ray? What was he doing? Did he have any comment about Carl? Was he still part of Twisted Wishes?

He fought his way to the elevators, head and heart pounding. That last question? Hit home a little. Technically, he wasn't part of Twisted Wishes at all. Ray said he was, but legally? Nope. On the outside, looking in.

Very much like he'd been the night of the release party.

He pushed through the reporters as they photographed him, shouted questions, and tried to get him to say anything that would make a good sound bite.

"No fucking comment," he muttered.

Thankfully an elevator was just opening as he got to the bank. He stepped in, and turned around just on the other side of the door. "Don't try it," he said to the guy who looked like he might push past Zavier and into the car, too. "Leave it alone, guys. I'm sure there will be an official statement soon enough."

With that, the doors slid closed. He pressed the button for their floor and stepped back until his ass hit the car wall. Shit. Off balance and angry was *not* how he wanted to reenter Ray's life, and the elevator ride was not nearly enough time to shake off the crowd of rabid reporters. But here he was, with the doors opening on their floor. He stepped out of the car and took a breath. A moment later, a security guy he hadn't noticed stood up from a nearby chair.

"Can I help you?" Dude crossed his arms, and his muscles bulged.

Wow. Okay. Made sense. This wasn't the normal band security, though. "I'm Zavier Demos. The drummer."

Guy didn't move. "Got ID?"

God, did he really have to do this? He knew it was a precaution. Likely the security company didn't know who the fuck they were by sight. But he so didn't need this right now. He pulled out his driver's license and handed it over.

In his mind, he turned over that shouted question. *Are you still part of Twisted Wishes?*

Security dude looked over his license, then made a call on his phone. "Got a guy here who says he's with the band." He rattled off Zavier's name.

With the band. *With.* The word cut into him, even as he chided himself at his reaction. He was reading too much into everything. Too many hours in his head, not enough of them asleep.

After a moment, the guy straightened. "Right." He hung up and gave the license back. "Sorry about that, Mr. Demos. Go right ahead."

See?

He tucked his license away and headed down the hall to their room. He keyed himself into the closer of the two doors —and when he entered, there was no Ray. The bedspread was rumbled to hell, and there were playing cards scattered on top.

So, his room had become the hangout. Which meant the other room hopefully held Ray.

When he got to the threshold between the rooms, the adjoining door was open slightly. He pushed it open, gripped the frame, and his breath caught in his lungs.

The light was soft in the room, and Ray was naked and kneeling on his heels, eyes closed, in front of an empty chair. His blond hair was wet and dark, and drops of water beaded on his shoulders. His breathing was slow and his smile beatific, and every toy from Zavier's duffle had been artfully arranged on the bed.

It was like a kinky rendition of some artistic masterpiece. A sculpture of an angel on his knees beneath a still-life banquet of erotic choices. His willing, submissive partner.

Ray flicked his eyes open and turned his head to meet Zavier's gaze. No words.

There didn't need to be any.

This man knows me better than anyone has ever known me. No other partner had ever had the forethought to think about Zavier's needs. Zavier's desires. And maybe that was something else he never considered—that what he and Ray had went in both directions.

He crossed to Ray and touched that damp head of hair. "I can't possibly use all of those on you tonight."

Ray leaned his head against Zavier's leg, but other than that didn't break his posture one bit. "I know. Pick what you want and use those, then."

Zavier traced his finger down Ray's cheek. "Oh, I will."

A sigh and a shudder, then silence.

Perfect. He stepped past Ray and took a seat in the chair. "I need this part more than you do tonight, I think. But forehead on my shoes, Ray, and hands at the small of your back."

Ray complied beautifully, and the arch of his spine was like art. Zavier palmed his hardening dick through his jeans, closed his eyes, and let his breathing and body still. His need for Ray didn't abate, but all the worries, all the fears nibbling at his mind vanished. What filled the void was warmth. Contentment.

No. He opened his eyes and studied Ray, his supplicant pose, his stillness. More than that. Joy.

Zavier spoke. "Up, please."

Ray sat up, his hands still tucked at the small of his back. God, that grin.

"I had never felt so much fear as that moment you fell into my arms at the party."

Ray's smile slipped away. "I don't remember. It's—" He struggled, shifting on his knees. "I hate that part. Not remembering."

Zavier nodded. "I'd want to know, too."

"I'm sorry I scared you."

He leaned forward and brushed a lock of Ray's hair off his forehead. "You weren't at fault. And it wasn't just the fear of losing you—it was the utter helplessness. There was nothing I could do."

For a moment, Ray's gaze turned inward, and he nodded. "I should—we should—figure out the legal stuff. Power of attorney, all that." He met Zavier's gaze again. "If that's what you want."

It was. They were already tangled together. Better to tidy things up legally. They could pool resources. Find a place to live. Ray's idea was a good one, but Zavier had a better plan, one with more protections for the both of them. One he'd *never* thought he'd ever suggest to another person. "There's a far easier way to handle the legal end of things than power of attorney. If you're agreeable to something a little longer lasting."

Confusion for a long moment, then Ray's eyes widened and he stared. Finally he opened his lips and spoke carefully. "It's more customary for the person proposing marriage to be the one kneeling, you know."

Zavier rose and loomed over Ray. "I like this better." He threaded his hands into Ray's hair. "And I think you do, too." He yanked. Hard.

A gasp and a swallowed moan. "Yeah. I do. It's us."

Exactly. "So?"

"Yes. Please marry me."

Good. So good. A weight lifted off his shoulders. Ray would be his.

Another thought followed—he'd be as equally Ray's. A little vertigo flew through him, and he loosened his hold on Ray's hair.

"You give me hope, Ray."

Ray furrowed his brow. "How so?"

"I've spent most of my life under the assumption that no one would ever come close to understanding who I am." He gave a huff of a laugh. "And here you are."

A little shrug of the shoulders. "But this is who *we* are. You and me. And I don't understand everything. But I—I *care*, Zav. I want you to be happy."

Ray *wanted him* to be happy. Ray cared. Zavier turned that over in his head and cupped Ray's cheek. Everything about this moment, from Ray kneeling to all the toys on the bed, carved that into his mind. "You have no idea how much that means to me."

His smile was sly. "Oh, I think I do."

And maybe he did. Zavier patted Ray's cheek. "Get the cuffs, all of them, and bring them here. Do *not* stand to do it."

Ray's eyes flickered and his grin widened—and he obeyed beautifully, crawling to the bed, picking up the cuffs and returning. Ray was glowing, eyes bright and face enraptured.

"May I ask for something?" Soft words.

Zavier took the cuffs and set the ones for Ray's ankle aside for the moment. "Yes." Because this scene was being run by both of them in some way.

"I'd like to bring you the collar, too."

Heat chased ice chased heat through Zavier's veins, and he shivered. Couldn't help it. Collaring Ray. He nearly spoke, nearly poised the question. *Do you understand what you're asking?* But of course he did.

Ray fucking grinned at him, but said nothing at all.

Zavier's voice was rough and his dick very, *very* hard. "Yes. Get it and bring it here."

A few seconds later, he was holding the leather collar in his hands. A significant moment. He gazed at Ray, who seemed to be trying very hard not to laugh.

"What?" Zavier fingered the collar.

Ray's face was joy. "I never see you like this. And I'm so fucking happy, I could fly."

Zavier parsed the second sentence before the first, since the first made no sense. "We've played this game before. You've seen me over you before."

The joy remained, but Ray's smile fell to an intense seriousness Zavier had only seen on him when he talked music. "We're not playing a game."

Oh. *Oh.* Zavier swallowed, and the world did one of those standing still things that sometimes happened in his life.

Turning points. Precipices. Moments when everything going forward would be *different*. Had happened when he'd opened that letter from Juilliard, when he'd first seen a man tied up and flogged, and when he'd walked into HR in Silverton to tender his resignation.

He'd asked Ray to marry him. In return Ray asked for a collar. No, they weren't playing anymore. Maybe they never had been. He'd wanted to help Ray from the moment he'd read that apology of his, wanted to see how Ray had grown and changed. Now? He was twined into Ray. Planted in his life.

"How long have you needed me?"

"Since high school. But I don't think that's the question you're asking." Ray suddenly didn't look at all submissive, despite kneeling at Zavier's feet. "*Need* means so many things. *Want*, too. All words have layers."

Yeah, he shouldn't underestimate a songwriter. Zavier tucked that away. "What am I asking?"

Ray chuckled. "There's how I'd phrase the question, and how you'd phrase the question. What you're asking, and how you'd say it, is 'How long have you trusted me?'"

Okay, that did sound a little like him. "And?" He raised an eyebrow.

Ray raised his in return. "I love it when you're imperious."

"I am holding a collar in my hand. I'm assuming you want it around your neck."

"I do, yeah. Because I want to belong to you and you want me to belong to you."

Lightning in his veins. Ray knew him perhaps better than he knew himself, at least in some things. "Not all the time."

"No. Not all the time in the whole Dominant and submissive way." Ray's smile was crooked and charming. "We'd both hate that."

Zavier slipped the leather collar around Ray's neck, and

Ray's eyes fluttered shut. He seemed to melt as Zavier buckled it on, tight enough. But not too much. "Now...how long have you trusted me?"

"Got two answers for that," Ray murmured. His voice, like his body was soft. Ah, subspace. "My head—the one on top of my neck—has trusted you since the night on the bus."

Zavier didn't need to be told which one.

"But my soul?" Ray opened his eyes and stared up at Zavier. "Since the audition, when you played 'White Hot Midnight.'"

Zavier yanked on the collar, pulling Ray up, even as he bent down. Their mouths met and Zavier devoured Ray and his moans. Or perhaps it was the other way round. Ray's fingers were caught in Zavier's shirt, holding, tugging, grounding them both in this moment.

Partner. Yes. That was the best word. At least until it could be husband.

Zavier broke the kiss. "We're going to need the bed you so neatly covered in toys cleaned off."

Ray laughed and slid back to kneeling. "Pick what you want to use on me, and I'll put the rest away."

There was that incredible flare of desire—Zavier wanted Ray in every possible manner right now. But that wasn't feasible, let alone practical. Someday soon, he'd make a list of his fantasies, check them with Ray, then begin to cross them all off, one by one. But tonight?

He took the rope, the flogger, and the crop. They'd played a bit with them before, but now there wasn't a need to be careful about how much skin he could or couldn't mark. He grabbed the bottle of lube and eyed the condoms. A notion, a heat flared in him. Yes, he wanted to possess Ray. Own him.

"Is there any reason why I shouldn't fuck you bareback?"

Ray's breathing hitched, and then he was silent. Zavier didn't turn, just kept staring at the condoms. Finally, Ray spoke. "No. I was tested for pretty much everything under the sun at the hospital. I'm good. Even my cholesterol." He let out a sigh that Zavier matched mentally with one of Ray's little shoulder shrugs. "Plus I've been on PrEP for a while now."

"Pretty much the same for me, sans hospital."

"Your cholesterol's good?"

Zavier laughed and turned. "I'm a tiny bit close to high, but it's all the good type of cholesterol."

Ray was smirking. His arrogant, lovely man.

"Clean off the bed, Ray." Zavier settled back into his chair, setting down his supplies on the table next to it, and enjoyed the view of Ray carefully laying all their toys back into Zavier's duffle. Including the condoms.

It was symbolic, of course. But also not at all. His fingertips itched and he wanted to touch every part of Ray. Bite him. Make him cry.

Ray? Ray wouldn't be naked and wearing a leather collar if he had any objections. Still, Zavier tilted his head and asked, "Safewords?"

"Traffic lights, Zav. I know. You've never done anything I haven't liked."

True. "Someday, though, I'll hit a limit."

Ray stilled and nodded. "Yeah, probably." He zipped up the bag. "You got one? A safeword?"

He did. He'd only ever needed it once in his life, when Nadia had tied him up. But he'd not spoken it then. Never said it to stop a scene. "It's *baroque*."

Ray blinked a few times. "Please don't tell me you chose it because of the whole 'if it's not baroque' joke."

Zavier laughed. Because yes, yes he had. For the sheer artistic fuckery. Because he was an asshole.

Ray shook his head, put the bag in the closet, crossed the room, and knelt before Zavier again. He put his hands at the small of his back and tipped his chin up. "Please fuck me already. Or flog me. Or both. I need to feel you. Need to know this is real."

As if Zavier needed a reason for his dick to be harder. "Oh, you will. And it is." He picked up one of the smaller cuffs. "Give me your wrist."

He did, and Zavier kissed the pulse point before buckling the cuff on. Did the same with the other, and by the time he was done, Ray was flushed from the chest up. Practically panting. "Turn around, Ray."

He used the tiny clip dangling from one cuff and secured the two together, locking Ray's hands firmly behind his back. Zavier spoke. "Face me."

The softness was back. That sweet touch of Ray giving everything over. All his trust. His body. Everything. Zavier stood and stepped in close, and there was the spark of recognition, the drop in Ray's shoulders.

"Oh god yes, please." Ray moaned the words.

Someone wanted a dick in his mouth. "Since you're not singing in the near future..." Zavier unzipped, pushed everything aside, grasped Ray's collar, and slipped his cock into Ray's very willing mouth.

They both groaned, and the vibrations around Zavier's shaft were something else. Yes, he'd let Ray suck him before, but this time? Ray was all in. Licking, sucking, taking him deep. Over and over, with an enthusiasm he rarely saw from guys who mostly topped.

"Fuck, Ray." Zavier tightened his fingers around the leather collar and slid his other hand into Ray's hair. "Where the hell did you learn to suck cock?"

Ray pulled off and licked the tip. So fucking good, that. "Glory holes." A flash of a smile, then Ray's hot mouth was back around Zavier's dick, and it took everything Zavier had not to empty his balls down Ray's throat.

Fucking Ray had been holding out on him, depraved soul that he was. Zavier tightened both his grips, holding Ray's head still, and thrust in. And again. And again, until he was fucking Ray's mouth and throat with abandon. Ray didn't flinch. He did moan and shake and make sounds that were so damn obscene they should be in a high-quality porno. So was Ray's stare, full of blinking and watery eyes and a look that seemed to say *I can damn well take anything you give*.

It was almost a pity to stop, but if he wanted to fuck Ray's ass like he intended, he needed to, or the evening would be over before he'd even started. He pulled out.

Zavier wasn't sure which of them was breathing more heavily, him or Ray. "Glory holes, huh?"

Ray's voice was jacked and rough, but still so beautiful. "Yeah. I—uh—may have gotten some of my seed money for the band from swallowing other guys'...well. Yeah." A little furrow between his brows. "That doesn't bother you, does it?"

He smoothed his thumbs over Ray's cheeks and those plump, ruddy, well-fucked lips. "Not in the least. Remember, I learned much of what I know about BDSM from a rather infamous madam." He paused. "And I may have made some money as an escort."

"May? Like you don't know?" A quirky little smile.

"Did make. Enjoyed it, too."

Ray's sigh was a happy thing. "Yeah. Ditto."

So much he knew about Ray. So much he didn't. This would be a grand adventure. One to last a lifetime. "Up, Ray. I'm tying you to the bed."

He wouldn't tire of that little happy moan in the back of Ray's throat. Ray rose with grace and moved like he hadn't just spent quite a bit of time kneeling on the carpet. Zavier took a moment to tuck his dick back into his pants—as much as he could, given its state—and to grab the lengths of rope he'd pulled from the bed. Arranging Ray was easy enough; Zavier bent him over the bed. He had to unclip the wrist cuffs to have Ray stretch his arms overhead, then reclip them. Ray was both squirmy and relaxed, his sinuous body moving just so.

"You better not be humping the bedspread."

Ray huffed a laugh. "I won't come until you say."

"You'd better not." Zavier could wield a crop for pain as equally as for pleasure. "And stop moving."

Ray did, though his muscles flexed a little before he gave in.

It took Zavier longer than he'd like to anchor the ropes to the bed. Once he'd managed, though, he tied Ray's arms overhead and each ankle—once he'd cuffed them, pulled toward the sides of the bed. Ray open and exposed for him. "Comfortable?"

"You have no idea," Ray murmured, and it was that faraway voice Zavier loved to hear.

"You're still wearing my bracelet." The leather band rode low on Ray's ankle.

"Reminds me of you."

Interesting. He smoothed a hand over Ray's ass, then up his back. He didn't quite understand, no. He'd never managed to fall into subspace, but this? It was a headspace of its own. The trust he'd been given.

He returned to the table by the chair and claimed the last of his items. Flogger, crop, and lube. The latter he set down on the floor, and set the crop next to it.

He smacked his hand with the flogger, and Ray twitched and moaned. "I wonder if I could make you come from just that sound." He did it again and, as Ray laughed, flicked the flogger across his ass.

That got him a much louder moan. "Shit."

"Just you wait." He worked over Ray's cheeks and thighs and shoulders, warming the skin, ruddying it under the ink. Ray was a delight of moans and twists and curses until he wasn't—and that was a glory, too. That moment when the motion and the pain swept over Ray and took him higher and higher.

"There you go." Zavier's cock throbbed and his mind whirled. Such strength in Ray. Such grace in submission. He slowed the flogger to stopping and switched it out for the crop. "Safewords?"

"Mmm. Red, yellow, and baroque." More like sleepy words. "Won't need 'em."

Zavier resisted the urge to land the first one hard. Still, he put enough sting into it that Ray jumped, his limbs twitching. "Shit."

"Mmmhmm." He upped the ante with the next and the next until Ray was gasping and moaning and twisting in a completely different way than he had under the flogger. Both the edge of pain and pleasure sounded in Ray's throat. Groans and pants. Curses.

"You like that?" He raised a few welts on Ray's shoulders. His marks on top of the ink. So nice. Zavier's blood was on fire with need. For Ray's tears. For his sobs. To kiss and fuck them away.

"Fuck no. Yes," Ray hissed. "Don't stop. Please don't stop!"

He didn't. Not until Ray's voice broke and Zavier got exactly what he wanted—Ray overloaded and weeping and begging for more and no more at the same time. He gave three last strokes, then stopped.

A few moments passed before Zavier realized he was shaking. Probably as much as Ray was. He dropped the crop and went around the bed so he could see Ray's face, touch his hair, and wipe away his tears with trembling fingers. "Shh. Ray. It's over. I'm here."

"Didn't want you to stop." Ray's eyes were rimmed with red. "Glad you did." He sighed and melted into the mattress.

Zavier kissed his cheek until Ray turned and offered his mouth. Lips against lips. Tongues tangled.

Then Ray was exhaling again. "God, that was so good."

For Zavier, too—in control and yet also out of it. Trembling. On fire. He traced the welts on Ray's shoulders. "I left marks. Bruises everywhere."

Ray shuddered.

Felt right to lean over and kiss that raised skin. Nibble here and there. Listen to Ray hiss and moan. Feel that lithe body rock under his touch. He worked his way back to Ray's ear and whispered into it. "I want my come inside you."

Full-body shudder and a delicious moan. "Fuck, Zav."

"Tell me you want it."

"Shit, Zav. I want everything you give me. Yeah, I want it. Fuck me. Claim me. Paint my insides."

He nearly came right there. Ray's stunning voice, all in pieces, muttering those words. He kissed him again, harder, before pulling away and fetching the lube.

He'd never fucked anyone without a condom. But lubing his dick, fingering Ray, then sliding into his body? Felt so fucking *right* Zavier couldn't catch his breath for a moment. "Jesus, Ray."

Ray shuddered and moaned. "Fuck yeah, Zav, I need—"

Zavier pulled back and slammed in deep. "You *need* to take what I give you."

The answer Ray gave was a gasp and a long moan.

"Yes, exactly like that." Zavier quickened his pace—he wasn't going to last long, given how tight Ray was. How he thrashed and humped and babbled. And neither would Ray.

He raked his fingers over the marks he'd left on Ray's back, dug his fingers into Ray's hips, and let himself go. No caution, no restraint. He fucked as if every piece of Ray belonged to him. Hot and tight and marked and beautiful. A mind that saw music and a soul that understood his. Zavier squeezed his eyes shut against the pleasure, and tears fell on Ray's back. He'd never been this high, never like he was about to shatter like dropped crystal. Heat and light cut into him.

Ray's moans turned sharp. "Oh *god*. Zav. Fuck! Yes, *yes*. That! Don't...don't—" The rest was lost in gasping and a long cry when Ray came, shuddering and shaking against the bed and Zavier's ropes.

Zavier broke into pieces, his own cry echoing in the room. Light blinded him and for a moment all he knew was Ray under him, Ray around him, and Ray taking his seed before he lost himself completely.

All his senses overwhelmed him, vision hazing, limbs burning, mind swirling into heaven. He could stay here forever, inside Ray, inside this bliss, and never ever worry about anyone ever again. They were together and the rest of the world could go to hell.

It took a little longer than normal to pull himself together. Even longer to come back down to earth. He was propped up on his arms, over Ray and still inside him. He peered at Ray's back.

Slow, even breaths from Ray, and complete relaxation.

"You still with me?"

"Mmmhmm." Ray's voice was a whisper. "You?"

Zavier tried to laugh, but it came out as a croak. "Yeah. Hang on, I'll untie you."

"'S okay. Like you like that. On me. Stay, Zav. Stay a little longer."

He didn't know why, but a knot formed in his throat. He did pull out, but only so he could crawl up and drape himself over Ray. He laid his head between Ray's shoulder blades.

Had to hurt—or maybe not, since Ray only sighed and melted down into the mattress. "Welcome home, Zav."

Zavier closed his eyes and failed at not letting the tears out. Fucking beautiful Ray Van Zeller. He'd marry the man to keep anyone else from ever hurting him again.

IT WAS A LITTLE WEIRD TO WAKE UP TIED TO A BED, BUT RAY didn't mind. Felt strangely secure, especially with the weight and warmth of Zavier's body over his. He could have stayed like this forever, if it hadn't been for something so mundane as hunger.

His stomach growled again. "Fuck."

Zavier shifted. "I should untie you." Lips pressed against Ray's back. "Should've earlier."

"It's not that, but yeah." The loss of Zavier's weight and heat was disconcerting, but not as horrible as Ray had imagined it might be. "Fucking stomach wants dinner."

"Well, it is dinnertime." Zavier peered at the other side of the bed. "A little past, actually." Then he bent and freed the rope from the wrist cuffs.

Ray left his arms where they were because it *still* felt good to be stretched like this. "Please do this to me again sometime."

A huff of laughter. "You really are perfect."

"*Me?* Fuck no. You're the one who's too perfect to be real. Rock-star looks. Rock-star name. Rock star—"

"Tied down to my bed." Zavier tapped Ray's ass, and even the light blow sent a tangle of pain and pleasure up Ray's back. "I should make you read some of the fanfic descriptions of you."

The rope holding Ray's left ankle slackened, then let go. Zavier undid the other rope, too. "Oh god." Ray pressed his forehead into the mattress. While his arms felt fine, his legs were another matter.

"I'll help you up. You need a shower anyway." Zavier paused. "We both do."

They smelled of sweat and sex and each other, and Ray loved it. "Should check with Mish and Dom to see if they've eaten."

Zavier grunted, and worked with Ray to get him turned over and sitting next to the rather large wet spot he'd created. "I'll text. I suppose we're doing room service?"

He so *so so* did not want to sit in the room next door and eat hotel food again. "No. I want to go out. Get dressed. Blow through the paparazzi and have a real meal in a real restaurant. Maybe even outdoors because this hotel air is *shit*."

A strange look, part amusement, part pride, appeared on Zavier's face. "You're feeling better, then."

He rolled his eyes. "Text them."

"You giving me orders?" A grin. "While you still have cuffs and a collar on?"

"Remember that part where I said I don't want us to be Dominant and submissive all the time, and you agreed?"

Zavier snorted—and texted. A moment later, his phone dinged.

"They say they haven't eaten. They were waiting for us." He eyed Ray. "I'll tell them to meet us in the communal room in thirty minutes."

Ray nodded. "And tell them we're going out."

A quirky smile from Zavier. "Where do you have in mind?"

He had no idea. "Fuck if I know this town. Somewhere good. With a patio that we can get seated on. I bet the concierge can make it happen."

Damn, it was fun watching Zavier's ever-shifting emotions. "Shall I call down, then?"

Shall? He laughed. "Would you mind, Zav? I guess I'm the one being imperious now." He paused. "But you did just flog and fuck me into oblivion, so I kind of feel like I can rule the world."

"In a collar and cuffs, no less." Zavier texted the others, then picked up the hotel phone and talked to the concierge.

Ray closed his eyes and let the murmur of Zavier's voice

pull him back into that warm, safe place where he was strong and—at least to Zavier—perfect.

Hands on his shoulders, Zavier's hot voice in his ears. "You're still not down completely, are you?"

Ray shook his head. "Not entirely. But enough. Let's get ready."

They did, Zavier helping him into the bathroom and shower, but by the time they were done, Ray had found his strength. They put on nicer clothes. "Interview clothing," Zavier muttered, and headed into the adjoining room. Dom and Mish were already there, looking equally as stylish and nice.

"We're busting out of this joint?" Mish had a feral look. "Zavier's idea?"

Ray shook his head. "Mine. I'm tired of hiding. We've done nothing wrong. The press is full of speculation, but generally on our side."

Dom—or rather Domino, since the makeup and hair were back, as was the leather and boots and collar—rubbed his chin. "Would also let them see you and know you're fine."

Getting fucked by Zavier was the absolute best thing in the world. Second best, though, was watching Zavier realize Ray was a step ahead of him. His face did all sorts of interesting contortions on the way to surprise and elation. "You're playing the game!"

"Damn straight. I tried playing it their way. I'm gonna play it mine."

Zavier's grin was like a fall of a flogger, all warmth and light. "Come on. The concierge got us reservations—yes, on a deck, Ray—and a car, and they should be here in about five minutes."

They headed out, and it was fucking glorious, like something out of a movie. The security called down to warn the hotel and security staff, so there were people flanking them as they strode through the lobby. Flashes from cameras went off.

Mish laughed. Zavier looked like a fucking god, and Domino walked in front, like he would run everyone over with his steel-toed boots.

Ray didn't answer any of their shouted questions, just waved and smiled—until Zavier casually put his hand on the back of his neck. Then he laughed and locked gazes with Zav. His fiancé.

When they were all settled into the hired car—which was actually a freaking limo—he grinned at Dom and Mish. "Hey, Zavier asked me to marry him."

Mish punched him in the arm, missing all of his welts, thank god. "You bastard! Good. About time you freaks worked it out."

"Freaks?" Zavier was grinning. "Honestly, it's for practical reasons."

"Of course it is." Dom leaned back and waved a hand. "Legal paperwork and all that. Not like you guys care about each other. At all."

Zavier blushed. Honest-to-god blushed. Deeply. Enough that you could see it in the passing streetlights. "It's not— That's not—" He sighed. "I'm not a romantic. At all. But this..." He gestured between Ray and him. "It seems right."

"My mom always said to marry your best friend." Dom was grinning.

Zavier's eyebrows shot up. "Ray's *your* best friend."

Dom made a sour face. "Ray's like my brother. Ew. Did he tell you we kissed once?"

"Once." Ray held up his hands. "And I did, yeah. He asked why we weren't fucking."

"Because you are entirely not what Dominic is looking for in a partner." Zavier had a knowing look. "Dominic is looking for someone tall and tweedy who can whisper about hidden queer nuances in old literature while jacking him off."

"Fucking hell, Zav!" Dom choked out.

"Yeah, but is he right?" 'Cause Ray had to know. And yeah, he so could see Dom liking that.

Dom muttered "fucking hell" a few more times before sighing. "Yeah. Pretty close. Bastard."

"Lord, you boys." Mish sighed dramatically.

Dom punched her in the arm for a change. "Oh, don't you start. You don't have a leg to stand on. And half the time my room's right next to yours."

She smiled like a Cheshire cat and sank into the leather behind her. "I am not saying *anything*."

Ray laughed until he was in tears, then wiped them off before they stepped out of their limo. The air was cool and electrified with lights and people and the low thump of dancing somewhere. Zavier put his hand around the back of Ray's neck again. His back and ass burned. His friends were here. His band. The man he loved. Ray couldn't keep the happiness in his heart. Felt like everything was cracking open and blooming. Reaching for the sky.

They had nowhere to go but up.

CHAPTER
TWENTY-FIVE

Ten Months Later

There were flowers in a cut-crystal vase on the kitchen island when Ray returned home from his errands. Dark red roses paired with tiny pale blue flowers of some kind. The vase sparkled in the lights of the kitchen. Seeing those colors together flipped his soul and made his limbs tingle.

"What do you see when you sing 'Dare to Be'?" The question from all those months ago came back, along with the strength of Zavier's arms and the whisper of his breath.

Ray set down his bag of groceries and stared at the flowers. *Burgundy with dots of sky blue.* "Dare to Be" flew through his head, this time with Zavier's drumming—they'd just finished nailing down that part—and every bit of Ray burned. These flowers were for Ray, from *Zavier.* He both understood and didn't understand the gesture.

Zavier didn't buy flowers.

There was a small envelope leaning up against the crystal vase. No writing on it, but that wasn't needed. Ray picked it up, opened it, and slid the thick piece of paper out.

Please put away the groceries and join me in my office.

—Zavier

Ray ran his thumb along the side of the card stock. An invitation. To a scene? To something else? He didn't know this time. At other times, it was more obvious whether they were orders Zavier left on his cards, or when they were simply little notes.

The flowers threw him, but Ray treated the note as the beginning of a scene, anyway. Hell, he wanted it to be the beginning of a scene. He put the groceries away, careful to place items in their proper places in the pantry. Zavier had insisted at least that part of the kitchen be orderly. Everything else—dishes, pots and pans, the fridge, drawers—those were kept at Ray levels of chaos.

The balance worked, and when Ray slacked off, Zavier got to remind him of their decision, usually bent over one of the kitchen stools with a wooden spoon that never seemed to be used for anything else.

Ray wasn't above shifting things out of order when he *wanted* the punishment. But he wouldn't do that tonight. He finished up, picked up the card, and headed to Zavier's office.

The room was dressed in warm shades of yellow and brown and black, like an old study or smoking room. Bookshelves lined one wall. Along the other was Zavier's desk, complete with one of those ink-blotters. Zavier sat in his brown leather chair, reading an actual hard-backed book, though there were also small piles of mail on his desk, along with a package that had been opened.

Ray hadn't been quiet in his approach, so when he reached the door, Zavier met his gaze, slipped a bookmark into his book, and set it aside. "Everything put away in the kitchen?" Soft voice.

Could be play or just an inquiry. Ray nodded, turning over the card in his hands. "You bought me flowers."

Color touched Zavier's cheeks. "So I did. I thought you might like them."

"I do." Burgundy and blue. "They're 'Dare to Be.'"

Ray had seen him blush before, but not quite like this, not with so much uncertainty. "Yes." Zavier took a breath. "Was that an okay thing to do?"

So maybe this wasn't a scene after all. Ray crossed the threshold from the hall into Zavier's domain, and sat himself down on his lap. "It was an incredibly thoughtful thing to do, Zav." Ray kissed him on the cheek. "I very much appreciate them."

Warm arms wrapped around Ray, and Zavier pulled him tighter, even as tension drained from Zavier's expression. "Oh, good."

Sweet man. Ray's heart tumbled over and over, like it always did. "You don't have to get me flowers. Or chocolate." That had been last week. "I'm utterly content with you and our home. With us."

They'd been living together since that night Zavier had returned to Ray. He'd been there through the legal wrangling with the record label, for the settlement and release from their contract, and for the satisfaction of Carl pleading guilty to criminal mischief. Ray'd wanted more, but as expected, plea bargaining had reduced the charge and the sentence. Zavier had consoled him in every manner he could and that had kept Ray so calm.

After a month back in New York City, they'd gotten married at the courthouse with only Mish and Dom present. As Zavier had said, a legal formality—much easier to tie their lives together that way than any other.

Zavier's aromanticism was as much a part of him as his drumming or Ray's singing or their kinky sex. Ray didn't want to change *any* of it. They were husbands, yes. But also friends and partners. Bandmates. And sometimes Dominant and submissive, when they felt the need.

But always, always friends. He loved Zavier so much it hurt sometimes. He still wore Zavier's bracelet on his ankle. Even under socks.

Zavier kissed Ray's throat. "I know that. But it's a little thing that makes you happy, so why not? I walked by this florist and saw the colors and thought of the other night. And maybe it made a little sense in my head to buy them."

Ray tossed the card onto Zavier's desk. "And here I thought you were gonna put me on my knees."

A deep chuckle. "Oh, I intend to do that, and quite a bit more before dinner."

Sparks everywhere, and that deep calm that Zavier could draw out of him in an instant. "I'd like that." He slid a palm along Zavier's chest and was rewarded by a nip at his chin and Zavier cupping his ass.

"You say that now," Zavier murmured. He pulled back. "I have plans."

"Do tell."

Zavier patted Ray's ass. "Get up a moment, and I'll show you what came today."

Ray slid off his lap, and Zavier turned to scoop up the little package. Anticipation tightened Ray's muscles and nudged him from his calm place, but he forced himself to breathe—and let the lust and thrill slip through him.

When Zavier lifted the item out of the box, it took Ray a moment to comprehend exactly what the metal contraption was. A moment later, he was on his knees, his mind in a whirl, blood hot and cock hardening. "Oh shit."

Zavier held a cock cage. Stainless steel, if Ray had to guess. It came with a small lock that looked a hell of a lot stronger than the ones used for luggage.

The glint in Zavier's eyes and the turn of his smile were a perfect mix of devilish desire and heartwarming amusement. "Should I take your gesture of submission as approval?" He stroked Ray's cheek, but his smile said he already knew the answer.

"Well—you're not going to get me into it, currently." He was too damn hard now. "But yes. I want to try." A different kind of bondage, another way to surrender his will to Zavier. He wouldn't be able to get hard caged like that. Might come, but he'd read that was pretty uncomfortable. Every vein danced with need. Yeah, he wanted the cage on him, much in the same way he wanted to be spanked or bound or anything that made him heady and forced the world away.

Fingers traced over Ray's chin and neck. "I think you'll love it. And hate it. And look glorious caged."

"Probably." He met Zavier's heavy gaze. "Gonna fuck me in it?"

A hitch in Zavier's breathing. Good. Yes. Nothing turned Ray on more than when he flustered Zavier. Mostly because he had a pretty good idea what would happen next.

"Get up, strip, and put your hands on my desk."

Yes—that. Those orders, whispered in that deep, gritty voice. Ray did as told, his whole body warm as his placed his palms down in the green blotter.

The signs of their life together were before him. Bills. Statements. Musical notation scribbled down on a pad. His own picture on Zavier's desk.

A kiss landed on his back, then the sound of Zavier stripping and fishing into a desk drawer, probably for lube. "I was thinking about spanking you, but I think I'll wait on that."

When Zavier trailed his fingers along his sides, Ray twisted, but didn't break his stance. "Getting soft in your old age?" That earned Ray a sharp smack that was part pain and all glory. He bit back a laugh.

Zavier breathed across his back and smoothed his palm over Ray's ass. "Oh, I'll make you cry like you want before the night's through. But right now? Let's just say that since I intend to be *very* rough later, I want to be gentle now."

He was, too. Lovingly so. Kisses along Ray's spine as he entered. Zavier moved slowly inside him, pressing deep with each stroke until they were both rocking as one, gasping together, and working the rhythm toward the light they both sought.

Zavier stroked him, a slightly different tempo, but one that pulled waves of pleasure and drowned all Ray's thoughts. "God, Zav..." Every time, it was like having lightning in his skin. Everything burned and built and threatened to spill.

A laugh. "You always feel so damn good." Skin to skin, they moved until neither could keep oblivion away.

Ray tried to whisper Zavier's name again, but could only groan. He was so close, nearly to the end of the world, because Zavier wasn't just fucking him—he was making love to Ray.

Zavier spoke, words thick and breathless. "I want your come all over my desk. I want to sit here and see the stains your jizz leaves when I'm reading, when I'm paying bills. I want proof of this. Of us." He thrust deep over and over again.

Ray lowered his head and moaned, his heart full, and shattered as waves of pleasure swept over him. He did exactly what Zavier had demanded, coming all over the pristine green blotter, turning the thick paper dark with his semen.

Zavier came a moment later, burying himself in Ray.

God, Ray loved that, too. The way Zavier shuddered and groaned as he emptied himself inside him.

They marked each other. Every time. Mentally. Physically. Emotionally.

Took both of them a little time to recover. Tissues cleaned up what the blotter hadn't caught, and eventually Ray was curled up in Zavier's lap again, this time naked and relaxed and so very sated. His heart beat in time with

Zavier's and was so full he couldn't keep the words from spilling out.

"I love you so fucking much. I hope you don't mind." He pressed his cheek against Zavier's, a little trickle of worry worming into his soul. "I can't help it."

That fear vanished when Zavier laughed. "I'd be a fool to mind," he said. "And I'm honored you trust me with your heart, given everything you know about me..."

Ray tried to speak, tried to protest, but Zavier's finger was on his lips, demanding silence and attention.

"Ray, seeing you happy, hearing you sing, watching you make our band into what it is—that's my *passion*. You're like drumming or fine wine or—"

"Really good sex?" Ray said against that finger, then licked it.

Zavier chuckled. "The best sex I've ever had in my life has been with you. You *are* sex, Ray Van Zeller. And yes, that's my passion, too."

"It's almost like you love me," Ray teased. They'd talked long and hard about the different meanings of the word and how they related to their relationship. What Zav felt wasn't romantic, but as Mish had said all those months ago, there were all kinds of love.

Zavier clicked his tongue. "You know that phrase doesn't do it for me. I don't know that it ever will."

That was pure Zavier, right there, and Ray adored him for it. He shrugged. "I'm wearing your ring." That and the leather band on his ankle were more than enough. Constant reminders that Zavier wasn't leaving him. Them. They were in this together.

"So you are." Zavier grinned. "And I'm wearing yours."

"So—friends with benefits it is?"

Once more, Zavier's laughter filled the room. "How about husbands with the very best of benefits?" He pulled Ray into a kiss that ignited the heat in his blood.

"I can live with that," Ray murmured against Zavier's mouth.

"Forever?" Zavier's eyes were bluer than the notes from any of Twisted Wishes's songs.

"And ever," Ray said.

His love and Zavier's passion. Together, they'd set the world on fire.

Want more Twisted Wishes? Check out the next book,
COUNTERPOINT!

ACKNOWLEDGMENTS

Second Edition: Much thanks to Layla Reyne for her support and help while I worked to bring this new edition out.

First Edition: As always, I have Lori Witt to thank for being a sounding board and alpha reader and my best friend. All of my books owe her a little piece of thanks. In addition, my agent, Jennifer Udden, has kept me sane through career changes and self-doubt. She remains my constant advocate.

Many thanks also to Angela James for bringing me into the Carina fold and to Mackenzie Walton for making this book shine brighter than I could have ever managed on my own.

And to Elyse Springer, for her friendship and support.

Most of all, thank you to all of my readers and fans. I'm always amazed and touched by you and your support.

ALSO BY ANNA ZABO

TAKEOVER

Takeover

Just Business

Due Diligence

Daily Grind

ON THE BOARD (WRITTEN WITH L.A. WITT)

Rookie Mistake

Scoreless Game

Shift Change (coming soon)

TWISTED WISHES

Syncopation

Counterpoint

Reverb

CLOSE QUARTER

Close Quarter

Slow Waltz (a Close Quarter short story)

STANDALONE WORKS

CTRL Me

Outside the Lines

Weave the Dark, Weave the Light

Cinnamon Roll

Love of the Game

ABOUT THE AUTHOR

Anna Zabo writes contemporary and paranormal romance for all colors of the rainbow. They live and work in Pittsburgh, Pennsylvania, which isn't nearly as boring as most people think.

They can be easily plied with coffee or a chance to see the Pittsburgh Penguins.

Anna has an MFA in Writing Popular Fiction from Seton Hill University, where they fell in with a roving band of romance writers and never looked back. They also have a BA in Creative Writing from Carnegie Mellon University.

Anna uses they/them pronouns and prefers Mx. Zabo as an honorific. They can be found online at annazabo.com.

X x.com/amergina
O instagram.com/amergina
BB bookbub.com/authors/anna-zabo
a amazon.com/Anna-Zabo/e/B00A7LA6OC